GUARDIAN

The second book in the City of the Gods series.

By M. Scott Verne
& Wynn Mercere

Book design & digital collages by Steve Crompton

RAVEN PRESS
PO Box 2018, Scottsdale, AZ 85252

CITY OF THE GODS: GUARDIAN

First Edition - May 2013
ISBN: 978-0-9836929-4-2

Acknowledgements

Special thanks to:
Ken St. Andre for the idea about Zeus & Odin (and more)
Jay Allen Sanford & Randy Lindsay for various suggestions.
And to all the Kickstarter pledgers that helped made this book possible!
Especially our **God of Patronage: Matt Selter**

Proofing & Advice from:
Anita, Molly Baker.
Randy Lindsay, Karen Reed, Marty Murphy, Sherry Ledington
Jefferson P. Swycaffer & Robert Kassebaum

Special appearances by;
Brett Bozeman, Niki Canotas, Julio Capa, Ellie Idol & Cynthia Teare

First Edition - May 2013

Contents

From the Journal of Jacques D'Molay

I've always been a restless man. When I lived back on Earth as a Knight Templar, I was constantly on the move. France, Cyprus, Jerusalem, Italy… looking back on it now, I realize when King Phillip of France had me unjustly imprisoned for seven years, it was the most time I spent in one place. I would have been there even longer, except for the fact he executed me in 1314. I'd been certain the Pope would free me and the rest of the Knights. Instead, we were all executed.

Yet even after my death, it seemed my wandering was not yet done. I awoke in a cold, gray realm known as Purgatory, where the souls from Earth waited for the judgment day. I became a restless wanderer there as well, a man on a crusade to explore this strange, sad place. I traveled for centuries and eventually discovered the three gates. Hidden at the far corners of Purgatory are the entrances to Heaven, the Inferno and the realm of the gods. But none of the gates could be opened.

Eventually, that knowledge allowed me to take a stranded god to the gate of his realm. The journey took years. Truly grateful for my help, this deity invited me to leave with him. I had seen all there was of Purgatory and by then, I had lost my faith. God had abandoned me, so I abandoned him and went to the realm of these other gods.

Once I got there, news that I had rescued a deity spread. Soon other gods employed me to find and deliver messages and artifacts across their realms. Since I had no alliances to any gods, they knew I could be trusted. It became my purpose, my vocation.

I earned a sort of immortality that the gods give to favored servants, even though I was a Freeman, under the thumb of no god or pantheon. I largely forgot my old life on Earth. But despite living in a place of wonders, my existence was an empty one.

One day, I found a girl lying in the street. She didn't know her name or where she had come from. She was so helpless and beautiful in a way that seemed strangely familiar. I took pity on her and soon became caught up in solving the mystery of her identity. We called her Aavi and I fought to keep her safe, as dangers grew ever nearer. For the first time since I had come to this realm, I had fallen in love. At least I thought so; but it was much more than that.

Yet despite my best efforts, I couldn't keep Aavi safe. She died a helpless victim of the gods Set, Ares and Quetzalcoatl as they battled to possess her. After her death, I lost my will to live . . . I truly wanted to die.

Then I discovered the truth about Aavi; who she was and how she'd gotten stranded here. I realized that everything that had happened to me had occurred for a reason. Aavi had been sent to me, so that I might help her return to her home and restore a faith I had so long ago abandoned.

I will always be in her debt . . . for she saved my life and my soul.

D'Molay's map of the Inner Realms of the Gods.

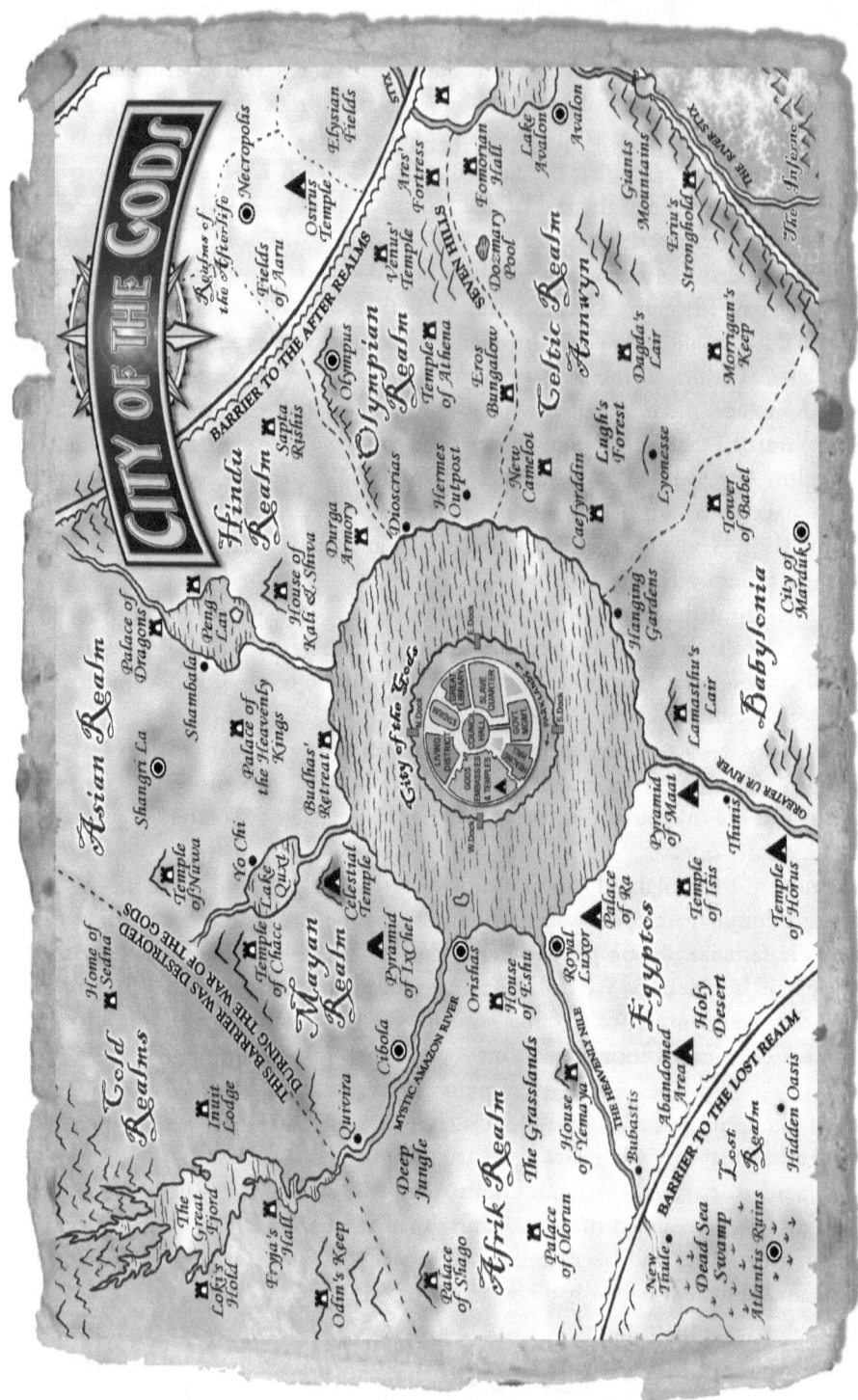

Chapter 1

Excursions and Encounters

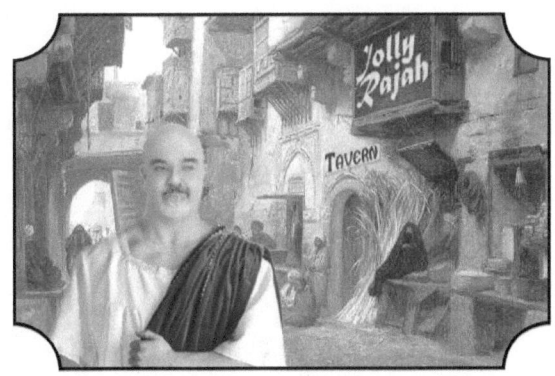

"*I* swear by Mithras you've had that ugly belt for 30 years."

The warm morning sun beamed through the open doorway and cast a pale orange glow upon the tavern room of the Jolly Rajah. D'Molay rarely visited this early, but he was comfortable in the shadows that stretched across the floor from the low angle of the light. His companion at the well-worn oak table was his old friend Sergius, who had just finished a jocular critique of D'Molay's wardrobe and kit. D'Molay wore dark leather boots and a matching vest. His beige cotton pants were tucked into the boots. Underneath his vest, he wore a loose fitting, long sleeved tunic that laced up the front. On the floor sat a traveling bag and a larger knapsack with a strap running along its length. There was no doubt that he was a man on his way to somewhere beyond the City walls. Sergius was a stark contrast; he dressed in a more decadent style that proved his tavern, and other under its tables pursuits, paid him well.

"So, where are you headed? Some new mission for the Council?"

D'Molay shifted in his uncomfortable chair. "Not this time. I made a bonded agreement, and now I have to honor it," he tried to say as casually as possible.

Sergius leaned toward him. "You bonded yourself? I thought you said you'd never do that again after what happened last time."

"It couldn't be helped. I needed some information. A bond was all I had left to offer in order to get it."

Sergius gave his old partner an appraising look. "Well, that's just one more reason I got out of the business and took over this place. I don't have to pledge my life to get a delivery of ale or wine." He leaned back in his chair and balanced it on the two rear legs, resting the chair against the wall as if to reassure himself that his tavern was still there. "What's this bond all about? Are you even able to talk about it?"

D'Molay took a sip from his mug. "I can talk about it. I have to find Circe and try to get her to reverse a spell she cast long ago."

"Circe? I've heard she's a sorceress who turns men into beasts."

"Yes, so have I. And worse. Have you heard any rumors about where she is these days?"

Sergius gave his familiar exasperated look, one that signaled disbelief that he would know the answer to such a question. "No . . . no, I can't say that I have. Are you sure she's even in the realms of the Gods? I mean, is she even a goddess? Maybe she died back on Earth, eons ago."

"Give me a bit of credit," D'Molay smirked back. "I checked the Great Library. Circe's listed in the book of

the favored, and that means she was definitely here at some point. I just haven't been able to track her down yet. You'd think finding a sorceress would be easy, but it's almost if she has gone into hiding or retired."

"Well, if anyone can find her it'll be you. Still, I think you're crazy for taking on something like this." Sergius tipped his chair back into its proper position as one of his serving girls brought a pitcher to refill their mugs. He glanced up at the woman, then said, "Hey, did you ever find that slave girl you were looking for?"

"Yes. I found her and freed her. Then she was killed at a battle at Ares' Fortress about a month ago. She sacrificed herself so that I . . ." His voice trailed off as the painful memories took over. D'Molay looked down at the table, unable to hold Sergius' gaze.

The sadness that burdened D'Molay did not go unnoticed by his old friend. "I'm sorry. I had no idea." Sergius seemed unsure what to say. They sat in silence for a moment. "Did she ever regain her memories and find out where she came from?" he finally asked.

D'Molay raised his head. "At the very end she did. But..." D'Molay seemed to almost be at battle with himself, like a stutterer unable to form a word he wanted to say. His entire body tensed up and his face started to turn red as he tried to speak. Finally he stopped and caught his breath. It was more a sigh of resignation as he accepted the fact he would not be able to say any more on the matter. Such was the power of the Council's magic. "I - I can't tell you any more than that, Sergius. It's tied up with matters the Council has ordered me not to speak of."

"A pox on the Council. See how they mess with our minds, our souls and our very existence? That's why I left. Being a pawn in their endless games is no way to live. I never knew if a task was really of use, or just some petty power play. I don't know how you continue to put up with it."

Sergius picked up his refilled mug and took a deep drink from it. D'Molay merely stared into his own ale as he answered.

"Maybe I just stopped caring. I was a good soldier. They gave me a task and I just did it. I never worried about the rest. It was a job and they paid me, regardless of the reason. I think that's why the death of Aavi hit me so hard. I cared about someone once again. I can't blame the Council for her fate, though. They had nothing to do with it. She died because I took her into danger and failed to protect her."

"Ah, you can't blame yourself for that. Only the gods can know the future, and I often have my doubts about even that."

"I should have known, Sergius. I should have . . ."

"Don't play the martyr. From what I've heard, you did enough of that back on Earth. What happened, happened. You can either move on or spend the rest of your life staring into a tankard of ale. I did that for years and I don't recommend it."

D'Molay looked up at Sergius. "Perhaps it had to happen. I'll never know for sure. I just need some time to get over her loss and my part in it. Maybe a hundred years or so."

Sergius decided it was time to change the subject. "So, where are you going next on this search for Circe?"

"I'm meeting Mazu at the north docks and then we travel back to the Olympian Realm. We have a few leads there to follow up on."

"At least you have a plan."

Just then a delivery man called out from the back of the tavern. "Where's the tavern master? I got a shipment of wine on my cart."

Looking up from the table, Sergius bellowed out, "Be right there!" He stood. "My day begins. I have to go. Be careful, D'Molay. If Circe is hiding from the world, she might not want to be found. Be wary of who you trust."

"All right - I will. Thanks for just being there old friend."

"Always. Well, except for now." Sergius waved farewell as he followed the man into the back of the tavern.

D'Molay finished his ale in one swig. He slung the large bag over his shoulder and picked up the smaller traveling bag he and Aavi had used just a few weeks ago. After walking out of the Jolly Rajah in into the morning streets, D'Molay hailed a carriage driver.

"Where to sir?" the man asked. D'Molay wondered how many centuries the thin old man had lived. In this world, he could be seventy or centuries more than that.

"Take me to the East Gate." As D'Molay loaded his belongings into the high compartment behind the driver, he heard the man sigh in response to the announced destination. The gate wasn't that far from the tavern and the man's fare would be accordingly low. D'Molay paid his coins and climbed into the carriage box.

The carriage rolled off, stopping only once to pick up another passenger by the Roman slave market. As a portly merchant boarded, D'Molay gazed out the window at the abandoned temple across the street. His trained eye caught the movement of several people ducking out of sight, retreating deeper into decrepit doorways. D'Molay knew he site was a haven for thieves. He frowned at the foolish risk the driver was taking by even stopping near it. Luck was with them, however, and the carriage moved on without incident. The merchant, after settling himself into his seat with a great deal of huffing, puffing and rearrangement of his wares, promptly closed his eyes to nap. D'Molay was grateful that the man had no interest in small talk.

Five minutes later they reached the gate. D'Molay eased out of the vehicle so as not to awaken the snoring man and retrieved his bags. He hoped that switching from the carriage to the boat might throw off or reveal anyone who might be following. Noticing the gate was relatively free of traffic he hurried toward it. Sometimes the entry was quite clogged with heavily loaded wagons delivering food from the agricultural dock and the sad procession of slaves from the single pier that allowed slaves to be offloaded into the City. D'Molay wondered if perhaps today was a holy day that restricted business. For the life of him, he could not keep track of all the festivals and random observances that affected affairs in the City of the Gods. But he appreciated his good fortune as he swiftly cleared the gate and headed toward the boat rental dock. D'Molay approached a middle-aged woman in an elaborately decorated Babylonian gown, who had constructed a podium of sorts out of a stack of empty crates, and hung upon it a sign painted with glyphs of people riding in ships. D'Molay was struck by her beauty, and wondered why a woman of her obvious good breeding was operating a boat rental station. Thinking quickly of his own unusual history, he suppressed his curiosity. Everyone in the City had a past that was probably as amazing and unconventional as his own. The woman looked up and smiled at him.

"Do you have a short-runner to the North Dock?" he asked.

"Of course." She glanced toward the agricultural dock. "My green boat is waiting for you." The woman pointed to the top of the box she stood behind and D'Molay looked down to

see a rudimentary chart of fares. A splotch of green paint had been applied next to a drawing of one of the City's coins. Nodding, he fished a matching coin out of his belt, realizing that perhaps Sergius had a point about its over-worn condition, and passed it to the Babylonian. In exchange, he received a small stone with some cryptic symbol on it. Assuming this was his ticket, D'Molay expressed his thanks and made his way to the small craft she had pointed out. Three other passengers were already on board, but he paid them no heed.

It was crewed by two young men who gestured eagerly to him as he came near. D'Molay held the stone between thumb and forefinger to show them what had been painted on it. The sailor with a tattoo of a roaring lion on his shoulder then pointed toward a pot with a hole in its lid. D'Molay dropped the stone through the hole and sat down on a ledge-bench that ran along the side of the boat. Chattering to each other in Panthos, the common language of the realms, the sailors put the craft quickly out on the lake and raised its sails to catch the wind that would propel it to the northwest. The boat carried him past the dense forest that shielded the northeast shore of the City. D'Molay allowed his thoughts to roam during the trip, imagining what mysteries the thick trees were hiding under their boughs.

When they reached the bustling North Dock, D'Molay juggled his kit and climbed up a short ladder as the young men held the boat steady against the pier. When his head popped up to dock level, an Asian man strode over and chastised the rental boaters for not tying their boat up properly. D'Molay laughed to himself as they bickered, the dock's man wanting payment for the use of his facilities, and the sailors insisting that they owed nothing for they hadn't actually docked. Their heated negotiations faded into the background as D'Molay moved on toward Mazu's boathouse. From the looks of it, little had changed since the last time he had been there.

To anyone else, the bright red octagonal building and surrounding garden was a serene way station overlooking the great lake. But to D'Molay, it was a reminder of the man he had murdered here less than a month ago and the pain that act had caused. Aavi had almost lost her sanity when she realized he had killed someone for her. At the time, her acute distress was perplexing; now knowing what she was, it made more sense. An angel wouldn't want others to die or kill for them. He looked up briefly at the clear blue sky as he remembered Aavi.

The first thing he noticed upon entering the boathouse was that its polished wooden floor was clean and shining. It showed no sign that it had been bathed in the blood of a Mayan warrior. Behind the familiar counter stood a bald Asian man wearing a small red cap and matching silk embroidered jacket. He looked like he was in his late twenties and was stooped over, reviewing a stack of papers. D'Molay wondered how the man might react if he knew that the assassin who left a dead man by the front door here had just returned.

"Good morning. I'm looking for Mazu," D'Molay said, walking up to the counter.

"If you need passage across the lake, I can arrange a ferry for you. Mazu is unavailable, venerable sir." The man rattled off this solution without moving his attention from his papers.

The hairs on the back of D'Molay's neck prickled as he recalled the similar conversation he'd had at this same counter with the Mayan. Instinctively, his hand rested on the hilt of his knife, which was ready and waiting in its leather sheath. He responded in a calm tone. "I don't need passage. I'm supposed to meet Mazu here this morning. Do you know where she is?"

The man shuffled his papers for another infuriating moment before looking up. "Many seek the goddess Mazu, but only the worthy find her. She has departed on a long journey and will not be returning soon."

D'Molay fixed his eyes on the smaller man. "Is that so," he said, feeling certain that the answer was a brazen lie. His challenge was met with silence and a smug smile.

Just then another older man dressed in similar clothes walked in from an adjoining room. "I recognize that voice. You are . . . D'Molay?"

"Yes. Do you know where Mazu is?" D'Molay turned toward the newcomer, whom he recognized as one of the men he often saw mending nets and sails around the boathouse. "What's going on here?"

The older man looked at D'Molay for a few seconds as if to size him up. "You can take him in, Quan. She's expecting him." Without another word the older man walked out the front door.

Quan tucked his papers beneath the counter and beckoned to D'Molay. "Come. I will present you to the goddess."

Still wary, D'Molay followed him though an arch and down a short corridor into a larger room. Ornate nautical instruments and fishing sup-

plies were stacked on shelves and hung from hooks. In the corner were a dozen wicker floor mats and a square stone fountain. Burning incense smoked up from pots set on the rim of the fountain. The light of many large candles cast a serene warm glow around the room. The juxtaposition of fishing supplies and a shrine drove home its purpose.

"Is this Mazu's chapel? And these things contributions to the goddess?"

Quan led D'Molay to the corner. "As you say. Please, sit. Mazu will attend to you when she is ready." He gestured to the mats. D'Molay picked one from the top of the pile and spread it on the floor. He lowered himself to sit, feeling a bit awkward.

Quan bowed and left the chapel as D'Molay sat on the floor, facing the only exit to the room. He waited, hoping Mazu would soon come walking in. After some time passed he began to worry about the delay. The room held no answers save the calm steady trickling sound of the water in the fountain.

D'Molay decided to try to relax, something he rarely did outside his own home. He closed his eyes and ignored the many questions that kept flitting through his mind. There was something about the soothing sound of the fountain and the feeling of security from the position of the chapel in the center of the building, protected from the outside, which put him at ease. For a few moments, D'Molay felt serenity that had hadn't felt in quite some time.

Then the voice of Mazu broke through his peace. "I see you have learned some degree of patience during these long years in the City of the Gods."

Startled, D'Molay opened his eyes and turned to see the water in the fountain rising up in a column and starting to take human shape. "Mazu, were you hiding in the water the whole time, waiting to see how long it would take me to get annoyed?" he asked good-naturedly. He was glad to see her, even if she seemed to be toying with him.

"I was waiting to see if you could reach a degree of calm in this peaceful place, and noticing how loosely your clothing fits these days." As she spoke, the column of water continued to become less transparent and take on her familiar form, the elder goddess of the water. She appeared to be as fully physical a person as D'Molay. A thin column of water shot out of the fountain and into her hand. The water turned to a staff of silver wood. Mazu stepped slowly down from the ledge of the fountain, her grey hair tucked under a broad pointed straw hat, her dark teal robe flowing around and behind her. She looked to be a graceful Chinese woman perhaps in her early sixties. Of course, she was in fact thousands of years old, as all the gods were.

Standing up, D'Molay offered his hand. She gently took it as she placed her sandaled foot on the wooden floor. He offered a sly smile. "So, you were packing for our journey in the fountain, were you?"

"In a manner of speaking. I have recently discovered a difficulty if I am to travel with you in our search for Circe."

"You're goddess. What difficulty could there be for you?"

"There is a one word answer to that question. Quetzalcoatl."

"Quetzalcoatl?"

"Yes. He is trying to capture me," she replied matter-of-factly.

"Still mad that you escaped from him, no doubt."

"There is more to it than his godly pride. I stumbled across his plan to take the great beast for himself while we were searching for Aavi. My knowledge of his dark ambitions puts him at risk. I am a loose end he plans to take care of one way or another."

D'Molay frowned, the sense of peace evaporating as Mazu spoke of this new threat. "But why should any of that matter now? The beast is gone and Aavi . . . Aavi is dead."

"Perhaps so. But rumor has gotten about that more gods than Set were involved in all that led to the battle at the Fortress of Ares. I know that Quetzalcoatl was involved and that makes me a danger to him. He did not rise to take a place on the Council by ignoring potential enemies." She gave D'Molay an earnest look that let him know that this was no idle political intrigue, but a deadly attempt to have her captured, or more likely assassinated.

"I still say you should go to the Council and tell them what you know."

She frowned. "We've discussed this before. I have no proof. It would be my word against his and he is a high-ranking member on the Council. They would take no action against him and I could be accused of making false accusations. I either have to find proof or wait until he makes a move that might prove his true motives to others."

D'Molay could see that Mazu had carefully thought the situation through, but one thing still puzzled him. "If Quetzalcoatl is so worried, why hasn't he just come here and captured you?"

"Because of the one thing in my favor at the moment. If he takes direct action against me it might appear he does have something to hide. Like the snake that he is, he will wait until the right time to strike and then do so quickly, so that others might not even see his involvement in it."

"I'm glad there is at least something in our favor." D'Molay was almost afraid to ask his next question. "Is there any more bad news?"

Mazu reached up and adjusted her hat. "Yes. My servants tell me there is a winged serpent flying overhead as we speak. It is the eyes of Quetzalcoatl, watching to see if I am here and where I might go next."

"So you can't even leave the boathouse? That's going to make looking for Circe very difficult, Mazu."

"I didn't say I can't leave. We'll just have to be careful about how I do it."

⌖

D'Molay dutifully waited inside the boathouse. Waiting was not something he liked doing, but Mazu had insisted that he, like she, remain out of sight. He'd wanted to help Quan and the other men load the small ferry boat for its journey. Instead, he spent his time in the chapel, trying in vain to re-experience that fleeting feeling of peace.

After about an hour, Quan reappeared, bowing to Mazu as he entered. "The boat is loaded. Where is it we're going?"

"Dioscrias," she smiled. "Bring me a servant's robe and an extra hat."

"A robe?" Quan seemed confused by the request.

"Yes. You'll see why soon enough."

Quan bowed again, quickly leaving the room on the errand.

D'Molay wondered what Mazu was up to. "Sounds like you have a lead on Circe."

"Not precisely," she said casually. "But I think I know where to get one. Ah, here's Quan."

Realizing that the goddess was not going to reveal her strategy right then, D'Molay could only guess of her plans. He had been to Dioscrias before. It was a minor port of the Olympian Realm and not a place with a reputation as a hub for gossip or intrigues. Rationalizing that they'd be there soon, he put his questions aside.

A few minutes later, two men emerged from the boathouse. Both wore traditional Asian garb and caps. One carried a small barrel of what looked like wine and the other toted a large dark jar. To any airborne spy, they looked exactly the same as the other men who had been busy loading up the ship with small items. However, as the minutes passed, these other workers left the boat in ones and twos leaving only the last two to board to cast off the ship. The boat pulled away from the dock; Mazu was nowhere to be seen.

"Pull that line, so we'll catch the wind," Quan called out from the stern.

"Right, got it." D'Molay grabbed the line and tied it off, his face hidden by the large hat tied underneath his chin. The robe that covered his normal clothes felt constricting, but he strove to move as naturally as he could manage in case the reports of Quetzalcoatl's spies in the sky were true.

Soon they travelled at a brisk pace, sailing east toward the Olympian Realm. D'Molay walked to the center of the boat and into the covered cabin area where there were two sleeping bunks and a small counter and cabinets. He bent down and pried free the lid of the barrel and opened the jar they'd brought on board. Almost immediately, the waters held by each container started bubbling out. Of their own accord, they merged into a single rising column of water which coalesced into Mazu.

"Ahhh, that's better," she sighed. "I don't like being separated like that."

D'Molay smiled. "Your trick worked. Welcome aboard. As long as you stay under this tarp, they can't spot you."

She raised an eyebrow "We must take more care than just that. Quetzalcoatl is not so easily fooled. But at least he'll be less likely to strike, for now."

Quan poked his head in through the other side of the cover. "Mistress, is all well?"

She looked over her shoulder, a slight smile on her face. "Yes, but that barrel smelled of wine."

Chapter 2

Plans & Schemes

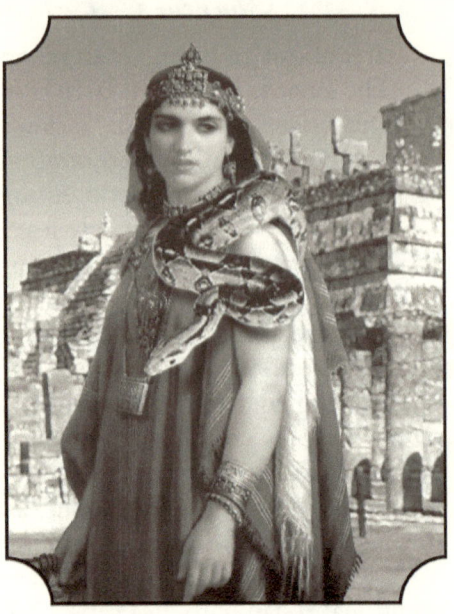

High in the mountains of the Mayan realm, above the humid jungles and wet-lands, was the stepped pyramid of the Celestial Temple. Built of solid stone and covered in white plaster, the huge edifice was a maze of rooms and chambers, with an observatory on the top. It was the place where the gods of that realm met to celebrate great deeds or discuss important matters. There was no doubt that today the gods were gathering for an official conclave, as one by one they started to appear in the round-domed observatory. The first was Ixchel, the beautiful goddess of the moon. None could miss her, for beside her perfect wide-eyed face and curvaceous figure, was her companion, a coiled green snake who rested upon her head as if it were a stylish beret. Her dark brown hair was intricately coiffed in the Mayan style and ran halfway down her back.

Soon, half a dozen other deities joined the two of them. Ixchel felt buoyed by the obvious show of support. Even Hunapu, one of the hero-ic twins, had joined her cadre. They all spoke in hushed, conspiratorial whispers about godly intrigues. Their discussions abruptly halted when Quetzalcoatl flew into the chamber in the form of a large feathered ser-pent. He hovered in the center of the observatory, his wings flapping slower, and his long red and green form coiling up on the floor. There was a burst of light; then Quetzalcoatl stood before them imperiously in his human form. There was little doubt that he was their Pantheon leader. Long ago, he had brought the disparate gods of various tribes together to form an alliance that dominated an entire continent on Earth. Together they had helped the humans build an empire and turn dangerous jungle into civilized land; but without the gods, the human empire had fallen into chaos and destruction. It was the unspoken regret of the entire Mayan Pantheon, for they were some of the very last deities to leave the Earth.

Quetzalcoatl looked around the chamber, making eye contact with all the attendees, his gaze fixing upon Ixchel. "I have come as you request-ed and will hear your words. Let the conclave begin."

The Mayan conclave was a formal event and it was expected that the deities would address each other in the proper manner, though sometimes in the heat of discussion the formality of the occasion was overlooked. Ixchel wanted to make sure she started off on the right footing. She stepped forward trying to remain poised and confident, addressing Quetzalcoatl by his title. "Thank you Kukulcan, for joining us this day. Ever may your wisdom and power keep our people strong. We have called for this gathering to discuss matters that are of concern to us all."

Quetzalcoatl stood proudly. "I accept your greeting, and return it to all assembled. I would know what concerns you wish to discuss." His multicolored headdress and elaborate jewel-studded kilt made a slight sound as he spoke, almost as if he were accompanied by a small group of distant musicians. His gaze remained upon Ixchel as he awaited her response.

"We have heard the reasons for the incursion into the Olympian Realm and the loss of many warriors during the battle, but we wish to know more of why such a thing occurred, and what we have gained from this action. We know that in your wisdom, Kukulcan, you always see beyond the valley of our sight. We only ask that you tell your brother and sister gods what you have seen beyond the mountains." Ixchel swallowed, and hoped that she had laid out her case in such a way that Quetzalcoatl would not take offense. She had used his Mayan title as a sign of respect, though she was putting herself at risk for daring to ask him to explain his actions, even though it was within her rights to do so. Quetzalcoatl's wrath was a terrible thing to behold. He could not kill her, but Ixchel knew that he could make her wish she were dead, if he so desired. He was much like the weather; there was no way of knowing if the day would be stormy or calm. The green snake on her head came slowly awake and it stared back at him, perhaps trying to gauge his mood.

Quetzalcoatl took time to consider his answer.

"Your words hold honor and your question is deserving of an answer, Ixchel. But you will have to trust that there are things beyond the mountains that I cannot fully reveal at this time. That is not by my choice, but the decree of the Council. No one is allowed to discuss some of the events of that day, though I will tell you all I can. Many of our warriors went to Olympia. I ordered this, not for my glory, but to stop Set from stealing something of great power, something that threatened not just our people, but all people in the realms of the gods."

There were murmurings from the gathered crowd. They had obviously not expected such a measured response, one that sounded so reasonable.

Ixchel tried to walk the narrow line between a desire for the truth and avoiding the wrath of Quetzalcoatl. "I am sure that all you have said is as it was, but why did you not consult the rest of us with such an important decision? I'm sure we could have aided you all the more in this important task you took upon yourself. Our charter sets out that invading another realm must be something that requires the agreement of the conclave, yet we had no such meeting."

"I would have called a conclave if I had thought there was time. But I didn't discover Set's devious plans until he was almost in Olympia. There was no time; I had to move quickly, before it was too late. Though many of our troops died in the battle, they did not die in vain. They gave their lives so that all of us could preserve our existence. You will have to trust me on this, as I cannot tell you more than that." Quetzalcoatl finished with a sorrowful wrenching of his hands to emphasize his grief at the loss of the troops and his apparent frustration at not being able to reveal more to his fellow deities.

It was obvious the crowd was impressed with Quetzalcoatl's answers. There was little doubt in the minds of Ixchel's allies that she was outmatched when it came to being able to influence others with smooth words and dramatic expressions, but she tried nonetheless. "I see. Still, we would know of any such actions in the future, regardless of the situation. It is at the very core of why we subverted our status in your favor and made you the Kukulcan of our Pantheon, Quetzalcoatl. We too expect a voice in such matters."

Quetzalcoatl bowed slightly. "I hear your words, Ixchel, and have no doubt your sentiments are shared by many here today. I promise you all that I shall consult with the conclave if and when the forces of the Maya are brought to bear. For now, I do not see that as likely, for we have avoided such with the previous foray against Set's ambitions. I will only add that the Council has banished Set and they thank the Mayan Pantheon for their quick actions to aid the Olympians in a time of great danger."

Ixchel bowed. "We can ask no more than that, Kukulcan. I thank you for hearing my words and understanding our concerns." She withdrew and rejoined her allies against the wall.

Quetzalcoatl addressed the other deities. "So,

are there other issues to discuss? If so, bring them forward." Soon various topics were debated, including how to replace the warriors lost in the battle, and rumors as to where the Egyptos god Set might have escaped, along with mundane matters like the fertility rites for the maize crop and the training of condors.

Ixchel and her supporters left the observatory as a group and found a more isolated area deep within the labyrinthine pyramid where they could speak more freely.

"You did well and asked what needed to asked, Ixchel. Quetzalcoatl needs to be reminded from time to time that we are also deities and not his personal servants," said Hunapu as he thumped his chest in support.

"Indeed, he was most conciliatory. Perhaps he is aware he overstepped his boundaries this time," said Itzamna. Ixchel had known Itzamna since she was a girl, for he was one of the first Mayan gods; the sky and sorcery were his domain. He walked with a slight limp, using a staff made of ironwood, decorated with semi-precious stones. Though she was flattered by his remarks, Ixchel had a different perspective.

"You may be right, but I think he has not told us everything about the battle and his part in it. There are too many things that do not align properly. I have it on good authority that he was preparing our troops many days before they left for Olympia and that he had sent scouts there many days before that. He would have had ample time to call us all for a conclave on the matter."

"Why did you not bring any of this up?" asked Hunapu.

She gave him a frustrated look and shrugged, "I only have rumors, gossip! Everything I said out there was based on things I knew to be fact, things I could have confirmed if Kukulcan had demanded it."

"Perhaps the Council really did forbid him from speaking of these things to others," suggested Yum Kaax, the lord of the forests.

"I hope you are right. Either way, we cannot be certain without gathering more answers," Ixchel replied as she removed her snake from her head and wrapped it around her shoulders like a shawl.

"Now he knows who his allies are and who questions his actions," said Nim Ac, whose head was that of a javelina.

Itzamna leaned forward on his cane, giving the group a wry look. "I do not question his right to rule, only his recent actions. We must be observant and see what we might discover from other sources. But know that Quetzalcoatl is no fool. He has always been aware of who has undying loyalty to him and who does not, so we must also be cautious."

Ixchel spoke again. "Very well. I hope that Quetzalcoatl is indeed working in our best interests. I want that to be the case. There is someone else I know of who might be able to help us learn the truth. I shall seek them out next."

"Who is this you speak of?" her mentor asked.

"I would rather not say, for now, but I feel as though our paths are fated to cross. I hope you will all understand."

The rest of the gods concurred, promising to keep an eye out for any further information and then left for their palaces and temples, uncertain of their next move.

Quetzalcoatl felt triumphant once again as he walked down the steps of the Celestial Observatory with several of his allies.

Chaac the frog god lead the way carrying his axe, awkwardly hopping down the stairs, which were too narrow for his bulbous body. Tlaloc walked at Quetzalcoatl's right, with Zipacna, he of the crocodile head, at his left.

Zipacna gnashed his teeth as he exclaimed, "How dare they question you, Kukulcan! You should drop them all into the bottomless pit of Xibalba, and let them suffer for a few centuries."

"Yesssss, very good . . . do that." Tlaloc hissed with amusement at the suggestion, his pink tongue lapping out in stark contrast to the green color of his reptilian skin. He became immediately silent once Quetzalcoatl began to speak.

"Ixchel and her allies are merely misguided rules followers, who only do what they think is correct and proper. They lack the vision to see the larger picture, and the bravery to do what must be done in a time of crisis."

Chaac looked concerned. "What will you do about Ixchel and her allies, Kukulcan?"

He smiled. "Sometimes you can catch a whole herd of llamas by simply taming their leader. It will do well if I can offer Ixchel some token of esteem or power to draw her towards our cause. We must look for such an opportunity. If she takes such bait, the others will surely follow her lead. But for now there are greater concerns. In fact, I need two of you for a very important task."

All were eager to help their Kukulcan. They gathered around him to hear of his plan.

et was weary, but fatigue would not override his reluctance to rest for long in any one place. Since fleeing from Ares' Fortress at the disastrous end of the war, he had kept on the move. The Council had done a thorough job of spreading the word about his crimes and tricks. Many sought to gain by capturing him, forcing Set to act with far more restraint than he was accustomed. He had resigned himself to travelling in the form of a dusty whirlwind, at night, when an airy pillar was less likely to be noticed; but the transformation required power, a resource that he was finding difficult to replenish in the forsaken wastes of the Lost Realm.

Set felt himself weakening at the worst possible moment: the hour before dawn when a Greek scouting force came dangerously close to picking up his trail. Their proximity was threatening enough to change his strategy. Hoping the Greeks had become accustomed to seeing the local creatures as they searched, Set sought and killed a snake-headed man. On the body, he found amulets, tokens, and a canteen of brackish water, but the garments were the only things of use to the fugitive god. With a snarl of disgust, he donned them and commenced stepping lightly across the wastes in the fashion of those creatures, keeping plenty of distance between himself and other nomads. He expended only enough power to keep a tiny dust devil spinning close behind him, erasing his tracks in the sand.

That day, he moved with no destination in mind. In fact, he tried to keep his mind as blank as possible, knowing that some gods were expert at snatching the very thoughts from another's head. He now regretted his hasty flight from the City. If he had stayed, perhaps he could have intimidated a faction of weaker gods to vouch for his innocence. Or perhaps he could have played protective politics as Quetzalcoatl and Lamasthu surely had. At the very least, he could have delayed his flight long enough to pack some useful potions and poisons. Yet here he wandered as an extremely ill-equipped refugee. He growled aloud at the indignity but quickly silenced his mental regrets lest his weakness be exposed to prying powers. The only sounds for an hour were the scrape of his footsteps and the occasional hum of a buzzing insect. Then he heard whispering.

At first, he wasn't sure it was a language he was hearing. The sounds were intermingled with sighs and weak wailing. Ghosts had found him.

Set stopped, listening carefully and using his keen eyes to seek the spirits. He could not see them, but could now catch some of their words. Most of them were in a tongue he did not know, one whose people had lost the power games and allowed their culture to slip into history. But he did pick out a few phrases in the speech of the Romans, a race adept at ordering others about. He heard "come," "now," and "she commands."

Set nodded his swaddled head in a faux subordinate bow and waited. The whispers ceased as the invisibles turned their attention to driving a round ball of dead brush in the direction of some standing stones to the south. Set took their hint and followed the tumbling flotsam. It was a risk, but better to know who was aware of him so that they could be summarily dealt with. As he closed on the rock grouping, he noticed a stone statue of a woman set inside it. He could not tell if the rubble around her had once been part of a temple or if the statue was planted among the rocks for some other reason. The rolling mass of brush bounced against the upturned toes of the figure's carved slippers and its motion ceased. The contact awakened a spark of life inside the statue, and that power in turn made the ghosts that had been impervious to Set's keen sight come into full view. Five misty forms of armored men flanked the woman made of stone. Set noticed that each one of them was connected by a tendril of energy that extended from their heads and disappeared into the folds of the statue's ornate robes. He could not tell if the being inside the rock was powering the ghosts, or vice versa.

"Well done, well done," a female voice cooed from deep within the stone. "This visitor looks to be a very special one." One of the spirits leaned in and whispered into her chiseled ear. Set thought he saw a minute raise of her eyebrow in response to whatever the ghost had said.

"I followed your minions here. What do you want?" Set said, reaching into the fine kilt he wore beneath the desert rags and drawing out a small bottle of nectar. If he was to be delayed by this being's curiosity, he would use the break in his journey well. Thumbing off the cork that was tied by a thin whip of black lacing to the exquisite blue-glass vial, Set tipped the bottle to his lips. This action triggered a longing sigh from the strange female, which he ignored.

"Ah. I see you don't want to know my name," she said flatly.

Set swallowed a small sip and put his bottle away. "Since I wasn't planning on giving mine that seems fair. I only wanted a look at you." He stared at the frozen woman for a moment, gauging her threat. His first instinct was to knock her down and break her into pieces. In his opinion, it was best to leave no witnesses even if those observers had no idea what they had seen. But leaving her destroyed body in his wake could give away his trail. Since there was no sign that she could move, and her ghosts had no more effect on him than the desert insects, he decided to do nothing. Without another word, he turned his back on her and continued on.

Her calls for him to come back went unanswered.

Chapter 3

The Old Goddess and the Sea

They sailed along for half a day as dark clouds gathered over the lake, blocking out Apollo's sun. The choppy waters became almost black; everything seemed gray and lifeless as a chill wind kicked up. D'Molay looked to the northeast and thought he saw a faint flash of lightning in the distance. "Smells like rain. I think we're in for a storm."

"The gods control the weather. They must have decided it's time for rain," Quan replied nonchalantly. The prospect of getting wet seemed of no concern to Mazu's servant, who after a short review of D'Molay's map capably set the ferryboat's sails to guide them toward the port called Dioscrias in the Olympian Realm. Quan's disregard for the wind and possible rain extended to his lighting of a pipe to smoke as they sailed along. D'Molay dug into his bag and donned a coat to keep the chill off his own bones.

With Mazu remaining concealed in the barrel and the jar, Quan and D'Molay passed the time with a little fishing. They had been at it for over an hour, with Quan proving he had a knack for the task at hand. Frustrated by his failure to catch even one fish, D'Molay was tempted to throw his pole into the lake as another annoying gnat tried to crawl into his eye. He swiped at his eyelashes and felt something squish. He growled. Quan laughed.

"No luck yet?" he goaded, wiggling his fishing pole as something nibbled on his line.

"I'm not a fisherman," D'Molay said, ramming the end of the useless stick he held between his knees as he reached for Quan's pipe. Perhaps a cloud of smoke would keep the bugs away, or even encourage them to go chew on Quan instead. As he puffed on the pipe, D'Molay shot a suspicious look at Mazu's favored man. He wasn't sure he trusted him; but he hardly knew the man, and such feelings were to be expected. Perhaps he had just grown too used to being Mazu's only traveling companion due to the many weeks they'd spent together in the past.

Quan pulled his pole out of the lake and detached a fish from his line. He tossed it into a bucket already populated by his earlier trophies. The boat barely rocked as the fisherman worked. D'Molay noted his skill and ease on the water with a touch of jealousy. Quan met his gaze and a grin spread across his oval face.

"That's five fish, Freeman," he said. "I'll let you eat one."

"Two," D'Molay bargained. "Mazu says I'm still too thin."

Quan scoffed. "She can't see how fat you really are under that coat." He hiked the long tail of his own thin silk shirt up around his hips as he settled in front of the bucket. Quan shook a long finger at D'Molay to caution him. "I hope you can float. Not even good Mazu could save you if you fall into the lake with that weight on your back."

"My coat's made of wool, not lead," D'Molay said wearily. "And it keeps me warm."

Quan began to clean the catch, his small knife glinting brightly. "I'm not cold because I am the most blessed one of the goddess," he said smugly. D'Molay frowned at him, but couldn't argue. If a different man were clad only in the silk threads that covered Quan, the day's biting wind would reduce him to a huddle of shivering flesh. He listened stoically as Quan soliloquized further about his favored status, fighting the urge to dispute the man's inflated view of himself.

Quan was still talking when D'Molay thought he saw something off in the distance that flickered and then vanished, presumably beneath the waves. As he wondered what it had been, he saw it again, closer this time. It was translucent, a shimmering ball of energy, floating just a few feet above the water of the lake. The glowing ball flickered in and out of view then vanished as if it had never been there at all.

D'Molay pointed toward the site of the orb. "Did you see that?"

Quan looked in the direction D'Molay indicated. "No. Nothing but the water of the lake. Sit back down. You'll scare the fish," he chided.

"I'm sure I saw a round ball of light." He kept staring at the spot where the shimmering energy had appeared over the water, hoping it would return.

"It was probably lightning. Give me back my pipe."

"It didn't act like any lightning I've ever seen." D'Molay searched the sky for other strange flashes from above, but the thick clouds kept their secrets. He thrust the pipe into Quan's wiggling fingers. "Mazu seems to think we're being watched. Maybe I saw a spell being cast, or caught a glimpse of something following our boat."

Quan took a puff and exhaled smoke, the corners of his mouth turning down in worried disapproval. "Years ago in my village, one of my neighbors started seeing phantoms and visions. It led him to no end of trouble. Eventually his family had to lock him away as he became a danger to himself and others. After a few months, the visions stopped and he was fine once again."

"What's the point of that story?" D'Molay shot back. "I'm no danger to either of you, and I'm not crazy. At least not yet," he added. "Forget I said anything." He sat back down. D'Molay realized his vision was giving Quan pause to doubt his judgment. Wisely, he decided not to press the point lest it cause trouble later. Still, he wished Mazu could readily appear and discuss the matter, but he knew they couldn't risk her being seen.

"Yes, perhaps that is best. However, if I see anything unusual, I'll tell you the moment I see it, agreed?" Quan attempted to look reassuring.

"Agreed."

"You should rest for now. I will get us to this 'Dee-ohs-cree-is' place you and Mazu are determined to travel to." Quan picked up the map and looked off in the distance. He made a course change, adjusting the rudder without another word.

D'Molay got back up, running his hand through his wavy dark hair as he walked back to the 'cabin' in the center of the boat. It was little more than an area covered with a thick bamboo curtain that arched over a cot and some cabinets that were attached to the floor of the boat. He stood at the counter and noticed a bowl of fresh water upon it. For just a second, he wondered if Mazu was hiding in the bowl, but knew she had returned to the larger containers.

Looking into the water, D'Molay stared at reflection of himself: a man who looked much younger than one who bore the long years of life that had been granted him by the gods. Had he really been alive for so many hundreds of years? He'd lost track of how long it had really been. He could see the lines around his mouth and eyes that hinted at someone who had seen and experienced a hard, long life. Thoughts ran by, like the babbling waters of a brook. *Maybe I'm just too worried about this bonded task, but I'm sure I saw something.* He looked into his own eyes in the reflection, hoping to see some hint that might reveal the truth. Finally, he came to a conclusion. *I look weary and hungry and maybe a little desperate.* He sensed a movement behind him.

Quickly, he turned to see who or what it was. Once again, there was nothing there. He splashed the cool water on his face. It was refreshing and he took a ragged, deep breath. Even the simple act of breathing seemed fraught with difficulty at times. Dropping down on the nearby cot, he closed his eyes, and made a silent prayer to God. He tried not to think about the ball of light or that they might be followed or his long list of self-doubts. There was little he could do about any of those things. Despite trying not to think, his thoughts ran around in his mind like a bee trapped in an upturned glass bowl. Mercifully, he eventually drifted off into a restless sleep.

D'Molay awoke to strong waves rocking the boat. Torrential rain poured down as he stumbled out of the cot and relieved Quan at the rudder. Quan nodded his thanks as he ducked under the bamboo covering. When he re-emerged, he had stripped most of his sodden clothing off and finally put on a coat.

The boat rocked violently, causing Quan to stumble as he scrambled to the stern. The battering continued and crests of water splashed against the deck.

"We'll never make Olympia in this!" he shouted through the pouring rain. "I can't tell our direction or hold our course!" D'Molay believed him. There was no telling where the sun was behind the dark clouds and pouring rain. They were no better off than a leaf tossed in a windstorm. Worse than that, the waves crashing into the boat threatened to rob them of anything not tied down.

"Stay at the rudder, we need Mazu!" D'Molay scrambled towards the cabin as another wave washed over the hull and almost knocked him out of the boat. As he fell against the rail he wondered why she wasn't helping. Even in her watery form, she had to be aware of what was going on. D'Molay crawled through several inches of rising water the rest of the way to the cabin. Once under the bamboo cover, he discovered why she had not appeared.

The two containers in which she hid had been encased in some sort of amber-like substance, much like tree sap. D'Molay tried to pick up the barrel, only to realize it was stuck to the floor. With great difficulty, he managed to pull his hands free from the glutinous mess as another wave crashed into the boat. Panicked, he searched the cabin for anything that might break through the covering. Grabbing a bottle, he smashed it hard against the side of the barrel. Glass shards flew in every direction, but the barrel remained undamaged, the sap completely blunting his attack. He stood up and tried kicking the barrel with the heel of his boot; the result was the same. The boat lurched, sending D'Molay sprawling back to the floor.

Magic . . . it must be some form of magic. Crawling back through the rising waters to the barrel, D'Molay reached to his side and unsheathed his knife. It was the only thing he possessed that had the power to dispel mystical energy. Quickly, he raised the knife over his head and plunged it as hard as he could into the top of the barrel. He turned the knife, attempting to open a hole, and then withdrew it. A steady spray of water came forth. Immediately turning his attention to the jar, he plunged the knife into the top of it in hope of releasing the rest of Mazu. Its water gushed forth, and soon the goddess formed before him as the ship tenuously held together in the storm.

"What's going on? I couldn't - "

"Later - we have bigger problems! We're in a storm and the ship is taking on water. You're a water goddess. Can you do anything to keep us afloat?"

"Yes, yes of course," she replied.

"Do whatever you can before we're capsized!" He looked down to emphasize the rising waters and Mazu immediately disappeared into the flood at his feet. Once she was gone, he scrambled for a bucket, beginning to bail water out of the floundering vessel.

While the storm raged above D'Molay made a silent prayer to the one god for their salvation.

*M*azu quickly flowed out of the boat, spreading herself around the outer hull as a buffer against the rough waters that were hammering it. She had to concentrate to keep her watery form tightly against the boat and compensate for the force of the waves as they slammed against the hull. As the waves surged, Mazu used her own watery essence to push back against them and keep the boat in a more stable position. It took every iota of her will to keep the boat steady and secure.

Quan, unaware of Mazu's aid, fought the rudder to keep the boat on a controlled course. D'Molay stayed near the prow as he continued to bail water. About an hour into the storm, a huge flash of lightning struck the mast. D'Molay fell back against the hull, his ears ringing from the huge thunderclap that followed the lightning. He saw Quan cringing on his hands and knees, lips moving in a prayer he couldn't hear. Then something was falling towards him - the mast. He stared up dumbly. There was no way he could react in time to avoid it falling on him. Suddenly, his feet seemed to slip on the wet deck of the boat as he slid several feet. The mast crashed down, breaking the roof of the cabin and splintering a section of the hull railing before flipping over the side and falling into the raging waters, dragging rigging and sails with it. D'Molay watched the debris, tangles of line holding it captive to the ship, bob in the lake. He was stunned, barely able to catch his breath as the rain poured down.

The bucket bounced against his leg as it bobbed up and down in the rocking boat. Grabbing it, he resumed bailing. He worked himself to near exhaustion, but could see he was making progress on an otherwise overwhelming task. The wind, rain and thunder continued. D'Molay wasn't certain if they would last the night, but he was certain of one thing. *We aren't going down without a fight.*

———————

Mazu held herself against the outer hull of the boat as the waves crashed into her watery form. Just before one hit, she would swell up on the side the wave approached and absorb the force as it surged against the ship. Mazu realized this technique was not unlike a mother holding her baby while in a carriage ride; she could compensate for many of the bumps in the road, but not all of them. She had to hope it was enough.

Staying beneath the boat through the night, Mazu flowed, pulsed and forced herself against the oncoming waves. Long hours passed as she endured the tiring labor. Eventually the dawn began to break in the distant east. Even under the water, Mazu could tell the sky above was growing brighter. Hope that the storm was over lightened her weariness. Mazu loosened her watery grip on the boat and noticed that a large part of the mast was floating nearby, attached to the vessel only by a tangle of rope and rigging. She coalesced into a more solid form, pulling away from the boat to swim to the surface. It was then that some unknown force grabbed her from behind.

She struggled to get free. Quickly changing from her human shape into pure water, she hoped to slip away. Her effort was fruitless, despite stretching herself into a long, fluid ribbon. Dragged into the depths, Mazu feared that something of great power had taken her.

She pulled with as much effort as she could muster, but it made no difference; she was still at the mercy of the strange force, like a fish caught in a line. Panic set in, and it may have been the only thing that kept her from collapsing of exhaustion.

Suddenly strange laughter echoed in her mind and she sensed the presence of another deity. "You belong to Tlaloc now. Cease your useless struggling."

"Tlaloc?" The name was vaguely familiar. Mazu searched her memory, trying to recall when she'd heard it before. It was long ago and had something to do with a meeting of all the water gods she'd gone to. Then she remembered. Tlaloc - a Mayan water god! *How can I defeat someone with the same gift I have?*

Fighting back her weariness from the night before, Mazu spread herself outward, like the spray of a decorative fountain, attempting to determine exactly what had her in its grasp. Creating a fragile spider's web of water, she was able to sense Tlaloc was as large as a house, and like her, was composed of water. His form was more solid than hers, almost gelatinous, like that of a jellyfish. His shape was vaguely humanoid. In fact, he held her in his hand.

"Are you finished wriggling, now? You only weaken yourself further. Chaac sent the storm to keep you busy last night. He has quite a score to settle with you, for you dishonored him with your trickery." Tlaloc's voice rang in her head mockingly.

Mazu shrunk back into a compact shape to save what remained of her strength. *Chaac? This is all part of Quetzalcoatl's effort to catch me!*

"I think I should make certain that you arrive at our destination safely." Tlaloc lifted his hand up to his gaping maw.

Horrified, Mazu realized what he was about to do. Calling up her last reserves, she made her arm and staff fully solid again. It was a strange sight as an arm appeared out of nowhere, then blasted the gigantic water god with a greenish burst of energy. The effort caused her to black out.

Tlaloc was stunned for a second by the bright light, but he did not let her go. Instead, he raised Mazu to his mouth and slurped her down as if she were a wet rice noodle. She had been swallowed whole by the god.

Her attack had no effect upon Tlaloc other than to make his watery skin glow slightly in the dark water. Smiling gleefully, he headed west toward the Mayan Realm.

Mazu awoke inside a semi-transparent chamber. She felt groggy, and every part of her ached with pain despite that she was still in her liquid form. Though the view was foggy, she realized that all around her was the lake; only now she was seeing it from inside Tlaloc. *I have been eaten, swallowed!* Too stunned and tired to consider what to do next, her form became more human shaped as she curled up in a fetal position and cried. For the first time since she'd learned of Aavi's death, she felt deep despair.

The huge water god swam for several miles while Mazu languished almost in a state of shock. She watched dully as he passed a school of fish, envying their freedom, something she now lacked. A couple of them had tried to nibble at the god as he swam by, the faint glow left by her earlier spell making him of interest to their appetites.

Gaining control of her emotions, Mazu stood up and struck at the stomach-shaped prison with her staff. After several minutes of hammering, she realized the gelatinous substance merely absorbed her blows. Next she became a jet of water, bouncing around the inside of Tlaloc trying to find a way to slip out and escape, but discovered her prison was sealed tight. Becoming semi-solid, she slumped into a sitting position to rest again. Looking up, she noticed the light filtering in from the waves overhead was bright daylight. I've been trapped here longer than I'd thought, she realized dejectedly.

I should be back at the boathouse, where my biggest worry would be the ferry schedule, or luring a good catch for the fishermen. Something about that thought rolled around in her mind, but she couldn't quite put the pieces together. It was like an itch that needed to be scratched.

Then an idea took root. *I lure fish by making then think there is plentiful food to eat. But what if I lured them and the food was really there?* Mazu broke out into a broad smile.

Concentrating as hard as she could, she projected thought after thought to call to the nearby fish. Soon, a few fish swam up, some of which took tiny nibbles of Tlaloc, bites that were far too small for the god to even notice. Then a large school of tuna appeared and began to feed. Mazu continued to announce to any fish in the area that easy-to-find food lay in the waters around her.

Within a short time there were hundreds of fish of all different types and sizes in a feeding frenzy. Mazu could see them all around her through the semi transparent body of Tlaloc. His voice echoed in her mind. "What are you doing? I will kill these foolish creatures, and you!"

Ignoring him, she kept sending out wave after wave of luring thoughts. Her mind was pounding with intense pain from the effort, but still she continued. Now there were thousands of fish swarming around Tlaloc, taking bites out of him. Mazu had painted the picture of the greatest, most delicious meal in the lake here waiting for them. It was the feeding frenzy of all feeding frenzies. Sharks, barracuda, tuna, dolphins, and octopus all roiled, jumped and passed each other by for a wondrous taste of Tlaloc.

The water god stopped swimming and began to fight the swarms of fish by battering them and blasting them with water, but it was like fighting against the fog. Mazu, her suffering increasing by the minute, watched him swipe hundreds away only to have hundreds more take their place

Soon a huge squid swam out of the depths and attached itself to the god, gnawing on his leg. Tlaloc howled in pain and anger. Stubbornly staying solid enough to hold Mazu in his belly, he pulled the squid off, casting it deep into the depths below. Yet still more fish came, each one taking another piece of him away.

Mazu was now screaming in pain. She clenched her eyes tightly shut, certain her head was about to explode. She felt the walls of her prison shake, and she forced herself to open her eyes. She saw nothing but squirming, wriggling blackness. The fish were inside Tlaloc now and they were taking chunks out of his stomach.

"Noo! Nooo!" Tlaloc's voice echoed through Mazu's totured mind as he cried in agony. Finally, he could no longer hold his solid form and popped like a soap bubble. One second he was a solid entity, the next, seemingly gone. Mazu felt him rush away in the form of pure water, as he fled to escape his attackers. Thousands of fish suddenly poured in all around Mazu and she too took the form of water and slipped away.

Free! I'm free!

She drifted slowly away from the huge gathering of aquatic life. With Tlaloc's gelatinous form now gone, the sea creatures turned on each other and the feeding frenzy continued on its own power. As pure water, the fish had no interest in her. Mazu had won, but she feared the victory might have cost her life. Never had she endured such pain, or felt so weak.

Barely conscious, she drifted with the current, unable to change her form or her direction. She hoped that the fish had consumed enough of Tlaloc to prevent him from attacking her again anytime soon. *I'm spent... I have nothing left to fight with.*

*T*he storm had ended just before the dawn. Quan and D'Molay lay sprawled on the deck, soaked and bruised.

D'Molay awoke to the odd feeling of his face being hot on one side from the sun beating down, and cold on the other from the water still saturating the boat. Dizzy, he managed to slowly sit upright to rest against the hull of the small craft.

"Ohhh . . . we made it." He winced, realizing that every bone in his body seemed to ache. As his head cleared, he realized the boat was still in serious trouble. It was a floating wreck. The mast had snapped in half and the bamboo that covered the center of the little boat had been shredded, leaving its contents exposed to the elements. He had little doubt that without Mazu's aid, the boat would have been capsized and broken up in the storm. "Mazu? Mazu!" he called out, but could see no sign of her.

His cries stirred Quan from his resting place and he too slowly sat up. "The boat! It's destroyed! Oh, no…"

"Quan, where's Mazu? Have you seen her?"

"What? No, not since she went to rest before the storm. Is she all right? Where are her containers?"

"I had to break them so she could go overboard to help stabilize us during the storm. She hasn't come back." D'Molay scanned the horizon, hoping to see some hint of her presence.

"If she is in her watery form, how can we to find her?" Quan leaned over the side of the boat and peered into the water.

"We can't. We just have to hope she finds us." D'Molay decided not to add 'if she is able to.' The sad state of the boat nagging at him, he decided to take command. "Quan, check the boat and salvage our belongings."

Quan scowled. "I am not your servant. If you wish to check the boat, then do so. I must find lady Mazu, first."

D'Molay rolled his eyes. He was really starting to dislike this acolyte of Mazu's. With irritation simmering, he gathered up their food and belongings himself, stacking them on top of the countertop so they could dry off. He collected other broken items littering the deck and piled them out of the way. D'Molay heard a shout.

Quan called out for his goddess and dove into the water. D'Molay shook his head as he watched the man swim around, diving and yelling Mazu's name. With endless water in all directions, he was sure Quan would find nothing. After a few minutes Quan gave up and swam over to the broken mast and rigging that the boat was tugging along. Noticing him fumbling with it, D'Molay came over to where he labored.

He looked at the mast and the shredded sail. "Well, you're the fisherman. Any chance we can fix this?"

Quan looked doubtful. "No, it's ruined, and there's not even enough fabric left to fix the sail. Still, we might be able to use some of it."

The two men worked together to cut free much of the rope and stow it on deck. They even lashed what was left of the mast more securely to the hull. D'Molay offered a hand to Quan and he came back aboard.

"We have some food. There's one fishing pole left, lots of rope, our travel bags are still in the cabinet. But everything's soaked. There are a few other odds and ends. I still have my knife. That's about it." D'Molay shrugged as he finished his report.

Quan surveyed the boat's rudder and made a disgusted sound. "It's broken. It must have happened while I was trying to keep us at right angles to the incoming waves." He moved the till back and forth. It was obviously no longer attached to the rudder.

"Can it be repaired?"

"Yes, I think so. We have a better chance of that than repairing our sail."

"Well, that's something. What do you need?"

D'Molay and Quan spent the next half hour improvising parts to get the rudder working again. The project distracted D'Molay from worrying about Mazu, until they were finished and Quan began to fuss again.

"Lady Mazu's been gone for hours! It's not like her. Something's happened," Quan said.

"She hasn't been gone that long," D'Molay said. "You know how Mazu is. She probably went off to help some other fishermen who got caught in the storm. Where are we, anyway?"

Quan went off to take their bearings. Despite his excuses, D'Molay had even more reason to fear that something had indeed happened to Mazu. Someone had tried to trap Mazu in the containers. D'Molay decided he wasn't going to share that fact with Quan unless he had to. The servant was agitated enough at the moment.

"We've drifted north, based on where Apollo is in the sky. Where's that map of yours?"

D'Molay got it from on top of the counter "Here. It's all wet, but you can still read it."

Quan looked at the map carefully. "We must be past the midway point between the City of the Gods and the outer shore, or we'd see both coasts. We can only see one and I think it's probably the coast of the Hindu Realm. We should head southeast to get to Olympia."

"I can't argue with any of that. How far?"

Quan cupped his hands around his eyes and stared off at the distant coast. "Without sails, it will take us days to get there."

"I was afraid you might say something like that. How do we move the boat in that direction - oars? I'm sure I've seen Mazu use them," D'Molay recalled.

"She has one special oar, but it's made from her staff and is part of her. So we don't have that." Quan delivered this news brightly, proud to show off how much he knew about his goddess. D'Molay much preferred this attitude and hoped it would stick with the man through their current trials. He looked about the deck at the assortment of broken gear.

"Can't we make an oar for each of us? They seem simple enough."

After sorting through their materials, and expending about an hour's effort, they managed to make paddles using the cabinet doors, some rope, the sticky sap that was on Mazu's barrels and parts of the boom. Finally, they had a pair of usable, if ridiculous looking, oars.

"I'll take this side," D'Molay said, settling himself on the right side of the boat. He watched Quan expectantly, but he wasn't making any move to get underway.

"I don't think we should go. We should stay here and wait for Mazu. If she really is helping other fisherman, how will she find us if we leave?"

D'Molay's grip tightened on his oar. He resisted a strong urge to use it as a bat. "If you felt that way, why did you help me make the oars?"

"Because we will still need oars when Mazu returns. I saw no harm in making them."

"We can't sit and wait," D'Molay said decisively. "Look at this boat. It's leaking. How long can we stay out here before we sink? We're days from land. Even if we leave right now there's a chance we won't make it. Mazu is a goddess. She can take care of herself. She would want us to get to dry land."

Quan paused for a moment before giving in. "I suppose she would. I'll lock the rudder towards the southeast and we can start rowing."

After an uneven start, the men found a rowing rhythm and were consumed by the tedium of rowing. D'Molay sighed at their slow progress. From what he could tell they were no closer to the shore after an hour of work that they had been at the start. He was tempted to complain, but kept his feelings in. To make matters worse, he noticed the water level in the boat rising again.

"We need to bail out more water."

Quan mumbled agreement as he put down his oar and grabbed an empty rice bowl. The two of them worked in silence as they scooped water out of the boat. They continued bailing for a few minutes and made a fair amount of progress. As D'Molay bailed, he noticed a small trickle of water running down the inside of the hull.

"Looks like we have a new leak." He followed its path up the side of the boat, suddenly realizing the water was coming from over the top of the hull. It wasn't a leak at all. "No, I think its Mazu!"

Quan hurried over. "Where? Are you seeing things again?"

"Look!" D'Molay pointed out the trickle and they both watched as the form of Mazu started to appear in the boat. To their alarm, she lay on her back as she reformed. Her human shape wavered as she fought to become solid again.

Mazu's eyes opened. "I - am gladdened to see you are both well. It would seem I and the boat are not."

34

"We prayed for your return, Lady Mazu!" Quan exclaimed as he bowed his head.

"What happened out there?" asked D'Molay.

"Another water god attacked me. I almost died. Perhaps I should have."

"Lady Mazu, you mustn't talk so! You will be with us forever!"

She looked at Quan from where she lay. "Nothing lasts forever, not even the gods. One day, perhaps tomorrow or an eon from now, I'll turn into liquid and never return from that state. I'll join with the rest of the water in this lake and that will be the end of me. That is the way of all things - even for gods."

"Every fisherman on this lake would give their lives for you, my goddess."

"You should never say such a thing. It is I who should give my life to the fisherman, not the other way around."

"What can we do to help?" D'Molay asked, worry etched across his face.

She forced a smile. "You can both keep rowing. It seems a long way to shore. But first, bring my traveling bag from the cabinet if it is still there. Then let an old woman get some rest."

Quan returned with the waterlogged bag and helped the goddess find a glass vial. After drinking its entire contents she laid back and closed her eyes. The two men returned to their tasks of rowing and bailing. Whether it was the return of the goddess or just dumb luck, the boat held together through the day. A slight, cool breeze eased the heat of the sun as the two men kept rowing towards land. In the afternoon, their efforts were rewarded.

"The shore looks closer now," D'Molay said, looking up to see the progress they'd made.

"We still have a long way to go," Quan groaned, shaking a sore arm.

"Just keep rowing," D'Molay replied, going back to the work at hand. He glanced over his shoulder to see Mazu still sleeping, using part of the damaged sail to keep covered and out of sight. An hour later they heard her speak.

"Ahh, I see we are all still here. I thought by now you two might have killed each other."

"Not yet. Glad to see you're awake again. How do you feel?" D'Molay asked.

"Lady Mazu, what can I get you?" Quan asked.

"I am fine. I don't need anything right now. When will we get to shore?"

Quan frowned glumly. "When we both grow another set of arms."

"Our muscles have about had it," D'Molay agreed. "We need to sleep tonight and strike out again in the morning."

Mazu smiled. "Yes. You've earned your rest. We'll get to Dioscrias in good time."

D'Molay and Quan rummaged through the food and improvised a quick cold meal before stretching out on the deck for whatever rest they could seize. D'Molay dreamt of riding on a swift ship, a phantom wind snapping bright sails and stinging his eyes.

D'Molay briefly opened his eyes. It was still dark. He closed them again with a sense of thanks that the morning, and its labors, had not yet come. He rolled over to ease a cramp in his back and listened to the sound of water lapping against the hull. He drowsily picked out the sound of creaking wood and a random splash of something hitting the water. Forcing himself to fully awaken, D'Molay sat up to see if the boat was filling with water again. He blinked at the sight of buildings a short distance away, their boxy shapes standing out in the dark thanks to a few nearby lampposts.

"How?" he muttered as he stood up and saw that the boat had arrived at the port of Dioscrias while he had slept.

"I got out and pushed."

The voice had come from the water beside the boat. D'Molay looked over the rail and saw Mazu floating there. He imagined an amused look on her face. The darkness prevented him from seeing the true set of her features. "My shoulders thank you," he laughed. Quan, unconsciously disturbed by their conversation, snorted loudly in his sleep before rolling over and beginning to snore in earnest.

D'Molay picked up a rope and hopped onto the old wooden dock to tie the boat to the nearest piling.

"While you slept the leaks worsened," Mazu explained. "I did what was needed. My powers allow me to push the boat or even shield it somewhat from leaks while I surround it, but I cannot seal the holes. We must put it on dry land so Quan can repair it for the return journey."

"As soon as the port opens he can buy what he needs," D'Molay said. "Can you hold the boat together until then?"

"Of course. And under a boat is a good place to hide."

When the sun rose and men began to appear on the dock, D'Molay nudged Quan awake. He grumpily stalked about the boat, gathering the clothing he'd discarded earlier in the journey. He shirked into it as D'Molay explained how the boat had arrived at Dioscrias. His face was beaming when it popped through the neck hole of his shirt.

"I knew Mazu would save us," he said happily.

"But it's up to you to get this boat fixed." D'Molay pointed to a ramshackle tent at the land end of the dock. "That's a marina shop. Take some gold and buy what you need."

"Aren't you coming?" he asked. D'Molay shook his head.

"I'd rather keep my eye on the boat," he said, "and Mazu."

Quan found Mazu's pouch and retrieved a handful of coins. "I won't be long," he promised as he climbed out onto the dock.

D'Molay noticed a hat lying in a tangle of supplies. He fished it out and donned it, adjusting it to hide most of his face. Then he sat down on a crate near one of the larger leaking cracks in the vessel.

"Mazu," he said softly toward the seeping damp. "Can you hear me?"
"Yes."

Her voice was faint and muffled, but D'Molay heard her answer. He reached for a nearby bowl and began to bail again so that anyone who observed him would think little of him being hunched over with his face downturned to the deck.

"Now that we're here, what next?" he asked. "At the boathouse, you hinted that we were coming here for information."

"That's right," she said. "Have you ever heard of a place called the Palace of Helios?"

D'Molay dumped a bowlful of water over the side. "Helios? Is he a Greek god?"

"His status is degraded," Mazu said diplomatically, "but his importance lies in that he is Circe's father."

"And if anyone knows where the witch is, it's probably him," D'Molay concluded. "Do you think he's hiding her?"

"It's possible. And that's what I will be going to his palace to determine."

"How are you going to manage that?" D'Molay hardly expected Helios to come right out with the truth, even if it was demanded of him by another deity.

"I will use my eyes and ears, of course," Mazu said. "From time to time, the City sends out teachers to the children of gods who live in the realms. I have been one of these tutors in the past and can use that status to gain access to the palace. Helios has many children besides his daughter Circe."

D'Molay was impressed with the plan. "Is he expecting you?

"Of course. But the attack has already made me overdue," she said. "As soon as Quan returns, I'll help you move the boat to dry land. Then I must leave for the palace, which is on a lake's island twenty miles east of here."

"All right. I'll help him get the boat fixed and then do some investigating of my own. One of us is sure to find a lead."

D'Molay bailed in silence for a few more minutes.

"Mazu? The god that attacked you. Was it Mayan?"

"Yes. As was the one who stirred up the storm."

D'Molay sighed. "There was magic on the lake. I saw strange flashes before I found your containers sealed. How did they see you when we were so careful?"

Mazu's voice held a gentle tease in its reply. "Perhaps I should have asked."

*A*res had chosen his most obedient soldiers for the mission to hunt down Set in the Lost Realm. They were ones who would never complain. The misery and danger of the lawless land was just another backdrop for another battle. They would execute their missions without question and without thought. Planning was Ares' job.

This time, he had an unusual consultant for his task, his mother, Hera. She was clever, and thanks to the foolishness of gods who thought nothing of talking unguardedly before a woman, knew some of the secrets, and certainly all of the rumors, concerning exiled deities hiding in the abandoned realm. After visiting her in her chambers on Mount Olympus, he left with a list of the most likely supernatural beings who might be aiding Set or might be willing to trade what they knew of him for the favor of Olympia.

Trusting his unit leaders to flush out and interrogate the low level mortals and creatures of the Lost Realm, Ares focused on the names of deities on Hera's list. It was a task for which he was not well suited. At times he felt he needed both the cunning of Hermes and the intellect of Athena to separate the truth from the likely lies that these exiles were feeding him. He worked hard to curb his impatience, practicing the art of politics, which he despised, to gather tiny seeds of information.

Ares had almost reached the end of the list. Most of the remaining names were gods of Egyptos, who would be found snug in their pyramids feigning ignorance of their kinsman's activities. He would seek and catch them later. There was, however, one goddess whom he knew would be found in this forsaken realm, and the leads he had shaken out of his other encounters had told him exactly where to look. Her seductive voice called out to him as he approached a mass of oddly-shaped boulders.

"Handsome Olympian," came the plea, "a drink of your water, please."

Ares stopped immediately, taking a moment to assess his surroundings. Although he did not for a moment believe that this goddess posed a threat to him in her current state, he increased his size slightly and allowed a flare of his power to course over his muscles before approaching the woman-shaped rock standing among the many stones. Her face was frozen except for her eyes, which rove freely and lustfully over Ares' body.

"Where do you carry your canteen?" she asked after finishing her visual inspection. He was unsure how she was speaking to him. He could hear her clearly, but her mouth was eternally carved into a saucy smirk. Ares noted the way the frozen flow of rock draped her almost in Roman fashion, but her stony gown was more primitive, and at the same time more decadent. Glassy points of quartz framed her head in a pseudo crown while pink tones of sandstone on her motionless face and hands hinted at life concealed inside. Of the names on his list, it was clear which one the woman matched.

"You must be Mania," he said. "Rumor was right about your hiding here."

Mania's eyes fixed Ares with a cool stare. "I am hardly hiding. You found me easily enough. As have many of my children." Her eyes rolled up into their sockets for a moment, giving Ares a keen moment of unease. As they rolled back into view, a hoard of misty figures began to form. "Yes, I am Mania, the mother of ghosts, the last goddess of dead Etruria left in the realms." The vaporous shapes came into focus. Ares lifted an eyebrow as he recognized many of them as soldiers from the battle at his fortress. Their ghostly armor identified them as remnants of the old Roman guard, some of the earliest mortals who had been transported to the City. Mania did not miss his inspection of her company. "You seem surprised that I am not alone."

"I am intrigued that there are still mortal souls who remember and choose you," he said. He thought her lips almost smiled wider at this admission.

"There are so very many. Do remind Hades I will take what he thinks is his at every opportunity," she declared. "Now, are you going to share your water, or not?"

Ares decided to bluff. The special water the gods favored was not cheaply obtained, and Mania had told him nothing worth such a boon. He took care to prevent his hand from skimming over the hollow grip of his sword which concealed a vial of the liquid inside it. "My cup bearer is not attending me on this excursion. So unfortunately, I cannot quench your thirst."

"Another selfish visitor," Mania said with resentment. "The last refused me water as well. And he didn't even bother to hide his, as you do. He flaunted it. That one is no friend of the dead. His reputation is built of lies."

Ares casually moved his hand and began to unscrew the secret cap at the butt of his sword, encouraged by the hints the ancient goddess was dropping. "I said I could not quench your thirst, but I can share a taste, at least. I would not want you to think me as rude as Set."

He watched closely for any reaction to his guess about her previous visitor, and was rewarded. Her ghosts began to curse the name of Set for his refusal to help their mother goddess. Ares slid the vial of water from its hiding place, stepping up to Mania and tilting a small libation of the life-liquid to her lips. Its power allowed her mouth to open ever so slightly before lapsing again into stillness.

"You hunt him? You seek to punish him?" she asked.

"I do. I will. Where is he?"

"He is vile, and deserves haunting. Since I could not pursue, I sent some of my children after him."

Ares took a good look at the spirits that ringed Mania. They didn't look like much. "With these weak ghosts?" he said dismissively. "I doubt he would even notice."

"Which is fortunate for you," Mania said. "These little ghosts can run straight to their brothers, who, I must shamefully agree, are likely not bothering Set in the least. They must seem like desert flies to such a great god as he." Mania managed to give Ares a wink

Immediately understanding and appreciating how the immobile goddess had endeavored to keep tabs on Set, the war god felt victory drawing closer. "Then there is strength in their weakness," Ares complimented. "I will be back immediately with my best men to follow the lead of your children."

"Good. And bring - "

"Yes, more water, of course," Ares called back as he shot off toward his army.

Dreams of the Past

fter helping D'Molay and Quan move the boat to a sheltered cove where they could affect repairs, Mazu joined with an underground stream which flowed to the west, reemerging from time to time to make sure she was traveling in the right direction. Her destination was an island in the middle of another lake. On it, sat the Palace of Helios. As she crossed the lake and took solid form on the island shore, she could see why Helios had built his palace here. The view was spectacular. The island stood in a sparkling clear lake that rose from the middle of a deep canyon of green-forested hills. Multi-domed buildings and long, red-tiled causeways surrounded a large central courtyard. It was much more opulent than the small port of Dioscrias, though still a mere country estate compared to some of the castles Mazu had visited in other realms.

A tall, white stucco wall surrounded the palace. Mazu could have seeped through it easily, but decided that would be bad manners and went to the main gate instead. The guard at the gate summoned the protocol priest, a tall, thin man wearing a deep blue robe and sporting a laurel wreath on his head. He carried a large scroll under his left arm. "Who are you?" he immediately asked.

"I am Mao-shi, guest teacher for the children," Mazu answered.

She'd obtained the teaching position under a false name, one she used with Aphrodite a few years earlier when she had worked as a governess. That had been a time of great political conflict among the gods, and Mazu had kept her godhood secret to avoid being drawn into unpleasantness.

She'd taken the name Mao-shi then, and did the same in this instance.

The man unrolled the top part of the scroll. "Mao-shi . . . Mao-shi. Ah yes, here it is." He rolled the scroll back up, his face an unreadable mask. "You were expected yesterday, but never mind. Follow me." He sharply turned on his heel and walked towards the palace. "My name is Celos. I manage the staff here. You are engaged to stay for a least a month, more if we are pleased with your interactions with the children."

"Yes, I understand."

"Good. I'll take you to Helios then show you to your room. Do you have any luggage?" He looked past her, apparently searching for it in vain.

"It will be arriving shortly. I'm afraid it was lost during my journey. There was a great storm on the lake and I was separated from my belongings."

"I see," he said. He escorted her though the gate and up a short set of stairs into the palace.

Upon entering the main reception room, Mazu could see Helios on his throne surrounded by courtiers. They seemed to be the usual hangers-on and sycophants that populated all royal courts. *One more reason to avoid such places,* she thought. Drawing closer, she could see that these people were even more unsavory than those one might normally expect.

She knew Helios once had been the beloved sun god of the Titans. Back on Earth, Helios had brought the morning dawn and guided the sun across the sky, but no longer. He sat now in his throne room and ruled this small kingdom. His brothers and sisters having all been enslaved or killed off, only he still remained free, but from what Mazu could see, he did not seem to enjoy this freedom.

He had once been quite handsome, one of the most attractive of the Titans. Those days had long passed. Though he was an immortal, time had not been as kind to him as it had to many other gods. He had gained a paunch and lost most of his once lustrous golden curls. His hair was now a graying brown and quite thin on top. His face, once handsomely chiseled and erudite, had become puffy and lined. He looked like he needed a shave, but lacked enough facial hair to call it a beard. The one bright spot in his otherwise worn appearance was his clothing. Helios liked to dress in the finest of regal attire. Custom made leather sandals that wrapped up to the tops of his calves, a deep, red velvet robe, and a golden laurel wreath that actually seemed to glow with some inner magic distracted from his overall shabbiness. He also wore an ornate golden sash encrusted with large gems, one for each of the original Titans.

Mazu tried to listen to what was being discussed as she and the priest approached him.

"But my Lord, we just don't have the gold to be able to pay for the construction materials or buy that many slaves. Perhaps we could continue some work on the foundation," said a short, portly man in a linen toga. Mazu noticed his white hair seemed frazzled as if he had been up all night, worrying about affairs of state.

"I don't care what you or the Royal Engineer think! I want it done as soon as possible - no more delays! Don't you understand? If we build the Colossus it will turn Dioscrias into a major port. Ships from all over the realms will flock here just to see it! My kingdom is floundering. Rebuilding the Colossus would make us important and wealthy. It worked on Earth and it will work here. The cost matters not.

The docking fees would pay for the lighthouse in no time. Find a way. Raise taxes, sell something. I don't want to see you again until you've worked it out. Now leave my sight!"

"Yes, my Lord. I - I will find a way." The man retreated from the throne, bowing as he went.

Helios slouched back in his throne, an irritated scowl on his face. "What else must I deal with?" he asked a retainer standing at his side. This man pointed haughtily at the priest, signaling him to speak.

"The guest teacher Mao-shi is here. She is the one recommended by Aphrodite," said the priest.

"Very well, bring her forward." Helios showed a hint of interest, but Mazu noted it quickly faded once he saw her. He was obviously hoping for an attractive goddess, not an elderly woman. He scowled, immediately finding fault with her. "You're not quite what I was expecting. You are from the Asian realm. What do you know of the wisdom of Olympia?"

"I have studied all the great philosophies and histories of the Olympian Gods. I taught some of Aphrodite's children, which is why she recommended me. I would be happy to demonstrate if you wish," Mazu replied, bowing slightly.

"I have no time for that. If Aphrodite recommended you, why should I argue? If you fail, I will hear of it and you will be thrown out of my palace." He quickly glanced around the chamber, clapping his hands twice and barking out an order. "Celos, take her to a guest room. She can start with the children tomorrow. Now leave me, all of you, I am bored with all this minutiae. Go!" Helios dismissed the courtiers and visitors with a wave of his hand as he glared at them resentfully.

Mazu followed Celos, who led her down the main corridor and deeper into the less traveled hallways of the palace. After a long, silent walk, he finally spoke. "You'll have to get used to his moods. Helios' patience grows thin very quickly."

"Surely he has the power to arrange things to his satisfaction," she remarked, truly curious as to the reasons for his apparently constant annoyance.

The priest looked at her out of the corner of his eyes as they continued to walk. "You must understand that Helios was . . . let's just say he was invited to retire by Zeus. In exchange, he was given this region to rule, but it is an unworthy lot for a sun god. He is quite justified to be angry. Not that this is of any concern to his servants," Celos said pointedly.

Mazu answered quickly. "I'm sorry if I offended in any way." She felt a tinge of annoyance at Celos' condescension, but knew it was the price of keeping her true nature a secret.

"No, no - far better you understand the situation now than provoke his wrath. Be respectful and brief any time he speaks with you. For now, get situated and tomorrow you can meet your charges." He halted at a wooden door then opened it. "This is your room. I'll send a slave by to see to any needs you might have."

"Thank you. For both you help and your advice."

Mazu entered the chamber. It was appointed in classic Greek style. The floor was made of tiny white tiles bordered with a geometric green design. What pleased her the most was the balcony, which opened out to the east, overlooking the small lake and majestic hills beyond. She wished her old demon companion General Thousand Miles Eye was with her. From this vantage point he could have easily seen how D'Molay and Quan were coming with the boat repairs back in Dioscrias.

She sat on the bed, gathering her thoughts. *I can only hope they get the boat fixed. I have the feeling that we might need to leave on short notice.*

After D'Molay paid the day workers they had hired from the dock, he bounced his purse in his hand. It was now lighter than he had planned it to be at this early stage of their journey. However, there was no avoiding the expense. It would have been impossible to careen the boat on the secluded stretch of beach without assistance. Ideally, he would have asked the extra men to stay long enough to help raise a new mast, but he didn't want strangers underfoot. Quan claimed to know enough about ramps and ropes to allow just the two of them to deal with a new support for the sail; D'Molay hoped this wasn't an idle boast. He walked over to Quan, who was examining the exposed side of the hull.

"How bad is it?"

Quan pointed to an almost imperceptible line that diagonally crossed a plank and led to a tiny crevice that gapped between the split board and its neighbor. "If I fix this and this, we can trust the boat again." Quan waved an impatient hand at D'Molay. "Get a fire going."

Determined to resist being ordered about, D'Molay did not move. "Is the blessed one of Mazu cold?" His barb earned him a scathing look from Quan.

"I need heat to melt wax. If you don't want to help, go away." Quan sat down and began tearing skinny strips from some scrap linen he had purchased from the sail makers in port. From time to time he looked up to give D'Molay an irritated glance. D'Molay dallied for a short time, but soon relented and built the requested fire, realizing Mazu would be disappointed in him for not cooperating with the repairs. This turned out to be his only contribution the entire day. Quan asked for no further help as he packed the split wood with linen and sealed it by slathering a stinking mixture of the melted beeswax and some sort of gum over it. By late afternoon, the project was finished, although it would take several days for the fixes to dry completely.

Quan, after his labors, had been unwilling to cook anything. D'Molay was accustomed to missing meals, so they ate a sparse dinner from their packs. D'Molay complimented Quan on his repairs which diffused their earlier standoff. By sunset, each man had picked out a place to throw down a blanket for the night. D'Molay chose a spot just within the tree line but in full view of the boat. Quan sprawled out on the open beach near the dwindling campfire. The stars were well established in the evening sky before D'Molay eased himself into slumber. Even then, worries about Mazu and their mission intruded on his dreams.

D'Molay was walking through a forest, a heavy bag slung over his shoulder rocking against his back. He was following a deer that danced ahead of him on the trail. The doe leapt joyfully in and out of the trees that lined the road. D'Molay had no desire to hunt the animal, but he increased his pace, not wanting to lose sight of the beautiful creature. He soon began to jog after it, the sack he carried bouncing against his shoulder.

The trail widened into a clearing. From above, bright sunlight illuminated a circle of golden sand. The deer jumped into the middle of the circle and the light danced over its hide. He approached the doe, the bag over his shoulder getting heavier with each step. D'Molay shirked the burden and swung it before him to see why it was causing him so much trouble. The rough, woven sack was soaked with blood.

D'Molay recoiled, dropping the bag. *What was I carrying?* He side-stepped the lumpy mystery which began to leak gore into the golden

sand. He took another pace toward the deer, which was looking away from him into the forest on the other side of the clearing. D'Molay matched its gaze. He heard branches being pushed aside. Someone was coming.

Aavi, the beautiful, innocent girl with golden hair emerged from the trees. She seemed more interested in the deer than D'Molay, although she did send a friendly smile his way as she closed the distance to the doe, gliding forward, her feet not touching the ground. D'Molay rushed toward her, frightening the deer which dashed out of the circle.

Aavi! Are you really here? Can you hear me? D'Molay found himself thinking, rather than voicing his questions. Aavi nodded to him, but said nothing. Reaching her, he extended his right hand and grasped her shoulder. The soft, white material of her robe, and the warmth of her body beneath it, was acutely real. Aavi raised a hand and laid it over

D'Molay's own, pressing down firmly to hold it tightly to her. He grinned at her, extremely pleased that she had returned.

Let her go! What are you doing?

A loud voice intruded on D'Molay's joy.

Take your hand away!

Growing angry, D'Molay tried to slide his hand out from under Aavi's to draw his knife and deal with the undesired visitor; but, his hand remained firmly pinned. *Aavi, let me go*, he pleaded. She shook her head, her lips forming a word. D'Molay heard no sound, nor any voice in his mind. Aavi began to fade away. The clearing began to darken. Something thumped him on the back where the horrible bag had been.

"Wake up! Are you crazy?"

Quan's strident words jolted D'Molay back to reality. He found himself standing against the boat, his fingers stuck in the drying sealant. He tugged them free with some effort, a chunk of residue pulling free and leaving an indentation.

"What have you done to Mazu's boat? I'll have to fix her again!" Quan frowned, folding his arms.

D'Molay stared at his hand. He couldn't believe he had been sleepwalking, that the vivid encounter with Aavi had merely been a dream. "I thought I was following someone," he muttered. "I was sure I saw . . ." He let his words trail off as sadness at his mind's deception began to sink in. Many pantheons worshipped gods of dreams, but D'Molay could not understand reverence for such ambivalent tormentors.

"Seeing things again?" Quan took a step back.

"No," D'Molay said sharply in defense of his reason. "It was just a dream. Forget it."

Quan eyed him sideways for a moment before returning to his blanket. D'Molay was jealous. The man would have a much easier time forgetting the incident than he.

---

*M*azu's first full day in the palace was unlike anything she had ever experienced in the halls of a deity. The pendulum of life with Helios swung from despotic control to utter anarchy. Depending upon the king's mood, which changed by the hour, his court was either suppressed with severe formality or abandoned to hedonistic chaos. It saddened Mazu to observe his children, who seemed either numb or ever on edge from the random state of their father's household.

As the teacher Mao-shi, Mazu made a point of trying to cheer the children of the gods. They had paid an unexpected price when their parents united their powers to create the City and the realms. The great work of creating the world had a critical side effect. None of the young deities brought there would ever age. The children were trapped. They would never develop their bodies or their powers beyond the state they were in when they entered the City. To make their misfortune even more tragic, the same restriction did not extend to mature gods, who were able to adapt, change, and enhance their traits, often by defeating other deities and forcibly taking their powers and skills. Some gods had even murdered their own children when they realized what Fate had consigned to them. Those parents thought it a kindness, but she found it utterly cruel. At least in this palace, her young charges were not divine. They were the result of Helios forcing himself on his slave women; because of that base origin,

Helios paid little attention to them. Circe was one of his few immortal children. Mazu hoped that status meant Helios was still involved with her.

When Mao-shi introduced herself, the older children were cautiously surprised that a teacher had even been provided, while the youngest were gleeful that anyone had come to spend more time with them than it took to shove a plate of food under their noses or herd them into an occa-sional communal bath. Yet while they were friendly, the children had developed no discipline for sitting still or listening, unless directly threatened by a beating, a technique one courtier suggested to Mazu when she was chasing down a boy who had snuck out of her class.

What the offended adult did not know was that teacher Mao-shi was being purposely lax in her control. Each time a child "escaped" was an opportunity for Mazu to leave the nursery wing and set her eyes and ears to work. In the drunken, gossipy court of the king, she was sure to learn something that would help find Circe.

"Oh, that brat!" she complained with false irritation as she hurried past the courtier. "Just wait until I catch him!"

The man lifted his cup in a sarcastic toast to Mazu's faux fury and drank sloppily from it.

That's right, keep drinking, Mazu thought. *Loosen your tongue.*

Chapter 4 - Dreams of the Past

s soon as there was sufficient morning light, Quan touched up the section of the hull seal that D'Molay had inadvertently disturbed the night before. Partly to apologize, but mainly as a distraction from the boredom of sitting in camp watching the boat dry, D'Molay went hunting. He set several snares and at day's end one had captured a rabbit. He presented it to Quan skinned, gutted, and ready to cook, unsure if Mazu's servant's culinary expertise went beyond the preparation of fish and rice. Quan spitted it over the campfire and took great interest in roasting it, managing to cook it without blackening much of its flesh. They spoke congenially during the meal about how well the boat repairs were setting. Quan hoped to get the craft back into the water in another two days.

No dreams of Aavi came to D'Molay that night, but in its darkest hour something stirred him awake. He realized his face was wet and immediately thought it was raining. He sat up. Next to him, a clear, slowly bubbling fount of water was rising from the ground and forming in the middle of the campsite.

"Mazu!" he exclaimed.

Within seconds the water took the shape of the goddess, then became solid. "I see you have found a good spot to make camp," Mazu said with a trace of a smile. "Good evening. Or should I say good morning?"

"Either will do. How are things at the palace, 'governess'?"

"Tense. It is not friendly, but all is well enough. I'm sorry I came at this hour, but I must slip away only when there is no chance I'll be missed." Mazu eagerly shared the news she had come to deliver. "I saw something today that might be of help."

"Let's hear it," D'Molay said, his interest piqued.

"Several of the children were looking at something out the window and when I saw what it was, I knew I needed to tell you."

"Well, what was it, then?"

"A harpy. It landed in the courtyard this morning and it was carrying an amphora of some sort. Not only that, but one of the children told me that a harpy comes once every two weeks with a delivery like that for the King."

"Circe's father." D'Molay added.

"Yes. Something else I overheard today makes me think the harpies might be working for Circe. Two advisors were talking and didn't know I was near enough to hear.

I didn't hear everything, but one of them said Helios needed more potions from Circe. Then the other said that 'I'm sure another of those flying bitches will land in the courtyard soon enough.' I'm sure he was talking about a harpy making a delivery."

D'Molay felt a shock of recognition upon hearing her news. "Aavi and I saw harpies last time we were here. The ones we saw took urns off the ship we traveled on."

"Do you think they're the same ones?"

D'Molay stroked his beard as he pondered. "No way to be certain, but it's the best lead we've had since we got here. Harpies don't usually carry stuff en masse like what Aavi and I saw, so there's something odd about them right there. The harpies we saw attacked one ship and all of them took the same thing - clay urns. I never told you about that, did I?"

"No. But a lot has happened since then."

"True enough. At the time, I never really gave those harpies much thought. It was just an odd thing that happened while we were traveling to the fort. This connection to Circe, it's worth checking out."

"I agree. Do you know where these harpies nest?"

"No. They flew to the east and we didn't follow them. Wait . . . there's someone in the village that might know, the blacksmith. She's also a huntress. Maybe we'll get lucky and she'll know where they roost."

"Good. I'd best get back to the palace. One of the children might need tending to, or a guard may come to check on me," Mazu said.

"I'll leave any news for you with Quan before I leave to track them down. If you need to find me for any reason, look for my marks. I'll carve them on trees along my path."

She nodded slightly as she started to become transparent, "I'll finish up at the palace and see what else I can find out. We'll follow you in a week or two. Try to stay out of trouble." As he watched, she transformed into a human-shaped column of water and melted into the ground.

"You too, Mazu," D'Molay said to the darkness.

In the aftermath of this visit, D'Molay found it impossible to get back to sleep. While Quan continued to snore, D'Molay began to plan. His thoughts raced with how he would approach Sophia the blacksmith about finding the harpies. He also considered better equipping himself for what he might encounter should they find the monsters. There was also the matter of keeping Quan and the boat at the ready should they need a hasty retreat from Olympian shores. By the time dawn began to break, D'Molay had decided several things that needed to be done. He set off along the path to the port as the first fishing boats began to appear on the great lake.

Though a small port, Dioscrias hosted enough commerce to inspire its shopkeepers to open early. D'Molay was able to purchase a fresh supply of dry biscuits and augment his small cache of spare arrowheads and barbed hooks before the sun was fully up. He even found the man who had headed up the crew who helped them careen the boat and rehired his gang to help Quan re-launch it the following day. There was only one merchant who dallied abed. D'Molay had to wait outside the shop of the oil seller.

From the appearance of his store, the owner was making enough money to set his hours to suit his own convenience. The prosperous shop even had small glass windows. Through them, D'Molay could view lamps of all shapes and sizes, from small fired clay oil pots in the style of Olympia to elaborate golden cages with inset panes of jewels that hailed from lands D'Molay had never visited. He stared at one of the fanciful fixtures, trying to work out how it had been put together. His eyes traced the metal strips that were riveted together with golden pins and he began to understand how they were folded together to form the crown at the apex. Then, he sensed someone coming up behind him. He turned from the window, expecting to see the oilman arriving to open the shop. As he did, he saw a reflection of Aavi in the glass.

After a pause of less than a second, D'Molay spun fully around. There was no one on the street. His hand went to his knife and his eyes darted up and to every side, trying to spot a supernatural enemy who was playing with his mind. He saw no one, save a sleeping sailor sprawled by a barrel. He turned back to the window and the face of the angel was gone.

D'Molay stepped away from the glass and leaned nervously against the wall of the building. Doing his best to collect himself, he nonetheless worried about these dreams and hallucinations. The thought of Aavi haunting him was ridiculous. It was far more likely that these experiences were caused by one of the gods angry with him over her escape with the beast. That was a more comforting notion than the alternative: that the sightings originated from his own tortured psyche, his guilt fueling madness over her death.

The shop door rattled at last and a young girl opened it wide for D'Molay to come inside. At the sight of her, his heart lightened. It had probably been she whom he had seen. She, too, was young, and had curly, straw-colored hair. Other than that, she bore little resemblance to Aavi, but in dim light through wavy glass . . .

"I need some wicks, flints, dry tinder, and a small vial of oil," he said cheerfully to the girl's father who was standing behind the shop's counter. D'Molay was greatly relieved that he had a solution to the day's mystery. The oilman rubbed sleep out of his left eye as he set about filling the order.

"You always this excited about shopping?" he asked, laying the requested items one-by-one before D'Molay.

D'Molay muted his happiness. "Sorry. I probably need more sleep. Do you want cash, or can we barter?"

He dickered for a few minutes with the shopkeeper and managed to obtain his items for one coin and the beads that decorated the wide hat Mazu insisted he wear as a disguise. He hoped the beads hadn't been worth that much; he had no eye for jewelry.

Now re-equipped, he headed back down the trail to the cove. The sun was fully up and he expected Quan would be too. As he stepped out of the trees and into camp, Quan rushed out from behind the boat, brandishing a small fish-gutting knife. D'Molay laughed at him.

"You really need to be more careful with blades. You might hurt someone," D'Molay said. "What do you think you were doing, for that matter?"

"Protecting Mazu's boat," Quan declared. "Why are you sneaking around?"

"If I was sneaking, you wouldn't have seen me. Put that knife away. Do you really think someone's going to steal a beached boat?" D'Molay was beginning to look forward to facing off with the harpies. It would be a welcome break from Quan's company. Quan settled down, watching as D'Molay began to add his new purchases to his traveling pack.

"Where did you go so early?" Quan asked. "Were you visiting Mazu?"

"No. She came to me in the night. She told me a rumor that Circe might live somewhere in the woods where the harpies nest."

"Harpies? How do they connect to Circe?" Quan asked.

"Mazu said they're delivering things to Circe's father, King Helios. Circe must be close enough to control them if that's the case."

Fear crossed Quan's face. "Harpies, witches. I don't like this."

"You don't have to. You're staying with the boat. I went out this morning and hired the men from the port to return to help you put it back out on the lake. Wait there for Mazu. She'll tell you what to do next."

Quan brightened at his part of the plan. "Ah. I can fish while I wait."

"Do whatever you like. Just keep the boat ready. I came back to tell you about my plans before I leave." D'Molay replied as he gazed back towards the distant hills beyond Dioscrias.

Chapter 5

Playing By the Rules

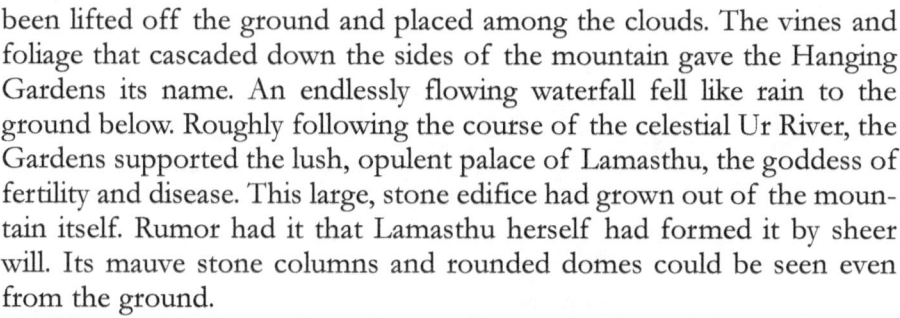

Floating over a thousand feet in mid air, the Hanging Gardens of Babylon drifted slowly across the sky. From a distance, it looked like a beautiful green mountain that had somehow been lifted off the ground and placed among the clouds. The vines and foliage that cascaded down the sides of the mountain gave the Hanging Gardens its name. An endlessly flowing waterfall fell like rain to the ground below. Roughly following the course of the celestial Ur River, the Gardens supported the lush, opulent palace of Lamasthu, the goddess of fertility and disease. This large, stone edifice had grown out of the mountain itself. Rumor had it that Lamasthu herself had formed it by sheer will. Its mauve stone columns and rounded domes could be seen even from the ground.

This morning, Lamasthu sat in a swirling, hot pool that fed into the waterfall. It was on the southern side of the Hanging Gardens, giving her a view of the distant shoreline of the Babylonian Realm she ruled. The warm water bubbled and flowed around her as she reclined against a wet, rocky ledge, half immersed into the grotto. The dark green tendrils on her head dipped into the waters as she tilted her head back and basked in the sunlight. Her eyes were closed and there was the trace of a smile on her lipless mouth.

Though the pool was open to the sun, most of the surrounding courtyard that led back to the main palace was in shadow. A large cavernous overhang of rock that extended from the main building, though it was seamlessly melded into the rock face, made it hard to tell where the building began and the mountain ended. A hooded figure emerged from beneath the poolside overhang. The messenger's leg-like appendages made a scuttling sound across the cobblestone floor.

Lamasthu barely opened her yellow eyes to slits to see who dared to bother her. As the thing moved forward, the light from the incoming sun lit up its deep red hood, identifying it as one of Lamasthu's trusted minions. It had been a man once, but Lamasthu had molded the man into the creature before her. Pale green tentacles emerged from the cloak. She could see it was carrying something at its side.

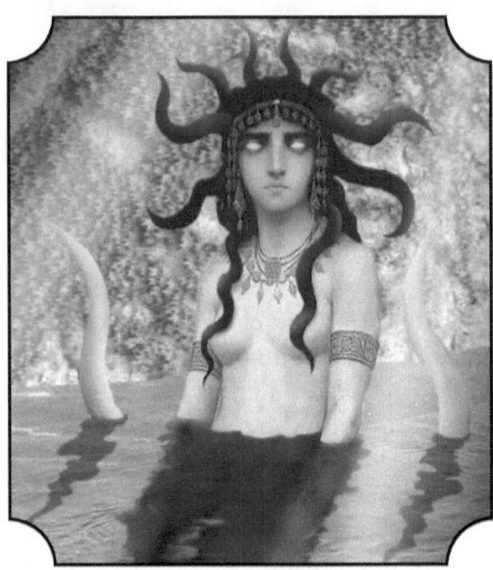

"What is it? Can't you see I am… busy?" she hissed.

The creature gulped air as it stammered a response. "I . . . sorry, mistress. You told me if the seed came to life." The man-creature held out a brown, oval-shaped item. Bright green clouds swirled on its surface.

"Bring it to me." Lamasthu pointed at him, the tendrils of her hand curling to command him to come into the pool and give her the seed. She obviously had no intention of moving from her comfortable alcove. The creature immediately complied, walking into the pool, getting the bottom half of its cloak and body soaking wet.

Lamasthu took the seed from her servant. "Get out, but stay close, so you can take this back when I am finished."

"Y-yesss mistress."

Lamasthu held up the seed and gazed into the shifting green pattern on its surface. She didn't have to guess who was reaching out to her; there was no doubt. As she looked, a face started to form and take on the jackal-like visage of the Egyptian god Set. His eyes gleamed as he turned his long dark snout and looked back at her. "Ah, Lamasthu. Good, these seeds I stole work."

"You didn't know if this would work when you gave it to me?" she asked incredulously. "Why are we using this ridiculous method to communicate?" Usually Set would project his Ka to form a ghost-like image of himself to speak with her.

"Spare a thought for me, great lady," Set explained, doing his best to ooze charm. "I don't want to risk having my Ka captured or used to track my current location. These seeds are a matched pair. I can contact you or you can contact me. We don't have to worry about the Council or others knowing our plans. You don't want anyone to know those, I'm sure," he added slyly.

"Very well. Where are you hiding now?" she asked, knowing he wouldn't tell her. Their relationship was built on mutual usefulness, not trust. Neither of them had faith in the other, but they had common goals, at least for the time being.

"We have more important things to talk about," Set said. "For instance, what have you heard from Quetzalcoatl and the Council? What did they do when they learned an Angel was in their midst? Are they taking any action?"

Lamasthu found his rapid questions incredibly rude and snapped at him. "Why should I answer, when all this time you have refused to fully share what you learned from our other friend?"

Set's face in the scrying seed took on the petulant look of a child who was expected to clean his room before he could have ice cream. "Yes, yes, I'll tell you what he told me about Earth."

Lamasthu smiled slightly, pleased. If Set would divulge those secrets, she could reveal what she knew. "Good. The Council has done little as far as I can tell. It is said they don't believe that Aavi was from the Heavenly Realm. If that's the case, then their lack of action is not too surprising. They are looking for you, but not because of Aavi. It's the attack on Ares' Fortress that marks you. Quetzalcoatl has honored his agreement and absolved me of any guilt. The Council believes that I was pursuing you after you invaded Babylonia. Nor has Quetzalcoatl been accused of crimes against another pantheon. None challenged his assertion that he was just trying to stop a war in the Olympian Realm."

Set's simmering rage was apparent even through the scrying seed. "The Council is a den of fools. Why must I take the entire blame for this whole affair?"

"Don't play the angry martyr. It doesn't suit you." Lamasthu reached for a pitcher of scented oil and allowed a few drops to fall into her bath. "You knew that would probably happen. It was all part of the plan."

"Yes, but we were supposed to end up with an Angel and the beast of God's wrath in our possession!" Set bellowed in anger. Their plan was much more nuanced then that, but Set had boiled it down to a simple statement.

Lamasthu remained unmoved by his outburst and managed to restrain a smile at Set's expense. In truth, she liked seeing him twist in the winds of failure. "We all knew it was fraught with risk, and yet the plan succeeded in several ways. The realms of the gods are safe for now. That was the most important goal, after all," she reminded him.

Set glared back at her. "It was important for you and Quetzalcoatl. Domination of the realms was my goal. We were so close! How did we fail?"

"You've only yourself to blame. You had the angel in your possession and failed to inform us. We might have been able to help you restrain her. But instead, she escaped and managed to get back to the beast."

Set looked away, a grimace dressing his snout with bared teeth. "She almost destroyed me that night. Aavi seemed so helpless . . . powerless. I still don't know how she got out of my prison. Someone helped her, or she was a much better liar than I thought."

"Quetzalcoatl told me she had some help from a tracker who works for the Council. He didn't have the whole story, but he knew they traveled to the fortress together."

"What was that tracker's name?" Set felt he'd heard it at some point, but in all that had happened in the last two months it was a detail that had slipped through the cracks.

"His name was D'Molay." Lamasthu rubbed her hand along the smooth surface of the seed as she answered.

"D'Molay. I need to repay that mortal fool for his interference with a slow, painful death!"

"Provided I don't catch him first. Now, you've heard my news, so it's time to speak of the devil," Lamasthu pressed.

"Very well."

Then Set began to tell her what Satan had told him.

The shadows of the temples and trees had just begun to stretch out as if they were reaching towards day's end. The street was its usual bustle of late afternoon activity, with stately priests, demigods, and merchants busying themselves with errands, deliveries or even ceremonies that had to be performed at that particular time of day.

Lamasthu held a scroll in her tendrilled hand as she walked along the tree-lined boulevard of the Temple District. Usually, she traveled with her own retinue of guards and priestly escorts. But while his reason for demanding her presence was vague, his instruction to bring no one else with her was quite specific. Moments before, she had visited the great Bank of Babylos to check the treasury vaults, but that was just a convenient excuse to cover her visit to Quetzalcoatl. He had summoned her.

As she passed the great Hindu Temple, Lamasthu was tempted to stop and see if there were any interesting ingredients for sale in the market stalls, but thought better of it, not wanting to be too late for her meeting. She continued on, letting her thoughts return to Quetzalcoatl.

Why does he want to see me? Could this be some sort of trap? No, he would do nothing to me here and now. It would be too obvious and there would be too many questions asked if anything happened to me. All my underlings know I am going to the Mayan Temple. Besides, I can take care of myself should he try anything. By the time she reached the meeting place, she felt more self-assured.

Lamasthu stood before the Temple of Time, as the Mayans called it, home to the official living stone calendar that marked the days of the Gods since the City had been founded. The temple loomed ever larger as she approached, a gray stone stepped pyramid that reminded her of the Great Egyptos monument in many ways, though the Mayan pyramid was smaller and the main entrance had been annoyingly placed at the top of the pyramid rather than at the bottom, forcing any who visited it to traverse a rather long flight of stairs. She walked onto the parkland that surrounded the temple, feeling the cool grass between her green-hued claw-like toes. She realized with delight that she enjoyed the sensation.

She passed by the small Lake of Remembrance and was soon ascending

the steps of the Mayan Temple. The huge, circular stone calendar floated over the top of the pyramid, a series of concentric icons and symbols all slowly moving in a clockwise fashion, with only the outer stone circle moving fast enough to be seen as it counted the seconds. At its very center was the carved image of Quetzalcoatl's face in his feathered serpent form.

When she reached the top, guards emerged from the smaller entry building and escorted her into the bowels of the pyramid. She was shown to a large, circular chamber completely covered in golden carvings of Mayan designs and icon glyphs. These were intricately connected and went from floor to ceiling. Lamasthu was unsure whether the walls were made of carved wood or of stone that had been covered in gold. They could even be solid gold. Even the floor was golden. All the reflections and carvings made it difficult to see where the floor ended and the walls and ceiling began. The overall effect was disorienting and threatened to steal her breath.

Quetzalcoatl did not immediately appear, so Lamasthu steadied herself by examining the many racks of scrolls lining the walls. She selected one to read and a white orb flickered into life, hovering above her shoulder to light the text. The symbols, colorful and vital, communicated something about harvest time, but Lamasthu was unschooled in the language of the Maya. She put the scroll back on the rack.

"Welcome, Lady of Babylon."

Lamasthu turned toward Quetzalcoatl's voice. He had taken his human form, and was seated cross-legged upon a very large, dark red pillow that floated three feet off the ground. Several other minor gods were gathered around him. Some held scrolls so long they touched the floor. Others manipulated long strings with knots and beads tied onto them. Lamasthu had heard that this pantheon used such strings to count and add numbers, much like the Asians used an abacus.

"I'm impressed that you journeyed so far just to see me," Quetzalcoatl began, cooperating in the deceit that their meeting was unplanned. "To what do I owe this visit?" He then gestured for his advisors to leave the chamber.

Lamasthu stood silently as his retinue retreated. The last one out of the room closed the large golden door. It made a heavy metallic sound as the latch clicked in place.

"You summoned me, as I recall," she intoned, holding up the parchment he had sent her. The yellow glow in her eyes intensified with more than a trace of annoyance.

Quetzalcoatl laughed. "Indeed, I did. It is time you and I spoke. Much has happened since the last time we were together and now one member of our trinity has been forced to flee, has he not?"

"You know he has. Set has lost his status in Egyptos - due to our efforts."

"Not our efforts. His own. Set's reach exceeded his grasp. He was foolish to try to move without consulting us. He has no one to blame but himself," Quetzalcoatl added.

Lamasthu paused a second or two. "I have to agree. If I had known that damnable Angel was being held as a slave in my own temple, I would have moved to put her under our direct control. Set knew she was there and decided to try and steal her for his own use. Then he made a foolish rush with his undead army to try and take the Angel and the beast from Ares' Fortress."

"Yes, and we had no choice but to follow him. He put us at great risk. If I were not on the Council, we would have been punished for our transgressions as well. I covered for you, Lamasthu. Do not forget that," Quetzalcoatl added.

"I forget nothing. And as much as I detest saying it, I am grateful for your efforts on my behalf. Still, it puts me in your debt." Lamasthu's fingers clenched the parchment, crumpling it. "I don't like being in anyone's debt. We risked everything to intercept that Angel. Was it worth it? Did we manage to avert the Olam Haba?"

"My people call it the end of the 13th B'ak'tun, but either way, it means the same thing. The end of the current age of man, and perhaps the end of the Realms of Gods. That, dear Lamasthu, is why I am here in this building. Right now, we are in the chamber of the next ages. It is here that one can predict future events and see what dangers or treasures the next cycle brings. One just has to know the right questions to ask."

"So have we averted the end of all things?" she asked again.

"The end date has come and gone, so in answer to your question, I'm certain that we delayed the end time."

"Delayed? So it can still happen? Will it come tomorrow or a thousand years from now?"

"It might happen tomorrow or at the end of the next B'ak'tun cycle in 394 human years. It might not happen until the end of the next Piktun, which would be in 2760 years. I've spent two weeks here with some of my fellow gods who are more skilled in interpreting these walls around us, but it has all been for naught. It seems prophecy will be of no use now in these matters. We are beyond the reach of the ancient warnings. This new cycle holds its mysteries well."

"So all we know for certain is that we have bought more time. Do any of the other gods know of this?"

"A few. Most believe what happens on Earth has no bearing on what happens to us, and therefore, anything we did is irrelevant. But there are those who would accuse us of crimes of treason. Attacking an angel is a violation of the treaty we have with the Heavenly Host."

"Who knew they even still existed?" Lamasthu gave him an appraising glance as she strode around the room, examining the various Mayan objects of power Quetzalcoatl had on display. She had almost missed them since they were displayed on small golden alcoves scattered about the room just below eye level. She picked up a crystal skull in her hand and felt a slight vibration beneath its polished coolness. Quetzalcoatl floated closer to her, as if he was concerned she might drop his curio.

"I do not deny my quest to maintain power," he admitted, "but saving the Realms and preserving our way of life was always my main goal in trying to capture the Angel."

Lamasthu had her doubts about that statement, but said nothing of it, instead deciding to move on to the matter at hand. "Well, I'm not sure how I can help you now. Prophecy was never my specialty."

"But you are still key to our agenda, Lamasthu. I invited you here for a specific purpose. Because it is the end of a cycle, Konohana is stepping down from the Council. Her term has ended. I have it within my power to nominate a new member. I could nominate you, if you are willing to pledge your loyalty to my concerns. But I need to know I can trust you."

Lamasthu was surprised by this turn of events. Though she had from time to time coveted a position on the Council, she had long ago abandoned the idea of being nominated due to her sardonic and independent nature. "I . . . I don't know quite what to say. I'm flattered you would ask, but worried about what the cost might be of such an honor."

"As with all things in life, there is always a cost. If you were on the Council, I would want your support anytime I had some important issue arise. Usually, I won't care how you vote, but there will be times I'll need you to vote my way. I suspect most of those times your needs will conveniently align with mine. We have more in common than you might know." Quetzalcoatl tried to give her a reassuring smile, which was only partially convincing.

Lamasthu paused, uncertain what to do or say. She considered the possibilities, finally coming to a conclusion. "Very well. I'm not likely to get another offer like this anytime soon. And you are correct. We do share many of the same goals." She carefully set the skull back into its niche as it grinned back at her. "For too long the Council has been run by inept fools. I will pledge my loyalty to you, but remember I am a leading goddess of Babylos, not some minion to order about. Let us work together as we have in the past."

She thought to herself, *I can always betray you later should the need arise.*

Quetzalcoatl smiled at her in approval. "I understand your concerns. This will be our chance to set the path and steer the Council away from issues that might hinder us."

A feeling of anticipation and excitement flooded Lamasthu for the first time in years. "Do you really think you can get me elected?" She couldn't help but smile a little at the thought of it.

"I think I can. They want another female on the council, and the candidate has to be from a Pantheon not currently a member. There hasn't been a Babylos god on the council since the death of Marduk. You'll need to reach out and make contact with the Pantheon leaders. You must be charming and make them comfortable with you if you are to win their acceptance. No doubt there'll be other candidates."

Lamasthu smiled at him. "I can do that. Am I allowed to kill the other nominees?" she asked, only somewhat sarcastically.

Quetzalcoatl laughed. "If only it were that easy! Let us go over the details and plan our next move."

⚜

*E*ros stood at the entrance to the Great Pyramid of Egyptos in the City of the Gods. Once again, he had been chosen by Zeus to work as a courier for a quick delivery and return of an important message. It wasn't something he liked doing, but somehow over the last few months he had gotten on the list of gods to call when messages needed to be formally presented. He wondered if his old friend Zephyrus had a hand in this prank.

After stating his business to the guards, Eros was permitted to fly directly to one of the balconies that were carved into the face of the huge pyramid. These platforms were almost invisible until one was fairly close to the huge, angled walls. Eros flew to the highest balcony on the west side. His wings spread out as he came in for a gentle feet-first landing on the smooth polished granite floor.

"I have a message written only for your lord, Ra-Horus," he told the two warrior priests he met there. They quickly made way when they heard a deep voice from the chamber behind them.

"Let him pass." Eros walked between the attendants and into the next room. There, Horus sat regally on a polished, red granite throne surrounded by advisors, a few guards, and some attractive maidens who worshipped at his feet. The dark haired girls giggled as Eros approached, his aura of passion and love immediately riveting their attention. Horus waved the maidens away. "Eros, is it not? We were told of your coming. Approach."

The juxtaposition of the two gods was intriguing. Eros seemed much like a man save for a pair of long white dove's wings, while Horus had the head of a beautiful hawk with a sharp yellow beak and large round eyes. Where his head merged into his shoulders he wore the traditional robes of an Egyptian ruler, festooned with gold and turquoise.

Eros bowed. "Ra-Horus." He held out a small parchment scroll that bore the wax seal of the Council. Horus nodded and one of his guards took the scroll and handed it to him, kneeling as he passed it to his sovereign god. Horus broke the seal and started reading in silence.

As he waited, Eros recalled the story that to help preserve the power of Egyptos, Ra had sacrificed his essence to many of his fellow deities. Horus was one of the gods who had benefited. At the time of the merging, he had formally changed his name to Ra-Horus, but most of the other Egyptos deities still called him Horus. Eros doubted the top god of Olympia, Zeus, would ever commit such a selfless act.

Horus made a happy, clicking sound with his beak which caused his advisors to look on expectantly. "Well, this is a good message for us. It appears that it is time for a new member on the Council, and Zeus has asked me to choose a candidate from Egyptos," he announced. His beak upturned in the semblance of a smile as his retinue clapped and voiced their approval. "Ahhh, but whom shall we choose this time?"

The advisors enthusiastically called out, "Lord Horus, Lord Horus!"

Horus waved them quickly to silence. "No. I've been on the Council already. Once is enough. I think it's high time we have some new blood over there. It's just a matter of whom to pick, and according to this parchment it should be a goddess." He looked to his advisors. "Make your suggestions . . . interesting," he encouraged the scholarly-looking men.

As Horus allowed his men time to confer, several of the maidens drifted back toward his throne, and from there, to Eros. They smiled coquettishly and reached out to stroke his wings and admire his beauty. Not wanting to offend Horus, Eros was happy to let them. He stood still, towering over his temporary devotees and smiling at them.

The three advisors murmured with each other and seemed to come to an agreement. One stepped forward. "My lord, perhaps your mother, Isis?"

"But she is involved in so many things. I fear she might not have the time for it. Still, not a bad choice," Horus replied

Another advisor suggested, "What of Meskhenet? She has little to do, Lord Horus."

"No. She is only interested in birthing and of little use in a meeting unless someone went into labor." The rest of the assembled onlookers chuckled at this.

The advisors glanced at each other nervously as their ideas were rejected. A third tried again. "What about Sekhmet, my lord? You spoke with her the other day on a matter concerning Set."

"Hmm, Sekhmet. The leader of the cats? Yes . . . Set and his kin are in our disfavor. It would be appropriate to reward those we are pleased with and those whom we favor." Then Horus turned his attention back to Eros. "Very well, we have decided. Tell Zeus that we shall endorse Sekhmet as our nominee for a place on the Council."

Eros bowed, managing to ignore the maidens as they continued to fawn over him. "Do you wish to confirm this with her first, Lord Horus?"

"Confirm? No. She is the nominee. It is my will and thus becomes Sekhmet's duty. She will no doubt be deeply honored. And if she isn't, she'll have to do it anyway."

The assembled crowd cheered and laughed their approval.

Elsewhere, the choice was not as popular.

<hr>

*H*era stormed into Zeus' Council room, her angry eyes fixed upon him and hands tensely balled up in fists. Despite her fury, she was still a beautiful goddess. She appeared to be a woman in her early forties, shapely of figure and youthful vigor gracing her face. Her auburn hair fell behind her like a dark fire trail from a comet.

"Ah, my wife returns. What concerns you today?" Zeus asked, knowing that she would not come for a visit unless she had a favor to ask or something to complain about. From her agitated expression, he suspected the latter. The female attendants at his side fled the room, knowing full well that Hera would not tolerate their presence.

Zeus and Hera did not see each other frequently. Although she had stopped being upset at her husband's many affairs with mortals, seeing him was a constant reminder of his infidelity. So, she now spent her time in any part of Olympia where Zeus was not. The two of them were only seen together at formal affairs where their mutual appearance was required, such as funerals, annual ceremonies or other regal events. Their personal lives no longer touched.

Hera marched right up to Zeus. "What were you thinking? Did you really just arrange a nomination to the Council without asking for anything in return? And why of all the Pantheons did you give it to Egyptos? Didn't they just invade our lands during the last lunar cycle?" she angrily spat out in an accusatory tone.

Zeus stood up to defend himself. "Egyptos didn't attack us - Set did.

Horus assured me of that. There were no other Egyptos gods with him when he invaded, only servants, creatures and undead warriors. They hold no blame, at least from me."

Hera seemed to ignore his answer. "And who is this 'Sekhmet' that Horus chose? Some new concubine for your harem? Are you putting her on the Council so she can service you during meetings? Really Zeus, I thought you kept your dalliances to humans and nymphs," she said disdainfully.

Anger flashed across Zeus' face. "You go too far Hera! I've never even met this goddess! Horus picked her because she is an enemy of Set. Besides, I've heard she has a cat head. She's not my type," Zeus added.

Hera stood her ground, crossing her arms and giving him a suspicious look. "That still doesn't explain why you gave Egyptos the nomination. Why?"

"You remember the last war in realms, the death and destruction it caused? The last thing we need now is a war with Egyptos. I intended the nomination as a peace offering to Horus, to let him know we hold no enmity toward his realm. The cycle has ended. The future is uncertain and unknown. We must proceed cautiously, not stumble forward like a raging drunkard."

"You sound like a conniving soothsayer," Hera scoffed. "Your words are weak. Did you know our son does not share your desire for peace? Ares is already seeking Set in the Lost Realm. He has forces near the Egyptos border, ready to strike if he finds him hiding there. Who can blame him? It was his fortress and forces that took the brunt of the attack."

"What? I told him to take no action against Egyptos!"

"Ares has taken no action . . . yet. But how long do you think he'll stand down?" Hera felt she had achieved some small victory for revealing something infuriating. "He, more than anyone in Olympia, has cause for revenge. Who could blame him? Certainly not I," she said haughtily.

"This cannot continue! Hera, we have to work together if we are to preserve the balance between the major pantheons. If our son can't see that, I hope that at least you can," Zeus said with the touch of pleading in his voice. Picking up a goblet of nectar he took a swig as he awaited her reply.

For the first time in quite a while, Hera saw a glimmer of vulnerability in her wayward husband. She had to admit to herself that she had misjudged his reasons for giving the nomination. Although it would be satisfying, perhaps Zeus was wise not to provoke Egyptos. His cunning over the eons had proved him a competent leader. Hera dialed back her resistance.

"All right, I'll talk to Ares and see what I can do. And I'll let others know what your reasons are, now that I understand them."

Zeus smiled. "Thank you my dear. I'd much rather we be a force for peace. War may yet come again, but there is no need to speed its arrival."

⊶⊰✦⊱⊷

Shiva walked into the glen. It was cooler here then he preferred, but the lush trees and spectacular waterfall more than made up for the inconvenience. He had traveled across the great lake from the Council chamber all the way to the Celtic Realm just to see her again. Walking on, thoughts of her beauty filling his head, he approached the waterfall. Pushing his way through thick vegetation, he found the cave entrance.

"Ceridwen, are you about?" There was no answer. "I came to speak with you on a matter of importance."

Just then, a beautiful woman with long red hair appeared behind him. Her hands rested on his shoulders as she whispered in his ear. "Importance, is it? Must be, for you rarely come here to see me, my blue prince. What brings ye now?"

"I've missed you," Shiva's hand reached back to rest upon hers.

She smiled. "You timed this well. The other two Matres went to see Cernunnos. I got your message, so I stayed behind. But what brings you? I thought we decided we shouldn't meet anymore." Ceridwen sighed, stepping back and smoothing the folds of her dark, green gown as she looked away.

Turning around, Shiva embraced Ceridwen, gazing into her violet eyes. "The new cycle has come. A new member on the Council must be chosen. I want it to be you."

"Me? Shiva, are ye mad?"

Hugging her all the closer, he replied. "Don't you see? We can be together that way. We'd see each other all the time and none would dare object."

She pulled slightly away. "You know we can't be together. It's a violation of Celtic edict. It's too painful. There you'd be, right there, only a touch away and yet, unreachable. I couldn't bear it, Shiva."

He ran his hand through her long, wavy red hair. "But we'd find time. A way for stolen moments for just the two of us. No one else would know."

"Everyone would know. How could they not know that I loved you and that you loved me? One look at us tells the tale."

"The City cares nothing for such things. Only your people do."

"You know what their punishment is! I would be cast out or entombed."

"Not if we're careful. I'll change my form when I come here from now on and we can remain distant when we are in public." As if to prove the point, he took a few steps away from her to keep a respectful distance. Then he shifted his appearance to that of a stranger to whom no one in Ceridwen's realm would give a second glance. Yet she still frowned.

"Even if we did these things, it's just wrong. What do I know about the politics of the Council or the affairs of the realms? Celts don't mix with the other Pantheons," she said as a tear of frustration ran down her cheek.

"That's exactly why I want a Celtic goddess as a nominee. I think the Council could use an outsider who could to look at matters with an untarnished view. Besides, I'll be right there to help you along." Unable to resist, Shiva leaned in and kissed her freckled forehead. For him, those freckles and creamy white skin were one of her most alluring features, as his people lacked such markings. They reminded him of a leopard's spots.

"Oh, Shiva, you make it sound like it's all possible, that it could all really happen."

"Of course it is, my love. We are gods after all. Never forget that."

Chapter 6

Hidden Huntress

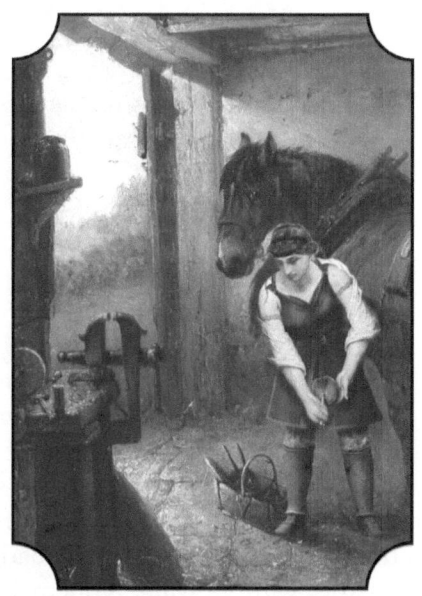

D'Molay walked along the dirt road that wound behind the shops that fronted the port. The way was creased with ruts from cart wheels and many muddled footprints stretched before him in mud still drying from recent rains. Although this was not the busiest part of Dioscrias, it seemed to be an active section of the town. He stopped under a sign with horseshoes and arrows painted on it. He and Aavi had been here not that long ago. In contrast to everything he had been through, here it felt the like nothing had changed.

From inside the large barn on which hung the sign, he could hear a familiar tapping sound. Entering, he saw Sophia bent over, holding the leg of a horse as she hammered the bottom of its hoof. He remained silent as she finished her task.

"That takes care of you now," she said to the horse. Without looking at D'Molay, she spoke to him as she led the horse into a stall. "I'll be right with you, hold on."

"No rush," he replied. D'Molay noted that she was dressed much the same as the last time he had seen her. She wore a brown leather apron with pockets in the front over a white linen, short-sleeved tunic which extended to her mid thigh. Her sun-browned muscular arms and legs were bare and she wore brown leather boots that laced up to the top of her calves. Sophia had a stocky build, but was quite tall, easily over six feet.

Closing the stall gate she wiped her hands on the leather apron. "So what can I do for you?"

"Good morrow, Sophia. You may not remember me."

She squinted at him for a second before recognition crossed her face. "Ah, yes. The traveler with no name. On your own this time?"

"My name is D'Molay, Jacques D'Molay. I'm sorry I couldn't tell you before."

"I suppose it didn't matter. But I'm sure you didn't come all the way back to tell me your name. What do you need, Dee-Mole-ay?" Apparently pronouncing his name slowly to make sure she got it correct.

"I'm looking for harpies."

Sophia gave him a strange look. "At my forge? Last time you were here you didn't strike me as feeble minded."

D'Molay's jaw tightened. He was getting extremely tired of others questioning his sanity.

"Of course not. I'm going to seek them in the mountains."

Sophia merely looked intrigued. "Harpies? Why would you hunt them? They don't make good trophies and to eat one... would just be wrong."

"I didn't say I was planning to hunt them. I'm looking for where they live. Do you know where they fly to when they pass over here?"

She gave him an appraising look. "What are you really after?"

He tried to speak calmly and earnestly though he felt irritated by Sophia's suspicions. "An answer. Last time I was here, my companion and I saw a large flock of harpies swarm the ship we were on. They stole some things off that ship and now I need to find out where they took them." Without knowing it, his time with Aavi had inspired him to find ways to say what he was after without lying. Nonetheless he would still lie if he felt he had to.

Realization passed over Sophia's face. "Ah, so that's it. Harpies have been known to take anything that catches their eye. Jewelry, weapons, food. What did they get from you and that flaxen-haired slip of a girl you were traveling with?" As she spoke, Sophia walked through the archery workshop and towards the back entrance.

D'Molay followed and, upon seeing the archery and fletching tools, couldn't help but smile as he recalled Aavi's astonished reaction to seeing an arrow fly loose from one of Sophia's bows. "We - I'm looking for an urn that the harpies carried off."

Sophia was still ahead of him as they emerged from the building and stepped onto the archery range. She looked up at the distant hills beyond the town. "I've seen them flying off in large flocks, off that way." She pointed to the east. "Some say they have a rookery deep in the woods. Mind you, I don't know of anyone who's ever seen it." There was silence and they both heard the distant caw of a raven as it flew overhead.

"Can you help me find them?" he finally asked.

She turned to face him. The wind blew her long dark hair across her face and it reminded him of Aavi once again. Sophia furrowed her brow a little. "Perhaps. But I can't go tramping through the woods looking for harpies. I have work to do here."

"Be honest, Sophia," D'Molay said. "Deep down you're a huntress. You'd like nothing better than to go off on a trek in the woods."

"Oh, would I now? What makes you so sure of that, D'Molay, if that's your real name?"

He smiled. "That is my real name and you're not the first Amazon I've met. You all love to hunt and travel the wilderness. Maybe I can make it worth your time. What if I hired you to be my guide?"

She raised an eyebrow. "Your guide? Why me? You can probably find a dozen men in town who could be a guide."

"But I trust you and I'm sure you know your way around in a fight."

"You'll need a fighter if you go after harpies," she said, casually examining one of her own arrows.

"I know. That's why I'll pay you three gold a day if you'll come."

Sophia gave him a sly look. "Four gold. Plus, you pay any expenses and I get ten percent of whatever we bring back."

Despite the higher price, D'Molay nodded in agreement. "All right, done. Four it is. How much time do you need to get ready to leave?"

She shrugged. "A day, maybe two. I need to see who can take care of things here while I'm gone. There are horses to be fed and some smithy work I have to finish before I can go."

"Anything I can do to help?"

For the first time ever, D'Molay saw her smile mischievously. "Do you know how to clean horse stalls?"

D'Molay spent the rest of the day performing a series of tasks for Sophia that he found rather insulting to his status. *I'm a tracker who holds a Council seal, not a servant boy,* he inwardly grumbled as she set him to cleaning horse stalls, sorting arrows, and counting horseshoes. When she told him to polish a long neglected and unimportant stack of saddles, he became convinced she was taking advantage of his desire to help her get ready. This had to stop.

"No, Sophia. I'm not going to waste my efforts on this old tack that obviously no one will ever use again," he said, lifting one of the saddles to point out the extensive damage to the leather.

"Are you tired already?" Sophia challenged as she left him standing by the saddles to load more fuel into her forge. "If today's light work has taxed your strength, I don't think I want to be alone in the woods with you and a nest of harpies."

D'Molay could not help himself. He strode over to Sophia and bluntly pressed his case. "I've offered to pay you well. I've done your tasks." His hand drifted to his knife. "Are you trying to cheat me?"

Sophia was not intimidated. Her eyes narrowed as she spoke to him firmly. "Do the saddles. Then we'll eat and plan this journey of yours." She lifted her hammer with a quiet assurance that communicated she would use it as a weapon if need be.

A short time and seven polished saddles later, the two of them sat at a simple but sturdy table in Sophia's home, eating a stew she had quickly put together and heated on the still-hot forge in the stable.

"Enjoy this. Tomorrow we'll be eating dried meat and hard bread."

D'Molay shoveled a large spoonful into his mouth, suddenly realizing how hungry the day's tasks had made him. He reached for his mug of water as Sophia stirred her own bowl idly, as if she had little appetite.

"Let's talk about this hunt," she went on. "You realize if the harpies still have your urn, they'll have opened it by now."

He swallowed a gulp of water and looked over at her. "I know. But I still need to find out where they took it and why."

"Harpies will take things because they can. That's why," she scoffed. "Locating their home may not tell you anything about the fate of your urn."

"I know. But if it's at all possible, we need to find them."

Sophia drummed the table with her fingertips. D'Molay could see she was beginning to get excited about the adventure in spite of her strong ties to her smithy.

"I know the woods up there well," she said. "I can't make any promises, though. We might not find the harpies' nesting grounds at all. And it may be too far to get there in the time we have, even if we do find out where they dwell. But I promise you I'll do my best. I'll stay out there for a week. Then I have to return."

D'Molay slapped the table, almost feeling like he had won a battle with the Amazon. "Good. Then I'm going to get some sleep," he said, pushing his emptied stew bowl aside.

"You can sleep in the archery room or here in the kitchen. I'll get you some blankets. Oh, and if you try anything, I'll kill you."

D'Molay merely nodded at the warning. He knew Amazons had little patience for men. There was no point in trying to change Sophia's opinion other than through his own actions, or lack thereof.

"I appreciate your hospitality. You don't need to worry."

She gave him a stern look. "I'm not worried. I just don't want your blood on my floor."

The next morning Sophia was already prepared to travel when D'Molay got up to pack. Her dark hair was wound into one loose braid that hung down the center of her back. She wore a short sleeved green tunic with a leather belt. On the belt hung a sheathed knife and a small leather pouch. She had a cloak wrapped around her shoulders and wore tights and knee high boots, and looked like a woodland warrior ready for battle. D'Molay decided not to compliment her for fear she might take it the wrong way.

While they were in the stables gathering supplies, a tall, older man appeared at the entrance. Unlike most of the denizens in this area, he was not wearing a toga, but a simple long-sleeved linen tunic with an open brown leather vest, which emphasized his protruding gut. He wore a sort of kilt that went down to his knees. On his feet were old leather sandals that laced up his calves. D'Molay noted they were the same type that Greek soldiers were issued. The man's shoulder-length hair was white, though the top of his head was mostly bald. His face showed the care-worn signs of a man who has spent most of his life scratching a hard living outdoors. He leaned on a wooden staff that doubled as a walking stick. "Sophia. I got your message, so here I am," he said.

Sophia set down the pack she was filling and walked over to greet him. "Markus. So you'll be able to take care of things here for a week?"

"I wouldn't be here if couldn't. Just come back on time. I have things to do too, you know."

Sophia smiled a little. "I thought you sold me this place so you wouldn't have anything to do anymore."

"Heh, I thought so too, but there's always something that needs doing. Where are you off to?"

D'Molay answered for her. "I've hired Sophia to help me track down the harpies' lair."

The man turned to D'Molay. "I'm Markus Perchius, retired smithy. So you want to hunt harpies, eh? I'd be careful if I were you."

"D'Molay. I'm always careful," he said, offering his hand in greeting.

Sophia patted the nose of a horse in a nearby stall. "Have you come across harpies in the past, Markus?" she asked, as she fed it a handful of grain.

The older man absently scratched his belly. "Long ago when I was a youngster, I came across a harpy in the woods. She couldn't fly. I think she had a broken wing. I tried to help her, but she was so vicious I couldn't get close enough to do any good. Finally I just had to retreat and leave her be. The creature shrieked like a banshee the whole time. I couldn't tell if she had any intelligence beyond that of a wild animal."

"Perhaps she was blinded by pain or fear," Sophia suggested.

"Never did find out," Markus shrugged.

"Did you know where she came from? Or where they live now?" D'Molay asked.

"Well, I've not been there, but I hear that flocks of 'em live in the mountains to the northeast. Mind you, that's only a rumor."

"Can you show me on a map?" D'Molay took out a folded piece of parchment from his traveling bag and laid it out on the workbench. The three of them gathered around.

"This is where we are now, Dioscrias," D'Molay indicated. "Where are those mountains you've heard of?"

Markus hemmed over the map for a moment, finally planting a plump finger on it. "I think they're near the Hindu border here, but I don't know how far inland. As I said, I've never been there."

D'Molay noted the place then refolded the map. "You've given us a destination at least."

Sophia touched Markus on the shoulder. "Now, let me go over some details on business matters for while I'm gone. The good news for you is you won't have to do any smithing work. Just take care of the horses and make sure no one runs off with the place." As she took the older man around the stables and told him the status of various horses and equipment, D'Molay put away his map and continued to make ready for their trip.

After a quick meal, they filled up the water bags and loaded the horses. Sophia and D'Molay mounted up and rode out of the stables. Markus gave them a friendly wave as he stood at the entrance, leaning against his staff.

"We'll take the north trail," Sophia said as she set off on a well-worn path that ran up the hills to the northeast. D'Molay followed, turning back to see the town and the great lake one last time before the view was lost in the thickening trees.

They rode for several hours, passing wineries and villas. D'Molay was surprised to see how many of them were run down or abandoned. When he and Aavi had traveled a route further to the south, all was prosperous. "Have you noticed all the abandoned houses up here?" he asked.

"Yes. It's been in decline for years. I've heard some enemy of Helios has cursed our region of Olympia. No one likes him, so who knows which god might have done such a thing. Of course, the taxes and corruption in the lands under his control are enough of a curse on their own," Sophia replied as they passed by another empty villa.

"Seems you didn't pick the best place to go into business. What was it that brought you to Dioscrias?"

"Nothing in particular. I wanted to make my own way in the realms. Dioscrias seemed as good a place as any. I knew horses and got hired by Markus to help at the stables. I worked for him a good many years. But since he was not in favor of the gods, he grew too old to work the forge and offered the establishment to me. Since I'm also skilled at making bow and arrows, I added them to the shop." D'Molay noticed she would not meet his eyes as she spoke, which made him wonder what pieces of her story she was leaving out.

"Fair enough. I'm glad it all worked out for you," he said, hoping she might reveal a little more. Instead, she asked him a question.

"You never did tell me what happened to your doe-eyed companion. Where is she now?"

He opened his mouth, but no words came out. Once again, the Council's spell was stopping him from revealing any information about Aavi. "She's not with me at this point. She's . . . I mean . . . Damn, I'm unable to say. The . . . C . . . It's a spell." He wasn't even able to mention the word Council to Sophia. The spell seemed to know how much the person he was talking to already knew about Aavi. Mazu knew as much as he did, so he could talk to her about her easily. He could speak to Sergius about Aavi somewhat as he had told him about her before the Council had put the spell in place. But he'd never even told Sophia Aavi's name or why they had been traveling together.

Sophia stared at him as he babbled. "Forget it. You don't want to talk about it. Fine. So we both have things we'd rather not discuss. Guess that makes us even," she said, coldly.

"That's not how it is," he shot back. "I'm prevented from speaking."

"Men. Why can't they ever just tell the truth?" she muttered, nudging her horse forward and turning her attention to the trail ahead. D'Molay exorcised the offense he felt at her dismissive attitude by drawing his knife and hacking his first trail marking on the nearest tree.

Once they got into the deeper woods, D'Molay made crosses more often on trees as they rode along the trail. Sophia shot him impatient looks each time he did.

"Must you do that?" she finally complained. "We have little time to travel as it is without you constantly stopping."

"These cross marks may save our lives. My friend Mazu's quite good at showing up when she's needed most."

"And it may cost us our lives if someone else is following," Sophia added with a frown.

"Who would be following?" D'Molay challenged, again seeking to draw out the woman's past. She did not take his bait, giving him no answer.

The trail began to take on a wilder appearance. As from the start, Sophia held the lead. "This way is seldom travelled. If we're going to find your harpies, it'll be in this region. Almost everyone takes the southern route since Helios had the village of Kalios cleared out."

"Cleared out? What do you mean?"

"Don't know the details. It happened long before I moved to Dioscrias.

I heard he closed all the businesses and made everyone move south to Scarrios. He probably had plans for some big project, but nothing ever came of it. About the only thing still active up there is Artemis' Lodge. We'll head there if we don't get a lead on the harpies. Someone there might know."

They continued along the trail for a half an hour in silence. Occasionally they could hear the cry of some distant creature or animals moving in the nearby brambles.

"What lives out here?" D'Molay asked.

"Keep an eye out for griffins, hydras or brigands," Sophia said authoritatively, as she manuvered her mount around a fallen tree.

"Brigands?"

"Or bandits, if you prefer. Those that follow darker Olympians like Pluto or Ares are always looking for ways to honor their gods. A few killings would suit them well, not to mention looting whatever goods their victims carried."

Having fought and defeated more human foes than he could count, the possibility of an encounter with those foes held little threat for D'Molay. He'd never fought a hydra or a griffin before, however, and wondered how either would match up with other monsters he'd dealt with. After experiencing the fight with Aavi's beast, he doubted either would even approach that challenge.

After a few more hours, they made camp and spent an uneventful night. They set off again in an early morning rain, but it soon cleared into a fine day. They saw a pack of wolves on a nearby hill and passed a beautiful waterfall, and at one point they thought they saw a harpy flying high above their heads, but it turned out to be a large condor.

They passed a few more abandoned homesteads as the vines and brambles grew thicker. D'Molay thought about all the displaced people. The whims of gods and the fallout from their wars were often the cause of shifting populations. But for the life of him, D'Molay could not think of a single realm he had traveled that seemed more crowded as a result of the gods' interference.

The day burned its hours away, the sun drifting off toward the horizon. Orange light put the trees in dark silhouette and cast long shadows across the forest floor. They dismounted among some old marble columns and the broken statue of a god. D'Molay watered the horses while Sophia took out some dried meat and pomegranates. Once he'd returned and sat down, she handed him his share of the food.

D'Molay looked up at their crumbling surroundings as he ate some meat. "What was this place?"

Sophia spit out a pomegranate seed. "I think that statue was meant to be Apollo. Helios had all Apollo's images destroyed when he took over this region. People say they were fighting over the sun. You know how gods are."

"Oh, I do," D'Molay said conclusively as he leaned back and looked at the broken statue, now mostly overgrown with ivy. He traced the rough surface of the stone with his fingertips, remembering something. Once, he had carved the image of the sun on his prison wall, thinking he might never see the real sun again. He'd even incised a crescent moon beside it, longing even for the cold light of that orb. But the skies of old Earth seemed empty compared to those above the realms. Two moons were rising, and soon more stars than he could name would dot the heavens. Sophia nudged him out of his reverie.

"As I was saying," she repeated, "since we haven't seen any harpies yet, we should talk to some other hunters. The Lodge of Artemis is about half a day's ride from here."

"We should head for it tomorrow, then," D'Molay said, shaking off his memories. Although he wished the detour wasn't necessary, he agreed with Sophia that the local hunters were their best source of information about where the harpies actually lived. As he rolled himself up in his blanket for the night, he imagined what the lodge might be like. He had never visited one before. It would be an interesting location to add to his map.

The next morning came with a dense fog. Vaguely remembering throwing off his blanket during the night, D'Molay was not surprised that warmer weather had rolled in. Unfortunately, it had brought with it conditions that clouded the ground. This slowed the pace of their ride considerably and made everything in the forest seem even more eerie and threatening. Sophia rode forward slowly, her eyes fixed on the ground to make sure they stayed on the trail. D'Molay followed closely, watching the woods even though he doubted he would see anything that chose to attack until it was right upon them.

After traveling for half an hour, they became more comfortable in the fog. D'Molay even rationalized that what he couldn't see likewise couldn't see him, putting him and his potential foes on an equal footing. Ahead of him, Sophia raised her hand, signaling that she was stopping.

"There's a slope ahead," she informed him.

"A steep one?"

"I can't see and I don't remember," she said.

D'Molay dismounted. "Then let's lead our horses down, just to be safe." He took the opportunity to slash another trail mark on a tree as Sophia got off her horse.

They moved on with care. D'Molay could hear many small rocks bouncing down the hillside as the hooves of their mounts dislodged them. He and Sophia tread gingerly, their boots slipping on the uneven, wet slope. The trip down took them into an even whiter world where the densest fog had settled in a hollow.

"I can't see anything," Sophia sighed. "We're going to have to wait until the sun burns some of this away."

"It'll take hours for the sun to reach this hole," D'Molay protested. "We should just push through." His horse stamped nervously as if it too wanted to move on.

"But I can't be sure which way -"

"Then let me lead." D'Molay pulled his horse forward and passed Sophia. "This fog could take all day to disperse. We don't have time to wait."

"You'll still be paying me if you get us completely lost," she called from behind him. He soon heard her and her mount trudging after him and smiled in satisfaction that he had gotten his way.

His smile soon faded as he found the going difficult. The path bent frequently to the right or left, signaling its turns by large trees or tall thickets that suddenly blocked the way.

"Damn," he cursed as the pack on his saddle became entangled in some thorny vines that had crept up a stack of boulders. He edged to that side of his horse to work his bags free when he heard something walking on the rocks above his head. There was the sound of a soft footpad, then the scratching of a claw. His horse nickered.

"Sophia," he whispered, freezing in place. She looked over at him and he pointed up. D'Molay saw her expression turn grim as a screech sounded and more scrambling noises came from the top of the rocks. He pressed tightly against the boulders as Sophia quickly tied her horse's lead to a tree and rushed to ready her bow. Taking her cue, D'Molay found a root sticking out of the boulders and secured his own horse. If they lost their mounts in this fog, they'd never find them again.

As quietly as possible, he edged away from the rocks and back toward Sophia, drawing his knife. Just as he reached her they heard wings beating above them. "Harpy?" D'Molay asked.

He was proved wrong as a griffin swooped low over them. D'Molay ducked and evaded the grasping eagle talons on its front legs, but a switch of its tail caught Sophia in the face. She staggered back against a tree and dropped to one knee, grasping the side of her head. He saw blood between her fingers.

"Give me your bow," D'Molay demanded, assuming she was too hurt to fight.

"Never," she said, glaring at him with a glint of excitement in her eye. "You'd probably shoot one of my horses."

They could hear the griffin circling above them, ready to fly in for a second attack. Another screech sounded, giving a clue to the beast's position. Sophia raised her bow and drew back an arrow blessed with her own blood. The lion-bird descended, its great claws reaching for them. D'Molay heard Sophia's bowstring snap. The griffin screamed and wheeled off to the left, crashing through the trees. They waited for a tense minute, hearing nothing more.

"Did you kill it?" D'Molay asked.

"It will be back if I didn't," Sophia said. "But it was a good strike, near, if not in, its heart. Wait here."

Sophia stood and moved toward the spot where the griffin had seemed to fall. Ignoring her instruction to wait, D'Molay followed. They found the creature thirty paces into the woods. It lay on its side, still.

"We were lucky," Sophia said. "It was old and slow. I wouldn't have been quick enough to shoot a younger one." She nodded in approval, noting the placement of her arrow in the griffin's chest. D'Molay watched as she stepped up to the corpse and began to yank feathers from its wings.

"If you want a trophy, why not take its head?" D'Molay asked.

"Because griffin feathers are light and tradable," she explained. "You can take the head yourself if you want the burden."

D'Molay found the suggestion unsettling. It reminded him of his strange dream about carrying a bloody sack. "No thanks." Instead, he knelt by one of the griffin's front legs and cut off several of its talons. "I'll take these."

Chapter 7

Days of the Hunt

Quan had caught more fish than he alone could eat. As the warm afternoon dragged on, he flagged down other boats to offer them a share of his catch. He collected a few coins and traded for some interesting trinkets, but his main reward was meeting people from realms far from his own. Even though Mazu had brought him into the City, he had seen nothing there beyond her boathouse at the North Dock.

He listened as oarsmen of a small boat with a prow decorated by a carved dragon's head sang a chant to coordinate their strokes as they passed by. If he and D'Molay had sailed with some of them in their crew, rowing to Dioscrias after the storm would have been easy. Luckily, Quan instead had the favor of Mazu, who had brought them to port safely while they slept.

The day Mazu had first visited his village remained the most amazing in Quan's life. He had been an old man; so old, that several of the younger men had been gambling on his death day for several weeks. Quan grinned while remembering that their game had been foiled by Mazu rejuvenating him. She had never told him precisely why she had done it. At first he thought it was in return for the small offering he had presented, but that token was hardly equal to another life.

Gods and goddess were beyond his understanding, though, and Quan had resolved not to question his benefactress. Her gift had more than earned his utter loyalty, and when a message came to his village to serve her in the City he left home with haste. He anticipated great honor and status as a favored servant of a goddess. Besides, since he had been transformed, everyone in the village had become a bit afraid of him. He didn't feel like he fit in anymore. After settling into life at the boathouse, Quan did not miss his home.

Lately, however, serving Mazu was placing him in dangerous situations. Quan had never particularly craved adventure, even as a little boy. When his friends played at fighting imaginary demons, he pretended to build great ships or palatial estates. Almost losing their boat was a terrifying event that he prayed would not be matched by future incidents. He enjoyed his new life and his second priority, after obeying Mazu, was preserving it at all costs.

He was half-dozing in the shade of the repaired cabin when he heard water splattering on deck. Quan rose with a curse, fearing his fixes had failed and caused the boat to leak again. He was relieved to see that it was not an encroachment of ordinary water, but Mazu. He watched as her stretched-out, liquid form flowed over the deck and pooled near his feet inside the cabin, where she could take her shape out of sight of any spies.

He bowed. "Goddess. Does your return mean we can go home?"

Mazu tipped the brim of her hat down. A splatter of normal lake water fell from it. "We've barely begun this journey, Quan. Be patient. Did D'Molay go harpy hunting as planned?"

Quan nodded. "Yesterday. He said he'd be a week away. Then can we go home?"

Mazu eyed him with a slight smile. "Quan, I know you prefer a quiet life, but a bit of adventure will do you good."

"I've had a bit already," he dared to say.

"There will be more," Mazu said. She then laughed at the dismayed look on Quan's face. "I do sound like a fortune teller."

"No. A fortune teller would make it sound better," Quan said. "Say something about treasure and beautiful women."

Mazu twirled her staff in her hand thoughtfully. "If you wish. I can guarantee you'll see both in our travels. Now, would you make tea for me, Quan? The palace servants cannot do it properly."

This was a task more to his liking and Quan set about it energetically. "What's it like in the palace?" he asked as he boiled water and carefully selected leaves from a lacquered box.

"Chaotic. The king does not rule well and that imbalance is reflected in every aspect of his household. Even down to the refreshments," she said, as she watched Quan begin to steep the leaves. "In spite of that, I think I will learn all I need to know soon."

"I'm glad you came back," Quan said. "But won't they miss you?"

Mazu accepted her cup of tea and held it to her nose, appreciating its aroma before taking a sip. "I have been granted a day off. I told the children that today I am hiding, so that they can have the fun of seeking me. There is so little happiness in their lives."

Quan sat down respectfully at Mazu's feet as she enjoyed her tea. "Is there anything else I can do out here?" he eventually asked.

Mazu looked about the boat. "No, not right now. You did well with the repairs. The boat is sound again." As Quan beamed under the light of her praise, Mazu casually examined him. His true age had not yet begun to erode her boon. Quan seemed as vital as he had when she first worked her power on him months ago. Mazu had no idea how long her gift would last. She had rejuvenated him on a whim and had often wondered if she had done wrong, or if the act was predetermined, a natural path to Quan's greater destiny. Her curiosity had inspired her to keep the fisherman close by. Mazu wanted to see what would happen to him. Perhaps he would remain young forever, though she seriously doubted that would be the case. She wasn't looking forward to telling him the truth about his state of being. He was so proud of his vitality that she hadn't the heart to say anything. But with the dangers they were sure to face, he might be killed before he reverted to old age and the problem would solve itself.

She finished her tea. "Thank you. I'll come again after D'Molay is back." Mazu stood, noticing some of the bartered items Quan had obtained from other boats on the counter. "Be careful who you talk to and what you say," she warned him. "Anyone could be looking for me."

Quan bowed and vowed he would be cautious. Mazu liquefied and flowed away. He stepped over to his pot and poured himself a cup of the aromatic tea. He used to drink it because people said it kept one young. Now he just drank it for the taste.

*W*ith one dead griffin in their wake, D'Molay and Sophia continued their ride. When the trail finally led up and out of the hollow, they got above the fog and could see the Lodge of Artemis off in the distance. Set on the edge of a small lake and surrounded by tall cypress trees, it was a beautiful sight in the middle of untamed wilderness. The lodge was a palatial two-story villa built of stone with a red tile roof and ionic columns all along the front. The building was a hundred feet across and perhaps two hundred feet long. There was an overgrown apple orchard and an elaborate arched stone entrance at the center of the compound.

"So that's the lodge. It's huge. I was expecting a hunter's shack, not a palace," D'Molay said, obviously impressed by the sheer size of the estate.

"This was all under the control of Artemis at one time, but it was another prize Helios managed to steal. He used to hunt these lands, but he stopped coming ages ago. Now only a few caretakers live here along with some other retired soldiers," Sophia said as they rode past the gate.

D'Molay noticed that one of the large gate doors had broken off its hinges at the top and was hanging at an odd angle against the archway. He also saw that small plants were growing between the cracks in the cobblestone walkway and on the tops of the stone wall. Debris and mounds of leaves had piled up against the foundation. As they approached the main building, D'Molay saw it had a neglected, decaying feel to it.

"It's a beautiful building, sad to see it like this."

"You can bet it looked better when a female goddess was in charge," Sophia said. "Let's head for the stables; we can pick out a stall for the horses."

D'Molay followed her off to the right and to another large run-down building. The stables had the same style and look as the main lodge, consisting

of an arched entrance with a carved marble frieze of running horses at the top. The frieze was stuffed with numerous bird nests, having been built in every available niche. Just beyond the archway were two rows of horse stalls, at least fifty on each side. As Sophia had predicted there was no one around, despite the fact there were more than a dozen horses already stabled there. They watered their own and headed for the main building, each carrying their belongings. As they took the weathered steps up to the entrance, two men walked out the double doors and came toward them. There was no doubt from the look of them that they were hunters. Both had bows and quivers on their backs, carried knives at their hips, and wore animal skins as outer garments. One of them broadly grinned upon seeing Sophia.

"Well, look what greets us at the end of the day - Sophia. What brings you up here? Didn't know you had time for hunting these days." The speaker was a burly, bald man with an uneven moustache. D'Molay suspected that he sported it to hide some defect with his upper lip. The man pointed to Sophia. "What happened to your head?"

Sophia reached up to the crust of dried blood on her hair from the strike of the griffin's tail. "I had a little trouble on the way. And you're right, Julio. I don't have the time I used to. I'm only here because I've been hired to aid him in a hunt. Sorry, this is D'Molay and these two Julio and his brother Capa," she said, nodding toward D'Molay. The three men exchanged greetings.

"So what are you after then? Certainly not a hydra. You'd need a hunting party for that. Perhaps a bear or a banshee?" Julio asked.

"We're looking for harpy nesting grounds," D'Molay interjected.

"Harpies?" Cupo exclaimed. His eyebrows raised in an exaggerated manner which only accentuated how far his hairline had receded. "Just the two of you? They travel in large flocks. You'd be mad to try to find their nesting grounds; they'll rip you to shreds."

Julio nodded in agreement with his companion. "I suppose you're tempted by their treasure, eh? Well, you aren't the first."

"Treasure? What treasure?" Sophia asked, looking suspiciously at D'Molay.

"We're not looking for treasure, just harpies. Do you know where they are?" D'Molay asked, trying to see if they could get some useful information. He was tired and mildly annoyed by the hunters' assumptions.

Ignoring D'Molay, Julio answered Sophia's question. "Aye, treasure. Harpies are known for grabbing things that catch their eye. Legend has it that there are piles of gold and jewels in their nests, waiting for any brave enough to find it."

"Oh, that treasure. If we see some lying around, we'll be sure to pick it up, don't worry," D'Molay said sarcastically. He'd heard the same tale about every dragon and ogre from Olympia to Valhalla.

Sophia just laughed. "Julio, that's just a story."

"Maybe," he shrugged. "No matter. It's just good to see you again. Blessings of the gods to you both." Julio turned to Cupo. "Let's get going. It's getting dark and if we don't clear our traps something will eat our catch during the night." They started off.

"Wait," D'Molay called after them. "You never said if you know where the harpies live." The gray-haired man turned back.

"Try the mountain area ta the nor'east. A friend of mine saw harpies there 'bout a season ago. Maybe their nests are there." The two men departed and Sophia and D'Molay moved on toward the double doors.

"Looks like you're known even up here," D'Molay said.

"Julio is one of my customers. Dioscrias is the closest place for men like him to buy arrows and horseshoes. And I spent a fair amount of time up here before I took over the blacksmiths. I had more time for sport then."

They entered the main hall of the lodge. It was two stories tall, with a high wood-beamed ceiling and large iron chandeliers designed to hold twenty large candles each. None were lit the moment, but heavy deposits of hardened wax hung in brittle strings from the sockets. The smell of wood and leather permeated the air. The room itself went back about forty feet and was about fifty feet wide. In the center stood a large marble statue of the goddess Artemis. She carried a stag in one hand and wielded a short sword in the other. Her pose gave the impression she was running, with the wind billowing her hair and her short dress behind her. It was truly beautiful.

The floor was tiled in fine polished marble and the stone walls were decorated with the preserved heads of over a hundred animals. D'Molay noticed a sphinx, a griffin, a crocodile, lions, stags, bulls, bears, swans, owls, and many other smaller creatures. He had never seen so many different trophies gathered in one place. They walked past a large niche in the wall which held the preserved bodies of a unicorn and a harpy.

"Look at this," he said to Sophia.

They stopped before the figure of the harpy. She had the torso and face of a woman, though her legs were like those of an owl, with strong, sharp talons. This one had no arms, only wings, and they were poised for attack, as if she had been frozen in place. D'Molay had never seen anything like it. The creature was so vital. "I've never seen a stuffed kill look so alive."

"This one is special. They say Artemis caught this harpy and put her here. How such magic works is beyond me. I wouldn't be surprised if she could bring it to life again." They stepped over to examine the unicorn. "These figures have been here for over a hundred years at least. There aren't many harpies around without arms anymore."

As they moved on, D'Molay took another look at the large marble columns and the sweeping curved stairs that led up to the second story. It reminded him of some of the palaces he'd visited long ago, traveling across Europe to recruit lords and dukes to embark on another crusade to the Holy Land. He could only hope that his current quest would be more successful than that one had been.

He felt Sophia's hand on his shoulder. "This way."

D'Molay followed her across the grand room to an alcove in the opposite wall. Sitting at a counter facing them was a young woman. She was plain with dark, straight hair pulled back in a ponytail. She wore a white linen frock that had seen better years.

"We need two rooms for the night," Sophia said.

The woman took on a fake, practiced smile.

"Alright. Do you want them separate or connected?"

"Separate and he's paying," Sophia took a half step back. D'Molay reached into his bag, but not for his coins.

"What will this get us?" He placed the griffin talon on the counter.

The woman's eyes lit up. "That should cover it," she said, grabbing the toe and talon before D'Molay could change his mind.

"I thought you wanted that as a prize," Sophia said as they were each handed a key with Greek letters denoting their room assignments marked on the leather strip secured to it.

"You were wrong," D'Molay said simply. "Besides, I wanted to drop a hint that I can handle myself in the woods."

"Really?" Sophia said in offense. "With evidence of my kill?"

D'Molay laughed. "They don't know that."

"Not yet," Sophia said pointedly.

The next morning, D'Molay knocked on Sophia's door. When there was no answer, he tried the knob. The room was unlocked. Entering it, he found his guide and her things were gone. D'Molay gathered his own things and went downstairs, where he found her in the lodge's tavern, talking to an older man with a gray beard. He was cleaning ale mugs with a small towel as they spoke. D'Molay took a seat at a table in the mostly empty room and listened to their conversation.

"I've heard tell of harpies in the Aeaean Mountains," the tavern keeper was saying as he cleaned a cup with a rag. "There could be a rookery up there, I suppose. The terrain would suit 'em."

"I thought if anyone might know, it would be you," Sophia said.

"Aye. I have good ears. And time to talk," he said with a wink.

"Thanks, Rantheus." Sophia turned from the old man and noticed D'Molay. She picked up her gear and walked over to his table. She was smiling for a change.

"Good idea, talking to him," D'Molay said. "Aeaean Mountains, is it?"

"I had to pay him fifty silvers for that," she said, holding out her hand. D'Molay fished her repayment out of his pouch.

"Fifty? I think he cheated you."

Sophia's grin only grew wider. "Oh, no. It was well worth it." She bounced the coins D'Molay handed over in her palm before dropping them into a pocket. "He's doing something else for me too."

"I'm afraid to ask," D'Molay said as he followed her toward the main doors of the lodge.

"He's going to tell anyone who asks the real story of how you got that griffin talon."

D'Molay froze in his tracks and looked back toward the bar. There, mounted on a block of wood and prominently displayed on the wall, was the griffin's talon he had traded for their lodgings.

*A*fter a brief bout of annoyance with Sophia's clever revenge, D'Molay found the ability to laugh at himself. Allowing the woman at the lodge to assume he had killed the griffin was just how he would have behaved in the courts of old Earth. Back there, one's reputation was often raised on the shoulders of others who did great deeds. This time, he'd been caught, and that was fair enough. Also, Sophia seemed quite cheered that she had put him in his place, so to speak, which made their ride toward the Aeaean Mountains less contentious.

"There they are," Sophia remarked, allowing her horse to stop and nibble on some greenery beside the trail. They stood at the base of a mountain range.

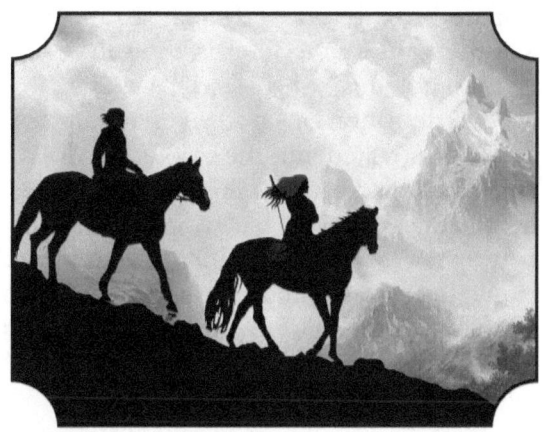

"We've come to the sloped side. That's good," D'Molay said. "I've seen mountains like these before. On the other side, there'll be a sharp drop. Let's hope the harpies have nested below the ridge line."

"I see plenty of food." Sophia pointed to a small group of goats perched on an outcropping and some grouse scratching in the shelter of bushes loaded with berries. "Maybe we'll see them come down to eat."

D'Molay frowned. The thought of cooling his heels and observing the scenery felt like a nature outing, not a mission. "Maybe we can lure them out."

"How?" she asked.

D'Molay mentally reviewed everything he had learned about harpies. "First, we kill one of those goats. Then, we'll add some other bait."

Sophia dismounted and stalked ahead while D'Molay remained with the horses. She targeted an old billy, dropping it neatly with her bow. The rest of the herd scattered as he rode over to join her.

"There's your goat," she said. "Now what do we do with it?"

D'Molay was off his horse and picking up the animal before Sophia finished her question. He slung it over his saddle. "See that flat rock sticking out by those trees? We'll put him there. Then we'll hide in the forest cover and watch the sky to see where the harpies come from."

Sophia took the reins of her own horse and walked after D'Molay as he led his toward the rock. "What makes you so sure they'll come? It's just a dead goat."

"It won't be, in a moment." They reached the place D'Molay had chosen and he heaved the animal onto the rock. Drawing his knife, he slit its throat so that the scent of its cooling blood was intensified. Then, he started digging through his pack.

"What are you looking for?" Sophia asked.

"Things that would catch a harpy's eye." He pulled out the glass vial of oil he had bought in Dioscrias, one of his flints, and several low value coins. "Do you have anything shiny in your bags?"

Sophia searched and offered him the silver fork from her cook set and a spare brass buckle. D'Molay arranged everything in a little pile facing just the right way to glint in the sun.

"What is this," she asked. "An altar?"

"Hardly. But if any god takes an interest, I won't turn down help today."

They retreated into the woods. D'Molay walked their horses a good distance away and secured them to sturdy trees out of view of their arrangements. Back near the bait, Sophia decided to climb one of the trees for a better view of the south. D'Molay returned and hunkered behind a thick trunk, his eyes scanning the skyline to the north. They waited.

A fox came. D'Molay threw a rock at it and it quickly retreated. The same scene repeated with a carrion bird. At last Sophia saw a harpy flying toward them from the south.

"Here comes one," she said softly.

D'Molay turned to track it with his own eyes. "Did you see where it came from?"

"Yes. From over the ridge near a burned copse."

They watched as the creature flew toward them. The harpy moved with great speed, closing fast. Sophia and D'Molay leaned into their cover as best they could to remain concealed. The harpy sped over them and past the dead goat. This surprised D'Molay, but it didn't matter that the creature wasn't tempted to linger. They had seen from where it had flown, which was the point of their efforts. Suddenly, as if it just couldn't resist the bait, the harpy wheeled back and landed by the goat.

This harpy was a very large but dreadful specimen. Grotesque lesions had spread across her face and a thick crust of seepage had dried in every furrow of her face and neck. This horrific condition made her look all the more vicious as she shoved and shook the goat to make sure it was dead. Satisfied it was no threat, the harpy pounced upon the items beside it, rifling through them. Sophia and D'Molay watched as her dirty fingers played with the buckle, then grabbed the oil vial.

The harpy squawked as her sharp nails poked at the cork in the bottle. She tipped the vial to her mouth and tugged the stopper out with her teeth. D'Molay noticed that despite her other miseries, her teeth were still bright and sharp. She tasted the lamp oil then angrily slammed the bottle on the rock in protest of its foul flavor. Broken glass and oil splattered over the coins. Then as abruptly as it had returned, the harpy screeched and fled. As D'Molay wondered what had frightened it away, he heard Sophia gasp.

"There's a flock coming!" she cried.

D'Molay turned and saw Sophia climbing as fast as she could out of the tree. Catching his eye, she pointed up. D'Molay looked to see close to two dozen harpies in pursuit of the lone outcast. Sophia dropped into hiding next to D'Molay, bow in hand, as he counted five harpies fly on to continue the chase. Unfortunately, most of the flock was as distracted by the goat and its treasures as their quarry was. The bird-women land-ed, pushing and snapping at one another as each tried to claim the prizes for itself. Soon a bloody brawl erupted.

Feathers flew and the eagle-like limbs that served as the flying women's legs kicked chucks of flesh into the air. A few of the harpies gave up quickly, flying off in the direction the first five had gone. But many remained, determined to fight to the end to prove their dominance in the flock. D'Molay picked out the one he thought was the toughest and watched as it punched another harpy already on its back hard in the gut. That one wailed and scrambled off the rock, rolling around in pain. It writhed across the ground and came close to their hiding place. Sophia turned her loaded bow toward it. D'Molay reached out to touch Sophia's arm, shaking his head. His warning was reckless, as he leaned forward he lost his balance, and scraped against a tree. Upon hearing the noise, the bruised harpy forgot its pain and humiliation and focused on the spies in the woods, calling to her sisters to announce there was more than a goat to eat. It surged toward D'Molay as Sophia's arrow flew.

This time, Sophia's shot wasn't fatal. It pierced the harpy's wing and barely slowed it down. She kept coming and D'Molay was forced to meet her. She pounced upon him with a wing-assisted jump as he drew his knife. One of her clawed hands encircled his wrist, trying to shake the weapon out of his grasp. D'Molay grabbed the shaft of the arrow embedded in her wing and twisted it. The harpy screeched in pain and let go of his arm, the only opening D'Molay needed to slit her throat. But the others were coming now, and even as he heard Sophia loosing arrow after arrow, he feared they were in serious trouble.

Two of the evil birds flew high into the air and circled directly over their heads while their sisters continued to attack from the ground. "I can't shoot everywhere at once," Sophia snarled, a touch of panic in her voice. D'Molay leapt up to grab the wing of a harpy perched on a limb above them. He surprised it, managing to drag it to the ground and plunge his knife into its heart. Unfortunately, he was equally surprised when a second harpy that he hadn't noticed dropped upon him from the same tree.

"Sophia!" he yelled as he felt talons grip the clothing on his back, their sharp bite reaching through to pierce his skin. As he tried to twist around to stab the harpy, she flew off, carrying D'Molay with her. He quickly sheathed his knife. If Sophia shot down the bird, his best chance for a safe landing involved having his hands free.

"D'Molay, don't move!" he heard her call. He froze, knowing she was taking aim. The crafty harpy twisted sharply to the right to avoid her arrow. D'Molay saw the ground getting further and further away. He struggled, hoping he could use his weight to impair the harpy's flight and force her lower. If he could give Sophia another shot, he might be saved. But his efforts only served to anger his captor. She used both hands to deliver a debilitating blow to both sides of his head. He hung limp and stunned as she flew on.

He regained his senses through a green haze of dizzying pain. Still in the harpy's clutches, he found himself far from Sophia. He dangled above unfamiliar terrain littered with wet boulders. He blinked at the steep mountainside they were zooming past. It was pocketed with dark crevices. D'Molay realized the harpy had brought him over the ridge.

Suddenly aware again of the deep pain in his back from the bird's claws, D'Molay moaned. The harpy barked out a grating sound and began to circle down to a particular group of rocks. D'Molay looked below and saw the picked bones of many creatures smashed over the stones. He was about to be dropped, broken open like a melon for the harpy's dinner.

Ignoring the agony in his shoulders, he reached up and behind him with his left hand and grabbed the harpy's leg above its talon. As he did, the bird released his right shoulder and swooped toward the cliff side with D'Molay dangling from her ankle. She steered him toward a ledge protruding from the mountain. With a sinking heart, D'Molay realized the harpy intended to crash him against it. He grabbed his knife. If he was going to meet his death, it would be on his own terms. Blindly, he sliced above and behind his head and felt his blade bite into the harpy's leg. The harpy screamed, flexing its talons to let him fall, but he held tight to her bleeding left foot and kept his hold until she kicked him in the head with her right.

D'Molay fell. A white hot surge of fear shot through him as he realized there was no way he would survive the drop. During these seconds of mental agony he cried out the name of God.

Then he saw Aavi appear out of the corner of his eye.

For a brief few seconds, his descent ceased and he floated directly opposite her in mid-air. She looked just as she had in his strange dream, and again her lips moved to voice words he could not hear. He caught his breath and started to speak, but before the first syllable left his mouth there was a flash of light. He felt himself tumbling again, but slowly, like a leaf drifting from a tree rather than a rock falling from the sky. His boots scraped the ground and he tipped forward, landing on his hands and knees. He laid back on the ground for a long time, catching his breath and giving a prayer of thanks to the one God.

An angel had saved him. Perhaps Sophia had been right. He'd indeed built an altar without knowing it, and survived certain death once again.

Chapter 8

In Pursuit of Set

*A*res brought help when he returned to give Mania the water she demanded in return for lending him her ghosts. His twin sons Deimos and Phobos and his niece Ioke accompanied him: Fear, Panic, and Pursuit. To Phobos, he entrusted a large jug of nectar. Deimos carried a special key, while Ioke bore the enchanted torch that brought those in hiding to light. Ares, the only one of the group strong enough to bear their weight, carried a pair of interlocking chains made by Hephaestus. The chains prevented the use of magic and suppressed divine power. He looked forward to wrapping Set tightly in their embrace.

But first, Set had to be found. When they returned to the lonely group of boulders, Mania no longer stood in the place Ares had found her stony body. A flash of anger flared in his chest, until he noticed that she had merely changed positions. Though still frozen in a rocky shell, Mania now reclined upon a flat rock, posed much like a celebrant at a banquet.

"You moved," Ares observed.

Although the expression on her face remained fixed, Ares had the impression Mania was amused by his remark. "Why shouldn't I? I was so tired of standing."

Deimos and Phobos traded looks as they experienced for the first time the odd sensation of hearing her voice without seeing her mouth generate it. Ioke even employed the power of her torch to assure herself that there wasn't another hidden entity behind the speech.

"Are your ghosts prepared to help me?" Ares asked,

stepping over to Mania. As before, her eyes disappeared up into their sockets. When they rolled down, two of the soldier spirits coalesced next to her.

"They're ready. Bring me the nectar," Mania said. Ares nodded and waved for Phobos to bring the jug. Phobos set it down on the ground, removed its lid, and stepped back. The phantom soldiers stooped down and, together, raised the vessel. They carefully helped their goddess drink. Swallow by swallow Mania became more lifelike. By the time the jug was almost empty, she looked much like Ares and the others, save for shards of stone at the tips of her fingers and a hint of hard plating across her chest and shoulders. She sighed in satisfaction and swung her legs around so that they dangled over the edge of the rock she had been lying on. As she looked down at her feet, her mouth quirked in dissatisfaction at the shabby appearance of her once-fashionable shoes. "That's mostly better," she said, her lips moving and her voice sounding in a normal fashion as she spoke.

Mania grabbed a tendril of smoky power that connected one of the ghosts to her and disconnected it from her body with a violent yank. She held the severed end of the cord out to Ares. He grabbed it, holding tightly as Mania snapped the second spirit free. "Make sure you don't let go," she warned. "I don't know if you or your friends have the proper power to see my children once they leave my presence. But you will feel their pull, and they will take you to their brothers who are stalking Set."

"Father, they'll be like hunting hounds," Deimos grinned. Ares nodded and gave his son a cursory glance.

"Which is why Ioke will hold their leashes. I don't have time for any mishaps, like you and your brother letting them run wild."

Deimos and Phobos both exclaimed mild curses as Ares passed the tethers of the spirits to Ioke. "I won't lose them," she promised, wrapping their cords tightly around her right hand.

"When you're done just let them go," Mania said. "They'll come back to me on their own."

Ares turned away, but was called back. "Wait, I'm so curious. What will you do to Set when you catch him?"

Ares wasn't about to reveal his whole plan, but in light of her help some generalities could be shared. "He'll be chained," Ares said, rattling the links he carried, "and locked away where he'll never be found."

"Oh," Mania said, sounding a bit disappointed by the answer. "Well, whatever you do to him, make sure he hates it, as a favor to me."

"That's a favor I will be happy to grant," Ares declared. "Let's go."

His group moved off, Ioke in the lead with the soldier phantoms float-ing before her. When they had traveled out of sight of Mania's standing stones, the ghosts did indeed fade away.

"Can you still feel their pull?" Ares asked Ioke.

"Yes." Her reply was confident. "Let's go faster!"

Ioke inclined her torch toward the invisibles, urging them to greater speed. She and the ghosts darted off, forcing Ares and the twins to race after them. They chased Ioke, her long black hair streaming like ribbons behind her. As they rapidly crossed the Lost Realm, the excitement of the chase began to affect Phobos. His golden hair morphed into a lion's mane and his mouth hung open to show lengthening, sharp, white teeth. His eyes glowed with bright fire. Noticing the wild display, Ares considered forcing Phobos to stay behind. His use of power might be enough to alert Set to their approach. However, it seemed even more risky to attempt cap-ture with one less god, so Ares allowed Phobos to run rampant.

They traveled for days across the barren lands, killing any man or beast that stood in their way. Day by day, they strove to close in on Set, who was able to just keep ahead of them. Finally, Set's luck began to run out.

The pull of the spirits veered Ioke to the left, toward the steep sides of a long-dry arroyo. Ioke jumped, disappearing over the edge of the deep gulch. As the others approached, a flare from her torch shot into the sky.

"She's found him!" Deimos shouted, eager for trouble. He and his brother flung themselves without hesitation into the deep ditch. Ares kept to the higher ground. Standing with his chains at the ready, Ares could see that the ghosts had done their job.

Set stood in a ring of jackal-headed warriors. All of them were clear-ly surprised by the sudden appearance of Ioke, Deimos and especially Phobos. Set shouted a command to attack and most of the jackals tried to obey. But they were fearful, pressured by the powers of Deimos and Phobos. Their attempted strikes were timid, showing their reluctance to commit entirely to the fight. Ares was disgusted by the sight of the dogs. He had hoped his fighters had killed all of them in the war. Perhaps he could finish them off now.

Ares shrugged the heavy chain from his shoulders and called out to the twins. "Get rid of the jackals," he said. "They're in my way."

Set backed up against the side of the arroyo as Deimos and Phobos used their powers of fear and panic to herd his minions down either side of the gulch. Deimos chased half of them north, while Phobos harried the rest south. Isolated, Set growled at Ares and began to change his body to a whirlwind of sand.

"Ioke!" Ares shouted. "Embrace him!"

The goddess threw herself into the midst of Set's dissolving form. Still holding her torch high, she threw her free arm around the swirling mass of particles that comprised him. The funnel of sand stretched high, tipped over, snaked and danced along the arroyo, but no move Set made could evade Pursuit. As the union skimmed beneath Ares, Ioke looked up

at him with a wide grin. Ares laughed. She was clearly enjoying the wild ride at Set's expense. Ares jumped down from the top of the ravine. It was time to put an end to the fun.

He caught Ioke's eye as he held up the chains. She nodded, and began to actively push Set toward Ares. She knew the god of war would not miss his throw, so the moment Set was in position she pulled back, releasing him. Ares pitched the chains at Set, directly striking the center of his dusty form. The links flashed on impact, taking on their own life. They spun, tightly wrapping around Set, interlocking their links. Immediately, the magical chains negated his spell and his whirlwind aspect fell away, leaving only his divine body in its place. Set flexed his arms in an unsuccessful attempt to break free of the chains. He tried again, more desperately, as Ares laughed at him.

"Keep trying, it's rather fun to watch you fail," Ares said.

"What are these bonds?" Set growled. "I suppose you got them from the Council. They couldn't capture me without such tricks."

"Actually, Hephaestus made these especially to fit you. I didn't feel it necessary to bother the Council with my personal business." Ares walked over and kicked Set to the ground.

Set tried to stand, but the chains continued to restrict his body, tightening and entangling his limbs. He turned a fiery eye up to Ares. "What personal business are you talking about, Olympian?" Set snarled.

"Have you already forgotten how you ran away from our duel? Or how much damage your creatures did to my fortress and armies?"

Set forced a pained grin across his muzzle. "I have not forgotten. Those memories keep me warm on the cold desert nights."

"Do they?" Ares shook his head in disgust and commanded Ioke. "Catch up with Deimos and Phobos. Then meet me at the tunnel. I already have men waiting there." Ioke nodded and sped off to the north to find Deimos. Set squirmed and managed to position himself on his knees.

"Do you have enough men?" he demanded to know. His arrogant attitude came close to angering Ares, but the Olympian was on his highest guard against his tricky prisoner.

"It only took a single female to subdue you, so I think my forces will be adequate," he said.

Set snarled and struggled in the chains. "My odds keep getting better," he observed. "Now we are one against one. You may have me at a disadvantage for a moment, but Olympia is weak in magic. My Egyptos power will eventually dissolve these pretty links."

Ares stepped over and took hold of a length of chain that dangled from Set's neck. With a hard tug, he yanked Set to his feet. As if understanding that motion was required, the chains adjusted their positions to allow their prisoner to walk. Set smiled as he felt the links shift. "You see. I'm half free already."

"Funny you should mention the power of Egyptos," Ares said. "Hephaestus was concerned about that. But after he consulted Horus, he learned many things - most importantly, the glyphs that suppress your spells."

"Horus is a beakless bird," Set spit. "He knows nothing of my arts."

"The chains say otherwise." Ares, using his great strength and the chain's supernatural properties, was able to swing Set out of the gulch to the lip of the ravine as easily as if the Egyptos god had been a sack of grain. Ares jumped up after him and dexterously reclaimed the chain as Set tried to run. "Wrong way, Set. We're going to the mountain."

"What mountain? That molehill you call Olympus?" Set staggered after Ares as he strode ahead at a brisk pace. The information about Horus' complicity in this insult churned red-hot in Set's gut. He'd have another god to brutally repay when the tide turned.

"You'll see soon enough," Ares said. "Now shut up and walk."

As they traveled, Ares tuned out his prisoner's periodic threats and complaints. He kept his attention fixed on their destination, a hidden fortress used long in the past to keep an eye on the Titans exiled to the Lost Realm. Since the Titans had become infirm, no one ever came there anymore. Within the mountain were secret tunnels and impenetrable dungeons. One shaft was rumored to lead to Tartarus. Ares chuckled aloud at the thought of dragging Set that far.

"What are you laughing at?" Set muttered.

"Besides you?" Ares jabbed.

Set dug his heels into the sand, but the power of the chains made his feet as light as feathers dancing over the ground. He trudged angrily after Ares, hoping for some break in the situation.

After a long walk, they reached the base of a rolling mountain. Ares continued on through the rubble of fallen boulders. Set was becoming disoriented by the frequent twists and turns.

"Do you not know where you're going?" he hissed. "Or are you taking me along this ridiculous path to confuse me?"

"Good," Ares said, turning to give Set a superior look. "I see it's working."

The god of war pulled Set around another rock pile. Waiting there was a contubernium, eight of Ares' most trusted soldiers. Deimos, Phobos and Ioke had also arrived. Deimos and Phobos were kicking a severed jackal's head between them to pass the time. The soldiers came to attention at the sight of Ares as the twins forgot their game and ran over to get a good look at the chains Hephaestus had contrived.

"Look how they hold him," Phobos said.

"He's like a pet dog," Deimos grinned.

Ares rolled his eyes. "Don't be foolish. Take Ioke and lead the way. You men, stay behind me."

The group assembled according to Ares' wishes and entered a long, dark tunnel which led into the mountain. Ioke's torch was their only light. Set was soon able to marshal some confidence. The claustrophobic passage was not unlike a pyramid shaft, an environment in which he felt completely at home. He walked along, seemingly unconcerned by his situation.

"How long do you really think you can keep me Ares? You know that I'll either find an escape route or I'll be freed by the Council or the Egyptos elders."

"You're assuming they'll know I have you. No one here is going to pass that information on, unless I tell them to. Oh, Zeus knows I'm out here in this forsaken land to find you, but no one knows I have you in my grasp."

Set's expression soured slightly though he tried to keep up a good front. "Oh, they'll find out one way or another."

"We'll see," came Ares' reply.

They walked in silence for a few more minutes until Ares pulled back on the chains as they came to a large, iron-bound, stone door. "Stop. Deimos, Phobos, open it." Ares pulled Set back so the door could be opened by the two gods. A moment later, they pried it open. Deimos slipped inside and pushed as Phobos pulled from the outer side. The door creaked upon on its ancient hinges as it opened for the first time in centuries.

Just then, Set tried to break free. He kicked Phobos hard, shoving him into the door and slamming it into Deimos. He managed to topple another guard that stood near him as he tried to spin the chains out of Ares grasp; but the war god was not to be taken so easily. Chains still in his hand, Ares made a fist, quickly striking Set in the side of the head. The blow was so powerful that sparks flew when the chains made contact with Set's stone-like skin. Set's knees buckled and he fell to the floor, unconscious. The other assembled guards had drawn their weapons and were ready to move in, should Ares call upon them.

Ares grabbed the door himself and flung it open. "I knew he would try something," he said, dragging Set along with him as he went through the doorway. Inside, he looked down at Deimos, who sat on the floor nursing several fingers that had been pinched when the door slammed. Ares glanced over his shoulder at Phobos, who stood rubbing his lower back where he'd been kicked. "You're an embarrassment to Olympia," he muttered to his sons. They were indispensible on the battlefield, spreading fear and panic, but strangely inept anywhere else.

Ioke stepped into the room. By the light of her torch, Ares pulled Set over to a primitive throne carved of gray granite, older and more worn than the sandstone of the walls.

Dust and cobwebs were disturbed as Set was thrown into the large chair. This lone seat of disgrace was the only object in the chamber.

"Deimos, lock his feet and hands."

Deimos rushed over and closed thick metal latches over Set's arms and ankles. The latches mystically merged into the stone, completely holding Set's hands and feet in place. Ares let the chain he held drop to the floor. The heavy sound roused Set. Red slits of barely opened eyes could be seen on his dark visage.

"Ah. Awake again?" Ares taunted. "Sorry, your desperate escape attempt failed. I probably would have tried the same thing, were I you. Except I would be free by now."

Set's eyes opened fully. "What do you want Ares? Power? Victory? Vengeance? I can get you all those and more."

Ares leaned in close. "Do you really think I'm that shallow? I brought you here, to this particular place, for a specific purpose. I want answers Set. I have lots of questions and I will get answers from you."

Set grimaced back at him. "I'll tell you nothing until you allow me to contact the gods of Egyptos as per the rules set forth by the Council. That must be done! I know my rights as a god, even a captive one."

"I don't think I need to worry about violating your rights. You see, you're sitting in the last known chair of Parrhesia."

Set's eyes opened wider. "Chair of Parrhesia? What is that, some kind of Olympian torture device? You're wasting your time. I've been tortured by far worse. I'll sit here all eternity before you get anything from me."

Ares smiled. "No, it's not a torture device. It does something far more useful. You see, the chair compels its guest to tell the truth."

Set stared at Ares in stunned silence. For the first time in centuries, he felt nervous. He dreaded what Ares might ask and feared being unable to resist the chair's mystic power. If only he could find a way to steal this chair and take it back to his prison in the City of the Gods. It would give him an incredible advantage against his enemies. *I would rule over Egyptos in a month, if I had such a chair,* he daydreamed.

Ares' booming voice brought him back to his current situation. "Question number one: I want to know why you invaded Olympia, the real reason!"

Set sneered. "None of your - " Bile rose in his throat as a sharp wave of nausea gripped him. But what came up instead were words, and not ones of his choosing. "Urrr gaak . . .baa . . . because . . ." Set tried to fight the compulsion to speak. He closed his mouth, but there was no stopping the flow of words. "I was after . . . the girl Aavi and the Beast . . . They were in your damned fortress!" Set gasped and panted from the effort of trying to stifle his voice.

Ares smiled and a smug look crossed the face of the goddess who held the torch. "Well, Ioke, the chair of Parrhesia still works as well as ever. I wasn't certain it would, after so long." Ares strode around the room like a gladiator taking a victory lap. "Question two: why did you want the girl and the beast?"

Set dreaded giving this answer more than the last, for this was something only he and a few others knew. Once again, he felt like he was going to vomit. "Naaa . . . sheee . . . she w-w-was an angel s-sent to . . . Earth. S-She was t-taking the beast there!"

"An angel? How is that possible? How did she end up in our realms instead of Earth?" Ares demanded.

Unable to stop himself, Set replied. "W-We intercepted h-h-her."

"And who is we? What other gods were involved in this conspiracy?"

Set threw his head back and forth and pulled his restraints, all to no avail. The words were magically pulled from his throat. "Qu- Qu-Quetzalcoatl… and La-Lamasthu!"

"The others who attacked my fortress. I should have known," Ares growled. "Why did they help you?

"I don't . . . know everything. D-different reasons."

While the chair had power to compel the truth, it could not extract information its guest did not know. Ares paused, considering a new line of inquiry. Ioke leaned to his ear and offered a whisper. He nodded, and resumed the interrogation.

"What was your reason for striking down the angel?"

Once again Set writhed for a moment, then said, "I-I wanted to h-harness her p-power to f-force other gods to o-obey me."

Ares smiled. "But we stopped you. You never did get to use her. And then she was gone, back to wherever she came from?"

"Yes . . . or destroyed."

"Why do you think Lamasthu aided you?"

"Naaa . . . She wa-wanted to save all the realms."

"And what about Quetzalcoatl?"

"He . . . He wanted p-power . . .Th-thought he was saving the realms. We all thought that . . ."

Ares interrupted. "That makes no sense! How would stopping an angel from going to Earth save our realms?"

"La-Lamasthu d-discovered that angel would be g-going to Earth to o-open the great s-seal and begin the end times," Set gasped out.

"End times? What are they?"

Set shook uncontrollably as he tried to resist the chair, but failed. "D-destruction. The Earth is w-wiped clean and a n-new age begins . . . La-La-masthu thought it would mean the end of this r-realm as well."

Ares seemed surprised by this answer. "So, they acted to save the realms. And you . . . you acted in your own selfish interests."

"I-I don't want the realms to end either," Set managed to say.

"No. I suppose you don't." Ares glared at him. "But, since we're all still here, that means you three were either all wrong, or that you're responsible for saving the realms. Either way, they followed you into Olympia. They were worried you'd get to the angel first, and use her power to double-cross them, weren't they?"

Set's weak nod of agreement seemed enough to satisfy the power of the chair. Set, exhausted, slowly regained his composure. The nauseous feeling faded as long as he wasn't answering any more questions.

Ares turned to his sons. "Deimos, Phobos. I would have your consul."

The three of them stepped away from Set and spoke quietly.

"What do think of his answers?" Ares asked. "Is there enough in them to help you feed terror into the Mayan and the Babylonian and their forces?

"Of course, if the chair is working and Set is telling the truth," Deimos said.

Ares waved the comment away. "These answers don't serve Set - that's how we know it's the truth."

Phobos then offered his opinion. He was slightly more cautious than his brother. "Father, ask him what their plan was once they captured this Angel and her creature."

Ares turned to face his captive. Set had rested long enough. Ares walked behind the chair and grabbed Set by one of his ears, yanking his head back up. "Did you think we were finished? What was the plan once you caught these two creatures you shot out of the sky?"

Set winced and tried to pull away, but there was nowhere to go. He began to feel sick again. "W-We were go-going to hold them hostage to get m-more power . . . m-more realms under o-our control. M-Maybe even force the H-heavenly Host to give us control back on Earth." Set wheezed as he finished. He fell limp after fighting so hard, and so use-lessly, against the chair's power.

"So now we have it all. Now we know just what you and your conspir-ators were up to." Ares seemed to savor the moment as he gloated over Set. Set's reply was weak, but filled with hate.

"You have everything you want. Now let me go."

The god of war gave him a flash of a smile as his brow furrowed. "Let you go? Oh, I don't think that's an option at the moment, Set."

"We should kill him, Father," Deimos said.

Set's red eyes widened as he suddenly realized there was a chance he might actually die at the hands of this Olympian god.

Ares smiled as he stared at Set. "It's a tempting suggestion, but I don't want that crime on our heads. Set's allies and who knows who else would know he died and then there'd be too many questions. No. We leave him right where he is. His fellow gods will assume he's still hiding out here in the Lost Realm." Ares leaned in closer. "You seem comfortable enough. Besides, we might have some more questions for you."

Set's jaws snapped at the god, scratching the side of his face.

"You mongrel dog!" He back-handed Set hard across the side of his head. Ares stepped back, wiping his own blood away with two fingers. His eyes burned with anger. "Enjoy your stay. Maybe we'll be back in a century or two." He turned to his retinue and started to walk out of the chamber without looking back. "Lock this place down - we're leaving." Everyone followed Ares out, Ioke and her torch the last to go, leaving the chamber in total darkness.

Set struggled and screamed from the stone chair as he heard the creak of the heavy door. "You can't do this to me! Egyptos will destroy you! You can't - "

The gods and soldiers outside heard Set's shouts abruptly cease as the door fully closed.

"That was fun," Phobos grinned. "When do you think we can put some other gods in that chair?"

Ares just smiled as they marched back out the way they had come.

Chapter 9

The Cave of the Harpies

D'Molay took stock of his condition after his miraculous survival. He was not encouraged. His packs were far away with Sophia, assuming she had been able to fight off the harpy flock after he was taken. He had no broken bones, but his back and shoulders were torn from the harpy's claws - claws that were filthy when they pierced his skin. He distracted himself from thoughts of disease and infection by being grateful for what he still had. That list was short: his knife, map, a few extra coins stashed in a special pocket of his belt, and the Council seal he always wore around his neck. His inconvenient hat had fallen off sometime during his flight with the harpy, but he didn't miss it much. He had no food, no water, and no rope or gear to help him climb back up and over the ridge. He stared morosely at the towering vertical cliff above him.

"Well, Aavi," he said aloud, "now what do I do?"

D'Molay watched and listened, but no response came from the angel. It seemed that though she had clearly saved him, he was going to have to find his own way out of this fix. He prayed to the One God for thanks then continued in.

He climbed around, over, and among the boulders where he had landed. The broken, bleached bones he had seen from the air were but a small sampling of the collection of remains on the rocks. Smaller piles of bone had settled at the bases of the rocks and lodged in the many crevices where one boulder leaned against the next. His foot slid as he trod upon a collapsed ribcage. D'Molay thrust a hand out to steady himself against a rock and looked for a safer spot to place his boot. A flash of color in the bleak skeletal landscape caught his eye. Just beyond his foot was something bright. It was an irregular red-orange shard about the size of his palm. Stooping to pick it up, he realized it was a piece of a clay vessel. He turned it over. A crust of something dark and thick coated the other side. Was it blood? He and Aavi had once found a broken urn that spilled blood onto the ground.

D'Molay scratched at this residue with a fingernail, but it was so old and dry he couldn't determine for sure what the pot had once contained. He tossed the fragment aside and pressed on, climbing over one of the rocks when he noticed some vines behind it. If they were strong enough, they might be a substitute for the rope he was missing. D'Molay reached the top of the rock and crouched there, surprised by what he saw. On the ground near the spot where the vines had taken root were larger broken pieces of pottery. He recognized them now. They were exactly like the urns that the harpies had stolen from the ship Hector - and just beyond them was a small opening in the cliff.

As he was about to push aside some vines and look into the dark hole, Aavi appeared next to him, floating a few feet above the ground. Her feathery white wings spread open and she put her hand out in an attempt to halt his progress. D'Molay's breath caught in his throat. What should one say to an angel? He took a step back, gathering his wits, and spoke to her, though he did not know if she could hear or understand.

"Aavi! Remember the clay urns? I think this is where the harpies took them!"

Her posture remained the same as she stared at him silently.

"Don't you remember? They glowed, and you wanted to know what was in them."

Aavi floated beside him, acting more like a statue than a living being. "I... have been sent here to be your guardian."

D'Molay was so startled to actually hear her speak he barely processed what she had said. "Guard me?"

"Yes. That is my task." Aavi smiled slightly, but seemed detached from the whole situation, distant. At length she noticed the clay shard in his hand. "The urns . . . they glowed . . . and something with wings carried them away."

"Yes, that's right. The harpies took them from the ship we were on. You wanted to know what was in them. It's blood, see?" He held the broken shard out to her.

"Oh yes, I . . . we need to know," Aavi replied dreamily.

Taking another step toward the hole, and pointing towards the entrance, he said, "The answer is in this cave, I'm certain of it."

This finally provoked a response. Aavi turned and gazed toward the hole. "Do not go there, D'Molay. I will not be able to guard you if you enter."

"You can't go in? Why not? What could possibly stop you from going where you wanted?"

She turned her gaze back to him, seeming to look right through him. He waited for a reply, but none came to explain her unwillingness to enter the cave. He pressed his case.

"I have to go in, Aavi. It's my only clue to Circe's whereabouts. I have no choice and there's no telling when those harpies will return. I won't be able to get in then. I'll be careful, I promise." He gulped in a breath to replenish the air he had used to push out his rush of words.

She hovered, expressionless. "You have free will. I cannot stop you."

"It's so wonderful to see you again and know you are near," he continued, wondering about her distant manner. "You saved me from falling. Thank you."

Aavi nodded. "It is my duty. For now I will pray for you and await your safe return," Aavi replied with a touch of sorrow in her voice. She looked downward, closed her eyes, and disappeared in a spiral of wind like fine sand trapped in a dust devil.

"Aavi, Aavi?"

But he received no response. He turned and entered the cave. The threat of danger lurking in the darkness kept him from noticing how much his heart pained him over Aavi's cool, detached attitude.

Without his supplies, he had no torches, but pushed on as his eyes adjusted to the darkness, feeling his way. He could hear small rocks falling and what sounded like a skittering somewhere overhead, but it was too dark to see what it might be. He pressed deeper into the cave, attempting to move in silence. Despite his best efforts, he could still hear the crunch of scattered bones as he walked along. A swooshing sound overhead froze him in his tracks and he dropped to the ground as quickly as possible. He felt a rush of air across his back and head as something flew only a foot or two above him. Whatever it was did not circle back, and after holding himself in a crouch until his thighs began to ache, D'Molay began to move again.

As he rose, the darkness retreated. D'Molay gave thanks that the sun had moved just enough for its light to stream into the cavern. Able to see better, he glanced back to make sure he hadn't missed anything on his way in. What he saw ruined his theory about the sun. A bright white globe was rising just outside the entrance. In the midst of the sphere floated the figure of Aavi. As he watched, a long shaft of golden light stretched from the globe and reached deep into the cavern. *She had found a way to help despite whatever prevented her from following!* D'Molay was elated, but his joy was short-lived.

The moment he turned to move on, he saw half a dozen harpies perched high on the walls of the cave ahead of him. He drew his knife and fell into a defensive pose, expecting to be attacked. But they completely ignored him. Were they blind? The globe was illuminating the entire cavern now. Suddenly, as if he heard a voice inside him, he understood. *Of course! Only I can see Aavi, so only I can see the light she's creating!* Nevertheless, he kept his knife at the ready as he crept on. Perhaps the harpies' eyes had been tricked, but he doubted their ears were shuttered as well.

Passing by the ledges of the bird-women was nerve wracking. D'Molay breathed as shallowly as possible and tried to tread as lightly as a cat. He made it almost all the way past them when suddenly one harpy decided to swat another, sending it tumbling off the wall. It landed with a whining cry less than two feet to his left. It was a small creature, a youngster. It continued squawking and D'Molay used its noise to his advantage, daring to move less cautiously to clear the area quickly; he feared the harpy's mother might come to investigate its cries and discover his presence. He ducked into a passage that curved to the right, losing the benefit of Aavi's light but gaining space and cover from the harpies. Aavi's light seemed to be fading, so he moved on quickly toward a different glow further down the passage he had chosen, saying a silent prayer of thanks for her help.

D'Molay made his way deeper into the mountain caverns. Faintly glowing lichens grew on the cavern walls, casting a greenish glow to help him see his way along. He passed small pools of clear water which he drank from. He sampled strange, spongy plants that grew from cracks in the rocks, but found then to be unpalatable and spit them out. From time to time, he heard the echo of falling rocks and distant murmurings too faint to be identified. When he reached a side tunnel that emanated a faint glow, his heart leaped; his first thought was that Aavi had found a way into the caves. Then he realized the light was flickering and was likely from a flame, or a torch. His long knife at the ready, D'Molay crept along the side tunnel as it curved off to the right. Carefully rounding the bend, he saw a dark metallic brazier, about five feet high, with a flame burning on the top. He wondered if it had been placed there to discourage any curious harpies from coming this far into the caverns. He remembered using a flaming torch to keep harpies at bay on a mission long ago in the realm of the undead.

He approached the bronze brazier. D'Molay observed that it was in the Roman style, and saw handprints in the fine dust that had settled on it. Someone had tended it recently. He was careful not to touch the object, for fear it might magically alert guards to his presence or even worse, be some kind of trap.

Leaving the brazier, he continued carefully. He passed several more braziers which were placed about every hundred feet. As he traveled further down this tunnel, he noticed the walls and floors were carved more carefully. The tunnel began to take on the appearance of a corridor in a Greek building, even though he was in fact deep inside a solid mountain of rock. His gut instinct told him he had indeed found the hiding place of Circe when he began to hear distant sounds of laughter or orders being barked out. However, they were still too far away to really identify. He came to an intersection of passages. Those with no lighting he ignored. At one point, he heard heavy footsteps and just managed to duck into one of those side tunnels before he could be seen. Hiding in the darkness, he saw the silhouettes of two men pass by. They were dressed in Roman armor. Each wore a large helmet. When D'Molay left his hiding place, he noticed an archway across from him, just a little further down the corridor.

Curious, he ducked through the darkened arch and almost knocked over something that was right by the entrance. As his eyes adjusted to the light, he saw that the entire room was filled with urns, just like the ones he and Aavi had seen on the ship a month or so ago. Rows of them completely filled the room in stacks that reached almost to the ceiling. Each urn was about four feet high and made of hardened clay. Like the ones on the ship, these were all sealed shut, and definitely filled with some-

thing. If the urn D'Molay had bumped had been empty, it would have fallen and made enough noise to attract those guards.

D'Molay wandered the rows of urns, old questions rising in his mind. *What are they doing with all these urns? Is there something besides blood in them?* He'd been vexed by this mystery ever since Aavi had first noticed urns like these glowing on the deck of the Hektor. Then, as now, he seemed no closer to an answer to that question.

He wished Aavi was there to see the urns. Deciding there was nothing else he could do there, D'Molay moved on to explore the rest of the tunnels, hoping his luck at avoiding the guards would hold out. He knew he was taking a great risk, but if he was going to find Circe he had little choice. Exiting the room of urns, he went along the smaller darkened corridor where he discovered another room, also filled with more urns. Soon he had counted eight rooms of urns. He continued on down the corridors past more small rooms and tunnels. Then he was spotted. Two burly guards made loud squealing noises and ran toward him with their war hammers at the ready.

D'Molay was stunned at their appearance. The two guards had the large brutish heads of warthogs or wild pigs. Their pointed ears and large tusks made their heads seem too big for their bodies, but this mismatch seemed no hindrance to their agility. As they closed, D'Molay stared into their angry red eyes. Finally managing to react, D'Molay turned and ran in the other direction. He ducked down the first corridor he came to, hoping to lose them. Unfortunately, the squeals of the pig-like guards had warned others of an intruder. D'Molay was faced with another guard coming at him from the other direction. Quickly, he  dodged into another chamber and ran right into another tusked guard who grabbed him. D'Molay stabbed the guard in the leg and broke free, but by then it was too late. The original two guards had caught up. One of them hit D'Molay's hand and he dropped his knife. The guard he'd stabbed head-butted him in the back, knocking him to his knees. Another guard put his foot on the loose knife; there was no way D'Molay could grab it again. Then he was forced to stand up and felt his hands being bound in manacles. A hoof-like hand shoved him in the back and grunted in slurred Panthos. "Forewaaard, huu-man."

He trod along, having no other choice. "Where are you taking me?"

"Cir-ceee," replied the one who'd spoken earlier. D'Molay felt a thrill of accomplishment mixed with an appropriate measure of uneasiness at this revelation.

"Good," he said. "I've come a long way to see her." This did not impress his escorts, who continued to roughly haul him down a maze of passageways. D'Molay did his best to mentally map the way. He'd been caught near the urn rooms then hustled along corridors with irregular slate gray tile floors. After that, the pigs had guided him through a large room with support columns spaced throughout it. It had a heavily guarded iron door at one end. D'Molay suspected a treasure room or armory lay behind that. Lastly, he was marched through an open archway at the other end of the columned chamber and into yet another room.

An attractive woman sat upon a backless throne. She had long, deep red-brown hair and her figure was voluptuous. Several animals lounged near her feet. A half-sleeping dog was trying to ignore a small monkey that was pulling on its tail. A tortoise with an unusual shell hungrily chewed on a melon rind. The woman removed a cat from her lap and stood as the guards shoved D'Molay to his knees.

"Let's get down to business," she said brusquely. "I want your name and how you found me."

"Are you Circe?" D'Molay asked.

"Are you deaf? Answer what I asked you." She stalked over, circling him. D'Molay felt like her eyes were boring holes in his back. One of the guards nudged him and a sharp pain shot across his torn shoulders.

"My name is D'Molay. A harpy attacked me while I was hunting and carried me over the ridge. It happened to drop me near your cave."

Circe laughed bright tones that rang through the room. "How convenient! And then you just strolled in. Who helped you past the rest of my harpies?"

D'Molay swallowed. He could tell her the truth about Aavi, but what would that gain? She, like the Council, would surely not believe an angel was in this world. Forced to implicate someone else, a ready name came to mind.

"I am under a magical bond put upon me by Glaucus," he revealed. With satisfaction, he noticed the woman's mouth gape open the slightest bit. "Perhaps it was that spell that kept your guardians from killing me."

"A bond?" Circe went back to her throne, sat, and rearranged her skirt around her legs. "For what purpose?"

"If you are indeed Circe," he said. "I will tell you."

She rolled her eyes. "Yes, yes, that is who I am. Now tell me why he sent you," Circe responded haughtily. "I'm not inclined to take in stray visitors as much as I used to."

D'Molay pulled on his bonds, but they were no looser. Telling her that Glaucus wanted him to take her head was out of the question. Her guards would probably take his instead. He settled on what he hoped could be an alternate solution. "I came here to ask you to remove a spell you cast long ago."

"A spell? What spell?"

"You changed a young woman into a monstrous creature. Her name was Scylla and she still suffers to this very day, out somewhere in the Lost Realm." Circe showed no outward reaction to Scylla's name. However, D'Molay noticed her fingers gripping the folds of her skirt tightly. She seemed to quickly catch herself betraying her feelings and waved a more casual hand at him.

"I've cast many spells. I'm not inclined to undo them. Why would I? No doubt I had good reason to cast that spell when I did it." Circe looked at him with an almost teasing look on her perfect face, waiting to see what he might say in reply. D'Molay guessed she was enjoying the back and forth of the discussion the way a cat might enjoy toying with a mouse before eating it. He decided it was time to change tactics.

"I wonder, can you undo one of your spells, Circe, or are they like an arrow let loose from a bow, with no way to undo once fired?"

She gave him a slightly annoyed look, her eyes gleaming in the light from the braziers. "That's ridiculous. Of course I could. But you've still given me no reason why I would want to. Undoing a spell takes time and effort. I have many other tasks to attend to."

"Perhaps I can perform one of those tasks in exchange for cancelling the spell," he proposed. "I'm an official courier for the Council. I could deliver something for you or retrieve something you have been looking for. As you've seen, I'm very good at finding people who wish to remain hidden."

"You did find me, I'll give you that," Circe smiled slightly, but behind that smile seemed to be more than a hint of malevolence. "I think you should stay a while longer to give me time to consider your offer. I need more time to decide what to do with you." Circe looked off to her right and called out. "Kira, take him to one of the guest rooms. Clean him up, anoint him, and get him some fresh clothes. He will dine with me this evening."

A petite, dark-skinned woman stepped out of the shadows and stood before Circe. She bowed deeply. "Yes Circe, I will see to it." She turned to D'Molay. "Rise, and follow me." She started to walk towards the archway to the left of Circe's throne.

D'Molay followed Kira out of the chamber. One of the pig guards followed closely behind, war hammer ready to strike out if needed. A glance behind him showed D'Molay that Circe watched them leave with an unreadable expression on her face. He was still uncertain of Circe's intentions, but at least he knew she was curious enough about his offer to not kill him on the spot.

He followed Kira along several hallways and up some stairs. They passed a large room filled with scrolls and another alcove that smelled of dried spices and herbs. Finally reaching a corridor of bedrooms, Kira entered one. The room was circular, about twelve feet across. It was opulently decorated, with fine dark lacquered shelves holding towels and bottles of oil. D'Molay counted three tables which must have come from the Asian realm. The plaster walls were painted with a mural of Romans at play and various animals gathered around a central female figure that could only be Circe. The floor was made from small tiles arranged in a circular pattern.

He stepped onto an intricate Persian rug. On it stood a long, narrow table the length of a man. The top of the table was made of smooth polished leather, but the legs were the same black lacquer as the other furniture in the room. There were no chairs, only a pile of large pillows against the wall. Kira produced a key that had been concealed in her clothing and held it up in front of her face as she looked at D'Molay.

"If you agree to cooperate and let me clean you up, we can dispense with your restraints. If you decide to run, you'll find it a short journey." The guard shadowing them grunted to emphasize her statement. "If you get past him, there are other guards at each end of the hallway. And if you hurt me, I assure you Circe will be very unforgiving."

"I'll cooperate," D'Molay said. He thought of the wounds on his shoulders as she walked behind him to unlock the manacles. He felt the cool metal restraints slide away from his hands. Getting those wounds patched up would be an unexpected blessing.

"Good. Now disrobe, lie on the table and we'll get started," Kira directed.

D'Molay grimaced as he peeled his shirt and vest off his slashed skin. After he had dropped all his clothing into a pile on the rug, he approached the table where Kira waited with towels and a bottle of oil. He hopped up to sit on the table, turning his back to show her his injuries.

"Can you help me with this?" he asked.

Kira nodded, unmoved by the gore. "Looks like you met the harpies in our cave."

"Yes, a harpy attacked me." He left the particulars of that instance vague. "She didn't like me much."

A few hours later, D'Molay was cleaned, bandaged and refreshed. He smelled of myrrh and fresh oiled leather. He was given a tunic and toga to wear; his hair was decorated by a laurel wreath. After some serious pleading laced with flirtation, Kira let him put the Council seal back around his neck. He was also allowed to keep his boots, after they had been brushed and oiled, when Kira was unable to find any sandals that fit him. His wrists remained free of the manacles, but he noticed that the pig-headed guards remained mere steps away.

Kira escorted him to a large dining room where a great table was loaded with bowls of fruits, platters of meats and cheeses, and baskets of breads. Kira stopped a short distance from the table, folded her hands behind her back, and waited. D'Molay was tortured by the sight and smell of the meal that awaited him. He sorely wished to take a sampling from the nearest plate, but he knew better than to take such an impolite risk.

A few moments later Circe made a grand entrance from the far side of the room. Two more burly guards with pig's heads accompanied her. Two peacocks, their large feather tails opened, strutted just behind her. She wore a burgundy robe that caught the light and reflected iridescently as she moved. The top plunged open and revealed the center of her chest all the way down to below her navel, covering just enough to be considered decent. Around her waist she wore an intricate golden belt that held a large emerald at its center. She had matching bracelets and a necklace. Her dark auburn hair cascaded around her face like a lion's mane. There was no denying Circe was a beautiful woman. She gazed at D'Molay, studying him as a hungry cat might look at a bird.

"I see Kira took good care of you. Now you look fit to be in my presence."

Kira bowed deeply and D'Molay followed her lead. Circe was the daughter of Helios, and a powerful sorceress as well as a deity. If he was going to convince her to undo a spell, he knew he would need to stay on her good side.

As she approached the table, Circe gave D'Molay a coquettish look. "Shall we dine?" One of the pig guards pulled out a chair at the head of the table and Circe moved to it with gliding steps. She outstretched her arms and sat down rather theatrically. Kira escorted D'Molay to a chair near her where he sat. The rest of the table was unoccupied.

Circe turned her attention to Kira. "Take a plate of food and leave us for now. I wish to get to know my guest. Move back, the rest of you." At her command, the guards and serving staff retreated, while Kira efficiently filled a spare plate with food from the table. Once she had bowed and left the chamber, Circe reached for a small loaf of bread, breaking it and handing half to D'Molay. "So, how did you come to find me . . . What was your name again?"

"D'Molay. I specialize in finding the lost or the hidden," he began, explaining his search for her and the journey that brought him here. Over their meal he told the truth of it, but left out the names of anyone who had helped him so that Circe's wrath would not be directed toward his friends. ". . . and then your guards found me. The rest you know," he concluded.

Circe peered over the top of the goblet she was drinking from. Her dark eyes observed him intently. "You're quite resourceful, for a man. I wonder what other talents you possess?"

He was spared the need to come up with an answer as Circe called out loudly. "I am finished!" Servants scurried back toward the table to remove plates and offer assistance as she rose from her seat. D'Molay had been forced to spend most of the meal talking, and he pushed his chair back regretfully, feeling he might have eaten several more platefuls of food if he'd been given the chance.

"I will call for you again in the morning," Circe said. "Stay in your room. From what you've told me, you've had more than enough adventures lately. Don't add to them by prowling about and tempting my guards to play with you."

"That is the last kind of play I would desire," he said suavely. Deep in his stomach a small knot protested his strategy of flirtatious wordplay with the witch. Circe laughed lightly.

"Shall I send Kira to you for the night?" She raised a finger tipped by a smoothly filed and shaped nail to her lips and tapped them as she considered the idea. "No, I think she's seen enough of you already. Sleep well, D'Molay."

Circe swept out of the room with drama equal to that of her entrance. D'Molay was left in the company of two of the pig-heads. Doubting they would stop him, he quickly reached toward one of the few trays remaining on the table and gathered a bunch of grapes and several crumbling chunks of cheese. He glanced down at the folds of the toga and spread a section of the bulky drape open as a makeshift pocket for the food.

"Lead on, then," he said, trying to sound imperious as befit his garb. Walking one ahead and one behind, the guards took him back to his room. They did not come in with him, but took up positions outside to guard the door. After eating all the food he had brought along, and checking to confirm that his guards were still in place, D'Molay resigned himself to being a prisoner for the night. He unwound himself from the toga, shaking crumbs of cheese from it, and removed his boots. He made a bed from the many pillows strewn about the room and fell into them, still wearing his tunic. Whether it was from exhaustion or some magic property of the cushions, he fell asleep immediately.

⚬━✦━⚬

*T*he smooth surface of the orb cast a pale yellow light upon Circe's fingers as the sorceress idly rolled it in her hand. She was intrigued by the man who claimed to visit her under the command of Glaucus. Causing her to remember the god who spurned her so long ago, when youth left her open to wounds of the heart, was not a point in D'Molay's favor. Soon enough, she would have her revenge for that reminder. D'Molay would join her zoo of other men transformed into base animals or interesting half-beasts. One of each sat near her on the floor beside her throne.

"Celias, come and amuse me," she trilled. Unable to resist her seductive voice, one of her favorite animal-men rose from the warm stones where he had been lounging to kneel at her feet. His strong Afrik body had been pleasing to Circe's eyes, and became even more so when the whim of magic replaced his ears with the prominent ones of a hyena, and appended a matching tail. She admired the dark stripes that framed his muscular torso as he abased himself before her. "You are a vicious wretch, aren't you?"

Celias lifted his face to look at her, grinning, unoffended. "That's why you like me best."

"So arrogant," she laughed. "Sit with me." Circe patted the open spot on the bench beside her and Celias quickly filled it. Smirking, he began to snake his arm around her waist. He was surprised when she elbowed it aside. "Stop it. That's not why you're here."

Celias inched back, apprehensive. "What is your desire?"

Circe laughed at him. "I see fear on your face. You must think I'm

going to make you do something horrible."

"It wouldn't be the first time," Celias said.

"Nor will it be the last. But settle yourself. I only need that evil, cruel brain of yours. I'm too annoyed to use my own today." Celias relaxed as Circe reached again for the orb.

The globe allowed Circe to spy on the City and its realms. D'Molay's talk of the pathetic nymph that Glaucus still sought had reminded her of how she had punished that rival. Truthfully, she hadn't given Scylla a passing thought over the eons, and without D'Molay's visit she would not have done so in the present. But once the bad memory had been resurrected, her intense curiosity drove her to spy. As she concentrated on the nymph she had exiled to a faraway land, images began to form in the glass sphere.

"She looks happy," Circe frowned. "I can't have that."

The monkey near her feet bared its teeth disapprovingly. It was the only way the former man could protest the cruelty of his mistress, as the witch had removed his voice along with his human form. Noticing his impudence, she kicked him hard, knocking him against a low table. Fruit tumbled from a platter; the ape grabbed several figs and fled.

Circe handed the globe to Celias and leaned forward on the cushioned bench, arching her back and stretching. She smiled, thinking of horrible things she could do to thwart the peace she had just observed.

Celias gazed at the scene. Circe was correct. The orb displayed a group of gruesome creatures wallowing in the slimy waters of a swamp. "Are they some kind of serpents or fish?"

"Happy little monsters. So disgusting," Circe said.

"You wish me to hunt them?"

"Don't be ridiculous," Circe snapped. "As if I would allow you to leave the cave for such a stupid errand. What I want is an idea for a new punishment. Just look at the big one, playing with her horrid babies. What in the worlds did she mate with?" Celias gazed again at the monsters. Once he got past their fearsome appearance, they did appear to be happily frolicking, not unlike a bitch and her puppies. Circe continued to complain. "Clearly she no longer minds being a monster."

"She?"

"Yes. The mother was a nymph who crossed me. I hate her." Circe ran her hand along the shapely thigh of Celias. "What would you do?"

Celias thought for a moment, enjoying the witch's warm caress. Although her hand was a bit distracting, several ideas came to mind. His ears twitched as he settled on the one he expected she would like the most.

"I would change her back. Let her see what she has spawned. And then watch her children devour her."

Circe's laughter echoed through the cave. "Oh, I do like that plan, except for the last part. Her misery must be eternal. I must break up this happy family."

Celias noticed the cold turn of Circe's voice as she spoke of family. Having no equal mate was an obvious sore spot for the one who enslaved him. He vaguely pitied the nymph, but being truly 'a vicious wretch' as she had said, Celias was more interested in what drastic new step Circe would take to torment her.

"I am so very sick of nymphs," Circe declared after a moment's thought. "The realms are thick with them. I will transform her into a woman, one who loves her ugly children as only a mother can."

Celias's ears twitched as his brow furrowed. "I don't understand. Won't they still be happy?"

"The whelps won't recognize a human as their own. They will flee, and break her heart." Circe considered her plan, fingers tapping on her servant's knee, and made one more alteration. "I will try a new shape-shifting spell I've been working on. It includes some protective magic that will strengthen her and ease the natural torments of the swamp. Let's keep her alive to suffer." She smirked at Celias. "Don't mistake this for kindness. There is a price for every boon."

Celias handed the globe back. The pictures were fading as Circe's concentration shifted. He watched as she fell into a deep trance, and backed away as mystical energy caused spinning halos of red light to form in the air, encircling her body. The power of the rotating bands allowed Circe's ethereal self to break free from her body. Her ghostly form then disappeared to enforce the new punishment she had decreed for the nymph.

Celias stared at her abandoned body. It was helpless as a corpse, but completely protected by the red power rings. Although he had favor with the witch, he never stopped fantasizing about the day that he would defeat her. This, however, was not that day.

<hr />

D'Molay had been awake for hours, but with no clock in his room he could only guess at the time. Already he missed the sun and the sky, and wished he knew what Aavi was doing, and wondered if she would still be there when he got out of this mountain.

When he had first shook off sleep and eased stiffly to his feet from his bed of pillows, he noticed his clothing had been returned, clean and skillfully repaired. He wanted to discard the linen tunic and toga Circe had selected for him and change into his own clothes. That, however, would surely give the witch offense. He would have to play along with her demands until she made a decision about his request.

One item was missing from D'Molay's returned wardrobe: his dagger. He frowned, remembering how he had lost it when tussling with Circe's guards. D'Molay resolved to request its return when he next saw Circe. Perhaps if he revealed it had special properties, she would want to examine it herself; and if she did lay claim to it, he would at least know where his dagger was.

When Kira arrived to escort him to breakfast with Circe, he was eager to go. Shadows of hope, dread and hunger followed him as he was led to a different room than the one he had dined in the previous night. This chamber was darker, lit only by smoky oil lamps. Circe, seated on a bench constructed of wood and leather, was squeezing a lemon and watching its juice drop into a mug already steaming with another liquid. She was dressed more practically than had been the case at dinner. She wore a plain blue robe belted with a wide sash. One large and several smaller pouches were tied to it. Her fingers seemed brightly pink, as if she had just vigorously scrubbed her hands. D'Molay noticed she looked rather tired. He wondered if she had been busy brewing potions while he slept. There was no table set for a meal, and only a camp chair for him to sit upon.

"Give him a bowl, Kira," Circe said. Kira walked over to a large cauldron that D'Molay hadn't noticed in the dim light. She shifted its lid to one side and dipped out a ladle of something that looked like porridge. This was deposited into a beautifully decorated bowl that was far too fancy for such plain fare. The serving girl handed it to him. "Sit and eat," Circe directed, and D'Molay lowered himself onto the small chair and raised the bowl to his face. It smelled of sweet oats and honey. He was given no spoon, so he tipped the porridge to his mouth to taste a mouthful.

"This is good," he said, somewhat surprised. The gruel's lack of visual appeal was balanced by its delicious taste.

"Is it?" Circe shrugged. "I never eat that dish." She stirred her hot lemon drink and took a delicate sip. "Did you sleep well? I found I did not. Your request about that spell - I just couldn't stop thinking about it."

D'Molay swallowed another portion of his breakfast carefully, watching Circe over the lip of the bowl. Her expression was hard to read. Rather than trying to guess the underlying message behind her words, D'Molay decided to take her statement at face value.

"Neither could I," he said, plastering a friendly smile on his face. "Did you decide anything?"

Circe sent an equally composed smile back. "Well, I decided there's no strong reason to deny your request, still . . ."

D'Molay waited tensely as she took another slow swallow of her morning drink.

" . . . I'd prefer to gain something if I help you. But you seem to have nothing to barter."

D'Molay wished there was somewhere to set his bowl down, but he was forced to hold it cupped in his hands as he appealed to Circe, feeling much like a beggar. "I do have something you may want, but your guards took it," he ventured. "My dagger. It's magical."

"Wonderful," she smiled. "Kira, go tell Celias to visit the patrol and retrieve D'Molay's knife. I'm sure he'll enjoy the exercise."

"Yes, Circe," Kira said. "I will find him now."

D'Molay noticed the two women share a knowing glance as he wondered who Celias was and what method he would employ to find the dagger. Deciding he didn't care to know, he returned his attention to his porridge. Circe leaned over to reach under her bench.

"If I choose to take your knife, I will give you this antidote in exchange," she announced, pulling out a fawn-colored glass bottle the length of D'Molay's hand. "If you're able to find Twila - "

"Scylla."

"That's right, Scylla, you will have to make her drink this entire elixir to break my spell. It won't be easy to get a monster to swallow this, but that isn't my problem is it?"

"No, it's entirely mine," D'Molay said, feeling a bit more positive. The pieces were falling into place. He would have to sacrifice his dagger, but he would gain an antidote for Scylla. Now all he needed was a way out of Circe's mountain. He ate more from his bowl as he thought about asking for her help getting back to Dioscrias. "Is there another way - " he began, but Circe interrupted him.

"Let's play a game while we wait," she said. "I'll ask you several questions. You can answer each with a lie or the truth. Then I get to guess how many times you have lied to me. Understand?"

D'Molay saw no point to the exercise, but nodded. "Those are all the rules?"

Circe nodded. "It's a simple game." She poured herself another hot drink and began her questions. "What is your favorite food?"

D'Molay had already decided all his responses would be lies. However, he resolved to appear to think about his answers to give the appearance that he was actually giving them due consideration. "Minted lamb."

"Would you rather fight a swordsman or a bowman?"

"A bowman, I suppose."

"How many women have you loved?"

D'Molay caught himself counting and quickly suppressed the urge to reminisce. "Five," he said randomly.

"What animal is most valuable to man?"

"A dog."

Circe sighed. "I would expect far more interesting answers from a man clever enough to find me. But as for the game, I think you have lied to me every time but once. Did I win?"

"I'm sorry, but you lost. I lied every time."

Circe gave him a knowing look. "Are you quite sure? Your answer about love rang true." Her expression darkened. "But men and women rarely agree on what love is, do they?"

D'Molay was rescued from what might have been an ill turn of the game by the arrival of a tall Nubian man whose head and legs looked like a hyena. The hyena man carried his dagger across his two open palms. From what he could see, it looked none the worse from being trod on by the pig guard plus whatever indignities had happened to it after that. Behind the hyena, Kira followed, awaiting her next order.

"You requested this, mistress Circe?" the beast rasped with a slight growl as a smile crossed his dog-like snout.

"Ah, Celias. This is our new visitor, D'Molay. The one I told you about. Come see what you think of him." D'Molay nodded at the man, but said nothing.

Celias walked slowly around D'Molay, sizing him up. "I heard you gave the guards a good chase. They are still grunting about it."

"They had their job, I had mine," he replied.

"And what is that job, human?"

D'Molay gave him a friendly smile. "Why, meeting your mistress, of course."

"She's met enough people for now."

Laughter filled the room as Circe displayed her amusement. "I love it when men fight over me. So what do you think of him, Celias?"

"He might make a good guard. He has the spirit of a fighter; that much is certain."

Celias presented the dagger with a bow. Circe examined it. "Are you still playing the lying game, D'Molay? This dagger isn't magic, it counters magic. Still, it could be useful."

"I have found it to be. Do we have a deal?" D'Molay asked.

"For now. Take the bottle. If you remain a pleasant guest, I will let you leave with it tomorrow."

D'Molay silently gnashed his teeth. He did not want to spend another full day stuck here, but he had little choice. "Thank you," he said, picking up the antidote. "May I put this away in my room?"

Circe nodded, waving him out. "Of course. Go where you wish, within reason. Perhaps we'll play a different game at dinner."

D'Molay stood up and gave Circe a small bow as he left.

Celias watched every move D'Molay made as he left the room. "Is there anything else you need of me, mistress?" he asked when he was out of sight.

"Don't be too jealous," Circe purred. "He's my new plaything, but you'll always be my favorite. When the time comes, I'll want you to properly train him, like the others."

"Of course." Celias gave her an insincere smile.

"Now go. I'm sure it's time to feed the menagerie."

He backed out of the room, bowing again.

Kira stooped to pick up the porridge bowl D'Molay had left on the floor.

"I want to watch," Circe said. "See that he drinks the potion when you serve his midday meal. When he falls under the spell, have the guards throw him in a cell. Then come for me." Circe idly twirled the dagger in her hand before tucking it away in the large pouch hanging from her belt. "I do hope he's not another pig."

"What about your other potion, my lady? I can retrieve the bottle from his room for you," Kira offered.

"Oh, the precious antidote?" Circe laughed. "Don't trouble yourself. It's nothing but colored water."

Chapter 10

Drunk With Power

Mazu looked up from her meditations and found one of the children standing in the arched opening to her chamber. It was one of Helios' younger sons, a boy of perhaps seven cycles. Mazu had not yet mastered all the children's names; she doubted King Helios himself knew all of them. However, she remembered that this particular boy had already earned a reputation for being extremely skilled at sneaking away from her classes. That made his visit to her now particularly curious.

"Come in," she said, remaining seated on her mat, hoping that not standing to tower over the boy might engender more trust. "Can I help you with something?"

The boy took several steps inside and leaned against a wall painted with a band of swirling wave designs. He stared down at his feet, carefully aligning the soles of his sandals to match the straight lines of the floor tiles. Mazu noted the boy seemed a bit reluctant to speak.

"Remind me of your name," she said gently. "I haven't seen you in class enough to learn it."

"Milos," he said. "Between Niklomidas and Alexander."

Mazu smiled at him. Apparently the male children had been taught by their father to describe themselves according to their place in the line of succession. "And why aren't you with your brothers on this fine day?"

"I . . . got away," he said, barely loud enough for Mazu to hear. When he looked up from his feet, she could see fear in his eyes. "My father . . . the king . . . he's yelling at everyone."

"Kings do yell loudly, don't they?" Mazu said mildly, standing slowly, straightening her robes. She held her hand out to Milos. "Show me where your brothers and sisters are."

Milos immediately reached out and hooked one small index finger around Mazu's pinky. He led her from her chamber and through the passage that led into an inner courtyard. When they crossed the courtyard and ducked into a wing of the palace that Mazu had not seen before, she could hear King Helios. His voice, though slurred, was boasting abrasively.

"Never forget that I am the most powerful god in Greece! I can kill any of you with a blink of an eye, and I'll show no mercy because you came from me!" she heard him rage. At the sound of this Milos hung back, and let go of her hand. She placed a kind hand on his head.

"Thank you, Milos. You can go now." Mazu was grateful that at least one child had found a way to escape the ravings of the king. As Milos ran off, she followed the sound of the king's voice down a hallway until she stood before an open, unguarded door. She found the absence of any courtly security odd, but perhaps Helios had ordered his men away so they would not observe his abusive behavior toward his children. She took a deep breath and positioned herself just outside the door where she could eavesdrop unobserved. She imagined her friend D'Molay would have done exactly the same thing, seizing the opportunity to learn something from the king's unguarded remarks.

"Be like Circe in all things!" Helios went on. "Your sister is the jewel of my court. Queen among sorcerers! Keeper of the great secret!"

Mazu heard something shatter on the hard floor. She pictured Helios waving his arms as he raved, perhaps knocking over an urn or a small statue.

"She keeps us strong. All of you! Line up on your knees and drink!"

One of the youngest girls began to whimper. When Mazu heard a sharp slap push the child's whines into full-out wails, she could stay hidden no longer. She entered the room, forcing herself into a pretense of composure as the king shouted at his daughter.

"Stop squalling, Iona! You worthless girl!"

Mazu smiled at Helios as if she had intruded upon a congenial family breakfast rather than the bizarre scene that confronted her. Today, he seemed to glow slightly, as if the remnants of his sun powers were trying to activate. He was garbed even more carelessly than usual. His royal over-robe was discarded in a heap in the middle of the floor. His long tunic hung crookedly from his shoulders and was splattered with wet spill marks. His beard and hair had not been smoothed or oiled. But under the grime of his face and hands, it was clear that the age, the puffiness and wrinkling, the weakening of vitality that was often so evident had been replaced with new vigor. Mazu chanced a glance at the queue of cowed children who were crawling like frightened, obedient dogs to lick the puddle of liquid that had pooled from several bottles that Helios had dashed on the ground. She immediately recognized the fluid as the gods' life water. What would happen to mortal children who drank it? The thought had never occurred to Mazu before.

"King Helios," she said. "I see you are busy with your children. Forgive my intrusion." Mazu bowed slightly, but made no move to retreat. The king looked over his shoulder at her, his eyes wild.

"Yes, I'm teaching them something more important than old tales. This is a practical lesson." He swung his foot, nudging one child away from the water so the next could bend and drink. "From the look of you, you might benefit from my teaching as well." Helios raised a finger and tapped the smooth skin beneath one eye, mocking the existence of the creases under Mazu's own.

"Are you appealing to a woman's vanity?" Mazu asked, forcing a flirtatious lilt into her speech. "I know what the life water does for us, but it's a rare and precious thing. You're a great king indeed to have enough to waste."

Helios smirked crookedly at Mazu. "A rare thing? Ha! My daughter, the most brilliant sorceress, brews as much nectar as I desire. And," he bragged, "chooses only the most delectable souls to mix into my personal supply." Helios stooped down for one of many small amber-glass bottles that filled a wooden box on the floor. He straightened abruptly, swaying dizzily. "A gift for you. Enjoy it."

Mazu took the bottle, then examined the liquid within. It looked just like the nectar of the gods, though perhaps a more potent form. "Forgive my old ears, King Helios. Did you say she brews with . . . souls?"

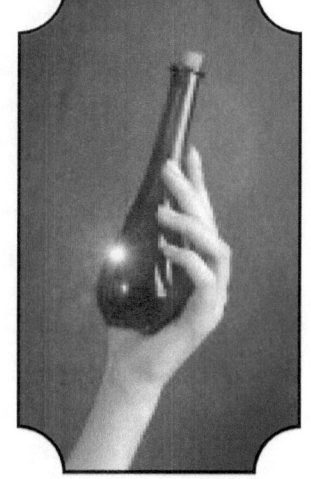

Helios threw up a hand and laughed. "Ah, the secret! I shouldn't have told you, but you are a teacher and a teacher should have all the facts. Did you hear, children? Your father is teaching your teacher!" Helios tipped forward and grabbed another bottle, thumbing its cork free with a violent jab and greedily downing another dose of nectar. He wiped his mouth with the back of his forearm and gestured at Mazu. "Drink, goddess! See if you can tell what realm's souls filled your bottle."

Mazu wrapped her fingers tightly around the little bottle. It disappeared within her fist, like an aberrant thing that should not be seen in the light of day. The claim of Helios was horrifying; the life water that kept the gods empowered in their post-Earth world contained mortal souls?

"You tease me, King Helios," she said, yearning for him to admit it was all a great joke. "How could our life water come from base humans? I've always heard that - "

"You think I'm lying?" Helios snarled. "You think my daughter Circe is a liar too?"

"I'm only saying this is news to me," Mazu said passively. "Forgive my ignorance." Helios raised an uncombed eyebrow as she dared to continue. "If Circe has achieved such an amazing thing, I would love to congratulate her in person."

"Would you indeed?" Helios staggered backward and fell into a chair, the intoxicating effect of too much nectar taking its toll. Mazu moved deliberately between him and the children, waving a hand at them behind her back. It was all the encouragement they needed to flee the scene. Mazu approached the seated king. A persistent twitch had taken root at the corner of his right eye and his jaw was clenched as he rode out the power of the nectar coursing through his veins. She released her grip on the bottle he had given her and opened it, stepping up beside him.

"I would. I will take her father's most warm greetings to her, if you only show me the way."

Mazu gently extended the bottle to his mouth and tipped more water of life over his lips. The pupils of his eyes grew wide and dark and his tongue industriously captured every drop of nectar from before he spoke.

"You'll never find her secret cave," Helios said sleepily as he slumped even further into his chair.

"I wager I can, if you tell me where to look." Mazu steeled her stomach, and forced herself to caress the king's cheek like a common seductress. The tactic worked.

"Aeaean Mountains," he sighed happily. His eyelids began to close.

"Where exactly," Mazu prompted, but she got nothing more out of him before he began to snore. She looked at the hand that had touched him with disgust. She dared to change it briefly to water to cleanse the taint of his skin. She still had a few more days to spend in the palace before D'Molay's scheduled return. Mazu hoped she could endure it.

Over the remaining days she continued her surveillance but nothing more was learned about urns or harpies or Circe's whereabouts. Helios had removed himself to the site of some ill-conceived monument where he could more directly threaten his engineers and workmen. While this prevented Mazu from prying any more information out of the king directly, it did provide her the freedom to steal into the royal library and consult its maps. Unfortunately, none showed any mountain range called Aeaean.

On the evening of her last day as Mao-shi, Mazu packed her few belongings and bid the children farewell. They did not look well. The nectar the king had forced them to drink had a lingering and debilitating effect. *The nectar is dangerous to mortals; any more than a little could be deadly.* Mazu was struck by a premonition that these children might not live long.

She walked away from the palace with mixed feelings. Although she had gathered some important clues and come to care for the children, she had found her stay to be repugnant in every way. D'Molay had been wise to split up their efforts. She hoped his foray into the wilderness had led to the witch.

Mazu walked along toward Dioscrias as Mao-shi. Ever mindful of the possible presence of Quetzalcoatl's spies, she did her best to blend in with the local people who were also returning to the port after their day's business at the palace. Many of them were pushing carts or carrying large sacks of goods on their backs. It was a simple thing for Mazu to position herself behind their bulk and make herself hard to pick out in the crowd. As twilight was taking over the sky, she arrived at the docks. She smiled when she saw the dark silhouette of her boat on the lake, her favorite lantern hanging with a shimmering glow on its new mast. She sat down on the dock to admire the scene until darkness fell completely. Then, when she was sure no one would notice, she slipped into the lake and flowed as liquid to the boat.

"Goddess!" Quan exclaimed happily as she reformed on deck. "Come inside and have a fish cake. I've been practicing my cooking."

"I'm glad to hear you've had time for it," Mazu smiled. Quan lifted the lid of a pan and showed her several flat discs made of fish and rice. They smelled quite good. "Are these all you've made? D'Molay could eat all of those by himself."

Quan looked down into the pan. "You're right. I forgot he's due back tonight. I'll make some more."

"Thank you," Mazu smiled. She settled back into the familiar surroundings of her boat and watched Quan work. It was very peaceful and normal, almost enough to make her forget she was still deeply embroiled in an unpleasant and unavoidable quest. However, her thoughts returned more strongly to that fact as the hours passed and D'Molay did not come.

By morning, even Quan was worried. "That crazy man is late. He probably fell down a hole chasing one of his hallucinations."

"Hallucinations? What do you mean?"

Quan made a circular motion with his finger next to his head. "He was sleepwalking and talking to invisible people. He even got stuck in my boat sealant. He's down a hole for sure."

Mazu sighed. "If he doesn't come by tonight, we'll have to go after him."

"You mean leave the boat?" Quan looked aghast.

"Unless you can make it sail through the forest, yes," Mazu said simply. "D'Molay promised to leave us a trail to follow if it came to this, so don't look so alarmed. It's all according to plan."

"I don't like this plan," Quan mumbled quietly.

Mazu, to be honest, didn't either.

⁕

Aavi had waited for days outside the harpy cave, but D'Molay had not come out. No matter what she tried, she could not gain access to the mountain. She felt sorry that she could not perform her duty of protecting the human who had protected her so many times.

Other guardians had counseled her about the challenge she would face in her assignment. She understood that she could not prevent every mishap. Men were willful and prone not to listen to their inner voice. They were so easily swayed by the word of another mortal. Aavi had been told that it was sometimes easier to push a man under the influence of other men than to guide him directly. Thinking of this advice, she remembered that D'Molay had companions on his journey, though they were far from him right now. But if she could lead them here, they could enter the mountain that had shut her out.

Reluctantly, Aavi flew back over the mountain ridge to the field where the harpy had stolen D'Molay. The strong woman who had fought by his side was no longer there. The bodies of dead harpies littered the ground, and Aavi recoiled, flying far up into the air where the sight and smell of the corpses could not reach her. She floated quietly for a long time, watching the clouds form pretty shapes and thinking.

Below her was a dense forest, where the woman had probably gone. She would be difficult to find among the dark trees. It was easy for her to stay near D'Molay, for she had a special connection with him. Aavi h a d no such chain to the black-smith. She drifted over the landscape, drawn to a bright sparkle on the horizon. It was the water of the lake.

Aavi loved water. Although many memories of her time as a human had faded, the joy specific things had brought her had not. She moved toward the Great Lake, remembering the excitement of her first trip on a boat. Aavi felt a thrill of happiness rise in her heart. She had a connection to the owner of that boat, Mazu, D'Molay's friend who had been so kind to her. Aavi could find her, and try to communicate D'Molay's plight. She flew toward Dioscrias and found Mazu and the man who had been on the boat when she saved D'Molay from the falling mast. They and three horses were on a trailhead that led into the forest. That was the extent of her success.

Aavi hovered near the two, unseen and unable to interact with them. She was certain that angels weren't supposed to feel frustrated, but she was, and there was no getting around the sense of uselessness she felt at the moment. However, even D'Molay had not been able to see her at first, so she did not give up. Eventually, however, she grew tired of shouting and glowing and flying into them with no results. Aavi withdrew, taking a seat floating over a limb of a tall tree, watching down on them sadly, pondering what she could do next.

Quan looked around at the forbidding dark trees as he nervously fiddled with his horse's reins. The old man at the blacksmith's shop had allowed them to rent the horses very inexpensively once Mazu had explained they were going after D'Molay and Sophia. He wished Mazu had used some of the money they had saved to hire some armed men to travel with them. Quan felt like he was riding to his doom and his resentment of D'Molay flowered.

"Must we follow him into these woods? Perhaps if we wait, he will return on his own, mistress," he said.

"We've already discussed this Quan. If you prefer to wait at the boat, you are free to do so," Mazu replied firmly. "I can move faster without you anyway." She rode forward without even glancing back at him.

Shamed by her declaration, Quan hurried after her. "No, my lady. I will stay with you to the bitter end."

A knowing smile graced Mazu's face as they rode on. Quan managed to hold his tongue for about ten minutes. When they were well into the shade of the dense trees, he began to complain again.

"I don't like these woods. I feel like something's always watching us."

"You're too used to being on the open water, so the woodlands make you nervous."

Aavi floated down and tried once again to make Mazu or Quan hear her, with no success. Sighing, she hovered for a while over the rider-less horse as they traveled along before fading away from their presence.

Quan resolved to reassure himself by voicing his confidence in his patron. "You're right. But I'm sure I'll always be safe with you, lady Mazu."

Mazu turned to look at him with the wisdom of many ages behind her eyes. "Do not bind me to guarantees I cannot keep, Quan. No one is always safe, especially in this realm."

The day wore on and the afternoon sun cast long shadows across the forest floor. Mazu and Quan had sought and found the trail marks D'Molay had left on the trees. They had passed the seventh far back on the trail but the eighth remained elusive.

"Did he forget to mark the trees or have we lost his trail?" Quan asked over the noise of a flock of loud, chattering birds.

Mazu paused, looking at the nearby oaks in hope she might see D'Molay's cross marks in them. "It's not like him to forget such a thing. Let's ride a little farther."

They continued deeper into the forest but still had no luck finding any sign of D'Molay having passed through.

"We'd better return to where we saw his last mark and make camp. We can try another direction tomorrow," Mazu decided. She turned her mount and headed back the way they had come. Quan followed. After an hour's ride back along the trail, they returned to the last tree they had found with D'Molay's mark. They set up camp, watered the horses, and Quan made a small fire as he chattered to Mazu about things they had seen on the day's journey.

Eventually he realized that Mazu was not responding to him. She was sitting very still, and although she faced Quan her eyes were looking past him and off into the distance.

"Mistress, what is it?"

Her gaze returned to him as she spoke very quietly. "We are being watched. Remain calm; make no sudden moves. I don't want whoever is there to know I sense their presence."

Quan sat as still as he could, his eyes bulging out in fear.

"Continue preparing our meal and wipe that look off your face. You look like a frog waiting for the crocodile to come." She smiled slightly in an attempt to lighten the tension. Quan continued his preparations with shaking hands, setting a noodle soup to cook in a pot over the fire. By the time its aromatic smell began to waft around the surrounding glade, the sun was starting to set in the west.

"Very good, Quan. I think it is time to invite our guest for a hot meal." Mazu stood up and looked around the circumference of the glade as she spoke in a loud, clear voice. "Please, won't you join us for dinner? I know you are out there. Surely you would like something to eat? We mean no harm. We are just traveling through these lands." She continued to stand, searching the area. Finally the rustle of foliage announced the arrival of a cloaked figure on a horse, leading another empty mount.

It was a woman. "Make no moves, either of you, or you'll feel my arrows. What are you doing in these woods? Neither of you look like you belong here. You are certainly not of Olympia."

"We seek a friend of ours who traveled here recently. A man with a beard and hair of brown."

"Why do you seek this man?"

Mazu detected a slight waver in the voice. "He is our companion and our fates are bound together."

The woman rode closer. She wore a green leather hunter's outfit, complete with bow and quiver of arrows. She was tall and muscular, her visage grim and determined. Her face was scratched and blood had dried in her hair. Her left forearm was bandaged and her clothing was torn. The woman's eyes narrowed and she stared directly at Mazu.

"What is this man's name?" she demanded.

"He is known as D'Molay the tracker. Have you seen him?"

The woman nodded, and dismounted. "Yes. My name is Sophia. I was his guide."

"Was?" Quan asked fearfully. Sophia nodded.

"I have dire news. He was taken by harpies, not far from here." Her voice trembled slightly as she spoke.

"Was he alive? Which way did they take him? Please tell us everything you know!" Mazu pressed.

The huntress tied her horse to a nearby tree. Mazu could see that she was tired, defeated and saddened. Mazu sat down and gestured for their

new visitor to do the same. "Please sit with us. You have nothing to fear. We wish only information. You must be the smith of Dioscrias. D'Molay told me he was going to seek your aid."

Sophia seemed slightly surprised that Mazu knew who she was. She came over to the cook fire and sat down on a log across from the two of them. "And you must be the two he carved those crosses for. D'Molay said you'd be following." She pointed with her knife at the tree behind them.

Quan couldn't stop staring at the muscular woman. He had not seen a mortal woman this tall or this strong looking before.

"We are, but we could find no more marks past this point." Quan gave Mazu a small bowl of the noodle soup, which she then offered to Sophia.

Their guest looked at the bowl. "I never eat food offered me until I see others eat it. You first."

"I see. No doubt a wise decision in a dangerous world." Mazu raised the bowl and took a good long sip and slurped up a noodle, so Sophia could see she had eaten it. Once this was done, Sophia accepted the bowl and proceeded to eat. After a few moments, she relaxed and seemed to enjoy the meal.

As Sophia scraped the last noodle from the bowl, Mazu began her questioning. "Please, what can you tell us of D'Molay?"

"He was taken at the foot of the Aeaean Mountains. We had set a trap to lure a harpy down from the heights so we could see where they were nesting. One came. But a flock of others followed it, and we were seen."

"You fought a whole flock?" Quan asked, amazed. Impressed, he scooped up another bowl of soup and handed it to her. She accepted it this time without suspicion.

"We were outnumbered, but not outmatched at first. Then one of them got lucky and grabbed D'Molay. It flew off with him leaving me alone to fight for my life."

"How did you survive?" Quan asked, his attention riveted by her tale.

"When I ran out of arrows I made it to a shelter under fallen trees where they couldn't get to me. I stayed hidden until they gave up. When it was safe to come out, I was able to find our horses. I searched, but there was no trace of your friend." Sophia looked at the ground and fell silent. "I have his pack, and a few of his other things left behind on my horse."

Mazu set her mostly uneaten bowl aside. "Was he alive when they carried him off?"

"Yes."

"Which way did they take him?"

"Over the mountain ridge." Sophia told them the rumors they had heard about where the harpies might dwell and described the way to the field where the harpies had attacked.

"There is still hope," Mazu said. "D'Molay is a survivor and he seems to live a charmed life. If anyone can survive being carried off by harpies, it will be him."

"I saw him pray to some god while we traveled," Sophia told them. "I hope someone was listening."

By the time they were done eating and discussing their journeys, night had fallen. Quan put away the food and dishes, while the two women continued to talk.

"No one should traverse these woods at night, Sophia. Stay here and sleep by the fire. Tomorrow you can head back to Dioscrias."

Sophia looked around at the dark. "I suppose you're right. I wish D'Molay had never come to me for this hunt. He'd still be safe now if I had refused his offer."

Mazu could see the guilt the woman was carrying. "No. If you had refused, he would have come out here alone. He told me as much the night before he left us. That's how I knew who you were. You mustn't blame yourself, Sophia. You did what you could." Mazu looked at her earnestly. "A few months ago, I felt just like you do now. Someone in my care was taken and carried off."

"Indeed? What happened?" Sophia asked.

Mazu smiled slightly. "We found her and she was safe." Mazu decided not to tell Sophia that Aavi died a few weeks later. "Let's get some sleep. We both have much to do tomorrow."

Sophia left early the next morning after leaving D'Molay's belongings and giving Mazu directions. "Good luck, I hope you find him. I must return to my forge, I'm already late."

Quan began to pack the cooking gear from their dinner. Mazu stopped him with a hand on his arm.

"No need to repack our things," she said. "I'll seek him alone, through the waters." Mazu noticed Quan's eyes brighten. "Don't look so relieved that you don't have to go."

He bowed sheepishly. "Sorry."

"However, you have not escaped too lightly. Stay camped here and let no one chase you off. I promise I'll return with D'Molay as soon as I can."

Quan blinked at her, not sharing her optimism. "Do you want me to dig a grave while I wait?"

"You are truly attached to the idea of D'Molay down a hole, aren't you?" she scoffed. "Leave the forest alone. Just wait, and keep our horses ready. I plan to bring him back alive." Mazu turned into water and disappeared into the ground.

Chapter 11

When Goddesses Battle

With the information gained from Sophia, Mazu now knew where the mysterious Aeaean Mountains lay. Locating underground streams that cascaded from their heights, she rushed along those waterways deep underground. Soon she would discover if King Helios had told the truth about the use of souls in the nectar of the gods. Mazu resolved to rely on her own observations before becoming too enraged. It still seemed hard to believe. She hoped it was merely the drunken ramblings of a god in decline. *Once I've found Circe, I'll know the truth of it.*

Further along the way, the small springs widened into a deeper channel. On its bottom, Mazu noticed fragments of pottery that matched the urns she'd seen around the palace. She flowed toward a dark hole in the bottom of the bank where a thick fan of shards littered the bed, flushed from some inner chamber. There she found an aquifer tunnel that rose to the surface. She moved into it, swimming against a strong current that carried more broken bits of pots, shreds of plant material, and murky swirls of unknown powders past her face. She did her best to dodge the discarded fragments of potions, unsure if the scraps would have any effect on her. Eventually the clutter became too thick to avoid. She powered through it, racing toward a bright glimmer in the water. Mazu reached the light, and emerged.

She had arrived in a torch-lit chamber. Above her, the round walls of a pit extended upward to a grated grill, a chute that delivered Circe's garbage into the river system. A nearby waterwheel powered a flushing current, redirecting a waterfall that spilled from the heights. Mazu struggled against the flow, fighting to force her watery form against the turn of the wheel, but tired quickly. She retreated. Realizing that someone had to keep the torches lit and maintain the waterwheel, she sought a more mundane way to enter and leave the pit.

Resting for a moment, she stooped and picked up a piece of a broken urn. The inner face of it was darkly stained. She could sense it once held blood. She laid it gently aside and shifted her attention to the area near the waterwheel. Footprints surrounded the machine, light impressions in the damp, sandy mud. Mazu followed them, coming to a dozen rickety wooden slats tied together with leather that served as a rudimentary door to a passage. She listened, hearing unidentifiable grunts and groans from the corridor she faced. Calmly reminding herself she'd encountered monsters of all descriptions before, she moved into the unknown.

Three steps in something flew at her. Mazu lashed out at it with a watery hand and whatever it was squawked and retreated. Other animal sounds signaled a reaction to the encounter, some of them sounding almost like garbled voices. Mazu stood still, expecting more creatures to accost her. She was, after all, an intruder here. A minute passed. Then slowly, singly and in small clusters, beasts crept out from nooks in the wall and climbed down from giant gnarled roots that bisected the ceiling and floor of the room. They gathered around Mazu, jostling for position, each of them angling for a spot closest to her.

A goose with a dark mark swirled across its beak nipped at a one-eyed brown dog, but the cur refused to give way. It snapped back at the fowl as a pig skirted their fight and ruffled its snout, snorting pitifully. Mazu looked closely at the swine, wondering if it and the other animals were hoping to be fed. A quick survey of the variety of beasts encircling her led her to believe they were not starving. Certainly they would have turned on one another if that were the case. This was Circe's lair; magic had to be at work.

The animals milled around her, tilting wide, intelligent eyes up toward her face. A long-haired ape bared its teeth in a grin, exposing the anomaly of a gold tooth. A vulture shifted from one foot to another to bring her attention to a ring encircling one of its talons. From these clues, Mazu realized that these creatures hadn't always worn their animal skins.

She stepped carefully through the gathering of beasts toward a section of the chamber that branched off into another narrow corridor. Flanking this passage were cells. In them were more disturbing results of the witch's work. These pitiful prisoners had not fully transformed into common animals. Parts of them were still men. Mazu's heart filled with pity as she observed their state. A young man who still retained his pretty face had nothing but a snake's body beneath his neck. He opened his mouth as if to speak, but only a bifurcated tongue came out. She looked away, her eyes settling on the cell across from his, where a seeming-centaur stood; but it was a man with the horns of stag, his deer body show-

ing the cuts of a whip. He had been blindfolded and gagged, and Mazu was relieved he could not see her as she forced herself to move on. The next little side room held something even worse. This man no longer had his own face, hands, or feet. These had been replaced with a horse's head and hooves. The horse-man staggered awkwardly up to the bars of his cell and beat the iron feebly with his hooved hands. He nickered and worked his jaw as if trying to force its brute noises into language. Mazu had always loved horses, and she sighed, reaching out a hand to touch his nose in comfort. As she did, noticed something hanging around the horse's neck that she had seen many times before: the Council seal.

"D'Molay?" she gasped. The horse shook its head up and down violently. Mazu immediately checked the locking bolt on his cell, but it was too complex to quickly defeat. He and the others would have to wait a little bit longer for their freedom.

"Listen, all of you men!" Mazu called out. The animal voices joined in a cacophony, as if all were overjoyed that this visitor had discerned the truth. Mazu did her best to quiet them, fearing the noise would expose her presence. "You're prisoners here, but not for long," she promised. "I will settle this and other business. Now which way leads to Circe?"

The long haired ape knuckled over and took her hand, pulling her toward a door. Mazu ignored D'Molay's alarmed neighing and beating on the cell bars as she left him behind.

Circe shook a shred of fairy queen wing from D'Molay's knife. The dispelling properties of the weapon allowed her to finally experiment with this dangerous ingredient, rendering it safe to handle for the short time it took to grind it into powder. The dagger was sharp as well, and Circe imagined she would use it frequently here in her brewing room.

From the corner of her eye, Circe noticed a long, hairy arm reaching tentatively around the edge of the door. Dirty, brown fingers spidered along the floor as one of her transformations wandered in. She wished that fewer of her captives would turn into apes, but more times than not the inner monkey of a man was the result of her transformation potion. The growing number of simians was a nuisance. She resolved to rid herself of them as soon as she completed this batch of nectar. It would be amusing to drive them into the woods and command Celias to hunt them with her. A thrill coursed through her blood at the thought of sharing such a game with her favorite man-beast.

Giving the monkey no further thought, Circe set aside the dagger and the cup of fairy wing and picked up a ladle. She reached for an urn that stood about waist-high and removed the vessel's lid. She glanced back once at a mixture simmering in her pot and judged the time was right for adding the key ingredient. She held the ladle in her right hand, stroking it with her left as she breathed over it, words of power ghosting from her lips. She thrust the ladle into the urn, scooping up thick, red blood. Turning slowly, she held the ladle of vital fluid just above the surface of her boiling soup of herbs and tinctures, watching as the blood began to warm. The vapors from the potion below thickened, rising up to intrude over the lip of the ladle. The blood cupped within it began to bubble at their touch.

"Come out, come out," Circe coaxed mockingly as the ingredients mingled. "Thirsty gods don't like to be kept waiting."

As if shamed by her words, the contents of the ladle began to change. The red, viscous blood began to lighten. Soon its color was almost clear and it crystallized into a rising icicle of faceted glass suggestive of boiled sugar candy. Circe watched eagerly as a frightened human image appeared behind each face of the crystal. As soon as an imprisoned soul had appeared on every facet, Circe dumped the delicate tower into a great mortar on her worktable. Taking a heavy stone pestle in hand, she cruelly shattered the crystal into a burst of tiny shards. She barely reacted to the agonized screams of obliterated souls, but she nearly jumped out of her skin when she heard a shout.

"NO!"

Mazu shot a forceful stream of water at the pestle, knocking it out of Circe's hand. The witch recoiled, clenching her stinging fingers into a fist.

"How dare you," she hissed. "How did you get in?"

"How dare I?" Mazu asked, incredulous. "Those are stolen souls, aren't they? How did you take them? You have no right!" Mazu charged toward the table, but before she reached it Circe waved her hand. A magical, shimmering curtain appeared, blocking Mazu from coming any closer.

"Don't I?" she challenged. "I have every right, whoever you are. Did you think nectar rains down from magic clouds? This is where it's made. I make it. And everyone drinks it."

Mazu's heart sank. Circe was confirming all the claims of her father. The revelation that life water - which Mazu had often drunk and had even given to the pure angel Aavi - was made from mortal souls caused her to steel her emotions and fix Circe with a cold stare.

"Then everyone must stop."

Circe's laugh rang out. "Stop? And have all the gods looking as old and used up as you? Why not take a drink? Let me see what you look like under all those wrinkles." Circe casually strolled to the other end of her work bench and picked up a large glass bowl of brewed nectar. Tauntingly, she dipped in a finger and raised it to her lips, licking it clean and making a satisfied noise. "It's a good batch. So fresh."

"Witch," Mazu said, taking care not to react to Circe's goading, "the blood in those urns. Where does it come from?"

"I'm sorry," Circe said with faux politeness, "I forget to ask your name. If we're going to discuss recipes like kitchen slaves I should know what to call you." Several red-eyed rats that had been watching from a shelf behind the sorceress beat a hasty retreat, sensing the anger building behind the words of their mistress. Mazu was not as easily intimidated.

"I am Mazu, Lady of Compassion, water goddess of the Asian Realm. And you are Circe, tormentor of nymphs and torturer of men. Now answer," Mazu said, advancing to the very edge of the curtain. She could see into the mortar where some faces still writhed within a few unbroken facets of the crystal. "How are you trapping these souls?"

"Really, who has time to squeeze blood from mortals like milk from a cow? Look around you." Circe waved the pestle at stack upon stack of blood filled urns lining the room. "My stock is the work of many harvesters." Circe folded her arms across her chest. "You're too ancient to be so ignorant of how our world endures."

Mazu searched within herself and found she actually agreed with Circe on that point. Until recent times, she had avoided the greater concerns of the gods and sought peace by working as a lowly ferrywoman. Now, she was faced with the type of choice she had hoped to avoid.

"Yes, I am ignorant," she conceded. "I've discovered I'm a hypocrite who urges compassion while existing on the stolen essence of those weaker than I. But there is one wonderful thing about being a compassionate fool."

Circe once again lifted her pestle and forced it down to crush the last remaining facets of the crystal icicle, half ignoring Mazu as she went back to work. "And what is that?"

"A compassionate fool is willing to die in order to stop evil."

Mazu raised her arms and closed her eyes. A second later her face disappeared. Her features were replaced by the swirling depths of a whirlpool as the rest of her body changed into a towering waterspout. Circe looked up in alarm, thrusting both hands out, shouting words to strengthen the curtain that separated her from the coming torrent. But water always finds its way. The magical barrier held for a few seconds as Circe turned to flee. Then it collapsed and Mazu fell upon the witch.

Slammed to the floor by the fierce attack, Circe screamed. She rolled away from the waterspout. Watching it as she sought cover, she could see Mazu's glowing form deep within it. The goddess made a vow. "I will tell the Council of your mendacity!"

"You are a fool," Circe called back. "Without me there is no Council! I keep them alive and imbued with power!" She scrambled back to her feet as her outrageous declaration made Mazu pause to listen. "These mortal souls are of no consequence when compared to preserving our realms!" Circe coughed out some water. "The Council had to find a way for us gods to survive and I provided it." After spewing out the explanation, Circe took a deep breath. "I gave them an answer. I keep their great secret. Whose side will the Council take if you get in my way?"

Mazu was overwhelmed. Anger, disbelief and betrayal fought inside her heart. The inconvenience of sharing the realms with a growing population of ghosts hardly called for every mortal being to be robbed of his afterlife for the sake of stronger nectar! But few could control the acts of spirits; the prospect of their anarchy must have made the legalistic Council pale. Yet that was no excuse for this horror. She thought of all the dying Greeks she had nursed at Ares' Fortress. To a man, they had faced their passing bravely with the prospect of their trip to the Elysian Fields keeping them strong. Unknowingly, Mazu had been complicit in deceiving them as she held their hands and bid them a fair journey. And what then? Who else had the Council enlisted in this horror? There must have been handlers of the dead to drain the bodies, transporters to smuggle the blood-filled urns as innocent freight. D'Molay and Aavi had seen the harpies steal them from unknowing merchants to bring to the witch. All the mortal dead of all the realms: the fallen soldiers, the sacrifices, the incidental victims of accidents and disease - this grand solution had taken them, and the power and reach of the Council had kept a lid on it all.

Her resolve wavered. What was the point of taking revenge for the truly forever dead? She looked away from Circe, staring down at a soggy bag of some unknown alchemical dust her advance on the sorceress had blasted to the floor. "The Council will stand with you, of course. And since that is undeniable, it matters not what I do," Mazu reasoned. Circe shook out the skirt of her sodden dress.

"Perhaps you are less of a fool than it appears," she said, victory coloring her voice. Circe's eyes darted to D'Molay's knife, which had fallen near her. Her hand slowly reached out to take it. Mazu noticed the movement, and recognized the object.

"You are nothing but a filthy, thieving rat and this is a plague house. It is time to wash away the evil you have bred here," Mazu said bitterly.

She closed her eyes for a second, calling upon all waters connected to

the witch's retreat to augment her watery form. A tide of water burst through every door in the brewing chamber while smaller founts split the walls and sprayed wildly. The dagger was flushed from Circe's fingers. In moments, the chamber became a roiling lake polluted with Circe's herbs and poisons. As if reliving the epic battles of the past, the goddesses fell to bitter fighting, while the only living things around them, the rats, struggled desperately out of the room for the minor goal of continued life.

"Damn you! I'll kill you, you watery hag!" Circe screeched in fury as Mazu and her waters began to destroy her workshop. She thrust her hand back toward the stacked urns of soul-saturated blood as an orange ball of fire formed at her fingertips. Spinning, she pitched it at the stack. The fireball ricocheted from one container to the next, breaking each pot open. Residual sparks from the ball drifted between the droplets, magically suspending the liberated blood in mid-air as the missile finished its work.

Mazu surged toward Circe, attempting to douse the strange, glowing blood. Before she could act, Circe danced so smoothly into the bright red rain that Mazu suspected she had enchanted her lower body into some aquatic form. Circe raised her arms, spun like a dolphin leaping from the sea, and drew the blood's energy into her body.

"You waste your power!" Circe yelled. The water rose high enough to lap against her breasts, yet she showed no fear. "I do the will of the gods. I cannot be stopped for long. Accept it!"

Mazu suddenly felt the waters change around her. Looking down, she saw swirls of blood, washed from the inner walls of the urns, corkscrewing toward her. Shards of power that had escaped Circe's grasp came to Mazu, as if the lost souls desired to see a more even duel between the goddess and the witch. Mazu recoiled, horrified at the prospect of complicity in the crime against mortal destiny.

"Drink, goddess," Circe ordered, "or I will force life water down your wizened throat." The sorceress threw out her arms again and the doors of the room, along with a high window, burst open. Water poured out through these spillways as the workshop began to drain. Mazu heard shouts of alarm coming from other areas of the compound as the water flooded in. The sounds caused no pain or alarm to Circe, who continued her taunts. "Still not thirsty? I think I hear my servants drowning. You could save them if you stop the water. But no matter. I'll just take their blood to replace the stock you've ruined."

A furious gasp escaped Mazu's lips. Anger and frustration beyond any level she had ever experienced welled up in her heart. Before she even realized what she was doing, she completely opened herself to the lure of the blood in the water. The energy powered her liquid body to towering heights. Her head burst through several stories of Circe's lair. At her feet, the witch stared up at her, shock upon her face. Circe cringed, throwing up an energy field to protect herself as Mazu lifted a foot to stomp down upon her. As the crush of the waters fell down, Mazu saw a ball of light shoot away into the next flooded room. She pursued Circe, caring not for the destruction she caused. Mazu no longer had to consciously call upon the waters to assist her. She had become a powerful magnet for nature, every trickle of every spring, every current of every local river, surging to her. Experiencing more power than she had ever felt before, Mazu gave in. She let the forces carry her forward, taking down everything in her path. Mazu closed her eyes, no longer feeling guilt or rage or purpose. A fleeting thought of how freeing it would be to let this carry her away, forever, tempted her to do just that. But the sudden image of a man with a horse's head stood in the way of that release.

She could not abandon D'Molay. Instead of casting herself into the oblivion of the waters, Mazu directed her body against the relentless current that was bringing down Circe's secret stronghold. At first, she feared the tide would present too much of a barrier for her to return to the general area where she had seen the imprisoned, bewitched, men. But there was nectar in the water, urns and urns of it that had been released from the broken vessels during her battle with Circe. Mazu could not avoid swimming through it, and as she did, she felt her body sucking it in greedily. Her strength surged, her powers increased. The contact with the abundant water of life was a heady pleasure and Mazu experienced the thrill to which Helios was addicted. Anguish from her knowledge of the nectar's source was compounded by her inability to avoid its touch.

The nectar empowered her greatly. Mazu sensed she would be a far stronger goddess for as long as the effect lasted; she hoped she could put the evil boon to good use.

<hr />

*D'*Molay could smell horses and the blood. His arm was weary, his hand felt leaden from the weight of his sword. He was exhausted, confused. Old battle companions and enemies appeared and disappeared before his eyes, and other faces that seemed somehow familiar but to which he could put no name tried to speak to him from time to time. Dreams and reality seemed to be shifting without distinction. Sometimes he thought he was the horse; sometimes he thought he was the blood. He stared with a troubled spirit down at the hard, black hoof that seemed to be his hand. D'Molay felt simultaneously alive, dead, mad and sane. Then he felt the rain. He heard a voice in his head that said, "Drink the rain from the heavens above."

He lifted his heavy head to the ceiling, allowing the moisture to slide over his skin. A trickle of dark liquid worked its way into the corner of his mouth. D'Molay tasted its bitterness, a strong flavor that caused him to recoil, shaking his head. The sudden motion brought everything to a point of clarity. He no longer felt lost in a fog of dreams. His situation was quite clear. He was a captive, as were other men in the cells he could see by some torches, which were beginning to sputter out from water dripping from the ceiling of the room.

Realizing where he now was, D'Molay banged on the cell doors and screamed to be let out.

An extremely muscular Nubian man walked over to the cell. He was excited, a joyous expression on his face. "I don't know how you did this, D'Molay, but we are all cured - I am no longer a hyena!" He shoved a key into the lock and opened the door. D'Molay grasped the forearm of his rescuer in a salute of thanks and the dark man nodded back, satisfied with his own efforts.

"You're Celias, but why - "

"I was trapped here just like you, long ago. Do you think I wanted to be a man-beast? Here, take this key and unlock all the cells. I'm going to the dungeons to check on the others. Go up those stairs and find your way out of this place. Get as far from here as you can, but hurry, the waters are rising everywhere!"

Wasting no time, D'Molay started to unlock all the cells as the water continued to pour down from above.

"The water from the ceiling is a cure, drink it!" D'Molay called out to any that had not already discovered this fact. As he opened the cells, he saw a warrior of noble appearance whose body was crisscrossed by the marks of a whip pick up a mouse and hold the small animal's head so that it was struck by the dripping water. The mouse began to squirm and grow, changing back into a man.

A lad raced in from another chamber. "You won't believe it!" he told an older man with enough of a resemblance to be his uncle, if not his father. "The waterwheel is spinning backwards!"

D'Molay joined several others who followed the young man to see this wonder. Just as he had said, a wooden wheel drew water from some underground source and propelled it upwards for an unknown purpose.

Calling out to the assembled men, D'Molay bellowed, "Follow me up the stairs - we have to get out of here before the waters drown us all!"

"Yes, we have to run before she catches us again!" called out the man who had been a mouse.

Sounding their agreement, the men grouped together and headed up the stairs and back toward a corridor that stretched away from the prison chamber. They quickly traversed a flight of stone stairs. On the landing, a strong stream of water raced inexplicably along the floor.

"Upstream or down?" wondered a Celt with a large moustache. He grinned at the others. "Trouble sends me to the highlands, so up I go." He strode into the current, waving for everyone to follow him. D'Molay took up the rear of the group and urged everyone along - for a time. When they reached a part of Circe's lair that he recognized, he split off and headed for his room. His last memory of it was Kira serving him some wine, perhaps the potion that changed him into a monster. He dodged around several corners, and up another staircase, encouraged by a lesser amount of water under his feet. By the time he reached the chamber in which Kira had entertained him, the waters was only knee high. His belongings sat safe and dry on a table, including the bottle of antidote for Scylla. *Damn, Circe has my knife! There's no time to look for it now...* He gathered his clothes and rushed back out as a great rumble shook the hall.

D'Molay staggered back against a wall, watching in alarm as a great crack appeared in the floor as a cascade of water rose. He hurried back the way he had come, dodging other panicked people who had been driven out by the flood. Two of the women screamed from within a room filling with water, its doorway mostly blocked by part of the ceiling that had dropped. D'Molay quickly calculated that the water would lift them enough to swim over the barrier if they kept their heads; he said a quick prayer for them as he hurried on.

The water rose quickly. Cushions, baskets, and soggy parchments tangled around D'Molay's knees. He ducked under an ornate archway just before it collapsed, allowing another wave of water from the heights to intrude. A torrent pounded behind him, flushing him off his feet and carrying him on. He was not alone. There were bodies in the water. A tangle of limbs coasted along with a raft of shattered furniture. A dead woman's face bobbed briefly before him; he realized it was Kira. He made the sign of the cross on his chest and quickly prayed for a safe journey for her soul, but that was all he could do as the waters continued to rise. In contrast to the death, several waterfowl zipped happily along, their quacking barely audible above the rush of water. He wondered if they were transformed men or lucky ducks that had been destined for a future meal.

He finally caught up with the other captives. They had made their way onto a large stone balcony that overlooked the plain where he had fought the harpies with Sophia, and beyond that, the forest. Here they were safe from the flood. The excess water poured across the balcony to drain over the edge of the precipice. D'Molay hailed them.

"Is there a way down? We can't go back," he said as he quickly began to dress. "Everything is collapsing."

"If there is, we haven't found it," admitted the Celt who'd led the group.

"Look for ropes, spikes, things we can lash together," D'Molay suggested. The men began rummaging through the debris that was being pushed onto the balcony.

He felt a slight turn, as if someone had grabbed him by the shoulders and faced him in a different direction. D'Molay stared at the ridgeline beyond the balcony and saw a lonely apple tree growing at the end of the cliff. He was immediately reminded of Aavi's fondness for apples. Quickly climbing down the balcony, he ran to the tree and then looked over the cliff side. He discovered that a stairway, well-disguised by a heavy growth of vines, was cut into the side of the cliff. He called out, waving to the men. "Over here!"

With freedom in sight, the mood lightened as the men hurried down to the woods, the sound of falling water echoing behind them. Looking back at Circe's compound, D'Molay saw walls collapsing as huge crests of water crashed against the buildings and rushed down into the valley below. He had never seen such a flood of wild water in his many years. "We need to steer clear of the valley. Those waters are deadly," he advised the men.

"Perhaps if you were yet a horse," Celias grinned, "you could run faster."

"And I'd beat you all if I still had my wings," bragged the Celt. "Hey, mouse, race you to the cheese!"

D'Molay might have smiled at their good fortune, but was too saddened by what he had seen inside the compound. The men he was with had been luckily restored, but what about the many others that Circe kept inside? He surely would have drowned if he had not been relieved of the head of a stallion and its heavy hooves. What had been Circe's purpose in turning him into such a monster? He philosophically pondered his role as a horse in the grand scheme of nature. Was he just a hauler of burdens and a carrier of his fellow men? And still he wondered what Circe had been doing will all those thousands of urns filled with blood. It was something he couldn't stop thinking about. He'd have to talk it over with Mazu. D'Molay suspected she must have had something to do with the flooding. And Aavi had been close at hand to aid him as well. This gave him a warm feeling of well-being as they all descended.

At the base of the carved stairs, he bid farewell to his temporary allies and warned them to watch out for the harpies and the still raging waters. He then struck back into the woods, retracing his journey from the spot where he had been carried off as best he could. "With luck, and perhaps a little more help from Aavi, I'll find my way back to Mazu or Sophia," he said to himself.

 small but expensive pleasure boat launched from the one remaining functional public dock at the base of the Palace

of Helios. Port access was always limited, for the king had priorities other than upkeep of his docks. It had become a running joke between the dock master and his decreasing company of shipwrights that the port would sink into the lake before King Helios diverted one coin from his wardrobe budget to its needs. From the second story window of his office, the dock master watched today's boatload of courtiers set out for a floating picnic. The silver and gold trim on their hats and cloaks sparkled brightly, belying the poverty of the kingdom.

". . . Uh, sir?"

The dock master turned, finding one of his men standing in the open doorway. He waved him in. "What is it? More complaints about late pay from the warehousemen?"

"It's the water. It's up."

"Up? What do you mean, up?"

The man shrugged, his weatherworn blue shirt lumping around his armpits. "Come look at the gauge."

The dock master, a dark-skinned man of middle age, followed the man downstairs. He was skeptical of his report, having seen the lake waters rise significantly only a few times in his career. Usually it was due to heavy rainfall, but occasionally the local naiads took offense at some human transgression and churned up the fresh water springs. Wondering how he might appease the nymphs if this were the case, he stepped out into the bright sunny day. A knot of men surrounded a bronze post sticking out of the water that lapped at the dock supports. Height lines notched into the pole were rapidly being submerged.

"Achilo," the owner of a trading ship hailed the dock master. "What do you think of this?"

Achilo took a close look and was alarmed by the water height indicated on the gauge. "When did this begin?" he asked the men, turning angrily to the underling who had come to his office. "How long did you wait before telling me?"

"I swear, it was only up three inches when I fetched you," the messenger insisted. "Right? Didn't I go at that exact moment?" He looked to the others, hoping they would confirm his story. Several of them nodded in support of his words. "Tell us what to do," he said, as the rest also indicated their readiness to confront the odd problem. Achilo scratched his head, looking up and down along the lakefront. High water could flood dozens of important operations, but to save any of them he had to choose which had the highest priority. Achilo didn't particularly like the conclusion to which he came, but settled his mind on it nonetheless.

The royal boat had sat unused for many months and was not in top condition. He ticked off its weaknesses in his head: rail rot, thinning sails, freshwater barnacle accretion. "See to the King's ship," the dock master ordered. "Get it ready to pull away. Make sure its mooring lines don't snap," he called after them. His command would keep the men busy while he tried to figure out what was happening. He watched the gauge. The water covered another notch.

"Where is it coming from?" he asked aloud. He looked to the horizon for storm clouds, to the hills for a sudden melting of high snow. No explanation could be seen. His feet suddenly felt wet. Looking down, he saw water seeping up through the boardwalk. Two shipwrights walked briskly toward him, their sandals flapping loudly over the growing puddles.

"Our shops are flooding," a young apprentice said. The teenager seemed rather amused by the strange event, but his master found nothing funny about it.

"We need to get the ships out. Now." This man, a white-haired, sun-tanned elder, pointed to a dozen boats bobbing nearby. The rising tide was lifting them from their places. If nothing was done and their moorings and anchors held, they would be swamped. If their lines snapped, they would be carried and dashed wherever the flood decreed. Achilo made another decision.

"Do it. Take all the sailors and boatmen you can find and get as many vessels as you can a safe distance away. But not too far. They might be needed. I'll go tell the king." The shipwrights hurried off as Achilo headed toward the steps that led up from the boardwalk to the lowest main street that circled beneath King Helios' palace on the island hill.

The local people he strode quickly past showed no alarm. They worked in a numb way indicative of the daily boredom and the spirit of decline that plagued the kingdom. Young mothers, vigorously tending their stewpots to keep their men and children fed, squatted by open doors and glanced wistfully at Achilo and his freedom to go where he willed. A few beggars held out their dirty cups as he hurried past, but he gave none a coin in return. Taking a shortcut behind a stinking butcher shop, Achilo darted through the backdoor of a dressmaker's operation and out its front, the annoyed complaints of several seamstresses following him. This put his feet on a wider avenue that led to the palace gate. He rehearsed a speech in his head as he approached the one guard who patrolled the entrance.

"Send for a - "

Only those three words passed Achilo's lips before the ground beneath his feet began to violently shake. He staggered back as the stones under his sandals lifted unevenly. He remained upright for a moment longer than the guard, perhaps due to his experience aboard heaving ships at sea. His balance failed him, however, when forceful blasts of water exploded through cracks that suddenly fractured the road. He fell, rolling down a hard slope that had been a flat walkway just a moment before, tearing the skin on his arms and legs as he tried to stop. His feet found purchase against the side of a wood frame building; he reached up, found an open window, and wrapped an arm over the sill. Like a crab, he clung with one strong limb to his haven as the street twisted and crumbled around him into a churning torrent. People tumbled past him now, half submerged, screaming. Finery from the palace swept by in a violent, aquatic parade. Beautiful fabrics, royal crests, hats and regal slippers embellished the flood. Achilo felt the wall he hugged shift and tip, falling toward him. He ducked through the window opening as a great section of the building smacked the water. Pulling himself onto a section of broken wooden wall which was now no more than a rickety raft, he was carried back toward the lake. Chunks of his platform sheared off as it collided with other debris. He could feel himself being lifted higher and higher in the air, the water rising inconceivably fast. He shout-

ed a prayer to Brizo, which, years later, he told his grandchildren accounted for his survival. When he was finally rescued by one of the boats he had wisely sent away from the island, he could hardly believe what he saw behind him. Only one flag from the tallest roofline of Helios' palace still stood to mark the existence of the settlement. It drooped, motionless, as if grieving for the utter destruction of the king's island home.

Chapter 12

Darkness

The darkness was total, engulfing. Time had become meaningless. Set pulled with all his might at the mystically charged restraints on his arms and legs, but it was no use. They would not yield, even to the strength of a god. He was trapped, deep underground, in a sealed chamber, chained to a throne. Set was the king of empty, black nothingness.

With his thoughts his only entertainment, he cursed Ares in all his forms. He planned horrible tortures to repay him for this captivity, but even the worst punishment he could think of seemed too light a sentence. His only comfort lay in his imagining Ares' agonized screams as he pictured the wounds he would inflict if - no, when - he caught the god in a similar trap. Set enjoyed the brutal acts that filled his mind, relishing every faux cry of his enemy. But eventually, a faint noise that was not of his brain's creation sounded on the other side of the heavy door.

Set came to attention, pulling against his bonds in the stone chair, listening. He strained to hear more, but there was nothing. He began to think he had imagined the tapping. Time passed.

Then out of the darkness came words. "I enjoyed watching your dreams," said a familiar voice that seemed to come from nowhere, yet everywhere. "Please don't stop them on my account."

Set welcomed a liberator, even if it was Satan. He had dealt with the Heavenly Realm's outcast before, and had him to thank for knowing where and when the angel Aavi would be crossing the realms with the beast. That information had allowed Set and his allies to intercept her on her way to Earth. That mission, he thought bitterly, had led to his current predicament.

He felt anxiety flare in his gut. He had never negotiated with Satan from such a lowly position. Even when he was free with all power in hand, he knew little about him, save that he was extremely dangerous. Satan's appearance was a shifting mask of deceit. Sometimes he looked like an Egyptian pharaoh of old Earth, other times more brutish with animalistic features. Here in the darkness, where Set could see nothing, the mask Satan chose to wear for this visit mattered little.

Set took a deep breath to steady his voice and replied with a feigned boredom. "Those scenes will be more enjoyable in reality. Free me, and you can watch."

Satan's soft laughter filled the chamber. "It's within my power to do so. But I need a better reason than that."

Set immediately understood. There had to be a price for his liberation. "What do want from me?"

"That's a good question. What is freedom worth to you?"

Set was slow to answer. A trickster himself, he knew the danger of promises. Satan was impatient.

"If you prefer, I can leave and you can hope someone else will come along. Ares might return. Someday," Satan replied from the darkness. Set still had yet to see him.

"Wait. I'll give you what you want. Release me." Set waited tensely.

"You don't know what I want. Are you certain?"

"Yes. I don't care. I want out!"

"Very well, Set. I accept your generous offer."

The bonds dissolved, the door opened, and the chamber around him disappeared as if his prison had been merely an illusion. Set stood blinking in the harsh desert sun, alone. He briefly wondered when Satan would again appear to collect his debt, but Set had a more pressing concern. He needed to get out of this realm before Ares found him again. He needed sanctuary. He needed Egyptos.

Konohana stood with Zeus in the center of the Council Hall, watching as her ladies began the task of removing her banner from its place of honor. Her colors hung far above the dais, suspended by the finest spun golden cord. In tandem, two of her women leapt upward, defying the gravity that pinned normal humans to the ground by powers granted by their family's dragon bloodline. Their

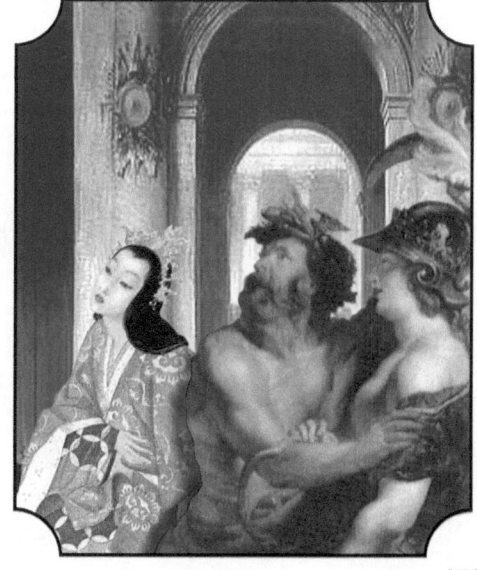

short knives flashed and the flag fell in artistic ripples as the dragon-girls glided down in pursuit.

"Are you sure you need to take them back with you?" Zeus asked with a wink. "I'll miss those two."

Konohana knew Zeus' fancy for her ladies would be easily transferred to the next pretty thing that graced the hall; she felt no regret at depriving him. "They need to return to my realm and their father's house," she told him. "He has been waiting my entire term to introduce them to their bridegrooms."

Zeus clasped his hands behind his back, the topic of marriage dampening his interest. It made him think of his own rocky relationship with Hera. "I see. Then I hope those men will be worth the wait." He continued to watch as the women carefully folded Konohana's banner. They then took hold of another long piece of fabric and flew back up to the ceiling to hang it in the empty space. This streamer featured a short poem in honor of Konohana's service, a traditional gift to those leaving the Council. Zeus was about to ask Konohana if she was pleased by the verse when a commotion erupted. Hearing a familiar voice shouting his name, Zeus turned toward one of the alcove doors to see his son Pollux knocking the chamber guards aside with his powerful fists, like a ball rolling through ninepins.

"Pollux, really," Zeus boomed at him, the gleam of fatherly pride in his eye almost completely negating the impact of his chastisement. "What have I told you about boxing mortals?"

"Sorry, Father. But they're in my way!" He raised his great fist toward the last knot of men. They wisely dodged and retreated, leaving Zeus to deal with his son's violation of protocol.

"What's so urgent, boy?" he asked as Pollux strode to his side, words flying from his lips.

"I've come from the lake of Helios. His palace is gone! The water around the island rose and - "

Zeus raised an exasperated hand. "Slow down. Just tell me exactly what ridiculous thing that old wretch has done this time. I thought putting him on his own island would keep him out of trouble. Apollo warned me it wouldn't be that simple. I should have listened."

Pollux shifted impatiently from one foot to the other through the entirety of Zeus' tirade, jumping in again eagerly when he got a chance. "It's not his fault. Someone else caused the flood. All but a few of his court are dead! Some sailors in an overloaded boat called upon me for help, and that's when I saw everything with my own eyes. I even fished Helios out of the water myself!"

"What!? He was attacked?" Zeus' countenance darkened. "Who would dare strike Olympia, especially now?"

Konohana gently interjected. "This is terrible news. I will inform Quetzalcoatl and Shiva."

As she left them, Zeus put an arm around Pollux's shoulder and pulled him in close. "What did Helios have to say? Does he know who caused this?" Zeus spoke quietly, hoping to keep whatever passed between them confidential. Pollux picked up on the cue and whispered back.

"He was so drunk on nectar I couldn't make sense of his story," Pollux

said. "He was crazier than I'd ever seen him."

Zeus nodded, as if appreciating his son's words. He carefully inquired about survivors. "Yes, he's quite mad. Did he happen to say anything about . . . what of his children? Did they escape? How about his eldest, Circe?"

Pollux shrugged. "I don't know. Do you want me to go back and check?" He smiled broadly. "I could fetch Castor and we could go together!"

Despite Pollux's enthusiasm for any excuse for an outing with his brother, Zeus denied his request. "No. There's a quicker way. Hermes!"

The moment he called for his messenger, Hermes appeared. "What is your will," he asked, in a dry, arch voice. The wings at his heels and on his cap beat continually, like the blur of a hummingbird's wings.

"There's been a disaster at the Palace of Helios. I want a report. I want each and every member of Helios' family found, along with any information you can glean about what happened there."

The corners of Hermes' mouth canted up slightly as he listened to the order. "Understood. Helios has always been a beacon for trouble. If not for his kingdom's main export, we'd be better off without him."

Hermes flashed away before Zeus could object to his opinion.

"Say, Father. What is his kingdom's main export?" Pollux asked.

"Nectar, or life water as some of the other realms call it," Zeus said lightly after a short, irritated pause. "It would be a shame to lose the convenience of having it produced within the borders of our own realm. But, I'm sure everything will be righted in a short time." He said nothing more, hoping his son would take his silence as a hint to leave, but Pollux lingered, gawking at the colorful banners and the other trappings of the Council Hall. He was still there when Hermes, by grace of his amazing speed, reappeared. Zeus did not like the serious look that had replaced the normal snideness that often played across his face.

"So? What have you to say?"

"Complete destruction of the palace and the mortal children of the king. The workshop of Circe in the caverns of the Aeaean Mountains is a total loss. Some of her servants who escaped say there was a battle there between the witch and another deity."

"Who?" Pollux asked eagerly, always interested in any type of combat, be it between gods or men.

"If I could ask her, I could tell you," Hermes replied, high snark returning to his voice. "Circe has disappeared. I cannot say if she still exists."

Zeus turned slowly away from Hermes and Pollux lest they notice the raw concern spreading across his face. After he had composed himself and replaced his fear with a mask of anger, he turned back. "You both may go. I must confer with the other Councilors about what is to be done."

He looked toward Shiva, Konohana and Quetzalcoatl who waited for him on the dais. The first two wore expressions of curiosity and sadness, respectively. In the Mayan's case, Zeus was infuriated by an expression he interpreted as outright amusement at the Olympian pantheon's newest problem. The election season had just become exponentially more complex.

<hr />

Molay was soon himself again, the strange feeling of being half animal faded. He had moved quickly into the forest, not stop-

ping to see if he would find Sophia's body at the site of their battle with the harpies. He wished above all that she had survived, but if she had perished, at least she'd died in a manner fitting to her Amazon heritage. Right now, he had to focus on his own survival.

Several times during the day he heard harpies screeching and circling overhead, causing him to take cover until they had passed. It was ironic that the creatures that had been so elusive on his way to the mountains were now showing themselves. The odd flood must have flushed them from their hiding places. D'Molay cursed himself for giving up his dagger to Circe, which left him without any weapon for defense. Stealth and speed were the only tools he had at hand. That night, he slept under a large tree on soft grass. He was cold and hungry, but it was far preferable to the cell and the horrible, helpless feeling of his body changing. He had a nightmare of transforming again, but Aavi appeared and healed him with her embrace.

The next day D'Molay continued further east and finally found one of the crosses he'd carved on a tree. He gave thanks to God that he had not relied only on Sophia's guidance during their journey. He wondered how long he had been changed and imprisoned by the witch. *Had Mazu tried to follow my trail?* He suspected she had. The watery demise of Circe's lair supported that, but it was not like Mazu to be a force of destruction. Then he wondered if Aavi had discovered a way to do something against his enemy. Thoughts of the two women who had been so significant in his recent life filled his mind as he continued through the woods. However, neither one of them was the first familiar face he discovered. D'Molay was drawn by the wondrous aroma of food cooking and found Quan. Mazu's servant whirled toward him, clutching a hot stick he'd been using to poke the campfire as D'Molay stepped out of the trees.

"There you are!" Quan exclaimed. "Where's Mazu?"

D'Molay strode over to the pot hanging over the fire and started scooping out a spoonful of stew. He was ravenous. He spoke to Quan between appreciative bites.

"I haven't seen her. How long has she been gone?"

"Only a day," Quan said, looking glum. "She went to rescue you."

"I'm pretty sure she did. I was saved by a timely flood. That probably wasn't a coincidence."

"Of course she saved you," Quan decided. "That is what she always does."

D'Molay ate most of the stew and then rested against a tree as Quan regaled him with tales of his dangerous journey through the dark woods.

A few hours later, Mazu appeared from somewhere behind the men. Quan's face lit up with happiness and D'Molay's was only slightly less pleased.

"Quan, pick up the camp," she said, forgoing any greetings. "We must leave as quickly as possible."

D'Molay took a good look at her. He immediately realized she looked younger and more vital then he had ever seen her before. She also seemed upset and withdrawn. "Mazu, you look so... different. Was it you that flooded Circe's lair?"

"I did what was necessary."

"How did you - "

Mazu shook her head. "I have no desire and we have no time to discuss all the details," she said. D'Molay watched her gaze shift to her hands, as if she didn't want to meet his eyes. She reached into her robe. "I retrieved this for you."

She held out his dagger.

"Mazu, Thank you! I had to trade it to Circe to get the antidote for Scylla." D'Molay hoped that announcement would spark some hope for success in their quest, but Mazu remained subdued and said nothing as Quan banged about the camp loading up the horses. D'Molay tried to draw her out. "I've lost everything but the clothes on my back. Getting my dagger means everything."

"Ha! I wish you'd lost everything," Quan said. D'Molay looked over and saw him struggling to load all the gear he'd taken on the hunt with Sophia onto one of the horses.

"How did you get my things back?" D'Molay asked.

"Sophia brought them," Mazu said. "We ran into each other as we followed you and she returned to Dioscrias."

"She survived? Thank God!" D'Molay was beginning to think their luck was truly turning. "You should have seen her shooting harpies." The memories of their battle sobered D'Molay slightly. "We'll need to be extremely careful on our way back. I've had to hide from harpies all the way here."

A short time later, D'Molay put his warning into practice. He guided Mazu and Quan through the woods, staying slightly off the trail under cover of the deep forest. Circe's harpies could be heard and glimpsed overhead from time to time. D'Molay often made Mazu and Quan stop to hide in brambles or among the rocks until the sky was empty.

As they waited behind a dense thicket, D'Molay prayed silently to himself for safe passage back to Dioscrias. A familiar voice responded.

I hear your prayers and I am with you.

D'Molay almost answered out loud, but he managed to keep his mouth shut as a harpy's shadow crossed over him. He twisted in his saddle, looking all around for Aavi, but this time he could not see her, even when she spoke again.

Wait. I will tell you when the way is clear.

A minute passed. Quan was watching D'Molay, waiting for a sign that it was safe to move on. Mazu gave him a curious look, having noticed him turning to and fro. Fortunately, Aavi then said all was well and he was able to ride out of the thicket before Mazu could ask any questions. Aavi continued to whisper to him throughout the day whenever danger was nearby. D'Molay was almost able to relax knowing that she was watching over them. But when the trees began to thin out the situation changed.

Aavi appeared in front of D'Molay, obviously very distressed. "You must ride as fast as you can. They have seen you!"

D'Molay sat staring at her for a moment, stunned to see her and a little slow to react to her message. Mazu must have noticed the odd look on his face because she stopped too, while Quan's horse plodded on. D'Molay snapped out of his shock.

"Harpies!" he warned Quan and Mazu. He pointed to a cliff about a half a league ahead. "Head for that cliff face! Use what trees there are as cover!"

As they all charged forward, Aavi flew along beside D'Molay.

"How many are there?" D'Molay called out.

"Half a dozen, perhaps more. If only I could stop them," Aavi replied in frustration.

"Just let me know where they are and how close," he said as he pushed his mount for more speed.

"D'Molay, are you talking to me?" Mazu called. "I can't - "

"Move to the left! One is diving at you!" Aavi cried out. D'Molay immediately pulled the reins, forcing his horse to the left. He drew his knife and slashed wildly in the air, hoping to slice the harpy in two as it dove at him. The creature was completely taken by surprise, neither expecting him to turn so suddenly nor attack. His knife caught the harpy's talons and cut both its legs off as it rushed past him. It plunged head first into the rocky ground after missing its target, dying instantly on impact. Wasting no time, D'Molay pushed his horse forward once again. Mazu and Quan were in front of him now; just where he wanted them to be.

"Keep going for the cliff! Look for a ledge, a cave, anywhere you can get cover. I'll be right behind you!" He shoved his knife back in its scabbard and reached for his bow.

"Two more are about to dive!" he heard Aavi warn him.

With the bow in one hand, he pivoted the horse around to face the oncoming attackers. He scanned the blue sky and saw the silhouettes of the two harpies heading toward them. Stopping the horse, he put the reins in his mouth, grabbed an arrow and notched it, taking careful aim. As they got within range, he took his first shot, which missed its target, but forced one of the she-birds to veer off to avoid the oncoming arrow.

The other one continued its dive. D'Molay managed to grab another arrow. There wasn't time to use it on the bow. Instead, he attempted to plunge it into the harpy as it dove at him. The creature sailed overhead and flew towards Mazu.

"Mazu behind you!" he cried out. She turned and blasted the harpy with a stream of water, causing it to fall to the ground, stunned. D'Molay drove his mount towards the cliffs once again, trying to bridge the gap separating him from his companions before the harpies made another attack.

Quan saw refuge ahead and frantically pointed toward it as he spoke. "There's a small canyon! I bet harpies can't get in there!"

"It's narrow, yes, that looks good," D'Molay replied.

Aavi appeared near D'Molay again. "No! It's not! Go to that outcropping a little bit further that way. What you need will be there."

"Are you sure?"

"Yes, it's where you need to go," Aavi told D'Molay with a degree of certainty that left no doubt.

"Wait - make for that outcropping!"

"But you just said the canyon was good!" Quan retorted, confused by D'Molay's contradiction.

"Just do it!"

"Do as he says, Quan!" Mazu ordered. "And hope he explains later."

Aavi flew alongside their horses. Her presence seemed to make the animals even lighter on their feet. "You must hurry! They are going to dive again!"

D'Molay pushed his horse all the harder, as the cliffs loomed closer. "Come on . . . Come on . . ."

Mazu and Quan made it under the ledge as several harpies swooped down. Aavi shoved D'Molay off his horse just as a harpy's claws raked the back of his mount. The animal stumbled and fell hard onto the rocks. D'Molay rolled across the ground, landing safely under the cover of the ledge while the other harpy joined its sister in attacking the injured horse. Quan and Mazu grabbed his arms, pulling him further away from the carnage. D'Molay got up and brushed himself off, completely unharmed.

"How did you do that? It was inhuman! You should be broken in a dozen places," Quan exclaimed.

In truth, he wasn't really certain what had transpired. One minute he was riding and the next he was flying off his horse. "I think I had some help." He stared at the dead horse as the harpies feasted on it. Aavi, floating nearby, turned away from the scene in pity and disgust.

"That poor creature," she whispered.

D'Molay could live with the loss of his horse, but not the things it had been carrying. "Mazu, can you distract them? I want to recover my bow and arrows."

"Of course." She pointed her hand at the harpies and blasted them each with water. D'Molay immediately ran out, grabbed his bow and traveling bag, and returned to the safety of the outcropping.

"I must admit, I'm beginning to enjoy shooting at those things," Mazu said grimly.

"That's good, because I doubt we've seen the last of them. At least now they can only come at us straight on." D'Molay notched an arrow to be ready for the next attack.

They watched as more harpies landed to investigate the dead horse. After a few minutes of squabbling with those who had got there first, three of them dodged toward the shelter. D'Molay immediately let loose an arrow, piercing one of the harpies through its torso. It fell to the ground making an earsplitting death screech. Mazu blasted the other two with water, sending them sprawling back.

Aavi looked at the dead harpy with sorrow on her perfect face. "Poor, tortured creature. I wonder what has brought it to this fate?"

"I'm sorry. It's us or them." D'Molay replied. He wondered if Aavi saw the harpies as distant cousins in some way, as like her, they were winged and female.

"Sorry? Why is he sorry?" Quan asked Mazu as he and his horse huddled behind hers.

Aavi's face became like a mask as she looked off into the distance. "Nonetheless, it is painful to see their deaths. You are safe for now. I can do no more." She began to fade away.

"Wait! Don't go yet!" D'Molay pleaded.

Quan looked even more confused. "Who's going anywhere?"

"He isn't talking to us, Quan, and you had best get used to it. He's talking to someone neither you nor I can see."

"I told you he was crazy," Quan asserted. "Why did we go here? The place I picked was larger than this cramped spot, and was probably safer."

D'Molay ignored him as he picked off the remaining harpies with his arrows then got on his knees. He leaned out, checking for any others lurking overhead.

"Quan's question is a good one, D'Molay," Mazu said. "Perhaps you should answer it."

"That's the advice Aavi gave me, so I took it."

"I see," Mazu said neutrally. "And what do you advise now?"

D'Molay pointed upward. "They're still up there circling. The longer we wait here, the sooner they'll bring reinforcements. Let's follow this opening and see where it leads." He was playing a hunch. Why would Aavi abandon him here if there wasn't another way out?

160

Quan, who eagerly led the way along the hillside away from the harpy threat, was the first to find it. "Mistress! There's a door!"

Seconds later they all stood in front of a large arch with a stone door that was built into the cliff. It was about nine feet high and eight feet wide. Next to the arch was a smoother rock face where Greek style letters had been carved. D'Molay ran his hand across them, spelling out a word. "N E K P O U A V I E O V."

"What does it say?" Quan asked nervously.

"Necro . . . I don't know the rest," D'Molay said. "Necro means dark or under. It's the name of something, maybe it's a tomb or a place to keep valuables, though this is an odd place for either. Usually they're near a town or a temple complex."

"It must be a tomb. We shouldn't go in!" Quan exclaimed

"But this must be why Aavi guided us here. It's a way to escape."

Quan rolled his eyes. "Can't you just ask her?"

D'Molay turned his attention to the door, and began feeling around for a way to open it. "No. She isn't here at the moment."

Quan started to make a scoffing sound which abruptly turned into an alarmed squawk as he noticed the silhouettes of harpies scrambling up the path toward them.

D'Molay pushed harder on the door as the harpies screeching got louder and louder. "It's locked."

Mazu took a defensive position, throwing blasts of water as several harpies jumped at them. "Both of you look for a handle or a lever!" she cried.

The men's hands pressed and pounded every inch of the door and its arched frame as Mazu fought the harpies. There was no ring to pull, no key slot. It didn't seem to be counterweighted or operated by a hidden switch. At last, D'Molay found a small, round niche carved into the stone door frame about six feet high. It suddenly dawned on him what it was. He grabbed the Council seal he wore around his neck.

"I found it!"

The harpies swarmed forward. Mazu sprayed most of them and Quan's panicked horse managed to kick one senseless. "If you are going to do something, you must do it now," Mazu called out, as a harpy jumped up on top of her horse, which reared in terror and threw it off. Holding the Council seal, D'Molay placed it in the niche by the door. It was a perfect fit. The ancient doors made a creaking sound as their bronze hinges groaned and the doors opened inward.

"Get in! "Bring the horses!"

Quan and Mazu retreated through the doors with the horses in tow, as D'Molay removed the seal. Once he did, the doors started to close. As they were just about to shut, a harpy leapt through the gap and fell upon him. Landing on his back, D'Molay managed to kick her off. The harpy slammed back against the now-sealed doors. Seeming to realize that it was alone, its claws scrabbled along the seam where the doors met. The harpy hissed in frustration and lunged at Quan. Mazu shot a ball of water at its head, and held it there. The harpy writhed desperately as it was completely cut off from the air. It soon drowned and fell in a heap at Mazu's feet. The goddess looked to D'Molay.

"Life is certainly never dull when I'm in your company. How bad is your injury?"

"Injury?" D'Molay sat up. Until Mazu mentioned it, he hadn't realized the harpy had done anything to him. "Just some scratches and a ripped tunic. I'll be all right." To prove the point he stood up, brushing himself off. "At least we're away from them," he added, nodding at the doorway. He noticed the Council seal on the floor. Picking it up, he realized that

the cord he'd tied to it had broken during the fight and tucked the seal into one of his pockets for safe-keeping. They could hear the other harpies hammering and scratching on the other side, but his two companions had already turned their attention to the tunnel ahead.

Mazu and Quan began examining their new surroundings.

Chapter 13

Into the Depths

"Where are we?" Quan asked, looking down the long dark corridor that seemed to lead endlessly into the distance.

"I don't know. All we can do is follow this and see where it goes. The fact that it could be opened with a Council seal makes me think it's more than just a tomb," D'Molay answered

"Indeed. The realms are riddled with caverns, much like an old stump has wormwood tunnels," Mazu added. "We just have to hope that this one will take us somewhere we want to go."

Mazu led the way, a swirling bubble of water at the end of her staff glowing with a wavering blue-hued light, much like the moon's reflection from a pool of water at night. D'Molay felt like he was in an underwater grotto rather than a dry tunnel. The passage continued fairly straight ahead, but at times constricted tightly. The two men walked the horses, Quan in the middle and D'Molay acting as a rear guard.

"Why did we bring the horses?" Quan said unhappily as he tugged on the reigns of his gray mount, which was reluctant to move further along a narrow stretch of the cavern.

"They can carry our gear and if we'd left them outside, the harpies would have eaten them. When we get out the other side of wherever this goes, we'll be glad to have them," D'Molay replied as he led the other horse, a brown one with a blond mane. "They've been more use than you have," D'Molay couldn't resist adding.

Every eight feet or so, they passed arched niches in the walls, each about seven feet high and five feet wide. A small ledge carved into each niche supported an assortment of items. Mazu examined several ledges closely. She found some bones, candles, and other small personal effects like combs, seeds, beads and dried food. Picking up a decaying peacock feather, Mazu held it up. "I believe these were left for dead friends and relatives. They're too small and personal for offerings to a deity." Putting the dusty feather back where she found it, she added, "Leave these gifts alone. They are for those that have passed beyond life. It would be not be wise to rile them if they still dwell nearby."

Quan edged a little closer to the horse he was resenting just a moment before, as if it could hide him from any restless spirits.

They continued walking for hours as the corridor descended deeper and deeper underground. The corridors were now winding back and forth into the depths like a flattened spring. They passed hundreds of niches, but no visitors had braved these depths, for only bones graced the ledges.

"Any deeper and we'll find the entrance to Hades," D'Molay half joked.

"What?! Does that mean we're dead?" cried out Quan.

Mazu looked back over her shoulder at him, sternly. "Keep your voice low, ere you wake the spirits. Of course we're not dead. Many of the living have entered Hades. Even in the Asian realms we know such stories."

"I was only kidding, Mazu," D'Molay said, surprised.

"I know you were. But I suspected this was leading to the Olympian underworld for some time now. However, I saw no point in bringing it up. We are where we are," she said calmly.

"What do you mean? Are we trapped here forever?" Quan worried.

"I have no idea," Mazu said. "We need to consider what we know about Hades that might aid us in some way."

D'Molay agreed. "We've been walking for hours. Let's rest and eat something. Who knows when we'll get the chance to dine in peace down here?"

Quan got their rations and they ate a quick meal as they sat in the middle of the corridor. Readily admitting he knew nothing at all about this land of the dead, he listened with great interest to what Mazu and D'Molay had to share.

"I remember Sergius telling me some tales when we traveled together. Hercules went to Hades and returned from it, and I think some others did too. Hercules went in one entrance and came out a different one, as we hope to." D'Molay took a bite of the dried meat and a swig from the water bag.

"I have traveled some of these waters. There are several rivers that run through the underworld and I believe mortals have to pay to get across them. I'm sure there are various ways in and out of this subrealm. All of them are in Olympia, save one. Some other water god told me that long ago," Mazu recalled.

"I still have a bag of coins, Lady Mazu. So we can pay to cross the rivers, but what about the dead? Won't they want to keep us here or take our lives?" Quan asked.

"We'll have to be careful not to upset them," D'Molay counseled. "I spent centuries with the spirits in a place called Purgatory. Most of the dead are too distraught to notice anyone else, but sometimes they can be very dangerous." D'Molay actually had more concerns about who else might not let them leave the Underworld, particularly Hades or his guardians, but decided not to make things sound any worse than they already were. "Just keep trying to remember anything you've heard about the Underworld that might help."

They started off again, continuing along the dark, twisting tunnels passing uncountable niches. As they rounded a corner, they saw the figure of a man in a roman toga shuffling along. D'Molay immediately realized he was transparent.

"There's our first spirit," he whispered.

They approached slowly. The spirit was oblivious to their presence and they passed by him with no incident. "Let us hope all such denizens ignore us," Mazu said as they rounded another bend. Her wish was granted. None of the other ghosts, whose numbers grew more numerous as they continued into the depths, showed any awareness of them.

"We are fortunate, for they seem more concerned with getting to the Underworld," Mazu pointed out as a few more spirits drifted passed them.

The corridor finally ended at a set of iron gates. Beyond those, they could see a cavern, lit by fire. It seemed to go on as far as they could see. Tendrils of smoke snaked out between the bars of the gate, as if the fire was beckoning them to enter. Numerous translucent figures slowly walked in the distance.

D'Molay examined the gate. He found its winch, a heavy chain wrapped around it, four feet away. "Quan, help me get this open."

No longer needing the light from her staff, Mazu made it disappear. She took the horses' reins while the two men operated the winch and raised the gate. Once it was up, several spirits drifted through the opening while Mazu led the horses through. Quan went next. D'Molay released the chain, running to dive under the gate before it crashed to the ground with a heavy clang. He barely made it.

"We are now properly in Hades' Underworld," Mazu said, passing the reins of the horses back to Quan. Turning back to the gate, D'Molay confirmed his suspicions with a quick inspection.

"Yes. And we won't be getting out the way we came." The inward side of the iron gate had no winch or other apparatus for raising it.

"Which way do we go, Lady Mazu?" Quan asked.

"Let's find that river I told you about," she said.

D'Molay led the way as they walked on, skirting the area of fire as they followed a steady stream of spirits through the gloom. Ahead of them, the ghosts seemed to drop into the ground, but when they reached the same point they found they stood at the top of a slope that stretched down to a wide band of dark water.

"Is this the river of the dead?" Quan asked, looking down at the water. Gray mist hugged its surface, only slightly more substantial than the spirits.

"Yes. When we reach it, do not drink the water, for it would be fatal to both of you,"

"What about you?" D'Molay asked.

"I don't know. I might be fine, or the waters could end my existence. Best we not tempt fate unless we have need to. "

"Agreed." D'Molay looked back at the locked gates. They were still plainly in view, about three hundred steps from the riverbank. He watched a spirit float through the bars and enter the underworld. He realized the gates weren't meant to keep intruders out; they were meant to keep anyone from leaving. "What now?" he asked. "Do we cross?"

"We should avoid that. On the other side is the realm of the dead of Olympia. Let's follow the river and hope that it keeps going to the east," Mazu suggested

They had barely reached the bottom of the slope when Quan called out. "Something's headed this way - a boat, I think."

Out of the fog, a longboat with a single figure on board glided silently across the waters and directly towards them. Half a dozen spirits gathered on the shore, eagerly waiting.

"That must be Charon. He ferries the dead across the river Styx."

"B-but we aren't dead, mistress." Quan struggled to pull the horses away from the river as the animals reached out their necks to drink the deadly water.

"Keep it up and you will be," D'Molay taunted.

"Hush, both of you," Mazu chided.

As the boat drew closer, they could better see its pilot. Charon wore a dark hooded shroud, which made his pale complexion look almost bone white. His eyes were sunken, cupped by dark circles, and he looked like a long-dead corpse. He stood perfectly still as he propelled the craft forward using a long, gnarled pole. Only his arms moved as the boat silently slid up on the shore. Charon stared at each them in turn as if looking for something specific. He frowned.

"Why are you here? You are not dead. Do you seek someone who has passed on?" His voice was a raspy monotone. D'Molay thought that perhaps he hadn't spoken in ages.

Mazu bowed slightly as a sign of respect. "I am the goddess Mazu. We wish only to travel down river towards the west. Can you help us?"

"...No." Charon responded slowly, as if making a reply took him a great deal of consideration.

"You won't, or you can't?" D'Molay asked.

The god stared at D'Molay, but said nothing.

"Mistress, he is a ferryman," Quan said. "Perhaps we must pay him first for his aid?"

D'Molay pulled out his purse and withdrew a handful of coins. He gave them to Mazu. She showed the coins, and the ghastly master of the boat looked at them.

"Here is our fare. Can you take us down river?"

Charon extended an open hand. "Can take you across."

"Across? No, we need to go down the river," Mazu clarified. "We are trying to get to the eastern coast of Olympia, or as close as possible. Can you do that?"

"You wish a katabasis?" The hand was withdrawn. "My task is here. I go across the river, not down it."

"Please, is there nothing you can do? Like you, I am deity who ferries travelers across the water. Won't you help me, as one ferryman to another?"

"I should not."

Despite the negative answer, D'Molay noticed hesitancy in making it. "Charon, is there nothing we can offer you to gain your aid?"

"Yes, is there something you need?" Mazu added

"I have few needs. I must go back to work now." Charon beckoned and several spirits drifted forward. He opened his hand again, and as each phantom entered the boat, a coin appeared in it.

"I guess we have a long walk ahead of us," D'Molay reasoned. "Maybe if we stick to the shore - " As he turned to Mazu to finish his statement, he noticed she wore a very strange expression on her face. He read great conflict in her features, and she seemed to be struggling with more than disappointment over Charon's refusal to take them downriver. "Mazu?"

Mazu stepped right up to the boat and stood so close that Charon could have touched her. "What about nectar?" she proposed. "Surely the water of life would have value to one such as you."

The cadaverous deity slowly swiveled its head to look at her. "You have nectar?"

"Yes. I'll give you the last I have if you'll take us to the nearest exit to the coast."

"Show me."

Quan protested. "Mistress, no. He'll steal them!"

Without turning around, Mazu held out her hand. "Get me the vials."

Reluctantly, Quan reached into her traveling pack slung over her horse and removed two vials. He put them in her hand.

Mazu displayed them to Charon. "You see? They are yours if you help us."

There was a long pause as Charon considered the offer. "I still will not take you. But if you truly are a ferryman, you can use one of my boats. That, is all I can offer."

"Very well, we accept." Mazu answered.

"Come with me, goddess. I will take you to the boat." Charon held out his hand to accept the vials. Instead, she placed them in D'Molay's hands.

"You can have these upon my safe return." She stepped forward and into the boat. The spirits jostled aside, making room for her. As soon as she was aboard, the boat drifted free of the shore and back the way it had come. Within a moment or two it was lost in the fog.

"What do we do now?" Quan asked.

D'Molay fixed his gaze on the spot where Charon's boat had disappeared. "We wait and we pray. What else can we do?"

The two men sat with the horses for half an hour. A few more spirits joined them on the shore, apparently waiting for passage across. Fortunately the apparitions seemed only mildly curious and largely ignored them. But under the surface of the water, other shades seemed to be watching them. Dim white shapes were gathering just beyond the shore.

"What are those things?" Quan asked, as he tossed a small stone into the river toward one.

"Why don't you jump in and see," D'Molay said, only half listening to the man. He kept his gaze fixed on the river, hoping for some sign of Mazu in the fog. He had indeed prayed for her safety several times, but was uncertain that the one god would aid one of the deities that lived in this place of many gods. But perhaps he had created them, so perhaps he might care in the same way he cared for people on old Earth. He tried to remember to ask Aavi about that, should they meet up face to face again.

"Charon said he wouldn't give us kata-basis. What is that?" Quan asked. The man was nothing if not persistent in his questions. At least D'Molay had an answer for this one.

"Greek soldiers use that term to describe an army's retreat down a hill. I suppose Charon meant our journey down the river, but that's just my guess." D'Molay saw the faint silhouette of a boat in the fog. As it drew closer he could see it had only one occupant. "Charon's returning, but I don't see Mazu."

"I knew he would betray us!" Quan exclaimed.

"Hold on. Let's see what he does. Maybe we can make him take us to Mazu."

"How? He didn't want to help us in the first place," Quan worried.

"Even gods can be convinced or tricked into doing things." D'Molay didn't like to admit it, but he had the same doubts as Quan. These fears lifted as he discerned another shape coming toward them. Behind Charon, a second boat came into view, just visible in the fog. "Wait - it's another boat. Looks like Mazu is piloting it. He kept his word."

As the two boats approached, more spirits gathered on the shore. Charon's longboat pulled up, but Mazu's remained out on the water.

"I will come ashore after he's done," Mazu called out. "Otherwise it may confuse the spirits."

The waiting spirits surged forward. But this time Charon ignored them and turned first to D'Molay. "You have a boat. Give me the nectar as agreed."

D'Molay stepped forward and placed the vials in Charon's outstretched hand. Charon's bony fingers rolled over them greedily and stashed them somewhere in the dark folds of his heavy robe. He again extended his palm and the spirits boarded, except for the last one. As she tried to step into the boat, she was cast out onto the shore by some unseen force.

"You do not have the fare, I cannot take you," Charon said coldly.

"Please, I must go with my family!" the female ghost cried out.

"No."

D'Molay fished out a coin from his purse and tossed it into Charon's boat. "I offer this as her passage."

His expression unreadable, Charon stared back. "Yes," he finally said.

The last spirit boarded and the ferryman guided the boat into the mist. He said nothing to Mazu as their two boats passed each other in silence. Mazu then brought her boat ashore.

"Take the supplies off the horses. There's no room for them in the

boat," she said.

"I suppose not." D'Molay knew she was right, as the small boat was only about seven feet long and fairly narrow. He worked with Quan to relieve the animals of their burdens, then took their reins and tied them to a half-buried dead log, near the gate they had come through. There was a small pool of water and moss growing there. *At least they can eat and drink.*

"What will become of them?" Quan asked as the boat pushed away and one of the horses whinnied at them.

"We'll never know. But they can't reach the poison of the river where they're tied. Perhaps some other traveler will find them. If half the stories I've heard about people passing through here are true, they may have a better chance than we think," D'Molay mused.

As Mazu guided the boat along the waters of the Styx, the scenery remained the same. Wandering wraiths dotted the shore but none seemed able to follow their boat into the water. Soon the shoreline ceased to exist.

"There's no way we could have walked out of here," D'Molay pointed out. "The shore disappears into solid rock." The boat drifted into a dark tunnel of water which eventually opened up again. On this segment of the river the fog had lifted. They could see tall stalagmites and the smoke of molten lava beyond the craggy hillocks of the opposite shore. Armored warriors, who seemed to be guards who kept watch over the dead, patrolled that side of the river. The guards glared at the boat but made no attempt to stop it. As they floated past, D'Molay also heard cries of anguish and sadness; it reminded him all too well of his long, empty existence in Purgatory. He felt an involuntary shiver run down his back.

Quan, who had been counting the ghosts to alleviate the grim nature of their journey, had just reached number one hundred and three. "Why do you think all these spirits aren't with the rest of the dead?" he asked.

"Probably for the same reason Charon wouldn't let that woman cross earlier. Their relatives didn't place any coins with them when they were buried," replied D'Molay.

"Such waste of money," Quan scoffed. "These Olympians have strange customs."

"Couldn't agree more," D'Molay replied.

As they rounded a bend in the river, Quan pointed off towards the shore. "Look, another boat, and isn't that Charon?"

"It can't be. We left him behind hours ago," D'Molay said. Yet as the other craft came closer, they saw that its pilot indeed looked just the same as the one they had dealt with eariler to gain their own transport.

Mazu smiled slightly. "Ah, I see now. It is Charon, or at least an aspect of him. He has split himself so that he can ferry the dead from all the gates that lead down here."

"Split himself? That sounds terrible," said Quan.

"How do you know that, Mazu?" D'Molay asked.

"Charon told me that I would see him again as we went downstream. Now I understand what he meant."

"Oh. So which one is the real one?" D'Molay thought that he would have trouble picking Charon out of a group of normal ghouls, let alone a group of ones that were as similar as thorns on a rose.

"All of them are. Each one is an equal part of him. It's similar to how I split myself so that I could be in two barrels."

"I don't understand how you do that either, but I'll take your word for it." The duplicate Charon stared at them sullenly as their boats briefly came near each other. "I wonder if he knows who we are?" D'Molay asked. "I mean, does this aspect know?"

"He might or he might not. It is difficult to tell."

They traveled for hours in the gloomy darkness, observed by spirits and guards on both sides of the river, but none of them took any direct action against them. At times an underworld being would cry out to them for help. Mazu and D'Molay ignored them, knowing it was pointless to become involved in their fate. Quan shoved his fingers in his ears when the screaming pleas became too intense.

In a stretch of the river where the banks were thick with spirits, they sailed past another gate. D'Molay noticed Roman numerals carved into top of it. "X-V-I-I," he said aloud. "That's the number seventeen. Do either of you remember seeing letters like that on the other gates?"

"Yes, I do," Quan said. "I know the gate we used had them."

"Do you remember if they were higher or lower than seventeen, Quan?"

"I can't read their language. How could I tell?"

"Well, I thought you - " but Mazu halted D'Molay's comment.

"Something is stalking us, look to the right," she said nodding her head in that direction.

D'Molay and Quan briefly saw a large creature with a long neck and a head like a crocodile skim across the water before disappearing under the surface.

"Was that a fish? It had blue scales." Quan looked to D'Molay, who shook his head.

"No, the Greeks call it a ketos. It's a sea serpent and it eats meat, including human."

"It's been following us for some time," Mazu told them. "I think it's sizing us up, waiting for the right moment to strike."

"What should we do?" Quan asked.

Mazu pushed on her staff to move the boat along more quickly. "We have few options. We can go ashore and hope it moves on. We can try to outrun it, or we can turn and fight it."

Rubbing his chin, and staring at the ripples in the water that betrayed the monster's location, D'Molay considered each alternative. "None of those sound too good. Let's try to keep moving and hope it tires of following us."

They traveled for another hour as the ketos slowly moved in. It made several passes near the boat as D'Molay stood ready with his bow and arrow. Finally, it came at them at full speed.

"Here it comes!" he called out as he let loose an arrow, which bounced off the creature's hide. His next shot struck it. The ketos shifted its direction, but still headed for them, the arrow protruding from its back. D'Molay swung his bow over his arm grabbed his knife as he shouted a warning. "Hold on! It's going to ram us!"

Mazu moved the boat away as hard as she could, saving it from a direct hit. The ketos scraped the side of the boat. Mazu's quick maneuver stopped them from being overturned, but they were rocked back and forth violently. Swinging his knife, D'Molay leaned over the side, putting a long cut in the creature's back. It roared in pain as blackish-green blood spurted from the wound. One of its large flippers smacked the side of the boat, violently rocking them side to side again. Quan, seated up front and held on for dear life, and Mazu, with her staff keeping her steady, managed to keep their balance. D'Molay was not so lucky. He fell head first into the water, still gripping the knife embedded in the creature's side. Gathering his wits, he withdrew the weapon from the beast while using his feet to kick off from the loathsome thing and push himself away.

The ketos floundered, apparently unused to fighting prey that was armed. It spun in the dark water between D'Molay and the boat. Mazu moved the boat away from the serpent. "Get out of the river!" she shouted. "Head for the shore, we'll pick you up there!"

Perhaps attracted by the sound of Mazu's voice, once again the ketos headed toward the boat. Mazu shot several water blasts, but they had little effect. A tall wake lifted the boat and that was all D'Molay saw before a new threat loomed. The ghostly white shapes that lurked in the water had found him. These wraiths circled him, drawing in closer and closer. D'Molay's hand was ice cold as it clutched his knife, a weapon which was of little use against a foe that had no solid body. Escape was his only hope. He swam for a gap between two wraiths but they closed in quickly. As he collided with one of them he instantly felt a stinging coldness like the strike of a whip made of ice. The wraith attempted to enfold him as it struck again. Ignoring the pain, D'Molay struggled free and kept swimming for the shore.

Because they were not solid, the wraiths could not restrain him. D'Molay could swim right through them, although this contact brought on the same deathly stinging cold as one of their attacks. Each strike weakened him, but he forced his body to fight on through the freezing pain. Several more wraiths swarmed around him, trying to halt his passage. Their icy grasp was agonizing and he began to sink.

In panicked desperation, he swung his arms out wildly, trying to force his way through and get out of the water. His entire body felt heavy and frozen, as it was if encased in ice. D'Molay kept moving, thrashing the water, but he was going slower and slower. The wraiths completely surrounded him, stinging him over and over again. Trying in vain to fight on, he was finally overcome with intense pain and a mind-numbing cold. As one hand clawed against the shore, his strength failed. His face fell into the waters of the Styx and he disappeared beneath the waves.

Chapter 14

Prophetess of Apollo

D'Molay awoke, feeling colder then he'd felt since the time he'd been lost in the mountains near Odin's Keep. As he slowly opened his eyes, he could see a woman, or more specifically, a woman's feet. They were clad in leather sandals with straps that ran up her calves. D'Molay dragged himself up into a sitting position, and looked up at her. She wore a pale red stola with Olympian symbols embroidered on its hem. Her hair was pinned up behind a tiara. Two ringlets of dark brown hair that hung in front of her ears framed a calm face. D'Molay scooted nearer the small fire that burned between them, greedy for its warmth. The woman noticed his stirrings as she threw a small leaf into the flames.

"You are most fortunate, mortal. Had I not been nearby and pulled you from the Styx, you would most surely be dead now."

"W-where am I?" D'Molay asked, shaking with cold.

"You are on the shore, across from the Fields of Asphodel, which is on the other side of the river." As she spoke to him, she kept her eyes fixed on the fire, as if she found the dance of its flames far more interesting than him.

"My ... Mazu and Quan, are they alive?" he asked, recalling that they had been in danger as well. A chill of fear passed over him.

"If you mean the two in the boat, I do not know. The ketos forced them ashore. The mists make it difficult to see the other side from here."

"I guess I should thank you for saving my life."

"Send your thanks to Apollo," she replied, as her eyes met his for the first time since he woke.

"I'd like to thank you. I'm sure I would have died in that river without you." D'Molay shivered uncontrollably from the cold that seemed to cling to his bones, like ice on the surface of a pond on a winter's day.

"You are welcome mortal. But since

you have fallen into those waters, my saving you may have only delayed the inevitable. You see, legend has it that anyone who swims in the Styx and lives to tell the tale will die before the year has passed. You may leave the Underworld, but death will pursue you wherever you go." The woman told the tale in such an offhand manner that D'Molay failed to find it too alarming at first. Then, he remembered that Mazu had also believed to touch the waters could be deadly.

"Do you know if that legend is true or not?" he asked as his teeth chattered slightly. Would he really pay such a bitter price?

"Few survive the wraiths of the water or the other dangers here. But it has not been tested since eons past, before I was named Cumean Sibyl."

"Cumean Sibyl?"

"That is my title. I am the prophetess of Apollo's Temple in Cumea. I come down here to console the spirits that cannot cross the river by taking them to Apollo. They call me Amalthea."

"I'm D'Molay, a tracker for the Council," he replied, trying to warm his hands by the fire.

"Is that why you have come to Hades - to search for someone?"

He tried to smile, despite the pain he was feeling. "No, not exactly. We came here more by accident. We didn't realize that the cave we entered would bring us here."

"Ah. That has happened in the past. There are twenty-four entrances to Hades, one for each hour of the day. Mortals occasionally enter, but almost never go beyond the gates."

"Well, we were foolish enough to - to enter where angels fear to tread." He'd suddenly remembered that saying, which someone had told him in purgatory at some point.

"Angels? None can be found anywhere in the realms. That is an odd saying, Da'Muu-lay. Though I think I take your meaning."

"Sorry. It means we're foolish to come down here." Not bothering to correct how she said his name, he set his mind on his comrades and how to get back to them. D'Molay knew with certainty that he could not swim across if they truly were on the other shore.

"Would you like to eat? I have goat meat. I bring goats here to read their entrails for my prophecies, but the rest of the meat can be used for other purposes." Amalthea offered him a stick with a large chunk of cooked meat skewered on it. He took it as she began to chant and sing a song of thanks to the gods for the safe return of Da'Muu-lay to the shore and of the food they provided for him. For his part, he gave thanks to God Almighty and prayed that Quan and Mazu were also safe. He devoured the meat, its warmth pushing back the bitter chill in his bones.

� decorative divider

*T*hey had made it safely ashore. Mazu wasn't entirely sure how. She was confident that it had more to do with luck than her skill as a ferryman. For the moment, they were safe from any denizens of the river. Their boat rested snug against a finger of sand that jutted out from the bank. While Mazu watched the glimmer of a small campfire on the other side of the river, Quan checked the boat carefully for damage.

"What if that monster cracked the hull?" he worried. On his hands and knees in the sand, Quan crawled alongside the boat in the dim light, checking its timbers.

"Let's hope not, for we have now set foot on the land of the dead. We will not be welcome here, of that I am certain."

"Ha! I was right. There are three broken . . . "

Quan's voice trailed off. Mazu turned to find him staring dumbly at the hull.

"What's wrong?"

"This boat is . . . alive."

"What do you mean?" Mazu stepped over and looked down over his shoulder.

"Look! The cracks are filling in and reconnecting." Quan and Mazu watched as Charon's boat repaired the breaks in its hull, by seeming to grow the wood over the gaps and holes. "How can it do that?"

"With magic. It makes sense down here," Mazu said. "I doubt there is a dockyard in Hades." She patted Quan on the shoulder. "Be glad the boat is enchanted. Let me know as soon as it has fully repaired itself. We must get back to D'Molay. That woman pulled him from the water, but we don't know his condition or what her intentions are."

After almost swamping their boat, the ketos had given up and fled to nurse its wounds. Mazu had sought D'Molay in the water, and spotted him struggling to the opposite shore. Waiting there was a woman. She made no move to help D'Molay. Mazu had initially thought she was another shade. But when D'Molay flung his arm upon the sand, she rushed to grab his hand and pull him from the river. Since then, mist had come up on the river and Mazu could see nothing of the other side but a dim orange glow from the woman's fire.

"Do you think he's still alive, mistress?"

"Do not doubt it, Quan."

As they waited for the boat to work its spell, spirits began to draw near. In a short time, a small crowd had gathered. One who carried the haughty manner of a Roman senator drifted right over to Mazu. "How dare you invade the sanctity of our realm? Get out. Be gone!"

"We will leave as soon as we can, I promise you," she said diplomatically.

The crowd grouped together and began to press in.

"No! No! Leave Now! Nooowww!" they droned as they swarmed forward as one.

"Get the boat in the water, Quan. We must leave!" She waved her arm in front of the spirits, creating a wall of water. She knew that they could pass through it, but they might not. Then she, too, turned into water, creating a second wall around the boat. The spirits paused, confused by the display, but then surged forward screaming like banshees.

Quan scrambled, quickly pushing the boat into the river. As he prepared to hop into it, hundreds of ghostly hands reached out to grab him. He jumped in and the boat drifted just out of the reach of their ghostly pursuers. The wall of water around him spun and became like a waterspout, which flew off the ground and arched into the air, landing in the boat, soaking Quan to the bone.

The water gathered up, merged together and transformed into Mazu. She turned to the shore and heard the spirits screaming and yelling.

"Die! Die!

"Cast off your flesh and bone!

"Never Return, blasphemers!

"May Hades curse you for all time!"

The spirits remained an unruly mob, but they were unable to leave the land of the dead to pursue them. It was the only reason that Mazu and Quan were still alive.

The goddess held her arm out over the boat; water flowed out of her hand and quickly turned into her wooden staff.

"What of the ketos? It may still be out here waiting for us," Quan worried.

Her expression stern and determined, Mazu shoved the staff into the murky water and pushed the boat forward. "It had best not be, for my patience has grown quite thin. Let's retrieve D'Molay and be away from this cursed realm as soon as we can."

Chapter 14: Prophetess of Apollo

*D'*Molay sat helpless and shivering at the water's edge, looking for signs of his companions. The fog still obscured the opposite shoreline, but there was no doubt that something was happening there. Even from across the river, he could hear the screaming and yelling of the souls of the dead.

Amalthea sat near the fire, arranging dried oak leaves with symbols drawn upon them. They reminded D'Molay of card decks he'd seen people use while he was in the near east on old Earth. Amalthea moved one leaf to cover another. "Do you see your friends yet? They will be here soon."

"Did the symbols on your leaves tell you that?" D'Molay asked. He wanted to walk over to watch her read the leaves, but felt too weak to stand.

"The leaves tell me many things. I use them to help find the lost souls who dwell on this side of the river. Ah . . . there are a group of them at the next gate." Putting her things away, the sibyl gracefully stepped over to him. Her hand lightly touched his shoulder. "I would ask a favor of you Da'Muu-lay."

"You saved my life. If it's within my power, I will grant your favor."

"I have not asked yet. You should be cautious about making such declarations, for they have gotten you in trouble in the past, as they will in the future."

D'Molay could not deny the truth of her observation. Raising an eyebrow, he asked, "Did the leaves tell you that as well?"

Amalthea merely smiled. "I wonder if you and your friends could take me to the next gate down river. There is only me and my bag."

"I don't see why not. There is certainly room for one more. Maybe you can warn of us of what's further ahead."

"Perhaps. Your companions approach." She looked back towards the river.

D'Molay saw the boat drifting out of the fog and his heart lifted in joy. With the help of Amalthea, he was able to stand up. Mazu and Quan looked fine, and the boat seemed to be intact. Mazu safely guided it ashore, her grim expression lightening as she saw D'Molay sitting there, waiting.

"I knew you would survive," Mazu smiled. D'Molay gestured to

Amalthea.

"This is Amalthea. She saved me, and wonders if we can take her down river a bit. I told her we would."

"Of course," Mazu said. "You saved someone we would have lost had you not been here. Quan, help them on board." He complied, though the suspicious look on his face was obvious to all.

"Easy, Quan. She's not a danger," D'Molay said. As he stepped into the boat, he stumbled, and would have fallen had not Amalthea been supporting him.

"What's wrong with you?" Quan wanted to know.

"That's the sting of the wraiths. It will pass with time," Amalthea answered. She and Quan had to work together to get D'Molay into the boat. Quan actually had to lift one of his legs over the hull while Amalthea held him up. When everyone had settled, Quan sat at the prow of the longboat, followed by D'Molay and then Amalthea. Mazu stayed at the stern to guide the craft. She pushed off from the shore and they drifted down the Styx.

"I must ask. How did you get this boat?" Amalthea asked.

"Through an honest trade," Mazu said.

The Prophetess cocked her head to one side, evaluating the truth of that declaration. "Never have I heard of the Ferryman aiding others for any reason, especially the living. If you weren't a deity, he would have probably just taken your lives."

"Luckily we found out what he wanted before he had that chance," D'Molay said, rubbing his legs in an attempt to ease his icy pain.

Mazu apparently noticed his discomfort. "How are you feeling?"

"I hope you won't need me to join any battles for a while," he replied.

"Hah. We are sailing down the river of Death in the underworld. What's the chance of that?" Quan said sarcastically.

Ominously, a sudden splash of water caused them all to stare into the darkness ahead.

"Probably just a stalactite that fell loose," Mazu said reassuringly.

As they reached the center of the river, a huge bubbling arose from beneath the water. Suddenly the ketos burst forth from below, rocking the boat and knocking Mazu off balance.

"It's the monster!" Quan cried out.

As the waves and bubbles subsided, D'Molay got his first close look at the carnage that followed in its wake. The ketos was floundering, struggling in the water as its own entrails streamed out behind it and floated on the surface. He could see the huge gash he'd knifed in its side as guts and blood drained out of it into the dark water.

"T-those things are eating it!" Quan cried out.

Dozens of the strange spider-like creatures, the size of a human head, each with a human face, were scampering over the beast, tearing chunks out of it with their long pincers. They shoved the pieces of flesh and guts into gruesome mouths on their backs, while the ketos tried to roll them off.

There was a large splash and several of the smaller creatures were thrown into the boat. The monstrous devourers began a keen screeching as they advanced on the boat's passengers. Mazu struck at one with her staff. Another rushed toward D'Molay and scuttled over his legs.

"They're in the boat!" Quan yelled as D'Molay stared into the female face of one of the screaming creatures. Its pincher darted at him and tore a piece of his clothing, drawing blood from the skin underneath. He quickly thrust his knife up through the bottom of the thing's body and pierced through one of its eyes. He brought his arm up and managed to fling it back into the water as it slid off his knife blade.

The third one landed on Quan and tore a small chunk out of his arm. He screamed in pain and horror but managed to slam the hideous thing repeatedly against the side of the boat until it fell off the side.

"Keep going, keep going!" D'Molay called back to Mazu. They continued to move away from the carnage as the ketos made its final death cry, its bloated body floating on the surface as the strange creatures continued their feast.

Amalthea had been surprisingly untouched by creatures, but seemed shaken by the event. She made a circular sign in the air. "May the blessings of Apollo protect us."

Shock and fear began to fade as they got further away, but D'Molay collapsed against the side of the boat, exhausted and shivering. Eyes fixed on the dark waters and unaware of his distress, Mazu voiced a command.

"D'Molay, get some bandages from the bag for you and Quan."

The prophetess looked back over her shoulder. I don't think he can." She pulled the bag over looking through it. "I see no bandages."

"I have them. They were in this bag," Quan gasped out as he unrolled the bandage.

"How bad is your wound?"

"It was more shocking than painful. The face on its back - staring and yelling at me. It was horrible," Quan said.

"Those may have been some of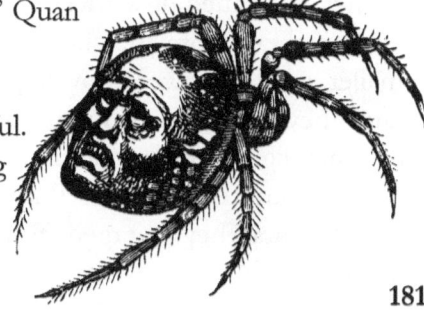

the most disturbing creatures I have ever seen," Mazu said turning back to take one last glance at the scene behind them as it faded into the fog.

"They are the Karkinos Katara, souls that sinned in the Underworld. That is one of Hades' punishments to those who disobey his edicts."

"Let us hope we don't do that," Quan said with a quaver in his voice.

"Can one of you check D'Molay?" Mazu asked.

Amalthea leaned forward and looked him over for a moment or two. "He suffers from the wraith attack. They have struck his soul and weakened him. When he wakes, he needs warmth, food and drink."

Quan looked over his shoulder. "We have very little of any of those."

"When we part ways, I'll give you what I can part with," Amalthea offered. She then wrapped one of her shawls around D'Molay in an attempt to keep him warm.

They traveled along the dark tunnel in silence for some time. Then Mazu's curiosity drove her to ask, "Amalthea, how long have you been a prophetess for Apollo?"

"For over a thousand years I have served as the Cumean Sibyl at his temple. It is my honor and my duty."

"Is that why you're down here? Is this part of your duty to Apollo?" Mazu asked.

"You could say that. I aid those who are trapped between the world of the living and the dead. Once a year, each of the sibyls must go on a pilgrimage to the underworld to escort souls who have no fare to cross the Styx. We bring them back to our temples, where our gods can care for them."

"I see."

Having awoken, D'Molay noticed an underlying anger in Mazu's terse answer; he wondered what had suddenly upset her. He decided that now was not the time to ask, and remained silent.

"It is a great honor to help those who are lost and the gods reward our temples in a variety of ways."

"I'm sure they do," Mazu added.

They continued downriver in silence, passing more of the spirits who watched them from the shores of Hades' realm. The vast cavern grew smaller, until they were traveling through a long, meandering tunnel. At times they were almost in complete darkness, the glow of Mazu's staff the only light source. In the dim light, they passed ancient temple entrances and monuments that had been long since abandoned. After several hours, they emerged from the darkness and entered a larger cavern much like the one they had seen when they first entered the Underworld.

"We are here. The next gate is around the bend," Amalthea announced. Soon they were back in the light and saw the large stone gate. Standing in front of it, near the shore, was a gathering of spirits. When Mazu brought the boat up to the shore to let Amalthea off, the phantoms surged toward it. Some spirits seemed merely curious but others anxiously pleaded for help.

Amalthea immediately left the boat to walk among them, her arms outstretched as if to embrace them all. "Fear not! I am the Sibyl of Cumae. Apollo has sent me to take you to him, where he will care for you."

The crowd was buoyed by this, many exclaiming their joy and praising Apollo. Suddenly another voice came forth. It was Mazu.

"Wait! Hear me out before you decide! I will ferry you across the river, for that is where you are destined to go. Everyone you knew who has passed on is waiting for you on the other side. Let me take you to them."

Amalthea turned to Mazu, clearly shocked

by her interference. "You cannot offer such a thing. It is cruel! Charon has already refused these spirits passage. You cannot take them." She turned back to the assembled spirits. "This woman is misinformed. None of you can cross the Styx. What she offers is not within her power. You would fade away before you reached the other side. Come! All you need do is pledge yourself to Apollo and I'll take you back to his temple at Cumae."

There was murmur of agreement among the spirits as all of them surrounded Amalthea.

"Will none of you go with me? I beseech you, let me take you." Mazu pleaded from the boat.

They all ignored her, except for the spirit of a little girl who drifted forward. "I'll go with you, teacher."

Mazu stared at the child. She couldn't have been more than four or five. Suddenly she realized that this was one of Helios' daughters, the one the god had slapped for refusing to drink the water of life. Mazu's eyes grew wide with horror and sorrow.

"Iona! What happened to bring you here?"

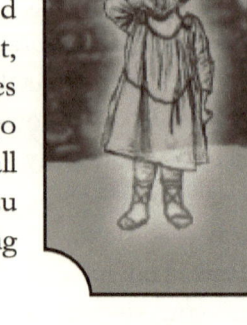

The spirit girl drifted closer. "I don't know. I was wet . . . and the wall fell down. I woke up here. I'm lost." Iona floated to Mazu and started to cry. Mazu was uncertain what Iona had meant, but it didn't matter at the moment; as her eyes welled up in sorrow. "Oh, Iona. Come. We'll go right now." She was determined to aid the small girl as best she could. "D'Molay, pay me." Mazu reached out to him as he sat in the boat looking back over his shoulder at her.

"What are you doing, Mazu?"

"I have the boat and I am a Ferryman. I am escorting her to the other side." D'Molay slowly found a coin and dropped it into Mazu's hand. "Iona, your fare is paid, it's time to go."

Iona looked up at Mazu, her eyes large and hopeful. "Thank you, teacher. I don't want to be alone." She drifted onto the boat, staying as close to Mazu as she could.

Amalthea stood on the shore, her hands bunched into fists. "You are upsetting the natural order of Hades. The Fates will not be kind to those who betray Olympia. You have been warned."

Mazu scowled back as she maneuvered the boat away from the shore. "I do what is right, Sibyl. It is you who are misguided. Just ask yourself, have you ever seen any of the spirits after you have taken them to Apollo?" She turned the boat away from the prophetess and headed towards the opposite side.

"Is this wise, Lady Mazu?" Quan fretted.

D'Molay, feeling cold and weary from his trials, raised a cautionary hand to quell his questioning. Quan hunkered down in the boat and said nothing else. Even so, the boat was not entirely quiet.

"What will it be like over there?" Iona asked Mazu.

"Well, you'll be safe with the other spirits and they'll help you learn what to do, just like I taught you things at the palace."

"Oh, that's good. I don't know about being a ghost."

"One day, your brothers and sisters will join you here too and you can help them," Mazu added reassuringly.

"I'll try, teacher."

"You are very brave. We'll be there soon." Mazu guided the boat around a stalagmite as they drew closer. A moment later, the hull made a slow rumbling sound as it slid ashore. She turned to D'Molay and Quan. "I want you two to stay here. Do not get out, no matter what you see or hear." They nodded their assent as Mazu and her ghostly charge left Charon's boat and walked into Hades' realm of the dead.

They followed a narrow path that was cut through the high rocks. The path twisted and turned, and the shore fell out of sight. As they rounded a bend, a ghostly guard in Greek armor confronted them.

"By what right do you enter the realm of the dead?" He pointed his spear directly at Mazu.

"This child was in my charge. I wish only to make her transition here less difficult. I need to get her to someone that might guide her." Mazu took on a more haughty tone in an attempt to use her status to get past the spirit guard.

"But you must go back! Even gods are not permitted past this point, unless by direct approval of Hades. But the child may enter." He took up a ram's horn that was tied at his waist with a long string. Like the spirit of the guard, the horn and everything he carried was also translucent and ghostly. He blew on the horn. Mazu heard no sound, but Iona flinched and covered her ears.

"Was that too loud?" Mazu asked, curious.

"Yes, didn't you think so?" the girl spirit asked, taking her hands out of her tangled hair.

"Well, I am very old and do not hear as well as I used to."

"Oh," came the simple response.

A few moments later, a wispy, female spirit rounded the bend of the narrow channel. She was tall and thin, with long hair that streamed behind her as she glided forward. Her gown was a low-slung toga and she wore a laurel wreath on her head.

"Why have I been summoned?"

The guard turned around, bowing slightly. "This goddess has brought a child to us, priestess." Mazu was encouraged by the helpful appearance of this phantom.

"Please, can you help little Iona? She was in my care, but something must have happened to her in my absence." They all looked down at Iona.

"I...I don't know what I'm supposed to do," she said softly.

The priestess smiled more broadly. "Welcome, Iona. I will take you the rest of the way. I'm sure there are familiar faces waiting for you. Will you accompany me?" The priestess held out her hand as she gently floated to Iona.

The child ghost looked over to Mazu. "Is it all right?"

"Yes, Iona. She will help you now."

Iona put out her hand. The priestess took it and addressed Mazu.

"Goddess you may be, but you must leave quickly, before Hades discovers you are here without permission."

Mazu nodded. "I understand. Thank you, and goodbye Iona."

Iona called out a tearful goodbye to Mazu's back as she returned to the boat. As she retraced her path, Mazu could not stop her own tears from falling, or still the thoughts that ran through her mind. What could have happened to the poor child to bring her untimely death?

Mazu arrived back at the shore and found several dozen agitated spirits, yelling and cursing at D'Molay and Quan. The men had been forced to push the boat away from the shore and were now drifting aimlessly in the middle of the river.

"... and never return, trespassers!" cried out one spirit.

"Curses be upon you!" shouted another.

Several of the spirits spotted Mazu. "There's another one! Kill her! Tear out her soul!" Many of them surged forward to attack.

Startled, Mazu immediately turned into water, flowed under them, and entered the river. Slipping through the dark water, she headed for the boat, suddenly realizing her mistake. Wraiths swarmed around her. Even though she was a virtually invisible stream of flowing water, the wraiths knew she was there. Mazu felt the icy sting of their attempts to drain her life essence. Nonetheless, she continued forward, managing to flow up the side of the hull and into the boat. Slowly reforming, she took her human shape.

Quan bent over her with great concern on his face. "Lady Mazu? We saw the wraiths go wild once you entered the river."

She gingerly sat up. "It was terrible. Most foolish of me to enter the Styx. Even as water, the wraiths were able to sense me and attack."

"Are you going to be all right?" D'Molay asked, as the two of them exchanged knowing glances; Mazu had just gotten a taste of what had happened to him.

"I feel very cold and drained, as though I had swum for miles rather than traveled a few feet. It would seem that even deities are not immune to those horrible things," Mazu said, pausing for a moment to assess her condition. "I'm well enough. I just need a moment to regain my stamina. Quan, take my staff." A stream of water flowed out of her hand and solidified into a long wooden pole. He took the staff as Mazu tilted her head against the side of the boat and closed her eyes. "Just keep us away from the shore."

"Yes, Lady Mazu." He did his best to keep the boat in a safe location while Mazu and D'Molay lay listlessly, shivering from a cold that reached into their very souls.

A short while later Mazu stood up and shuffled to the back to the stern. "I am ready now." She held out her hand as Quan gave her the pole and went to the prow of the boat, his movements waking D'Molay. As the boat glided forward, he sat up, turning his attention to Mazu.

"I see we're on our way again, thank the one God."

Quan responded with a scoffing laugh. "You should thank Mazu, for she is the one goddess moving this boat."

Ignoring Quan, D'Molay asked, "There's still something I don't understand, Mazu. Why didn't you let Amalthea take the ghost child with the other spirits to Apollo?"

"Yes, Lady Mazu," Quan chimed in. "Why did you leave her spirit in this cursed place?"

Mazu frowned and her eyes narrowed with indignation. "Trust me when I say this. That child's spirit is far better in Hades than with Apollo. I cannot say any more than that."

D'Molay shrugged. "I always heard Apollo was a great god. Wouldn't she be safer - "

"Enough!" Mazu snapped. "Iona was under my care not long ago and now she is . . . gone," Mazu's voice trailed off as tears streamed down her face.

D'Molay and Quan exchanged looks, but remained silent as the boat sailed out of the large cavern and into a dark tunnel ahead.

The boat continued along as the sound of its wake and the occasional dripping of water from stalactites echoing off the rocky walls surrounding them. A slight mist hung in the air. It brought with it the stench of decay and mud.

D'Molay was starting to worry about his condition. He realized he wasn't feeling any better. He was cold, painfully cold; his arms and legs felt numb and listless, as though anvils had been tied to each appendage. It was not something a man of action like himself was used to. *Could those wraiths have stolen a piece of my soul? Is that what it feels like?* D'Molay kept these fears to himself. He knew Mazu had her own sorrows to deal with. His gloomy thoughts were cut short by Quan.

"These tunnels go on forever. Will we never be out of this place? I yearn for the sun and the sky. And a hot meal."

"What food is left?" D'Molay asked.

Quan grabbed one of the bags and started rooting through it. "Three pomegranates, some dried meat, two apples and . . . that's all. Nothing else."

"You're not holding out on us, are you?"

"It is you that are a thief. That is what you do for a living, you steal things for the gods. Tracker - Ha! D'Molay the Thief should be your title."

D'Molay allowed his anger to bubble up. At least there seemed to be some power behind it, unlike his physical strength. "You useless whiner," D'Molay accused, attempting to kick Quan. He only managed to shove him forward a little due to the numbness in his legs.

The servant quickly turned, throwing a pomegranate, which hit D'Molay on the side of the head then splashed into the brackish water.

"You idiot! I ought to kill you!" D'Molay screamed back as he pulled out his knife. Deep down, D'Molay knew he shouldn't be taking this action, but it felt so right. He grabbed Quan's shirt and pulled him closer. They started to struggle. Despite his weakness, D'Molay managed to force Quan down and hold the knife at this throat. "I've had enough of your nattering!"

Suddenly Mazu's voice boomed out. "Stop it! Both of you! Put that knife away. Aren't we in enough danger?"

"Yes and he . . . he . . ." D'Molay suddenly realized he'd lost control. "I'm sorry, I don't know why . . ." He slowly pulled the knife away from Quan's throat and slid it back in its sheath.

Quan bowed and scraped. "My Lady! I beg a thousand pardons. I did not mean to throw the food away so carelessly."

D'Molay's ire was instantly rekindled. His hand went back to the knife as he realized Quan had only apologized for wasting food, not for throwing something at him. But Mazu's stern expression stilled his tongue. She stood over them with the imposing look of an inquisitor etched across her face. At times like this D'Molay could truly see Mazu was indeed a goddess of great power and knowledge.

"It is clear that we can-not stay down here much longer. The food is almost gone and this place brings on dark feelings of dread and distrust. I suspect that the longer we are down here, the worse those torments will become."

D'Molay ran his hand across his face as if trying to wipe away his bitter hatred and paranoia. "You may be right. I can't even tell how long we've been down here. I feel so confused and drained. Maybe it's time to go, while we still can."

"Whatever you decide, I will follow," Quan added as he prostrated himself to his goddess again.

"Very well. We should leave at the next gate we come to."

"By now, the harpies must have given up looking for us," D'Molay added, as he felt another icy twinge of pain in his legs. Privately, he worried about his ability to walk all the way out of the vast tunnels and back up to the surface, but decided to try when the time came. There was no other option. D'Molay's exertion left him exhausted and he fell into a restless sleep.

⬦

*T*he journey continued through endless tunnels of darkness and mist. Wraiths continued to trail the boat. Quan did his best not to look over the side and meet their dead eyes. Sometimes just catching a glimpse of one of them made him fear for his life. He kept his head up, his eyes forward.

"Look, there's Charon again," Quan said, as they came to a wider stretch of river.

Mazu guided the boat into a larger cavern. Compared to the inky blackness they had just passed through, it seemed almost as bright as daylight there. Charon, or his aspect, was over a hundred feet away and half obscured by the mist.

"His boat is full, and he sails toward Hades proper," Mazu observed. "We must be near another gate." *All the better for us, for we are out of food and water,* she thought. "Wake up D'Molay. We may be able to get off this boat once and for all."

Quan nudged D'Molay as he lay motionless in the boat. Getting no response, he shook him harder. "D'Molay . . . Wake up. Hey!"

Mazu watched the shore carefully, taking care not to miss any upcoming gate. She half turned her head to chide Quan. "Don't jostle him. He is injured from his trials."

"But he won't wake up. And he's very cold."

"What?" Quickly Mazu turned her pole into water and allowed the boat to drift as she knelt over D'Molay to see him for herself. She touched his brow. "He's dying. We have to get him away from here as soon as we can. Try to keep him warm."

"How? We have no blankets."

Mazu's brow furrowed as she resumed her place. "Wrap yourself around him; keep him warm with your own body's heat." Water flowed from her hand turning in to a wooden pole again.

"But . . . he . . . I'm - "

"I'd do it myself, but I'm the only one allowed to navigate Charon's boat. Now hurry! Don't be squeamish - his life is at stake," she snapped back.

Dubiously, Quan lay down on top of D'Molay. He grabbed the man's hand and tried to puff warm air on it. Then he vigorously rubbed D'Molay's arms, hoping to bring life back into them.

"That's good, we'll build a fire once we're on shore," Mazu said as she pushed the boat forward. "Is he still breathing?"

"Yes, but there's no warmth left in him."

Mazu headed with determination toward the gate. The boat bumped against sandy mud. "Let's get him out."

Quan helped Mazu pick him up and carry him to a dry patch of ground not far from the boat. As they went back for their travel packs, Charon's boat approached.

Mazu called over to the dark god. "Do you know me? I spoke with your avatar up river. He lent me this boat."

This Charon glared at her, his expression a mask of dread and foreboding. "You should not be here."

"We will leave through this gate as soon as we can. We are done with the boat, if that is your concern," she added in hope of getting some hint of his intentions.

"Must be on the other side." He pointed slowly back across the river. Mazu stared at the dark expanse of water, regretting the time it would take to move the craft across.

"Can I tie it to the back of your boat so you can take on your next trip across?"

"No... You must take it." His answer left little room for further discussion.

"I see. Will you bring me back if I do this?"

Charon stared at her but made no reply.

Quan tugged fretfully at her sleeve. "My Lady, do not forget he may require a fare for you to return."

"What does D'Molay still have in his bag?" She waited while Quan rummaged through the pack and found a handful of coins. Mazu took several from him.

"If only we could buy food down here with the rest of these," he said miserably, handing them to her.

"We will use them when get back up to the surface," Mazu promised. "For now we must remain hungry. Stay here. Try to keep him warm and to ignore any spirits that get curious."

"Yes, Lady Mazu." Quan bowed his head slightly as she walked back to Charon and got in their boat.

"I'm ready. I will follow you to the other side," she said pushing the boat away from the shore with her pole.

Quan watched them leave then turned his attention to D'Molay. His skin was pale and bluish. He put his hand on the man. He was cold, and when Quan then put his hand right in front of D'Molay's mouth and nose he was sure he had stopped breathing.

Panicked, Quan rummaged through the travel bag and pulled out a small vial. Guilt and uncertainty vied for control of his emotions. He had held the bottle back when Mazu had demanded all of her vials for Charon, fearing his goddess might need one in the future. He had never expected to be considering giving the precious nectar to the tracker. Nectar was meant for the gods; he'd even heard that it would kill a man who drank it. He shook D'Molay's icy, unresponsive body one last time. He already seemed dead. Satisfied the nectar could do no harm, he popped the cork from the vial, opened D'Molay's mouth, and let a single drop of the clear thick liquid fall into back of his throat. Quan placed the cork back in the vial and hid it safely away. Obedient to Mazu's commands, he rubbed D'Molay's chest and upper arms, trying to put some warmth back into them. "Come on, come on, bring him back."

Suddenly D'Molay took a wheezing gasp of air. His eyes flew open in apparent shock. He went limp and moved no further.

"D'Molay! D'Molay?" Quan put his hand back by the man's mouth and waited. He could feel his breath. Then he felt D'Molay's chest to confirm that his heart was beating, Quan sat back nervously, waiting for Mazu's return. "Neither of them need know that he died while in my care," he whispered.

———

*M*azu followed Charon through the mist and across the river. As they approached the shore, he pointed to sandy spot where he apparently wanted her to leave the boat. Not far away a large group of spirits lingered, a greenish glow surrounding them. Mazu pulled the boat up and stepped ashore. The boat seemed to twist and melt, roots grew from it and sank into the ground. It became a heavy log on the muddy shoreline, with no hint that it had ever been a boat at all. It was then Mazu realized that the ferryman had not moved his boat any closer. She was now stranded on the opposite shore in the realm of the dead.

"Charon? Charon!"

"Your friends will join you soon," he intoned flatly as his boat began to move back into the mist.

Mazu then heard the moans and screams of the spirits closing in behind her.

"Kill her! Kill her!"

Chapter 15

What Lies Ahead

D'Molay finally opened his eyes. He felt a little better for a change as he looked slowly around and turned on his side. He stared into the flames of a fire right near his face. Immediately he felt a wave of panic, fearing it was too close and that he was in danger of burning, but the fear passed as his eyes focused beyond the flames to Quan. Mazu's servant sat crossed-legged, chanting, a knife in one hand and what looked like an old root in the other. He saw no sign of the goddess. "Quan?"

"Welcome back to the land of the dead," Quan said ruefully.

"Where are we? Where's - ?"

"She left with Charon to take his boat to the other side of the river. I'm praying for Mazu's return so we can get out of here. If you have any sense, you'll pray to that one god of yours as well."

"He's not my god. He's the god of us all." D'Molay was a little surprised at how easily those words rolled off his tongue, wondering where he had found an extra reserve of energy to spend on theology. The effort seemed wasted on Mazu's man.

"You have your god, I have mine," Quan argued. "The difference is my god is real and yours is in your imagination."

D'Molay's body ached, but he couldn't resist giving an answer. "You have it all backwards. All the deities here are in the one god's imagination, for he created them and us." D'Molay shifted into a more comfortable position, closed his eyes, and whispered a prayer for Mazu's safety. Then he made the sign of the cross over himself and slowly sat up.

He stared at the fire again. He felt its warmth, and found he was truly glad for its presence. "How did you get that going?"

Quan smiled. "I found your flint and lit some strips of clothing. I used these dry roots and lichen to feed it. Are you feeling better?"

"Yes, somewhat. Is there anything left to eat?"

Quan reached into the bag and pulled out an apple. "This is the last thing. Mazu ordered I keep it for you," he handed it over jealously.

D'Molay took a bite and its sweetness was almost intoxicating. His mind drifted back to the times he'd eaten apples with Aavi. They had been one of her favorite foods. He realized, like Aavi, the apple was gone far too soon.

"I see Charon. There." Quan pointed towards the river, where D'Molay saw a faint silhouette emerging out of the mist. As the solitary figure drew closer, D'Molay could see him thrashing around in his boat, seeming to beat at some unseen force with his pole.

"What's he doing?" D'Molay wondered. Quan had a different concern.

"Where is Lady Mazu? She should be with him!"

"It looks like something's in the bottom of the boat and he's trying to kill it," D'Molay theorized, mentally cursing the infinite dangers of the caverns.

"Is he beating Mazu? No! Stop!" Having leapt to his conclusion, Quan ran to the shore's edge, yelling. He grabbed stones and started tossing them at Charon. All of them missed their target due to his excited state.

"Quan, stop!" D'Molay tried to get up to follow but fell face-forward onto the ground, unable to walk. "Damn it," he hissed.

As the boat drew closer, he could see that Charon was struggling with a column of water that kept rising from the bottom of the boat. Charon's pole slashed through the water as it attempted to spiral up. His strike made it fall back down, only to rise again.

"It's Mazu!" Quan exclaimed.

"Get back here!" D'Molay called out. He was relieved to see Quan retreat a few steps as the boat got within a dozen feet of the shoreline. Charon dropped his pole and tried to grab Mazu as she resumed her human form. His hands went around her throat but grasped nothing as she changed back into water and dropped again into the bottom of the boat. Immediately after, a column of water reappeared at the back of the boat coiled like a spring, jumping out over Charon's head and splashing onto the shore, where it rolled on the ground and took on the form of Mazu. Quan raced over to help her up.

"Quickly, to the gate!" she exclaimed.

D'Molay, with intense effort, managed to get to his feet as Quan seized their two remaining traveling bags. Charon stood indignantly in his boat, glaring at them.

"It is your fate to join us!"

The ferryman pulled a long, dark rib bone out of his cloak and threw it onto the shore. As soon as it hit the ground, it burst into flame and started to grow. Mazu didn't wait to see what it was doing as she ran towards the gate, with Quan close at her side. The burning rib quickly sprouted numerous other spurs and protrusions as D'Molay watched in horror. He saw that it was becoming some kind of creature as he stumbled after his friends. He estimated that the gate was easily three hundred feet away, but reaching it was their only chance. D'Molay fell again, and resorted to crawling forward. He lost sight of the burning thing near the shore, but he could hear a strange unearthly creaking and cracking as the thing grew and Charon called out, "Kill them! Kill them!"

Mazu and Quan turned back and hurried to help him. "Get him to the gate!" Mazu called out.

Quan, overburdened with their packs, bent down and awkwardly heaved D'Molay up from under his arm. "Come on, we have to run!"

D'Molay stumbled forward, his uncooperative legs providing some support as Quan dragged him forward. A deep growling sounded in the distance. Glancing over his shoulder, D'Molay saw a gigantic three-headed dog, its breath smoking of flames. He recognized it as Cerebus, one of the guardians of the Olympian underworld. The dog snarled as it charged up the trail toward Mazu, who had stayed behind to confront it.

"Mazu!" D'Molay cried out.

"Go - Go!" she called back.

As the two men struggled forward, Mazu stood before the ravenous beast. Two of its heads barked at her while the other kept its steely gaze fixed upon the men running away. Cerebus was easily ten feet tall. His bark was like the sound of thunder right overhead. Mazu directed a strong blast of water across the dog's faces, causing the demonic canine to step back a few steps in surprise. The flaming breath faded for a second, but returned in strength and blazed on. Cerebus shook the fluid off as anger replaced confusion. The dog snapped at Mazu, who just managed to change into water as its vicious teeth snapped at empty air.

She reformed further away from the gate, throwing another water blast at the beast, this time hitting it on the hindquarters. Cerebus turned, snarling as it ran at her. Mazu took a quick glance at the gate to see if the two men had made it, then quickly turned into water again.

"Come on, come on!" Quan yelled as he half-dragged, half-carried the burden of D'Molay along.

"I'm trying, damn these legs!" he exclaimed as they refused to move properly. Fear and excitement had seemed to help some, but he already felt exhausted, ready to collapse to the ground and give up the effort.

"We're almost there. A few more steps!"

They both fell against the gate, grabbing the bars to prop themselves up. Quan dropped the bags he was carrying at their feet. "Made it," D'Molay gasped, trying to catch his breath.

Quan looked over his shoulder back the way they had come. "No!"

D'Molay turned to see Cerebus charging up the trail right towards them. He saw no sign of Mazu. *It must have killed her,* he feared.

Now they faced the slavering jaws and massive form of an unstoppable killing machine. D'Molay could see no escape this time. *I've no strength to fight, and nowhere to run!*

"Th-That thing will kill us!" Quan exclaimed.

D'Molay leaned back against the gate, unable to support his own weight. "I know. This is the end."

Quan turned to his companion with a final confession. "I - I always thought you were crazy..."

Staring at the oncoming creature and resigned to his own death, D'Molay replied, "I never really liked you, Quan."

Just then, the gate started to shudder and clang as the portcullis slid up and the two men fell backward onto the dusty ground.

"Grab the bags, hurry!" they heard Mazu call out. Quan barely managed to snatch one of them as a head of Cerebus snapped at him. He quickly pulled the bag under the gate as it shut with a heavy metallic clang. "Get back, get back!" she called out. D'Molay reacted instinctively, rolling further away from the entrance. Quan was not as quick. The claws from the massive dog's paw rammed in between the bars of the gate, slashing Quan on the arm. He screamed and fled toward Mazu.

Mazu took the remaining bag from Quan. "Hurry," she urged. The two men followed, now supporting each other, half stumbling, half dragging themselves a bit further into the tunnel ahead. Cerebus howled indignantly as its prey escaped. The sound was ear splitting, and it ceased only when the beast decided to rip the travel bag they'd left behind to shreds. Once they were around a bend, the three of them collapsed in a heap, exhausted beyond words. They lay on the dusty stone floor, gasping for breath. D'Molay realized he felt safe for the first time in over a week.

"We . . . we made it. I thought you were dead," D'Molay managed to say as he sprawled on his back, his eyes closed.

"No," Mazu explained. "I was just trying to keep it busy. I changed into water and flowed right past you two and under the gate. Then I reformed on the other side and opened it."

"We are eternally in your debt, Lady Mazu." Quan gasped out.

"I'll second that," D'Molay added.

"Quan, come over here and I'll clean and bind your wound. Perhaps we can rest here for a while."

"But what of Charon and that dog?" Quan asked as he slid over to Mazu.

"I don't think they can pursue us past the gate or they would have done so by now. In fact, Charon may not even be able to set foot on this side of the river. I never saw him do it. Now, get me a bandage from the bag," she added, nodding to D'Molay

D'Molay dug through the remaining bag, his face growing frustrated the longer he looked. "We have none. The bandages were in the other bag, along with what remained of our water, and extra clothing."

"Do you have any other bad news?" Quan asked, wincing in pain as Mazu washed his wound with a wave of her watery hand.

D'Molay regarded the others, worry on his face clearly evident. "Yes, we have no food either. I guess I ate the last apple."

Surrounded by long forgotten memorials to those who had passed into the Underworld, Mazu, Quan and D'Molay had huddled together in the darkened corridor and slept like the dead. The glow of Mazu's staff kept the chamber from being pitch black.

When D'Molay slowly opened his eyes he saw Mazu next to him tending to Quan. She turned, her dark eyes meeting his. Gently letting go of Quan's arm, she smiled wanly and whispered, "It would appear you got some well deserved rest."

"I guess I did at that. How long was I asleep?"

"Hard to tell. A few hours or perhaps a day. I slept too. It would seem we all needed it."

"I feel better, too. At least I think I do."

"The wraiths' effect on us might fade now that we are past Hades' Domain. We may continue to recover the further away we get."

"I was so angry," D'Molay admitted as he analyzed his past feelings. "Despondent, hopeless."

"The Underworld is not a place for the living, as we have just experienced."

D'Molay nodded towards Quan. "It's a miracle we survived. What about him, will he recover?"

"I expect so. Another few inches and he would be missing his hand and wrist. We should get to a healer as soon as we can."

"Can we make it? We've still nothing to eat and no water."

Mazu smiled. "We always have water. Just nothing to put me in."

D'Molay blanched. "I'm not sure I could . . . drink you Mazu. I can't."

"I've heard you pray. Isn't there something about drink this in remembrance of me, this is my blood? I'm not sure what that all means, but it sounds like drinking those you love is part of the process."

"That's only done as part of a ceremony for salvation," he said. "And the difference is . . ." Mazu raised an eyebrow as if to dare him to try to repudiate her answer.

"My water is salvation. If you and Quan don't get some, you'll be sick, then dead. Now here, drink." Mazu held her hand above his face and a trickle of water ran down his forehead and over his lips.

Though he tried not to partake, his body's thirst betrayed him. He could not resist taking in the life-giving water and drinking it down. After a moment or two, his immediate need was quenched and he raised his hand to stop her. "Enough. Enough." He looked at her as anger, gratitude, repulsion and then serenity passed through his mind all at once. They exchanged a look of understanding that transcended anything they could have said aloud.

Mazu slowly stood up. "Time to rouse Quan and be on our way. We still have a long trek back up to the surface." She shook her servant awake and gave him words of encouragement.

D'Molay was uncertain if he would be able to walk or not. Bowing his head, he made a silent prayer for the strength to do so. Trying to raise himself up from the floor, he realized that the effort was futile. "I can't get up. My legs still feel frozen."

"Take my hand," Mazu ordered. "Quan, help him."

Quan went to the other side and took D'Molay's arm. Together they pulled him up as he wobbled between the two of them.

"See if you can move one of your legs now," Mazu suggested.

His expression grew pained from the effort, but he managed to slide his right leg forward.

"There. Progress. Now the other one," Mazu encouraged.

D'Molay concentrated again and slid his left leg. "Thank god for you two."

"Do you mean us, or your legs?" Quan asked.

"You and Mazu," he was forced to admit.

"We will continue like this for as long as we need to," Mazu vowed as she took a step forward.

"This is going to be a long walk," Quan complained.

They continued moving forward one slow step at a time for quite a while, but as they moved higher up  the winding corridor, D'Molay gained more feeling in his legs and was able to shuffle forward a little easier.

"You are going faster now," Mazu said, pleased.

"I still need you to keep me up, but perhaps that will change."

After another half hour of walking, they stopped to rest. Mazu turned to them. "You both need some more water, please take of me."

As she poured herself into his cupped hands, Quan exclaimed, "I am honored by your sacred water, Lady Mazu."

She stepped over the D'Molay and gave him an expectant look.

"All right." Despite his misgivings, he cupped his hands and took the water. "Doesn't it weaken you to surrender part of yourself like that?"

She gave him an unreadable expression that contained the slightest trace of a smile. "Me? I can always absorb more water into my being to replace what is lost. There is water to be found in these very walls. I have but to reach out to it."

Having refreshed them, Mazu sat down between the two men, putting her staff against the wall. "How is your arm?" she asked Quan.

"It hurts and is still bleeding, but at least I can still use it," he said looking past her and directly at D'Molay.

She examined his arm closely. "I fear there is little else we can do, for now."

Leaning back against the wall as he sat, D'Molay looked up and down the corridor. "Have you two noticed something missing?"

Quan rubbed his stomach. "You mean food?"

"No. Spirits. We haven't seen any the whole time we've been walking. When we first came down the other tunnel, we saw them every few minutes."

"You're right. Perhaps there haven't been many deaths in the area near this entrance," Mazu suggested.

"We should be glad those things aren't around," Quan insisted. "All their screaming and moaning - I've had enough of that."

Mazu's brow furrowed. "They are not 'things' Quan. They are the souls of the departed. One day you will be a spirit. You would be one now, if I had not renewed your body."

Bowing as he sat, Quan pleaded, "I'm sorry Lady Mazu, I meant no offence, please forgive me."

"Just remember to give proper respect for the dead," she chided.

"I promise," he bowed over and over.

D'Molay could tell that she seemed touchier about spirits now than he had ever seen her. He wondered what she had experienced in the moments she was separated from them.

"Let's move on. I'm ready to walk. Can you two help me up?" D'Molay asked, hoping his request would end Quan's ceaseless bowing and scraping.

They resumed their trek up the winding corridors, passing long abandoned shrines that had begun to crack and crumble. D'Molay was now actually lifting his feet instead of shuffling. They went along the twisting tunnel as it slowly rose up at an angle for another hour, D'Molay feeling better as they went. As the three of them rounded another corner, they were suddenly stopped dead in their tracks. Mazu stared in mute silence at what they saw.

"No, this can't be!" Quan cried out as he fell to his knees.

D'Molay lost his balance and slumped against the wall. He couldn't take his eyes away from the pile of rubble and rocks that filled the corridor in front of them. Dread and despair flooded through him like a freezing wind on a winter's day. "Now we know why there are no spirits. The tunnel collapsed."

"Then we're trapped, trapped down here like the dead!" Quan exclaimed.

Quan prostrated himself and wept silently while D'Molay sat on the stone floor amongst the debris and dust of the collapsed tunnel, still in shock at discovering their way out was completely cut off from the surface. "What do we do now?" His question was meant as much for himself as his companions.

Mazu walked further up, getting as close to the pile of boulders and rocks as she could. Finally she answered, "We can always go back and try to get to another gate."

"Cerebus will be waiting for us; and even if he isn't, Charon's not going to let you use his boat a second time. We have no way to get to another gate." D'Molay picked up a small piece of debris and tossed it against the wall, as he sat on the floor in frustration.

"Then we must move forward, somehow," Mazu replied as she ran her hand slowly along the rocks.

Noticing her actions, D'Molay slid a little closer to her. "What is it? You have an idea, don't you?"

"Perhaps. Though it might be very risky," she warned.

"Just about everything we've done the last two months has been risky. What are you thinking?"

"I can pass through that rubble in my watery form. I might learn something to help us, such as how far the tunnel collapse goes." She began tapping and probing the spaces between the rocks with her staff.

"If the rock fall blocks only a few feet, we might be able to move enough rubble so that Quan and I can get to the other side," D'Molay theorized.

She turned away from the boulders to look at him. "Actually I wasn't thinking that. However, it is an excellent suggestion. Let me see how deep this rubble pile is." Before he could ask what her alternate idea was, Mazu changed into water and flowed into the rocks.

Gritting his teeth as a twinge of pain ran through his legs, D'Molay stared at the spot where Mazu had just stood. "Let's hope you find some good news," he said to the wall. Quan remained on his knees, bent over, mumbling incoherently.

D'Molay decided to put his own plan into action. "Let's move some of these rocks. Quan - Quan!"

"I hear you. I was praying to the elder Chinese gods for our deliverance. Mazu is in need of additional help from her brethren."

"Finish that and help me up."

Quan gave him a doubtful look. "If you can't stand, how can you move rocks?"

"Just get over here."

Reluctantly, Quan came to D'Molay and helped him stand. "Now what?"

"Help me get to the edge of the cave-in. We'll start moving what we can."

D'Molay knew he was an impatient man, and he would rather futilely try to clear a path than sit and do nothing. Although walking was still difficult, D'Molay found he was able to use his upper body strength to roll some of the rocks out of the pile to Quan, who shifted them out of the way.

"This is all well and good, but for all we know, the entire tunnel has collapsed and there is nothing but rubble," Quan complained.

"If you wanted to rest, why didn't you just say so?"

A trickle of water flowed over D'Molay's hand and rose into the air, forming and growing. Mazu took her human shape as she leaned against her staff. Her face was grim.

"Lady Mazu," Quan bowed.

"So what lies ahead?" D'Molay immediately asked.

She frowned. The lines in her face seemed more apparent from the faintly glowing light of her staff. "The tunnel collapse goes on for over a hundred feet. I'm afraid I see no way past this point."

D'Molay was crestfallen. He leaned back against the rocks, staring at them helplessly. "That's it then? We're trapped. Trapped with no way out?"

"I fear so." She answered. Quan fell back to the floor and started to quietly sob. Resting her hand on Quan's shoulder, Mazu said, "You have served me well, Quan. I never should have let you accompany us on this journey."

His face turned up to hers, his eyes reddened by tears. "It has been my honor to serve you, Lady Mazu. I'm sorry my service to you is over."

"It may not yet be over. We'll just have to go back," she said.

"Back? It means certain death," Quan mumbled.

"What choice is left to us?" Mazu asked.

D'Molay watched them. It was hard to believe that something as simple as a cave-in had doomed their quest. But the beginning of an idea nibbled at the edge of his thoughts. He kept trying to bring it all together as though looking for the missing pieces of a mosaic. "Tell me again what you found," he finally said.

"The cave-in goes at least a hundred feet ahead. I don't think there is any way we could move those rocks, even with my water abilities. There's just too much debris."

"Did you try all directions?"

"I went back and forth four or five times, looking to see if there were air pockets I could widen. But there aren't enough gaps to make that work. That was my original plan. I hoped to build a tunnel for you two to swim through."

"What about up?" D'Molay pointed towards the ceiling.

"Up? What do you mean?"

"These tunnels wind around back and forth, always rising. What if the cave-in doesn't block the tunnel section above us? Maybe we could make a path upwards to that next level?"

Mazu's mouth opened, a look of surprise etched on her face. "I never thought of that. We'd have to hope that the upper section is close enough for that to work. I'll check right now." Mazu quickly turned into water and flowed along the rising pile of debris. Finally the last of her slipped into a crack and disappeared.

Looking up, Quan asked, "Do you really think there's a chance for this idea of yours?"

"It is our only chance," he said. This time, it was D'Molay who got down on his knees and made a prayer that Mazu's search would be successful.

They waited what seemed like endless minutes.

A stream of water suddenly flowed out of top of the rubble pile and onto the floor, becoming Mazu. "I think we can get up to the next level!" she exclaimed.

Quan's eyes opened wide. "You mean we can escape?"

"Where do we start digging?" D'Molay asked eagerly.

She pointed up at the ceiling on the left side of the tunnel. "There. If we move enough debris, we should be able to get to the tunnel above."

D'Molay walked right over to the spot, with some slight difficulty.

Mazu smiled. "You did that on your own."

"I didn't even think about it, I just walked."

Quan smiled. "Good, now we won't have to carry you the rest of the way. How far is it to this tunnel above us?"

"Perhaps five feet. We must be careful though, or we might cause a further cave-in," she reminded the two men. "I'm going to go back up

and work from above." She flowed back up the rock pile. D'Molay immediately set to work pulling rocks down, with Quan moving the new debris
to the sides of the tunnel.

Several times during the course of their efforts, small rocks and dirt
rained down on them. With D'Molay being at the top of the hole, most
grazed his head. Once he felt dazed and saw stars, but he wouldn't let
anything slow him down. Every so often, Mazu would flow down and
then back up the gaps, trying to widen the space. D'Molay worked
doggedly to get the tunnel finished. He had trouble breathing. Several
times his vision narrowed and he felt dizzy, but he said nothing.
Eventually the three of them cleared enough debris to make a shaft just
wide enough for them to crawl through. D'Molay was covered in dust
and his hands were bloody from moving all the rocks, but he rejoiced that
finally there was a way out.

Mazu stood in the upper tunnel and lowered her staff into the opening. "Take hold, I'll help pull you up."

Quan immediately grabbed for the staff. Though he didn't say so,
D'Molay wasn't sure he'd be able to climb up without both of them helping to pull him through. His legs felt numb and heavy. D'Molay helped
push Quan up into the opening. Within seconds after Quan's feet disappeared, something hit D'Molay on the head. His legs gave out from
under him and he collapsed into the pile of rubble.

The next thing he was aware of was Mazu looking down upon him, a
concerned look on her face. But she looked strange, out of focus. He felt
her hand on his forehead. She was speaking, but he couldn't comprehend
what she was saying at first.

" . . . don't have any rope. We'll have to wait until you can climb up on
your own."

"Whaa…" He tried to ask what had happened, but seemed unable to
form words or even a complete thought. Like his vision, everything
seemed fuzzy and distant. He wanted to close his eyes and sleep, but
fought the urge - he had to know what went wrong. Raising his hand, he
pointed up at the ceiling. "Uhhh whaaa," was all that came from his tongue.

"There was a cave-in, you were knocked out. It's all right, the opening
is still above us. Quan is up there now. Once you've rested a bit, you can
try to climb out." Cool water flowed from Mazu's hand onto his forehead
as she tried to make him a little more comfortable.

He nodded his understanding, put his head back on the soft dirt, and closed his eyes, falling unconscious almost immediately.

Mazu stood up. "This entire journey down here is like being attacked by a swarm of bees," she proclaimed. "No single sting is fatal, but with each attack, moving forward becomes more and more difficult."

"You speak great truth, my goddess," Quan called down the hole. "I double-checked. The rope was in the other bag."

Mazu looked back up at him. "Look around in some of the alcoves. You may find rope that was tied around an offering or used to support a beam. We need get him up there in case the tunnel collapses. It is precarious at best."

Quan quickly disappeared from sight.

Mazu gazed at her unconscious companion, wondering how much more he could endure and what further cost they would pay to complete their task. She bent back down to clean the steady trickle of blood from the right side of his head. She took the silk belt off her robe and wound it around his head in an effort to stem the bleeding. "We'll need to get you and Quan to a healer as soon as possible," she said softly. "Humans are so fragile at times."

Quan's voice came from above. "Mistress, I found rope but it's very old."

"Excellent. We have to hope it will last long enough for our needs. Hand down one end of it." Quan complied and she soon had the rope wrapped around D'Molay's torso and under his arms so they could pull him up. Carefully, she positioned him under the opening and signaled Quan to start hauling.

The movement woke D'Molay. "Uhhh? Ahh!" For a moment, he had no idea where he was. He panicked, thinking he'd been captured as he felt the rope around his chest. He started to struggle.

Mazu quickly put her hands on either side of his face, forcing him to look at her. "It's me. We are going to haul you up to the higher tunnel. Do you understand?" She spoke in a slow clear voice.

He calmed down as recognition of his situation dawned upon him. D'Molay nodded affirmatively to her and squeezed her hand. She smiled. "Once we get you to the opening, do what you can to scramble through and avoid getting hurt. I'm going to go help Quan pull you up."

Nodding, he watched as Mazu held the rope in her hand, became water, and flowed up it. Shortly after that, D'Molay felt the rope tighten under his arms as he began to lift off the ground. Somehow, his instinct for self-preservation kept him aware enough to make it easier for them to pull him out. Most importantly, he managed to avoid hitting his head again. It throbbed with a dull pain as he scrambled through the hole and emerged, gasping for breath on the floor of the higher level tunnel.

"We - we did it," Quan wheezed out.

"Indeed. Even I had my doubts," Mazu added as she sat back against the wall.

D'Molay almost immediately slipped again into unconsciousness. After Quan had rested from his efforts, Mazu sent him ahead to scout their way. As she sat beside D'Molay she began working the rope into a net, fearing they would be forced to drag D'Molay the rest of the way out. She was worrying about finding a healer to tend him and wondering how long his recovery would take as she heard Quan's footsteps coming back along the hallway.

"Quan?"

He rounded the corner, his face beaming. "The exit is only a few more corridor lengths to go. We are very close!"

"Good. Help me with this rope and we will be on our way." Despite her reserve, Mazu was as excited as Quan. A few moments later, they had created a sort of stretcher. She had separated her staff into two parts and they tied the rope net between them. She laid it flat on the ground. They picked D'Molay up and gently placed him on it.

Mazu saw a large pool of blood on the floor where D'Molay's head had been. For a moment, she felt tears well up in her eyes, but repressed them, trying to remain strong. "Take the back, I'll take the front. We have little time."

They picked up D'Molay and headed along the tunnel toward the exit. A few moments later they stood before a large stone slab that was the door to the outside world. Mazu saw a small niche next to it, just like the other entrance had. "Put him down. We need the seal." Mazu opened his tunic. "It's not around his neck. That's where he always keeps it! Look in the bag."

Quan rummaged through their remaining bag. "It's not here! It must have been in the other one!"

Mazu felt her stomach knot up in anguish. "No. It can't end like this. Wait. His pockets!" Mazu quickly got down on her knees and started going through D'Molay's clothing. She found some coins, his map, and then her hand felt the cool surface of the round seal. "Here it is, thank the Fates."

"I give all my thanks to you," Quan said.

Mazu took the Council seal and placed it in the niche next to the stone door.

Chapter 16

The Horsemen

The ancient door shuddered. For a moment, it looked as though it was not going to move at all, but finally it slid three-quarters of the way open. Quickly picking up D'Molay, they stepped out into the light of day. They'd become so used to the darkness that the sunlight was bright and disorienting; they couldn't see anything. Mazu heard murmuring voices, smelled fresh grass and the aroma of farmland animals.

The voices got louder and they heard men on horseback approaching.

"Zilac! Al seleitala acasv ve avil!"

"The humans won't understand Etruscan. Use the common tongue," a second strong, male voice said, adding, "Hold, humans! Go no further."

Mazu and Quan put D'Molay on the ground. "We mean no harm," Mazu replied.

"Only a fool would believe the words of strangers who emerge from a forbidden entrance to the Underworld. What is your purpose here? Has Hades sent you?"

"Hades? Certainly not," Mazu answered before thinking about whether it might have been better to say 'yes.' Her eyes adjusted to the brightness enough to see to whom she was speaking. They weren't men on horseback; they faced a dozen centaurs, some armed with spears, others with arrow-set bows at the ready. The sun was still so bright that it hurt to look, but she couldn't resist the urge to fully satisfy her curiosity. Beyond the guards, she could see at least fifty other centaurs, male, female and children, all staring in rapt attention. She had been uncertain what they would find on the other side of the gate, but had never expected to appear in the middle of a centaur enclave.

"Why have you come forth, woman?" the warrior asked.

"We are only weary travelers who have escaped from the depths of the Underworld."

"Get the elder," called out one of the older warriors. "He will know the truth of this, whether they be human or demon."

Mazu saw one of the females gallop off.

"Say nothing, Quan. Let me do the talking," Mazu whispered.

"Y-yes, of course," he stammered out, his shocked expression virtually carved onto his face. She could see his fear as the centaurs pointed their spears directly at him.

The party of guards said nothing more to them while they waited for their elder to arrive. A few minutes later a dignified, older centaur with curly white hair and a matching beard trotted up, followed by the female centaur that had gone to fetch him. The horse part of his body was a silvery gray with flecks of black; his long tail matched the color of the hair on his head. He wore nothing save a belt around his torso that had a knife and small carrying pouch attached to it. In fact,

almost all the centaurs wore little other than jewelry or belts. He looked at the three strangers with an expression of wary curiosity. "That door to Hades has not been opened in half a millennium. It is said only gods and heroes emerge from the Underworld. Which are you?" he asked.

Mazu quickly wondered what D'Molay would do in a situation like this. Then, like the sun coming up over the mountainside, the answer came to her. Her face took on a haughty mask of godliness.

"We are both hero and god. I am Mazu, deity of the Great Lake. This is my servant Quan and this man we bear is a hero. We went into Hades itself to bring him back to the world of the living. He is known as D'Molay the Tracker and works for the High Council." Mazu held the seal out for emphasis. "Our journey has been a difficult one. We bring no trouble. I ask only for hospitality and aid for these two men. They are in need of whatever healing you can provide. I can reward you for your help. Then we will be on our way, back to the City of the Gods where duty awaits us." As she finished with her pronouncement, she watched the assembled centaurs, gauging their reaction.

Several of them bowed as her gaze met theirs. Some looked suspicious, while others seemed to be waiting, uncertain what to think. The older centaur took a step or two forward, bowing slightly. "I have heard of this D'Molay. Was it he that found the great beast that ravaged our lands last season?"

"Yes. He also fought at Ares' Fortress against the hordes of Egyptos. It was there he lost his one true love. He has been heartsick ever since. He lies before you now, in need of your help." Mazu looked sadly down at her unconscious friend. She wasn't sure if centaurs had romantic emotions, but in her opinion it seemed as if all Olympians were overly sentimental and dramatic. She didn't think it would hurt to emphasize that in D'Molay's case. Everything she had said was truth, albeit stretched a little here and there.

The elder centaur turned back to others. "We will go to the Creche. Quickly then, gallop to the healer and tell her we are coming. Arrange food and drink for our visitors."

Mazu smiled. "I thank you Elder. Have you a name?"

"I am Carystus. Come with me to our place of healing, goddess Mazu. First though, I ask you close this cursed door to the underworld."

"Gladly." She turned and placed the Council seal in the outside niche. The door rumbled once again and slowly closed. As it did, Mazu gave a sigh of relief. "There. Your people are safe. I suspect it will be another millennium before that door opens again."

She noticed Quan was now smiling despite the fact his arm was badly cut. She was glad he'd remained silent. Leaning over to check on D'Molay, she noticed his breathing appeared to be shallower.

"You and you, put away those bows and carry this fallen hero," Carystus ordered two males, who immediately complied. He led the way, Mazu walking at his side and Quan behind her, while the two warriors carried D'Molay between them. As they approached the Creche, other centaurs gathered, wanting to get a look at what had come through Hades' gate.

They proceeded across an open plaza toward a large building, which Mazu guessed had once been the area's main temple. It stood directly across from the entrance to the Underworld. The village it dominated was a series of villas and other Roman-style buildings all arranged in a circle with a large fountain in the center. Mazu suspected that at one time the fountain had been just for decoration, but now the centaurs were using it as a source of water. She saw two females dipping buckets into it as she walked by.

The group passed marble columns and ornate statues of people that looked completely out of place among the unadorned centaurs, all of whom seemed concerned with basics like gathering food or making wooden tools rather than worshipping or keeping up the appearance of a once ostentatious temple complex. Most of the grounds had become overgrown with ivy and moss. The statues were weathered and stained by the passage of time and neglect. "Was this a sacred place in the past?" Mazu asked.

"Yes, but it was abandoned long ago, once the priests could no longer use it for burial rights. Eventually all the humans left and we took it as our village. It has been ours for over four hundred years." He pointed to the larger building. "This is our Creche. The healer dwells here." He motioned at the ramp up to the august building, which, though run-down, seemed little changed from how it must have looked when it was a temple save for one detail: the stairs had been covered over with hardened clay. They now formed a ramp. Mazu assumed it made it easier for the centaurs to come and go, but said nothing as they ascended.

They entered a rotunda, whose small, opening at the top let the sun in. There were many centaur children in the shelter. Several male and female adults supervised them, teaching lessons or caring for the needs of the youngest. As Carystus entered, all stopped what they were doing to stare at the procession.

"Bring him this way," Carystus said, crossing the chamber and heading towards an archway on the other side of the intricately tiled floor.

The group followed into the next chamber, which Mazu guessed had been a worship or prayer room. Carystus pulled aside a curtain and revealed an elaborately carved marble altar, large enough for a centaur to lie upon. She noticed shelves with glass jars of ointments, baskets that held tree bark or dried flowers, rolls of bandages and other tools of healing. A table with scrolls and other jars of liquids stood against the back wall beside a wooden door. Mazu saw no chairs, quickly realizing the centaurs would have no use for them. There were several clay jugs and buckets on the altar which Carystus quickly removed.

The two warriors placed D'Molay on the marble slab. Mazu and Quan stood at his side. She put her hand on his chest, feeling for a heartbeat. "It's slow and erratic," she said, looking off towards the entrance, hoping the healer would arrive.

"Find Perca, quickly," Carystus ordered the two warriors.

A moment later two young centaurs, a boy and girl, entered. Each carried a tray. One held assorted fruits and nuts, the other held two mugs. "Elder, we brought refreshment for the strangers."

"Place it on the table." Carystus pointed. Then, addressing his two guests, he added, "Help yourselves if you wish." Walking back towards the curtain he escorted the children out. "You two can go now. In fact, all of you go back to what you were doing. You'll hear all about all this soon enough." He pulled the curtain shut to give the four of them a modicum of privacy. Before he had time to turn around, Quan was already at the tray, eating.

Though hungry, Mazu had other concerns. She noticed a small pool of blood on the altar beneath D'Molay's head. Part of her feared he would never awaken.

A moment later from behind them the door opened, followed by a strong female voice. "What are these humans doing in the Asclepeia?"

They turned to see a female centaur enter, carrying a basket of mushrooms and flowers. She had very long brown hair that wrapped around her torso almost like a shawl. Her hindquarters were chestnut brown.

Carystus pivoted to face her. "Where have you been, Perca? I sent half the village out looking for you."

"I was in the deep woods, gathering rare herbs. Why are they here?"

"These travelers have need of your skills."

She glanced briefly at D'Molay. "I am not in the habit of treating humans. They care little for us. Why should we care for them?"

Perca kicked the door behind her closed with her back hoof. Then she put the basket down on the same table where the food was placed, pushing Quan out of the way.

Carystus put his hand on her arm. "I know what humans did long ago, but you cannot blame all of humanity for the sins of a few."

"Can't I? As healer I choose who to treat and not treat."

"His life is at stake. Please." Mazu dared to interrupt even though she knew doing so might anger the healer even more. Carystus interceded, pointing to D'Molay.

"This man tracked the beast last season. He helped Ares catch it. Would you so easily let him die after he saved our brethren? I'm asking you as herd Elder, Perca. Help him."

Unable to hold his gaze, she looked down. "Very well, I will do this for you."

Perca walked over to the altar and examined D'Molay. "Slow heartbeat. Head trauma. He's lost a lot of blood." Ignoring Mazu and Quan, she addressed Carystus. "I don't know if I can save him. He looks to be a lost cause to me."

Mazu had finally had enough. She grew in size and took on a translucent watery sheen. "I am not a human. I am a goddess and will not be ignored!"

Perca and Carystus took several steps back, fear written on their faces. Even Quan was surprised and retreated.

Carystus held his hand up in fear. "No, please, wait . . ."

"I have just come through Hades itself to bring this hero to the surface. I will not be thwarted by a centaur who has forgotten her duty. You are a healer - here is your patient. Heal him!" Mazu stayed large, her expression one of disfavor and indignation. She stared down at Perca, waiting for a response.

Chapter 16: The Horsemen

"I - I'm sorry goddess, I didn't know . . . I will help." She covered her face in shame and fear.

Mazu resumed her regular size and became solid once again. Her face turned calm, though her manner was terse. "Now. What can be done to aid him and what might you need from me? As I told Carystus, we are willing to pay for your assistance."

"We can worry about that later, goddess," Carystus said quickly. "Perca, do whatever need be done to save him."

"Yes. Yes, I promise. Hand me bandages from the shelf behind you. I'll mix a salve to heal his wound. His old bandages need to come off."

Her demeanor changed and the centauress acted the way Mazu would expect a healer to. She stepped forward. "I can remove them. You mix the salve."

All of them, even Quan who disposed of the old dressings, worked in concert to treat D'Molay's wound. Perca quickly mixed a variety of dried herbs and flowers with a mortar and pestle. Once she had completed that task, she poured the powdery substance into a different jar which held a dark, gooey substance. She then reached for a small silver box, which fit in the palm of her hand.

Her eyes darted to Carystus, who nodded. "Use it Perca. He would have approved."

She opened the lid of the box and a bluish glow came from inside. Perca then poured the contents of the box into the jar. To Mazu, it appeared that the box had held something like grains of wheat, though there were very few of them in the box. Each grain seemed to glow as it rested on the surface of the jar's dark contents.

"What is that?" Mazu couldn't help but ask.

"These are the last seeds of life. They were given to Chiron by the Titan, Kronus. It is said that they can only be harvested from the Elysian Fields by a Titan, so they are incredibly rare."

Sealing the top of the jar, Perca placed it on the altar. "Whoever cares for this human the most needs to shake it for three minutes. Keep thinking about how you care for him, as the magic will be more powerful that way. The jar will get very hot in your hands. Do not drop it, I cannot make more. There are no seeds left."

"I will do this." Mazu picked up the glass jar and started to shake it gently back and forth.

"You must shake it more vigorously than that, and don't stop."

Perca placed various metal instruments on the altar next to D'Molay. Some of them resembled small knives while others looked like spatulas or spoons. She carefully cleaned D'Molay's head wound, switching back and forth from one tool to the next and using clean rags to soak up his blood.

Quan drifted back over to the table, alternately drinking from the mug and eating whatever food his hand found on the tray.

After about half a minute, Mazu started to feel warmth coming from the jar, which was also glowing a little more than it had before. Soon it went from warm to hot, its glow also increasing. Mazu was tempted to run water onto its surface to cool it down, but worried that it might need the heat to work properly. As she continued shaking, the jar grew very hot and her hands started to smart. Then the heat became nearly unbearable. Mazu furrowed her brow and kept at it. She looked at D'Molay to remind herself why she was enduring the pain, focused on how she wanted him well again. "Ahh," she hissed out through gritted teeth.

"Mistress?" Quan put down his food and went to her side.

"It's . . . just . . ." was all she managed to say. She was certain her hands were on fire. The pain was incredibly intense but still she continued to shake the jar. The glow was so bright that Mazu couldn't see her hands.

"That's enough, put it down," Perca called out.

Mazu immediately complied, quickly slamming the jar down on the marble slab. Once she'd done so, the glow started to fade. She could see the vessel was now cracked in several places. Perca used a cloth to hold the jar and uncork it. Looking at her hands, Mazu saw no damage, and the pain of the heat was fading.

Carystus spoke a prayer in the language of the Etruscans, its words unknown to Mazu. He kept repeating it as Perca attended to D'Molay.

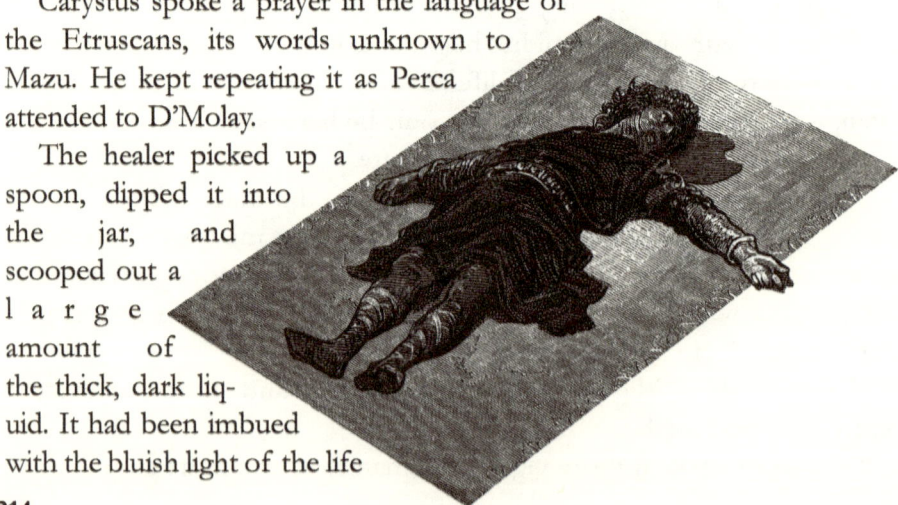

The healer picked up a spoon, dipped it into the jar, and scooped out a large amount of the thick, dark liquid. It had been imbued with the bluish light of the life seeds. She let it drip onto D'Molay's wound, then got another spoonful and repeated her actions.

"I must hurry. The healing magic fades quickly." Perca worked efficiently, dabbing the back of the liquid-drenched spoon on any other cuts or injuries she could see. Using the spatula-like tool, she smoothed more of the glowing liquid around his head wound as if filling a hole in a wall with wet plaster. "Hold his head up. I need to apply the bandages."

Mazu lifted D'Molay's head while Perca wrapped it with a linen strip, tying it securely in place. Stepping back, the healer crossed her arms and took a look at her handiwork. "That's all I can do for him now. This man of yours has been though quite a lot. Frankly, I'm surprised he's alive at all." Perca's eyes shifted to Quan. "What about him? His arm looks like it could use some healing. There's still a little of the salve left, but its power fades with every moment."

"Please." Quan stepped forward.

Perca picked up the jar and stirred the contents. "Clean his wound, but hurry before this congeals."

Peeling the wrappings off his damaged arm, Mazu could see that it was gangrenous and septic. "Quan, you should have told me it was this bad."

"You had enough to worry about, Lady Mazu," he replied proudly.

Letting her hands become water, she quickly washed his arm as Carystus stepped forward to dry it with a clean cloth.

"Give me your arm. Hurry." Quan extended it, closing his eyes tightly, while Perca poured the remaining salve on. Then she spread it around the wound to fully cover it. Mazu could see that the salve was only glowing slightly as Carystus began to speak the ancient prayer once again.

"What did this to you?" Perca asked.

"It was - a dog with three heads," Quan answered in between winces of pain.

She finished treating his arm and stepped back to rest for a moment. She'd concentrated her entire being on the task at hand and now seemed to be catching her breath. Finally she turned to Mazu. "Goddess, I've done what you asked." She bowed slightly.

"And I thank you, truly and deeply. What are their chances?"

"I can't guarantee that either of your servants will fully recover, but I did all I could do for them. I even used the last of our sacred seeds. If they fail, I don't know what else might succeed. D'Molay will have to rest for a while. How long will depend on his will to live, the blood he's lost, and the strength of the salve."

"I know you did your best, Perca. Of that I have no doubt. Allow me to pay you as promised. What is your fee for the healing you've just done?"

"Fee?" Perca gave Mazu a disgusted look. "I don't take money for what I do. I heal the members of our herd, or sometimes centaurs from other herds, but to accept payment for saving life, is . . . is barbaric. It is not our way. That is the human way. I did this because Carystus asked it of me, and because your anger was great. I did not want your vengeance to leave this room to wreak havoc among our people."

"I see. Then I must apologize for using my status to force you into acting. I am in your debt. Is there nothing I can do to repay you?" Mazu asked, her arms opened like that of a convict begging for mercy before a judge.

"Unless you can get more seeds of life, I can think of nothing I have need of. I'm sorry I didn't want to help. My grandfather was Chiron. He taught mankind the healing arts and his reward was to be betrayed by those he aided. And when I was young, men killed my father. So I hope you'll understand my misgivings about helping humans or accepting anything from them." Perca's face grew red and hers eyes glistened as she spoke.

Mazu bowed her head. "I see. Humanity is often less than humane. I have seen that aspect of them myself. Even as a goddess getting more seeds is not something within my power."

Carystus interjected. "Perhaps you can provide something else of use to the entire herd. Might that be a solution that will satisfy you both?"

"You are the elder," Perca said. "I give this debt the goddess feels to you. I care not what the two of you do with it." She looked back over to D'Molay. "This human should rest here at least until the morning and one of his own should stay with him. Hopefully he'll be fine on the morrow and you can be on your way. I am needed across the pasture. Sethra is in early labor and I need to be there for the birthing."

"Give her my blessing," Carystus replied with a smile.

"Certainly. She will be pleased to have it." Perca reclaimed her mushroom basket and began to add some other supplies from her table to it. "I may be gone for a day or two. If you humans have further needs, you can send for me."

Mazu wished her the best of luck, but she couldn't help but wonder if Perca needed to leave so soon. It seemed more likely she was just extremely uncomfortable around humans. She remained standing at her table with her back to them packing, as if they weren't even there.

Carystus broke the tension with a gracious offer.

"May I show you the village? The herd will be curious about the strangers who opened the gate and we can discuss your plans."

"That would be most kind," Mazu said, "but we should stay with D'Molay until he's well."

"I will stay with him, Lady Mazu," Quan spoke up, taking a swig from his mug. She smiled at him, suspecting he was reluctant to be parted from the food.

"Alright. Can you see that my servant has more food and drink? Then I will go with you," Mazu acquiesced.

"Of course." Carystus walked over to the curtain and pulled it open. The boy who brought the tray earlier was still loitering about, perhaps eavesdropping or just waiting for further orders.

"Ahh, good, Larce. Bring another tray of food and drink. When you return, give it to the man with the bad arm."

"Yes, Elder." He peeked past Carystus who noticed his eyes linger on Perca.

"You want to ask Perca something?"

"Please."

He trotted over to the centauress. "Healer Perca?"

She turned. "Are you worried about your mother?"

"Yes. Will she be all right?"

Perca put her arm around his shoulder and gave him a hug. "Don't worry, I'm going there now. She bore you well, I'm sure she'll do fine this second time." Perca picked up the basket filled with supplies. "I'll be at her side in a few minutes. Now you must do what the Elder has asked of you."

"I will." The young centaur, reassured about the birthing, galloped off on his new mis-

sion. Perca nodded to Carystus as she left out the back door.

Carystus looked over his shoulder at Mazu. "There. Now let me take you for a tour."

Mazu followed him down the ramp as the locals gaped at the goddess who'd escaped from Hades.

Carystus led her to the edge of the hill where the old temple had been built. Mazu gazed out over the countryside. Scattered cypress trees and mighty oaks grew in lush, green grasslands. She could see other centaurs in the fields, gathering berries and grapes just down the slope. "Your village is lovely and the land so peaceful and pastoral. No wonder your people have stayed here four hundred years."

"We are wanderers by nature, but call these lands home," he said, waving to one of the centaurs below.

Looking out over the scenic view reminded her of something she'd been meaning to ask. "Where are we? How close is the Eastern shore?"

"Not too far. A day's ride. There is a map of Olympia in the vault of knowledge. I can show you. Come." Carystus turned and headed back to the main plaza. Mazu followed and they walked to another building with numerous marble columns at its front and another ramp that led up to the entrance. "We keep our learning and history scrolls here. We'll look at the map and get some refreshment." As they entered he added, "I would love to hear more of your journey. To have survived the rigors of Hades you must truly be a powerful goddess. You know, our ancestors helped Hercules on his journey to the Underworld, so we've heard many tales of it. How did you survive down there?"

"I am hardly a powerful goddess, though perhaps in my old age I have become resourceful." She told Carystus a shortened version of their adventure through the underworld, glossing over some details and changing the reason for going down there. "I owe D'Molay a great debt, so I took it upon myself to rescue him from Hades. It was not his time to die, for he has many other tasks yet to perform for the Council," she concluded.

"He is lucky to have you as benefactor," Carystus replied with a nod of approval.

They walked into the vault, which reminded Mazu of some of the nicer villas in the Olympus quarter of the City of the Gods. The polished marble floor was littered with leaves and debris which may have fallen off the centaurs' hooves or blown in from the outside through the two large, propped-open doors. They then entered a larger room with a wooden table in the middle and many shelves of scrolls on the walls.

Carystus walked over to a shelf and chose a rolled parchment. Untying the binding string, he unrolled the scroll. It was a map of the local area and the shoreline of Olympia, though it was written in a language Mazu was unable to read. She suspected it was also Etruscan, like many of the names she'd heard today.

"Our village is Pelion, right here," he said, pointing at a spot on the map. "You are perhaps a day from the coast. There is a trail here that leads to one of the main trade roads. Once you get to that, go east."

"I see. What do you think is the best way to get to Dioscrias? Our boat is harbored there." She noticed Carystus frown a little as she mentioned their destination.

"It is farther north in Helios' lands, up the coast. That is another day's ride." He pointed to a location in the far north of the map. "Beyond that is the Hindu Realm."

The young girl centaur who'd brought a tray into the healer's chamber entered, carrying a pitcher and two mugs. "H-Here is some pomegranate juice, Elder," she said awkwardly, staring at Mazu the whole time, her eyes as big as saucers. The girl quickly trotted out, her task complete.

He poured them both a drink. "Do water deities get thirsty?"

"This one does." She picked up the mug and took a sip.

"You asked about transport. Some of our warriors might be interested in an excuse to take you. We rarely go north. Helios has little patience for our ways, so we keep our distance." He took a big swig from his mug.

Mazu nodded in agreement. "Before we go any further, we still need to decide how I might reward you for your aid. I had hoped to use my powers in some way, but you seem to have plenty of water. I know Perca would not accept payment in coin, but what of you? Would you like some gold?"

Carystus smiled. "We have little use for gold. We do use silver to make things we need. That would be acceptable if you have any."

"We do. You shall have all the silver we still carry with us. Shall I pay you now?"

He shook his head negatively. "Our ways are different from those of men or gods. You will pay the people on the way back to the Creche."

"I would be honored to."

Mazu asked for more detail on the suggested route and what to avoid on the journey. Their discussion complete, and their drinks finished, Carystus rolled up the map and put it away. "Let's go back out. You can be rid of your silver, and I'll see if I can find any who are willing to transport you to Dioscrias."

Their next stop was the fountain in the center of the village. Most of the villagers had seen the goddess at this point, but many still stole glances at her when they thought she wasn't looking.

"Do you have the silver?" he asked.

"Yes." Mazu got out D'Molay's pouch of coins.

"Place one piece at a time around the stone edge of the fountain until you run out of coins." He walked along the fountain as he spoke.

Scrupulously she placed them as he'd requested. When she finished, there were forty-seven coins arranged in a small arc along the ledge of the fountain. As they gleamed in the sun, she could see why men were attracted to them. Mazu thought they resembled a multitude of tiny pools of solid water, reflecting the daylight.

"What happens next?" she asked.

Turning back over his shoulder he said, "We go to check on your D'Molay."

Mazu gave him a confused look as she caught up to him. "And what of the coins?"

"They will be there for those who feel they need them. None of my people will take more than one. Some of those coins might sit there for days before they are picked up. That is our way. We take what we need, when we need it."

She smiled as they walked on. "Your ways are different. Those coins wouldn't last two minutes in any human village."

"Man is a flawed creature. Weak of body and spirit." As they walked on, he continued, "Like Chiron, the first centaur, I wished mankind well and tried to be a part of their society. Now, I keep our people at arm's length from humanity."

Mazu looked down. "Yes, I know of what you speak. But we gods are hardly any better. We argue, steal and get jealous, just like mankind," she said as they walked up the ramp into the Creche.

After they crossed the rotunda, she couldn't help but notice a warrior had been stationed just outside the curtain of the healer's area. She didn't bother to ask why he was there. *I suppose I can't blame them for being cautious.*

The guard parted the curtain to the healer's chamber and held it open for them.

Carystus stopped. "Check on your people and rest. I'm going to see who might provide transport. The children will bring more food and drink if you need it."

"Thank you. You have truly earned our gratitude. If there is anything else I can do, you have but to ask."

He bowed as Mazu walked past the guard. She fixed her gaze on D'Molay, who was still lying motionless on the altar. Quan was curled up on the floor. Her eyes widened as she realized he seemed hurt. Hurrying over, she bent down to check on him. "Quan?"

"Ohh," he moaned. His face was pained as he kept rubbing his abdomen.

"What happened? Were you attacked? Poisoned?" She looked closely but could see no blood or wounds.

Slowly he opened his eyes. "Mistress, I... I." Then he simply pointed towards the table where the trays had been left.

Looking over, she took note of the trays and walked over to them. Her brow furrowed as realization crept in. "Quan, did you eat all the food they brought?" She turned around, waiting for an answer.

With guilt and pain he nodded his head affirmatively.

"Oh, you greedy dog! Serves you right. Perhaps next time you will show some moderation in your actions! Sometimes you can be so - Human!"

"I am sorry," he whimpered. "It was so good I couldn't help myself."

"Ah, then it is the food's fault and not yours? You will just have to suffer for the sin of gluttony. I suppose a tiger cannot change its stripes. Though you are hardly like any tiger I have come across."

Disgusted with her servant, Mazu

checked to see if D'Molay's condition had changed. Gently, she placed her hand on his chest. His heart was beating normally and his breathing was good. Examining the bandages around his head, she saw no more blood escaping from the wound. Straightening up, she took his hand. It was warmer too. The seeds of life were working. Letting out a sigh of relief, Mazu felt like she could finally relax for a moment.

She found a stray apple slice that Quan had somehow missed and popped it in her mouth. She had forgotten how good food tasted and realized it had been days since she'd eaten.

"You, you love him, don't you?" Quan's voice sounded weak, piteous and resentful.

"What? Quan, don't add lovesickness to your upset stomach. I may look younger, but I am still an old goddess who is too tired for romance. He is a compatriot. Certainly I care about him and for now our fates have become entwined - nothing more." She let go of D'Molay's hand. "Perhaps I should send you both on your way and live here in peace with the centaurs. Let us both rest. I am suddenly desperate for the silence of sleep."

Mazu lay down on the floor, and soon was as unconscious as D'Molay.

<hr/>

D'Molay awakened to morning daylight streaming into the unfamiliar room. Slowly he sat up, remembering Aavi's old complaints about waking up in strange, new places. The sight of Quan and Mazu sleeping on the floor quickly comforted him. *Mazu got us out of Hades!* His spirit rose in joy and relief. Attempting to give thanks to God with a prayer, only a wheezing rasp came out. He coughed, waking Mazu.

"Welcome back to the world of the living."

He couldn't help but smile at her and tried to speak, but only managed to wheeze.

"I'll get you some water." Mazu turned and retrieved a mug from the table. "Here."

D'Molay drank it down eagerly in one continuous draft, then handed the mug back. "Ah . . . better. Now I can speak. I can't believe we're out of that hellish realm! How did you do it?"

She smiled as she regaled him with their efforts in the tunnel and their arrival in the centaur village.

"Centaurs? I've had very few dealings with them," D'Molay replied.

Mazu smiled, "That may be, but the town elder knew who you were. It helped belay their trepidation once we emerged from the Underworld. It would seem that even unconscious you were able to help," Mazu said with a joyous lilt to her voice.

"Glad to be of use. Is that food? I'm famished."

"They must have brought more in while we slept." Mazu got the tray, placing it between them. "Quan has been eating everything in sight." She chose a bunch of grapes to eat as D'Molay joined in. They said nothing as both quickly consumed most of the items on the tray. "We'd better stop, or we'll get sick like Quan from eating too much."

D'Molay laughed lightly at his rival's misery. "So what's next?"

"Well, the Elder of the village said he was going to try to arrange transport to get us to Dioscrias, but if he can't, I think we'll just have to hike to the main road and seek another way to the coast." Mazu put the unfinished tray back on the table.

"Sounds good to me," he replied, preparing to get off the altar.

She gave him a look that reminded him of a nun who'd tutored him as a child. "Be careful - you haven't really been able to walk for days."

"Right." Slowly he eased himself off the marble altar and stood up, still resting against it for support. Then he took a few tentative steps. Within moments, he was walking fine. "I feel great! I don't know what the centaurs did, but I haven't felt this good in years. Whatever it is, they should bottle it."

"Yes. Well, I don't believe they'll be doing that anytime soon."

"Day's greetings," came a voice from the other side of the curtain.

Mazu turned. "Please come forward, Elder Carystus."

"Ah, I see you've recovered from your ordeal," he said to D'Molay.

"Yes, thanks to you and your people." D'Molay bowed slightly.

"Since days of old, we have pledged to aid the heroes of mankind. It is part of our tradition," Carystus added with great flourish.

"I will never forget your help, even if I don't remember most of it." D'Molay replied earnestly.

Mazu approached the Elder. "Did you find any volunteers for our journey to Dioscrias?"

He smiled broadly. "I did indeed. There were several who offered. I chose the one that had traveled that way in the past. Now, when do you wish to leave? Velthur can be ready in an hour."

D'Molay and Mazu exchanged glances. "Yes, we can be ready in an hour, if that works for him," Mazu answered.

"I'll tell Velthur. Go to the fountain, he'll be waiting for you. I hope you have found your stay a good one. If only all humans were so well behaved." Carystus bowed slightly and left them. The guard let the curtain drop.

Speaking in hushed tones, D'Molay said, "He seemed to be in a bit of a rush."

"All the centaurs here are like that. I don't think they like the company of humans. It's only because you are a hero and I am a goddess that they are putting up with us at all."

"I'm a hero now?" he asked.

"Of course you are. Let's wake Quan and make ready. I want to clean up this room before we leave. The healer was most distressed to find us here and I want no evidence of our presence left behind to offend her. She made a great sacrifice to save your life. Cleaning is the least we can do."

"All right. You'll have to tell me about what she did," he replied.

"Do not fear. We have two days' travel ahead of us and time to share such details. Let's wake Quan and get ready."

An hour later the three of them were standing at the fountain, ready to leave. A few of the other centaurs had gathered to see what was going on.

D'Molay had his first chance to look at the village and the beautiful surrounding countryside. The aroma of trees and flowers was intoxicating. He was constantly smiling as he took everything in. "Reminds me of southern France . . . breathtaking," he said approvingly.

"Why are our coins sitting on the fountain like that?" Quan asked, pointing along the edge.

"They are a gift to the centaurs. Leave them alone," Mazu cautioned.

"But -"

"Leave them," she admonished, while giving him a disapproving glare.

The Elder and the young girl centaur walked across the plaza. This time she was carrying a basket of food while he carried a wine skin. Behind them came another male centaur pulling a two-wheeled cart.

Mazu smiled as they approached, while D'Molay tried to remain stoic, like a soldier going off to war. For some reason, that was how he felt. Like going on a crusade, he thought.

Carystus addressed the assembled crowd. "There is an old saying among our people: **'Ita tmia icac he ramasva vatieke astres.'** It means, Go forth, hero and finish thy good deeds. Heroes are few and far between, but your journey has brought you to us and we are honor bound to aid you. Thus we offer sustenance." He nodded and the young centauress presented the basket of food to Quan, who took it, smiling at her.

"We offer refreshment." Carystus gave the wineskin to Mazu. She nodded and slung it over her shoulder. The Elder stepped over and held out a scroll that was tied with a string. "We offer knowledge." D'Molay took the scroll, nodding gratefully. Then Carystus stepped back as the cart came forward. "Finally, we offer transportation."

The cart was small with two-wheels on one axle. D'Molay guessed they used it for hauling hay or bushels of grapes. It had an open back and a bench that ran the length of it. Unlike a regular horse-drawn cart, there was no place for a driver to sit at the front and no reins or bridle. Because it was pulled by a Centaur, such things would be unnecessary. The horse was the driver, he realized.

"Velthur has volunteered to take you to Dioscrias. I have shown him the map and he knows the way." Carystus bent over and picked up seven of the silver coins and handed them to Velthur. "Put these in your belt bag. If you need to pay for a toll or a repair on the way back they might come in useful."

"Yes, Elder," the dark-toned centaur replied.

Mazu and Quan climbed aboard and took a seat. "Thank you all. You have been wonderful hosts," she said, while Quan could not resist peeking into the basket of food, despite his recent discomfort. Carystus grasped D'Molay's forearm and looked him straight in the eye. "Think well of us, and let it be known that we still honor the good greatness in man."

D'Molay returned the gesture. "I will, Elder. That is a promise."

Then he got in the cart and they rode off down the hill, past the grape fields and meadows. The mid-morning sun beamed down upon them like a warm blanket of light.

Chapter 17

The Favor of a Goddess

Though he couldn't really see much in the darkness, D'Molay inhaled deeply, taking in the fresh salty aroma of the Great Lake. "Here we are, back at Dioscrias."

"Can you take us to the dock? It's over there," D'Molay pointed out.

"As you wish," Velthur answered.

Though it was night, there were still enough people around to notice the unusual sight of a passenger cart being pulled by a centaur.

"Heh, now there's sometin' ye don' see ever day. I wanta ride too! How much ta go ta Athena's Temple?" one old man called out.

"Hey mister, your horse lost its reins! Ha ha ha ha!" yelled another. Others pointed and whispered at the spectacle as the cart passed by.

They pulled up at the dock entrance. "Thanks, Velthur. I'm sorry about the sailors. Maybe I should teach them some manners," D'Molay fumed.

"Do not. At least now I understand why we are told to avoid this place," Velthur replied tensely.

Quan hopped out. "Even I am offended by their foolishness." He bowed to the Centaur. "Please accept my thanks for your people's generosity towards us."

Mazu stepped out last. "Thank you for bringing us so far. It was a lovely way to travel. Will you be all right getting back to Pelion?"

"Certainly. I may take a few side trips on the way home. This trip gave me a reason to come north. I love to travel the lands, even with a cart tied to me. I'll take my leave of you now. Good journey to you."

"And to you," D'Molay added as Velthur trotted off into the night.

"I think he just likes to travel. The destination seems unimportant to him," Quan said.

"You can't blame him for not wanting to stay here after that reception," D'Molay added.

"Sadly, that is true," Mazu agreed.

D'Molay turned to Quan. "So, what did you do with the boat?"

"I did just as you advised. I paid the harbormaster two months docking fees and some extra to keep an eye on it. So it should be there, waiting for us."

"Good. I'm glad you occasionally take my advice. Let's see if we can get some supplies and be on our way."

"You wish to leave right now?" Quan asked incredulously.

"Have you already forgotten Circe and her harpies? For all we know they're still looking for us. The sooner we're away from Olympia, the better."

Mazu gave them a worried look. "And we do not know who else may be searching for us. After all, Quetzalcoatl is still angry with me, I left Helios' palace with no explanation, and we spent a week in Hades' Underworld. Anyone or any thing from any of those places might also be tracking us down for various slights. I think we should keep moving if at all possible."

"You two find the harbormaster. I'll get supplies," D'Molay said. As he walked towards the shops that remained open a thought suddenly struck him. *I wonder what happened to Aavi? That reminds me, I'll leave a note and some gold on Sophia's doorstep to let her know I survived and to thank her.*

<hr />

Finally they were underway. Although no one seemed to be pursuing them, it still felt like they were fleeing as the boat left the small harbor of Dioscrias. They traveled for several hours, constantly on guard for harpies or some other threat, but none came. Soon the excitement of the day's events faded and D'Molay started to think about their next move. After relating his adventures in Circe's lair to Mazu and Quan, he took out his map and looked at the spot where they had heard Scylla now lived, deep in a swamp in the Lost Realm.

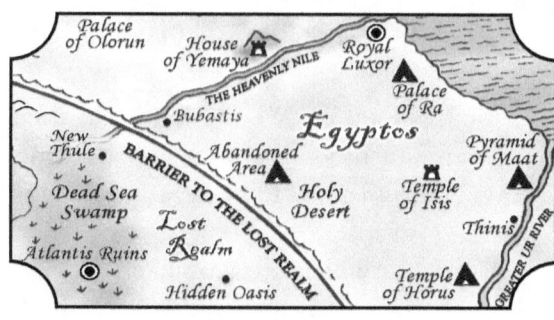

"So, now that we have an antidote in hand, we go to Anagar, wherever that is." He tapped his finger on a section of the map. While it did not indicate any swamp called Anagar, the terrain drawn there suggested a boggy place. "I have a hunch it's near here." He looked up at Mazu. "It's a good thing you are a diety, Mazu."

"What do you mean?" she asked.

"To get us in," D'Molay said, confidently.

"I cannot open the barriers. I thought you had a way through," Mazu replied with surprise.

"But, I'd heard that a god or goddess could open these sorts of barriers. I thought it would be something you'd be able to do."

"The only barrier I can open is the one to the Asian Underworld. I have no connection to the Lost Realm. I've never even been there."

"Why would Lady Mazu be mixed up with any of these horrible places?" Quan asked.

D'Molay and Mazu ignored him. Mazu stared out over the water. "We'll have to find a deity who has access to that realm and is willing to go with us to the barrier to open it." Mazu turned, concern evident on her face. "I'm trying to think if I know of any deities that owe me a favor. I've spent so much time avoiding them that I do not. I spend most my time with the local fishermen or ferrying people across the lake."

"And we are most gladdened by your presence Lady Mazu," Quan interjected as he pulled the sail round to better catch the wind.

"How many barriers are there?" D'Molay asked.

"There used to be four, but the barrier to the Cold Realms was destroyed in the War of the Ascendants. There is another, which I can open, at the entrance to the Asian underworld. Then there's the barrier to the Realm of Flame. There are a few lesser gates as well in scattered places. I don't know much about them. There are rumors of other barriers at the far ends of the outer realms, but they are only spoken of in legend. No one's ever returned from the edges of the outer realms."

"The Council has access to all the barriers," D'Molay said.

"Can't you use that seal of yours to open these gates then?" Quan's brow furrowed in frustration.

"No. I was told when they gave me this seal that it wouldn't open the mystic barriers between the realms."

"It is unlikely any on the Council will aid us. We are hardly in their favor - Quetzalcoatl wants me dead, and based on what you told me, they consider your story about Aavi being an angel to be heretical," Mazu added dejectedly.

"We'll have to find some other god, but which ones are likely to have access?" D'Molay shrugged his shoulders.

"I'm afraid there may be even more to it than that. If the Lost Realm's barrier is like the Asian barrier, a mystical key is also required. So the deity must have that as well," Mazu said, a touch of regret in her voice.

D'Molay nodded in understanding. "The gates of Purgatory were the same, come to think of it. I didn't really give it much thought at the time."

"Who opened that gate for you?"

"It was Vitiris. He was trapped in Purgatory and I was his guide to the right gate."

"Might that deity aid you again?"

"Even if he was willing, I doubt he would have access to the Lost Realm. He dwells in the Celtic Lands and its gods prefer to stick close to home."

Mazu let out a little sigh. "I think we are stymied for the moment. Perhaps with some sleep, an answer will present itself with the new day."

"Most wise, my Lady," Quan added.

She smiled slightly at him and then turned her gaze to the distant horizon, while D'Molay coiled up some rope that was lying on the deck.

"Well then," D'Molay said, "how about your story? You haven't told us what happened when you went against Circe."

Quan turned toward them eagerly. "Yes! I want to hear how you defeated the witch, Lady Mazu!"

"And how you stole my dagger back," D'Molay smiled.

Mazu said nothing at first. "Another time, friends," she said at length. "I've just realized how tired I am. I think I will go back into the barrels and rest. We should not let ourselves get careless."

D'Molay noticed she wouldn't meet his eye as she moved toward the containers. He stepped up to the barrels and removed their lids for her.

"Mazu," he said softly. "What happened there?"

She turned to water without answering and filled the two casks.

"Mazu," he said again as the last of her disappeared. Quan stuck his head into the covered section of the boat.

"Stop pestering the goddess," he snipped. D'Molay shot a dark look toward him which inspired a retreat to the other end of the deck. With nothing else to do but think of an answer to the barrier problem, D'Molay spread out his blanket and lay down, hands folded under his head. Before a solution came to him, he dropped off to sleep.

$\mathscr{D}'$ Molay was awoken by a circular glow. He sat up in the cot and Aavi appeared before him, a glorious angel bathed in light. Her wings spread open and her hand reached out to him.

"Something brings you happiness, I am glad."

"You do, Aavi! I've missed you so, but I knew you were nearby, helping us."

She hovered about a foot above the deck of the ship and smiled upon him. "Where are you going with Mazu and her servant next?"

"Don't you know? I mean - as my guardian angel, don't you know my inner thoughts?" he asked her, truly curious to know the answer.

"It doesn't work like that. I can see the emotions and intentions that swirl within your soul, but I cannot read your thoughts." She gave D'Molay an intense gaze. "I can see you are anxious and worried, but about what I could only guess. You wish to leave quickly for somewhere?"

"Yes. We have to go to the Lost Realm. It's on the other side of the Great Lake, east of Egyptos. We didn't go there when you were here last, so you won't know anything about it.

A concerned look crossed her face. "It's a dangerous place. You must be very careful."

"How do you know that?"

"I just do. Some knowledge is given me by the Heavenly Host. There

are many things I know about the Realm of the Gods, although some of it seems . . . out of date. It's difficult to explain."

Aavi's hesitant answer reminded him of the helpless girl he had first found in the streets of the City. "It's all right Aavi. I'm just glad you're here by my side. I feel truly blessed in more ways than one."

"Must you go to this realm? Perhaps there is another way to complete your task."

"No - I wish there was. It will take us a long time to get there."

"I see. If you must go, look to those to whom you have given aid in the past. They may be willing to help you in the future. Take care, I will be near." Aavi began to fade away.

"Aavi wait!"

Suddenly he sat up. He was still in the cot. *Was it just a dream, or had Aavi found a way to reach me while I slept? And she seemed to be more like the way she'd been when she was alive. Did more of her memories return the longer she was here?* There were no certain answers as he tried to go back to sleep.

When he next awoke, their boat had crossed many miles across the waters. D'Molay guessed they were still over a week away from the shores of Egyptos and Afrik. Off to the north, almost out of sight, was the island that held the City of the Gods. Quan was at the tiller as D'Molay left the shelter, the man's youth and blessed status sustaining him over the hours D'Molay had rested.

"Anything happen while I slept?"

"No, thank the goddess. And I did not see your angel floating about either, so there is no point in asking."

"I wasn't going to ask," D'Molay sighed. "I realize no one can see her but me. I can't blame you for not believing."

Just then Mazu's voice interjected. "You two aren't bickering again, are you?"

They both turned. She stood at the doorway of the cabin, just under the eave of its rooftop, still wary that Quetzalcoatl's agents were watching. Quan answered first as he bowed. "My Lady. I greet and honor you as a flower greets the day," quickly bowing again.

"No bickering yet," D'Molay said. "But don't hold me to it."

"I'm sure you'll do your best, D'Molay," Mazu smiled. "Now, I've been thinking about that barrier we need to breach. Our most likely deity will have to be one whose realm borders the Lost Realm. That means we should look in Afrik, Egyptos or Babylos. We have to find a god or goddess from one of those realms who has access to a key."

"But who? And at what price?" D'Molay wondered.

"I have a few in mind, but they are remote chances at best. D'Molay, you've done many tasks for many gods. Aren't any of them indebted to you in some way?" she asked hopefully.

"No, I'm always paid and . . . Wait. There is! I do know one that owes me a favor!" D'Molay exclaimed. He looked off in the distance towards the south. "Turn the ship. We need to make a stop back in the City of the Gods."

"I know that look on your face. You have a plan of action," Mazu said.

"I partly got the idea in a dream I had last night. I'll go back to my house, get the parchment she gave me, and return it to Sekhmet," he said with enthusiasm.

"Joyous news! Do you know where she is?" Mazu queried.

"I think so. I just hope her offer was earnest and not just an idle compliment."

Mazu looked to her man-servant. "You heard him, take us home Quan." This was an order he heartily approved. Mazu retreated back under the cover of the cabin and away from any prying eyes as Quan hurried to the rudder. He called out to D'Molay.

"Grab that sail line, we need to come about." After some effort, they brought the boat back to the Northern dock where Mazu's boathouse awaited. Mazu returned to the barrels and Quan and D'Molay smuggled her off the ship. Once inside her boathouse, she resumed her normal form.

"Quan and I will wait here while you contact Sekhmet," Mazu said.

"I'll return as soon as I can." D'Molay picked up his traveling pack, eager to put his plan in action.

"Please, take your time," Quan grinned. "Don't rush back."

Ignoring Quan, D'Molay bid Mazu farewell and hurried down the dock to a carriage stop. After a short wait, a carriage returned from a trip and D'Molay engaged the driver to take him to his home in The Settlement. He actually enjoyed the ride, easing back comfortably in the seat, relieved that for once the responsibility of travel fell to someone else. When the carriage reached his neighborhood, D'Molay got the driver's attention and asked him to stop.

"Stop at that house with the dead garden," he indicated. The carriage ceased its motion and D'Molay stepped out. He passed the driver some extra coins. "Wait here, I'll be right back."

The woman made a quick count of the payment and smiled down at him. "Whatever you say," she promised. D'Molay smiled at her and made for his front door. Several broken roof tiles lay near his doorstep, but he had no time for such things. Reaching the door, he had to use a shoulder to open it. He'd been away long enough it had become warped from disuse. *Guess that's better than coming home with the door wide open and everything stolen.*

Dashing inside, he sorted through his belongings and found the scrap of parchment Sekhmet had given him upon their first meeting. He grabbed a clean shirt, stripping off his torn and bloodied one. After pulling it over his head, he caught a glimpse of his windblown and tangled hair in a wall mirror. He grabbed another hat and settled it on his head, repacked the travel bag for the journey ahead and left, returning to the waiting carriage.

"Take me to the Great Pyramid," he told the driver.

The carriage made its way through the busy streets, past gleaming temples, elegant water fountains and huge governing edifices. By mid-morning he had entered the Egyptos temple compound and gained access to the Great Pyramid by showing Sekhmet's parchment. D'Molay now stood outside the same golden door he had been to before. He noted guards, minor priests and serving girls loitering in the hallway, as if waiting for someone or something. Ignoring them, he knocked three times as he'd been instructed. After a few seconds, the big door slowly opened and he saw a familiar face.

"Oh, hi there!" A short, pink demoness with long black hair, bat-like wings and gazelle-sized horns hopped toward him and hugged him closely.

"Tenh-Mer!" D'Molay exclaimed. In his focus on getting to see Sekhmet, he had all but forgotten her succubus companion. He was instantly reminded, however, of the effect Tenh-Mer had on any who strayed within the range of her seductive power. Unable to resist, he hugged her back. After an overly long embrace, the pink demoness pulled away from his grasp and looked him eye to eye at arm's length.

"It's so good to see you again. But what's your name? Didn't it start with a D?"

He stared back at her, having trouble gathering his thoughts. He could only think of how beautiful she was and how he wanted to be with her in every way. Finally her words got through his emotional fog. "I . . . I'm D-D'Molay. You helped me and Aavi escape from the prison."

"That's right, Dee-Mo-lay. Silly, I remember the prison thingie. It was your name I forgot. I guess you're here to congratulate my mistress, like all the rest, huh? Come on in then," she said brightly. Tenh-Mer turned around and walked back into the darkened chamber.

Confused and at a loss for words, D'Molay followed her in, unable to take his eyes off her swaying hips and pink tail as it swished behind her. When he had first met Tenh-Mer, she had been dressed in almost no clothing at all, but this time, she was wearing a sleeveless, long-flowing gown made of white silk cut low in the back so her wings had room to protrude. She wore matching gold arm bands, an ornate necklace that looked like it was a pair of wings, and fine bracelets that jangled as she moved. Around her waist, she wore a belt that looked like a golden serpent had wrapped itself around her. Although his eyes were distracted, D'Molay's ears registered the murmur of voices over the sound of Tenh-Mer's cloven hooves tapping on the polished stone floor. As the two of them crossed the chamber, D'Molay could see a gathering of Egyptos dignitaries and a few animal-headed deities.

D'Molay had the overwhelming urge to grab Tenh-Mer's pink, pointed tail as it rhythmically swung back and forth, just out of his reach. As he was about to give in to temptation, she looked back over her shoulder and whispered. "You'll have to wait till Sekhmet is ready for you. Oh, and don't say anything about me helping you with the prison escape." This was the sort of obvious statement that would be annoying if said by anyone else, but from Tenh-Mer it was somehow endearing. Somewhere in the back of his mind D'Molay realized the mystic aura of desire she generated excused much, but at the moment, he didn't care. Tenh-Mer stopped walking, and pointed ahead. His eyes lingered on her outstretched arm, tracing the lovely limb from shoulder to fingertip before noticing what the demoness was trying to show him.

Ahead of them, seated on her ebony stone throne, the goddess Sekhmet was dressed resplendently in a shimmering golden gown. It was encrusted with small red and blue gems. Golden Egyptos jewelry adorned her arms and neck. Similarly styled bracelets from which loosely draped fabric from her dress was attached graced her wrists. D'Molay and Tenh-Mer stood silently waiting as a dozen or so assembled dignitaries continued their discussions with her. D'Molay's genuine curiosity over why they were all here had him trying to take in every word.

A cat-headed god with black fur was the first god he heard. ". . . is truly wondrous news. You'll need to reach out to the other pantheons if you are to get their votes, of course."

"I hope that I'm up for the task, but I will do everything I can, Ptah. I can only hope that some of the feline deities from the other realms will put in a good word for me," Sekhmet said, as she tried to look calm and controlled, but even D'Molay could tell that she was slightly overwhelmed by all the attention.

"Oh, mother, I'm sure you'll be great on the Council," said a female cat goddess who bore a striking similarity to Sekhmet.

"Indeed milady, there can be no doubt of that," said a rotund man who was probably an Egyptos priest of some sort. The other deities surrounding Sekhmet all agreed in unison, clapping or exclaiming their support.

Sekhmet seemed to blanch at all the praise. "Please, let us not go too far with this. I've only been nominated. We have a long way to go before we can start speculating on such things." It was then the goddess looked beyond her assembled admirers and to Tenh-Mer, perhaps hoping to change the subject. "And who have you brought into our chamber now?"

Tenh-Mer took a step to the side, in order to give Sekhmet a better view of their newest visitor. "It's the tracker D'Molay, who brought you Geb's ring. I think he wants to congratulate you?" Tenh-Mer said questioningly.

"Step forward tracker," Sekhmet said formally. She gestured and all her guests parted like the Red Sea leaving an easy path for him.

D'Molay swallowed nervously then stepped towards the seated goddess. He bowed. "My lady Sekhmet, I do congratulate you on your nomination, though that's not why I have come to see you."

Sekhmet raised an eyebrow, "Oh? Then what is your purpose here?"

His gaze met hers. "When I delivered Geb's ring to you a few months ago, you gave me a favor that I might use sometime in the future. In truth, I never intended to redeem it, but now I find I have no choice. My cause is just and my need desperate."

The dark cat-headed god turned to him, raising a corner of his lip to show a bright, white fang. "You dare come now, upon her nomination to the Council? Sekhmet has no time for granting favors that were given only as a courtesy."

"Ptah, it is for me to decide the value of my favors, is it not?" Sekhmet interrupted.

Ptah stepped back, somewhat reluctantly. "It is. I spoke in haste."

Sekhmet nodded her acceptance of his quasi-apology. She turned her attention back to D'Molay. "What is this 'just cause' you speak of,

D'Molay? And then I would know what favor you wish of me. It may or may not be within my power to grant."

Speaking as succinctly as possible, D'Molay told her of his quest to find the nymph Scylla to break her curse, leaving out any mention of Circe or Glaucus. One never knew what prejudices one deity held against other gods, so D'Molay rarely mentioned the name of one god to another in his daily work. Then he asked his favor. "In order to save this poor woman, I must enter the Lost Realm. My companions and I need a deity who has the proper key to open the barrier so that we may pass through."

There were surprised murmurs from the assembled guests who fell immediately silent as Sekhmet replied. "I see. This would be a time consuming task, of that there is no doubt. And I do not have such a key as you require. Due to my nomination requirements, there is no way I could go to the barrier of the Lost Realm at this time."

D'Molay noted the smug look that crossed Ptah's face. He lowered his head. "I understand Sekhmet. I know it was much to ask - "

She held up her hand to interrupt him. "Nonetheless, I do find your cause just. I will be true to my word and find a way to aid you. Can your task wait till days end? I need time to ponder the matter."

D'Molay bowed deeply. "Yes. Of course."

"Then return at sunset and you will have aid from me in some form."

A grateful D'Molay was escorted out of the chamber by Tenh-Mer. "She's very honest about things like that you know. I'm sure she'll find a way to help."

"I see she is honorable too, as are you. Thanks, Tenh-Mer."

As they stood in the hallway she gave him a quick hug and he felt dizzy once again. "Take care, and if you do go to the Realm of the Lost, be very careful. It's dangerous out there. Really." Then Tenh-Mer popped back through the golden door and was gone.

Evening was many hours away.

D'Molay wandered out of the Great Pyramid as many thoughts, pressed aside in favor of necessary actions, now had time to reassert themselves. He wanted to know why Aavi had come back to help him, and where she had now gone. He wondered what Mazu wasn't telling him about Circe, and even found himself curious about Council politics, and how Sekhmet had come to be nominated. But being a man of great practicality, D'Molay did not allow himself to waste too much time in speculation. There were still steps he could take that might help him in the days to come.

D'Molay decided to visit the Great Library in search of more information about the Lost Realm. The scribes were willing to pull out every dusty scroll and torn map that touched on the subject. D'Molay spent most of the day reading about the realm's dangers, sketching old maps, and taking special note of anything that mentioned gates or barriers.

At one point, he ran across some ancient texts that looked very similar to the writing on the scroll the centaurs had given him. *I left that at home. I'm going to have to get that translated. Ah well, next time,* he concluded.

He was so engrossed in studying the Lost Realm that it fell to his stomach to remind him of the time. With a powerful groan, it announced that he had not eaten all day. Looking up from his pile of books, D'Molay noticed through the windows of the library that the sun was going down. After thanking the scribes for their help and leaving a donation, he hurried outside to a food cart to get a quick bowl of bread and

meat, which he ate while riding back to the Great Pyramid.

He once again was brought before Sekhmet. This time, only Tenh-Mer and Sekhmet's feline-faced daughter stood at her side. As usual, Sekhmet remained regally seated on her throne.

"I have spent some time on the matter at hand, and we have come up with a way to provide you with the aid you require," she announced, getting right down to business. "My daughter Bast has generously agreed to go with you in my stead. She has a pyramid not too far from the barrier, and Ptah has given her the location of a key. So your favor will be granted and I will be able to remain here to manage other pressing affairs." Sekhmet gestured to Bast. "You two can work out the details."

Bast remained close to her mother, leaning against her chair. Her appearance was more formal than her mother's, and her eyes were as fathomless as any god's. D'Molay had the sense she had seen more than her share of hardship and pain.

"When do you plan to leave for this journey?" the younger cat goddess said.

"In the morning if possible, but if you need more time . . ."

"No. In fact, the sooner we can complete this task, the better. How do you plan to get to the Lost Realm?"

"We are taking a boat."

"And to reach the barrier?"

"A caravan across the desert."

Bast swished her tail, stirring the folds of her multi-layered ivory colored gown.

"That will take too long for me. Bring the rest of your party here and we shall travel via air barge to my pyramid. You can hire camels from there."

Sekhmet added, "Then it is decided, I know that Bast will serve you well in my stead. Will this satisfy the favor I granted you?"

D'Molay bowed deeply. "Yes, Goddess. It most certainly will. You'll have saved a poor woman's life."

"Do not account to me what is your responsibility, D'Molay," she said. "Now go. Gather your comrades and supplies and prepare for a journey through the skies."

"Of course. Thank you. When should I return?"

Sekhmet turned to Bast for an answer. She shrugged. "I'll walk him out and we can go over the details. I don't even know how many are in his group. Hopefully they'll all fit on the barge. Come with me, Tracker." Bast walked down the three steps in front of Sekhmet's throne and past D'Molay towards the door.

Tenh-Mer called out to them as they passed. "Good luck, take care of each other!"

As they left the chamber, he heard Sekhmet say, "My blessings to you daughter. Be safe."

D'Molay caught up with Bast as she got to the door and opened it. "So how many are going to the barrier with you?" she asked.

"Four," he said hastily, accidently counting Aavi. "I mean, three of us."

"Three? You're going into the Lost Realm with just three people? You must have a death wish."

"Not at all. One of them is a goddess and I have centuries of tracking experience."

Bast gave him a sideways glance. "Well, it's no concern of mine. I only have to get you there and give you the opportunity to return if you are able to. Now, if you go out the main entrance of the pyramid, you'll see a place off to the west of the courtyard where the royal barges dock. Be there tomorrow when the whole sun has crested over the horizon and we will leave for Egyptos. Bring what supplies you'll need for your overland journey. Don't bring any pack animals. You can get them in Bubastis, my temple village."

"All right, we'll meet you here then."

Bast reached into a small pocket in her vest and pulled out a metallic disk. She handed it to D'Molay. "Here is my token, show it to the guards when you return and they'll let you in. Have you any other questions? I have to get ready for a meeting of the felines."

"No, Lady Bast. Thank you for doing this for me."

"I'm not doing this for you; I do this for the honor of my mother." Bast turned and walked back towards the golden door without another word.

D'Molay hailed another carriage back to the boathouse. He walked up the dark dock. Most of the fishermen and tradesmen had retired or closed for the evening, but the lanterns hanging outside Mazu's boathouse still glowed to light his way. Quan looked up from the counter as D'Molay came in.

"Visiting a goddess took you all day? You've been at the gambling houses or the brothels, haven't you?"

"What if I have?" D'Molay said dismissively, walking past him and back into the room with the fountain. Quan followed. They found Mazu sitting at the edge of the fountain looking into its waters. Her arm had transformed into a flowing tube of water that ran from the fountain to a dirty jar of water that sat on the ground at her feet. As they drew closer, D'Molay could see small fish swimming in the water tube, up from the dirty jar, through Mazu's watery arm and then into the waters of the fountain. Mazu noticed the two men enter the room, but her attention remained focused upon the fish.

"What are you doing?" D'Molay asked.

"A child found these small fish in puddles near the lake and he brought them to us. They were washed ashore after a tidal surge. The trauma of their journey and the shallow muddy water almost killed them. I am sending them to cleaner water and healing them. Once they are recovered, we will return them to the lake."

D'Molay leaned in and could now see that swimming within the watery tube from the jar to the fountain were numerous small silvery fish.

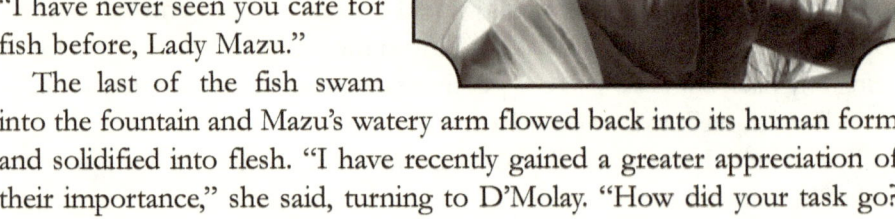

Quan looked on in surprise. "I have never seen you care for fish before, Lady Mazu."

The last of the fish swam into the fountain and Mazu's watery arm flowed back into its human form and solidified into flesh. "I have recently gained a greater appreciation of their importance," she said, turning to D'Molay. "How did your task go? What news do you bring?"

D'Molay smiled. "Good news. Sekhmet agreed to offer us assistance, even more than I expected."

"What do you mean?" asked Quan.

"The goddess is sending her own daughter, Bast, to obtain the key and open the barrier for us. She also will be taking us to Egyptos via one of the air barges reserved for the use of the Egyptos deities, which means we'll get there in a few days rather than weeks."

"But I spent all day getting our boat ready," Quan protested. "Do we have to fly? That's for gods, not men."

"I'll tell you what. You take the boat, and Mazu and I will travel on the air barge. You should get to the coast of Egyptos three or four weeks after us."

Quan frowned. "You'd like that, wouldn't you?"

Mazu lifted her arms to get their attention. "Enough. You two remind me of a pair of grappling suitors I had long ago. We will travel on the air barge that has been so kindly offered. No more discussion is necessary. This is indeed all good news. Now, what must we do to prepare for this journey?"

"The barge leaves tomorrow morning after sun crest, so we need to get all the supplies we'll need for desert travel," D'Molay replied.

Quan sighed glumly. "I have all the supplies on the boat."

Mazu tried to suppress a chuckle. "Good, then we know where to collect them. We just have to move them onto the horse cart."

D'Molay smiled in triumph as Quan shuffled out to do as Mazu directed.

"Well, get going," Mazu said teasingly to D'Molay. "Quan can't do everything himself."

After helping Quan reload their supplies, D'Molay caught a few hours sleep before the next day dawned. When he rose, the air was still touched with morning dew. Low clouds had drifted in from the lake, creating small banks of fog in the City streets. The cart that would take them to the Egyptos compound was a bright red, four-wheeled vehicle, pulled by a pair of large furry Yaks. Its driver, a man with a long ponytail, wore a gray coat that almost made him blend into the mist. Their ride was a slow one, yaks being not the most light-footed of draft animals. Quan dozed, Mazu hid silently in a water barrel, and D'Molay tried not to worry about the journey ahead of them. At last the driver tugged on the reins and brought the cart to a halt in front of a group of guards, who quickly moved to bar the cart from proceeding any further.

"What's your business here?" a dark-haired Egyptos soldier called out.

D'Molay leaned forward from his position behind the driver. "Meeting the goddess Bast at the Royal Barge. We're expected." D'Molay tossed him the silver medallion with Bast's symbol stamped on it.

The guard looked at it. "Let them pass."

The driver prodded the yaks. As they pulled the cart loaded with supplies forward, the guard tossed the medallion back to D'Molay. The metal piece slightly overshot him, but Quan caught it as he leaned up against the same barrel that D'Molay sat upon.

"Hah! Finder, Keeper," Quan said triumphantly.

"You can keep it until we see Bast in about a minute, when she'll want it back," D'Molay said.

"Ah. You keep it." Quan dejectedly shoved it back in D'Molay's hand.

As the cart took them through the compound, it passed impressive stables and fine tethered horses. The yaks' appearance was a stark contrast to the smaller Arabian stallions the soldiers of Egyptos preferred. The red cart crossed the stone-paved courtyard in front of the Great Pyramid, finally stopping a dozen feet away from the barge. Neither Quan nor D'Molay could take their eyes off the impressive craft.

It looked almost exactly like one of the royal barges that sailed the waters of the realms. Over one hundred fifty feet long and about twenty five feet wide at its center section, the barge tapered at each end, coming to points tipped by large golden mastheads. A raised area near the back of the barge had the look of an outdoor royal court, complete with a throne, ornate awnings, carpets and other luxury furnishings. A room stood behind the throne capping at least two decks below. Completely lacquered in black and gold, the barge was ornately decorated with hieroglyphs and designs. It had two sails, the largest emblazoned with the symbol of Bast in turquoise blue.

D'Molay noticed that the barge floated about a foot off the ground. It reminded him of Aavi's habit of floating in midair. A ramp extended from the side of the barge near the front of the craft. The crew was going back and forth with cargo for its journey. He glanced at Quan, who was staring slack jawed at the sight. Amused, he nudged him hard.

"What do you think now, Quan?" he asked. "Do you still prefer a simple boat?"

"It's beautiful," admitted Quan as he hopped off the cart. "I've seen these ships pass over my fishing village, but they looked so small and far away."

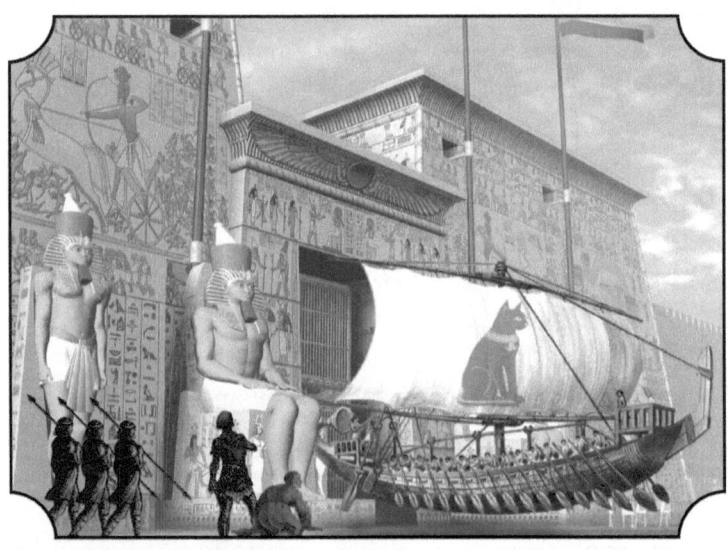

"They are something," D'Molay said. "Perhaps one of the most elegant things in the skies." D'Molay too climbed out of the cart. He scanned the ship and saw Bast at the rear section of the barge, giving orders to the crew. She pointed at the cart and one of the men left the barge and headed towards them.

"You are the Tracker, D'Molay?"

"Yes. Everything in the cart is to go on the barge," D'Molay replied.

The servant nodded and then called out, "Eck Ta Fa-oull. Hish!" Four slaves ran over to the cart and began to unload it.

As they started to pick up Mazu's barrel Quan became agitated. "Be careful with that - its contents are valuable!" The slaves, used to quibbling masters, merely nodded quick bows as they carried it off.

Once everything was unloaded, Quan signaled the driver, who then prodded the large yaks to circle around the courtyard and head back the way they had entered. Quan and D'Molay watched the slaves carry their supplies onboard until the servant who had set the slaves to this work

addressed them again. "Goddess Bast wishes your presence."

D'Molay and Quan were escorted up the ramp to Bast, who was now seated on her throne, under the sun cover. A muscular Nubian guard with a large scimitar stood behind her, as did a scribe with a writing tablet and stylus. Quan and D'Molay were subtly encouraged to bow by the slave who escorted them. Taking the hint, they bowed to Bast and D'Molay held out the token she had given him.

"So. There are only two of you now? You'd better keep that token. You might yet need it." Bast shook her head at them. "You won't last five minutes in the Lost Realm."

"Mazu is with us. But prefers to remain hidden from potential enemies who might be following," D'Molay said as diplomatically as possible.

Bast's eyes narrowed. "We do not allow stowaways on the Royal Barge. I will see this Mazu. Bring her to me now or your journey ends here."

The two men exchanged glances. Quan was shaking his head firmly in the negative, but this was a fight D'Molay did not want to start. "She's in the wooden barrel that we brought aboard."

Bast turned to the servant who'd escorted them. "Have it brought to me immediately," she ordered.

"How could you betray Mazu like this?" Quan whispered. "You are without honor."

"This Royal Barge is under Bast's control. If Bast were on Mazu's boat, then Mazu would be in charge," D'Molay reasoned. "That's how the gods keep peace."

Bast turned a wary eye on them. "Cease chattering. If this is an elaborate trick, I'll have your heads displayed at my temple."

"I promise you Bast, this is no trick," D'Molay said. "Just a misunderstanding."

She looked past both of them. "We'll soon see."

A few minutes later, two slaves carried the barrel up the three steps to the throne area and placed it before Bast. She put her hand up and beckoned to the guard with the scimitar. "Open it."

The large Nubian walked up to the barrel, raised his weapon over his head with both hands, and brought the scimitar down with massive force.

"No!" screamed Quan, lurching forward, but D'Molay held him back.

The scimitar smashed into the barrel as splinters of wood flew into a hundred directions. The Nubian was quite surprised when the water in the barrel remained steadfastly in place, maintaining the shape of its broken container.

"M-Mazu?" Quan choked out. Bast and her underlings watched intently as the water began to grow, take on the shape of a person, and finally solidify into Mazu.

Bast looked at the gaping guard with the scimitar still in his hand. "It seems we have wasted a perfectly good barrel." Waving him back into his place, the feline goddess then confronted Mazu. "Why did you try to steal away upon the Royal Barge?"

Mazu immediately bowed to Bast. "I am pursued by a rival deity. I meant no disrespect to you." Bast's whiskers twitched as she weighed this explanation. Appearing to accept it at face value, she waved her hand, allowing Mazu to rise. "Lady Mazu, I'm sorry for the inconvenience, but I was uncertain who or what these two brought on board. I had to know, for this barge belongs to Horus. Right now it is my responsibility and I'll let nothing put it at risk," she said firmly.

Mazu smiled benignly at Bast. "I understand. I hope we can forget all this and begin our journey."

Bast stared at the three of them for a moment, as if still trying to detect some trick. "I believe we can. Get us in the air," she called out to her crew.

The crew bustled about, setting the sails and untying the lines that kept the barge from floating away. Men shouted orders and the barge started to slowly rise.

"Go to the rail sides of the barge. You will get the best view of the city as we leave," Bast told her three passengers. They walked over to the edge of the craft, Quan lagging behind, uneasily.

"Are you certain this is safe?" he asked.

"Of course. It's no different than being on the water," D'Molay replied as the barge rose beyond the tops of some nearby palm trees.

"Yes, but if I fall out of a boat, I can swim. I don't know about you, but I cannot swim through the air." Quan edged slowly to the rail, as if he had to force himself forward.

"Well, try not to fall out of the barge then, Quan," Mazu counseled, a slight smile on her face.

Soon the barge was higher than the Grand Pyramid and it began to move toward the west. They could see the entire city and the scattered fog banks as the morning sun gleamed in the sky. "The city is beautiful from up here," Quan exclaimed, the spectacle overcoming his fear. They traveled in a serene quiet for several minutes, until the scribe who had stood behind the throne approached them.

"Lady Mazu, Bast would speak with you privately."

Mazu followed the scribe back to Bast's throne.

Quan looked at D'Molay. "Shouldn't we follow too?"

D'Molay rested his head on his arms while leaning against the rail, keeping his gaze on the city below. "No. They either have god business or woman business to discuss. Neither is for our ears."

The beautiful barge continued to drift higher and further towards the west, while an invisible angel followed closely behind.

Chapter 18

Sekhmet's Celestial Warning

As the Royal Barge pulled away from the City, the excitement of Sekhmet's nomination had turned into determined planning to win the empty place on the Council. Sekhmet had met with numerous advisors and ambassadors all offering advice or hoping to gain favor. Tiring, she retreated to her private rooms in the Grand Pyramid. She had been dressed in formal attire all day and wasted no time changing into more casual dress, a jeweled halter top and thin cotton skirt with hieroglyphs painted on it. She fell very informally onto her throne, leaning back with her legs crossed, her head back and eyes closed, yet still wearing her Egyptos headdress. The one advisor she trusted the most, Ptah the god of craft and skill, stepped out of the shadows just as she had settled.

"I should have known there's no sneaking away from you," she said. Her statement was delivered mildly, for she counted Ptah among her closest friends.

"Fault my curiosity, Sekhmet. Did I hear correctly that tracker D'Molay was the one who returned Geb's ring?" Ptah asked as he poured them both a drink. His black cat fur made his golden eyes and white linen robe all the more obvious in the darkened chamber.

Sekhmet's hand instinctively caressed the ring on her left hand. "Yes, it's all I have of him now."

"Hard to believe, really. That there was a time when canines and felines lived in harmony." Ptah handed her an alabaster goblet filled with nectar. She sipped, her eyes focusing not on Ptah but looking inside herself, to the past.

"It was a unique time when Geb and I ruled. Though perhaps not all lived in harmony." Sekhmet had a faraway look as she remembered that time.

"As history shows, your time of joint rule with Geb led to peace in the Nile kingdoms on Earth. I see why the ring means so much to you and why you granted that tracker your favor. Has Bast taken him away?"

She took another sip from the goblet. "Bast was due to take the Royal Barge this morning and I haven't seen her all day, so I believe she's left." Sekhmet looked up at Ptah as he paced across the room and wondered if she had made the right decision in telling everyone that Bast was Geb's daughter rather than Ptah's. No one knew of her deception, and the lie had helped to keep the dream that Dog and Cat could live together harmoniously. Bast was so happy to be Geb's "little kitten" that Sekhmet didn't have the heart to destroy her childhood memories. She wondered if on some level Ptah suspected that Bast was indeed his daughter.

"Sekhmet?" Ptah asked again.

"Hmm? Sorry, I was . . . just remembering something from long ago."

"Ah. I was just asking if you knew how he obtained the ring?"

"No. But the deepest levels of Necropolis must have been scoured to find it, that much is certain. The least I could do was to honor my favor and help the man on his task. Especially since he asks not for his own gain, but to aid another."

"I see your point. You are just and wise. One more reason you should be on the Council."

From the other end of the room, Sekhmet heard the clicking of Tenh-Mer's hooves. Glancing toward the sound, she could see her carrying something. "Tenh-Mer, attend me. I need to ask you something."

The pink demoness approached nervously. Sekhmet had taught her to stay far away when important gods came to visit; her aura of attraction was too likely to cause problems. With this in mind, Tenh-Mer edged to Sekhmet's side.

Ptah took several steps back, trying to put distance between him and Tenh-Mer, as he had often experienced the lustful effects of her proximity. Even ten feet away, Ptah seemed unable to take his gaze from the petite, winged creature, proof that both gods and men were subject to her mystical attraction.

Sekhmet seemed unaffected by her companion, though in truth she also felt the urge to be closer to the succubus. "Do you know if Bast left this morning on the Royal Barge?"

Tenh-Mer smiled broadly, apparently relieved that she wasn't about to be disciplined for some mistake or indiscretion. "Oh. Yes, she did. I mean I wasn't there or anything, but one of her handmaidens who stayed behind to care for her cats told me she had left."

Sekhmet smiled. "Very good. Now. What are you carrying?"

"Oh, these? Well, Bast left her cats here and I'm using these curtains to make a bed for each one of them."

Sekhmet and Ptah exchanged bemused looks. "Well, I'm not sure that her sacred cats will use beds make from old curtains, but I suppose it can't hurt to try," Sekhmet said as she tried to restrain a grin.

"Do you need anything else my goddess?"

"No, No. Go on with your task." She waved Tenh-Mer on her way and the demoness left the chamber.

Ptah walked back over to Sekhmet again. "I see why you keep her at your side. She seems an endless source of amusement."

Sekhmet smiled. "There is that, but in truth, Tenh-Mer has served me well for many years. She is far more than an amusement. You just haven't seen that aspect of her yet."

"Perhaps you could send her to Zeus as a present? He'd be certain to vote you onto the Council after meeting her," Ptah said half-jokingly.

"I have considered bringing her to the council nominee gatherings. But there is no way to control her power. As you know it affects everyone in her vicinity."

"Yes. Maybe you could take her to a private meeting with Zeus or Shiva. I'm not sure if her power would affect Quetzalcoatl," Ptah wondered aloud.

Sekhmet gave him a serious look, raising an eyebrow at the suggestion. "Is that really how we want to gain a spot on the Council? Shouldn't the Council pick the next candidate based on their wisdom and knowledge, rather than some trick or sexual favor?"

Ptah laughed. "Well, that's how they should do it of course. But that's not how it's done. You can be certain that the other candidates will use whatever powers and advantages they have at their command. You should do no less, if you are to be competitive."

Sekhmet seemed crestfallen at his answer. "I was afraid you'd say something like that. The sad thing is I know you're probably right."

Ptah decided to try another approach. "We can decide how far you are willing to go to get on the Council later. Let us instead focus on what you must do. Have you made arrangements to meet with any of the Pantheon leaders yet?" Ptah asked, taking another draught from his goblet.

"There's a reception tomorrow at sunset's end. I thought I'd arrange meetings then."

"Logical as always. One of Horus' civil-priests is putting together a report on each of them. I'll get those to you in the morning."

"Thank you, Ptah."

"Remember, you have to win them over, let them get to know you and become comfortable with the idea of working with you. You already have experience working with felines from different realms. Make sure they know this about you. If we can't trick them, perhaps we can impress them with your abilities, loyalty and honesty. The stakes are high and the dangers are real. I don't want you hurt in any way, Sekhmet." His eyes filled with concern for her.

She went to him. "Ptah, without you, I would not even try to get on the Council. You have always been my greatest supporter." she reached out and embraced him.

Ptah held her close and the two of them stood in a gentle embrace for a long time. Sekhmet shut her eyes against reality and enjoyed the fleeting moment of security and peace. However, a bright glow played about the fringes of her eyelids as Ptah stirred.

"Sekhmet, look."

A large, magical sarcophagus had appeared in the room. The box stood on end, glowing brightly. As Sekhmet looked at it, the sarcophagus opened and she felt an irresistible pull to step inside it.

"I have to go, Ptah," she said.

"Travel safely," he replied. "It seems I am not the only one who has advice for you."

Sekhmet entered the sarcophagus. Its power lulled her to sleep almost instantly and she neither saw nor felt the Sesem-Xex arrive to take it into the heavens. These dark, winged creatures had no form beneath the stars, but in the heavens their black shapes could be discerned as that of two winged stallions. They drew the ornate box behind them by fiery chains that sparkled like comet tails, landing after several hours on the second moon, known in the City as Heliopolis. The Sesem-Xex shirked off their chains, leaving the box on its back, as they merged into the dark emptiness of space.

The sarcophagus opened and Sekhmet awoke, sitting up to peer at her new surroundings. She found she was upon a huge glassy platform of some sort. Carefully, she arose and stepped out upon what appeared to

be a clear, smooth, pane. Far below her, she could see the all realms laid out like a gigantic flat piece of papyrus that went off as far as she could see. All around and above her were the stars and other objects of the heavens. After getting her bearings, Sekhmet realized that she was walking on the other side of the second moon, which was in fact not an orb, but a gigantic circular platform. From the activity she observed around her, it became clear that the platform was the working home of the celestial gods who needed to dwell in the heavens. In the distance, she could see a few structures. There were pyramids, observatories and many other strange buildings and towers that she didn't recognize at all.

Above her was the night sky, but it seemed so close, so sharp and almost alive. As she gazed up, she saw the large eye of a woman open. Then the sky coalesced and gathered overhead. The features of a blue face appeared around the eye. Soon Sekhmet saw the figure of a woman slowly descending, like a bottle of dark turquoise ink poured from a bottle. She recognized her as Nuit, goddess of the sky.

"Welcome to Heliopolis. It has been long since last we met," said the woman who had flowed from the heavens.

Sekhmet bowed deeply. "I am honored that you asked to see me." She raised her eyes to look upon Nuit. The goddess was just as Sekhmet remembered her, tall and lithe, with deep blue skin scattered with thousands of tiny diamond points of light. Her dress also sparkled and she wore a necklace with a golden crescent moon symbol. Her long black hair was the only part of her that was not scattered with star-like diamonds. Catching herself staring at Nuit for too long, Sekhmet looked away. "I've never been up here before," she said. "It's wonderful."

Nuit smiled bemusedly. "And I almost never leave, so one becomes used to the serene beauty. I thought I would never get used to living up here, away from the skies over Earth, but now, I wouldn't go back. This is my home now." Nuit gestured for them to walk and Sekhmet took the hint, though her steps were tentative.

"It's odd to walk on a floor that is invisible and so far up in the heavens."

"Yes, I suppose it does take some getting used to. Try to think of the realms below as the floor," Nuit advised.

Sekhmet looked down in several directions. "I've never seen the realms like this. They seem to go off into the distance forever. Where do they end?"

"It's difficult to determine. I've heard that if one were to try to travel to the edge, and you get further from the central realms, it gets darker and colder, until you feel like you are walking upon the night itself. I'm uncertain of the actual size of the realms, but I can tell you that they are shrinking at the edges. I know that, because I don't have to spread myself as far as I used to in order to cover the central realms at night."

Sekhmet turned away from the amazing view to face Nuit. "Shrinking? I've never heard such a thing."

"Few have. It is hardly common knowledge." As they walked on, Nuit said nothing more about the edges of the realms and Sekhmet did not press the issue. She patiently waited for Nuit to reveal the reason for bringing her here. The Goddess of the Night Sky placed a hand on Sekhmet's shoulder. "I must confess, I wanted to see you shortly after your pardon from the Egyptos tribunal, but was so engaged in stellar responsibilities that time did not permit it."

"I fully understand. I know that the Elders realized that I had no hand in Geb's death, but I always . . ."

"Wondered if I had forgiven you?" Nuit interjected.

"Yes." Sekhmet looked upon the floor, unable to keep Nuit's gaze.

"Geb was my brother and my closest companion. I have to admit, I was jealous of your relationship with him. When I heard you had been accused of causing his death, I was first in line to curse your name and I voted to have you banished," Nuit admitted.

"Everyone thought I was guilty."

Nuit turned Sekhmet's face to look her eye to eye. "Perhaps, but I reveled in your suffering. Then as time passed, it was revealed that Set was the true villain in the death of my brother and that you had been framed for the murder. So, not only do I forgive you, but I ask for your pardon for my error in judgment and my selfish jealousy. Will you forgive me?"

The two of them exchanged a look of deep understanding then, with tears in her eyes, Sekhmet leaned in close and embraced Nuit. "Oh yes, of course. Of course. I never blamed you for my fate. You had no way of knowing I was innocent - how could you? How could anyone?" Sekhmet suddenly realized that she'd had a similar conversation with her own daughter Bast, not too long ago.

Nuit hugged Sekhmet for the first time in several thousand years. Then she held her at arm's length and looked her in the eye. "I know that Geb loved you very much and that you loved him. For that I am grateful, for true love is hard to find. Come, let's share some nectar, for we have other matters to discuss."

They walked to the center of an area set with beautiful Egyptos furniture and potted plants. Two servants stood by waiting for Nuit's slightest request. There were no walls, and to Sekhmet it felt like they were sitting in the center of a vast, flat plain in the middle of the night. Nuit gestured toward a golden chair with a soft, padded seat. "Please, sit. I've heard you were nominated for the Council."

Sekhmet sat and a goblet was placed on the small table next to her. A servant filled it with the nectar of the gods. "Yes. Horus nominated me. I had no idea such an honor was forthcoming. I don't really know why he chose me, to be honest."

Nuit sat directly across in a similar chair and was also given a goblet, which she picked up and took a sip from. Her long dark hair cascaded around her blue figure as she sat. "I'm sure your part in saving the realms a few cycles ago had something to do with it. Tara spoke well of you shortly after the events of those days, and many pay heed to her words."

"I haven't seen Tara in a long time. I wonder how she is."

"Like me, she is deeply involved in keeping the realms stable and safe. I suppose that's why we are friends. Both of us are completely devoted to our tasks, so we understand each other." Nuit looked upward at the stars overhead, as if checking to make sure they were still in their proper places.

"The rest of us should be eternally grateful for both your efforts." Sekhmet enjoyed the nectar, which had a slightly spicier taste than the mixture she had shared with Ptah. The goddesses spoke for some time about family matters, including the death of Geb, the punishment of Sekhmet's exile and her reconciliation with her daughter Bast, and gossip concerning other Egyptos relatives. Finally, Nuit brought up her true reason for delivering Sekhmet to her heavenly retreat.

"Long ago I was on the Council. There are things you need to know should you get accepted into their inner circle."

Sekhmet's ears pricked up. "I didn't know you served on the Council! I'd love to hear anything you could tell me. Horus told me some things, as he too was on it once."

"So you know the basics then. Did Horus tell you about the mystical limits on what you can say or even what you might know while you're a member?" Nuit asked conspiratorially.

"Mystical limits? What do you mean? Will there be limits on my mystical abilities?"

Nuit raised an eyebrow. "No. I mean that once you are a member, they can limit what you know and what you can say to anyone not on the Council. That is an important detail for Horus not to share. Perhaps it was wiped from his mind."

"I'm not sure I know what you are talking about," Sekhmet said, uncomfortable with the direction the conversation was taking, but curious nonetheless.

"It's hard to explain. You see, the Council holds many secrets, and over the millennia they have created a system that keeps those secrets locked within the Council members themselves. Those who serve have wide-ranging powers that allow them to control any knowledge connected to the Council's actions. When I was on the Council, I know we enacted decisions that made a huge difference in the way all the realms operate, but I can't tell you about most of them. Once I was no longer one of them, many of my memories regarding such things were taken from me, so I truly don't remember. I can tell you about minor decisions and proclamations, but much of it I just can't recall. While you're on the Council there will be things that you will be unable to discuss with anyone else. It's all part of a bonding spell they cast on you. It's done to anyone who joins."

Sekhmet was shocked to hear this. "I . . . Horus didn't say anything like that. Why would they do such a thing and what could be so secret that even the members of the Council don't know what they did after they leave?"

Nuit gave no reply for a moment, as if she were searching her memory for some clue as to what was taken from her mind. "I don't know the answer, Sekhmet. I only know that is how it has been for as long as there's been a Council. But I feel like it is something you should know, now that you are a nominee." She took another sip of nectar.

"Thank you. I don't like the idea of surrendering my memories or voting for things I'll later not know anything about. It makes me wonder if this is really something I'm willing to do." Sekhmet set down her goblet, finding the taste in her mouth suddenly bitter. "But I've made a commitment to Horus and should see it through to the end."

Nuit nodded. "Well, at least you'll be entering into this knowing what will be expected of you. My duties up here require me to see the realms from a different perspective than most. I tell you that there are things going on that few ever notice, let alone understand."

"What kind of things? What have you seen, Nuit?"

The goddess slowly shook her head, "It would be too hard to try and explain it all. The realms are like a tapestry filled with tiny threads, and over time I've seen the threads change and unravel."

"I thought these realms were eternal. What could change?"

Nuit noticed Sekhmet's rapt expression, and seeemed to decide sharing one secret couldn't hurt. "Well, I've noticed that mortals have been slowly disappearing."

"Disappearing? How?"

"There are many different reasons. Wars and disease count for some of it, but there are many unexplained mysteries. Perhaps it is of no concern, but it seems like a larger purpose is at work. Entire regions of Egyptos have been emptied of servants, farmers, all kinds of people. There are villages that were once filled with humanity. Now they're deserted. It's the same in Olympia, Babylonia and the Mayan Realm. Things vary across the Pantheons, but there's a sort of pattern to it. As I said, it's hard to explain, unless you have been observing it all for a long time and from a great distance."

"But the City of the Gods is teeming with people. It's crowded Nuit."

"Yes, but I didn't say people are missing everywhere. But out in the hinterlands it's very obvious, especially from my vantage point up here."

"Maybe they are just growing old and dying off, and they don't have children to take their place?"

"Sekhmet, we goddesses can no longer produce children, but humans can and do. No . . . something else is at work. It's all part of a larger tapestry that someone unknown is weaving."

"I - I don't know what to say," Sekhmet said in earnest.

"There's so much more I could tell you, but I would be here for days explaining all the things I've seen and how they connect. But the stars are turning and I am required. I hope you understand."

Sekhmet stood. "Yes of course. And I greatly appreciate that you invited me here and shared your concerns with me. I promise that I'll take heed of all you've told me and see if I can discover some answers to these mysteries."

"When you are ready, the sarcophagus will take you back. Feel free to stay and enjoy the view if you wish. Good luck and be careful, Sekhmet."

From her seat, Nuit raised her arms straight up over her head and her entire body stretched upwards into the heavens. It kept going and going until only her impossibly long legs remained. At last they too rose from the glassy floor and joined the rest of Nuit in the sky above. Sekhmet turned and walked back to the sarcophagus, armed with new knowledge and many new questions.

Voyage on a Royal Barge

After leaving them to gaze down at the realms from the heights for about an hour, another of Bast's slaves respectfully approached D'Molay and Quan. They were taken to a room one deck down and told to remain there. It had two small beds, a table with a washing vessel atop it, a narrow wardrobe, and two fine sconces on the wall with vents behind them to draw off the smoke from the burning oil that illuminated the windowless cabin. Quan immediately began to investigate the room, looking under the beds and opening all the doors of the wardrobe like a curious child. His initiative paid off, as he found a small bowl of fresh fruit and nuts and a pitcher of water on a small table that stood hidden on the far side of the wardrobe. The men shared the snack as they waited.

"It's odd," D'Molay said. "I can barely tell we're moving at all."

Quan's hand paused as it lifted a grape to his lips. "You're right," he said. Concern crossed his face. "What if we're falling? We'd never know until we hit the ground!"

D'Molay laughed at him. "Somehow I think we'd notice. Besides, if it came to that, wouldn't it be easier not to know?"

Quan popped the grape into his mouth as he pondered this. "It would seem so," he mused, reaching for another grape, "but I'd like to hear what Lady Mazu would advise."

D'Molay heard movement in the hall and looked toward the cabin's door. A moment later Mazu herself stood in the open doorway. "How was your meeting?" he asked.

"Pleasant," she said, stepping inside and looking about the room.

Quan quickly spit out a grape seed and gave her a courteous bow. D'Molay wondered what had passed between the goddesses.

"So, what did you two talk about?"

"I cannot tell you, D'Molay. That would betray the trust Bast has honored me with. I hope you understand," she said, giving him the kind of look that said 'Don't even try asking again.'

"All right, fair enough. Where is your stateroom?"

"I'm at the end of the hall. Apparently the larger rooms down there are reserved for deities and dignitaries."

"This cabin isn't huge, but it suits us fine. It's far better than Charon's boat." D'Molay picked up a pillow and casually tossed it on the bunk.

Even Quan smiled at that comment. "We can agree on that, certainly."

The muscular Nubian guard who had broken open Mazu's barrel appeared in the open doorway. "Mistress Bast asks that Lady Mazu and her tracker dine at her table in one hour in the galley. Use the water-clock in the hallway to check the time. It is hour ten. Luncheon begins at hour eleven."

"Enjoy those grapes while I'm eating lunch, Quan," D'Molay smirked.

Quan deflated a bit. "I understand. I am only a servant, especially in the eyes of a goddess like Bast. I'll wait here for your return."

"True, you are my servant," Mazu said, "which means I have every right to order you to see to my stateroom. I noticed a fine assortment of honey cakes and seed bread on the sideboard there. You may eat as much of it as you wish, as long as you clean up after yourself. I don't want to see any crumbs on Bast's reed mats. And don't get sick again."

"Yes, Lady Mazu!" Quan's eyes lit up and any disappointment over missing luncheon with the others vanished.

An hour later, Mazu and D'Molay went up on deck and the Nubian escorted them into the room behind the royal court area. The galley took up the entire space inside, save for a set of stairs at the back that went down to the kitchen. A large oval dining table stood in the center of the room. Like the exterior of the barge, the table was black, lacquered with gold inlaid hieroglyphs around the inside edge. A large symbol of the eye of Ra, in turquoise, was inset in its center. Silver plates, green malachite goblets and matching finger bowls had been laid at each guest's place. D'Molay recalled that Egyptians ate with their hands and used the finger-bowls between courses. There were already a few priests and advisors seated. The table had a dozen chairs placed around it. The elaborate throne-like chair was obviously where Bast held court.

"I will take you to your seats," said the guard. "Lady Bast chooses where each guest shall dine."

Mazu was shown to a place of honor next to Bast. D'Molay was seated next to Mazu, which surprised him somewhat. He expected to be seated further away, perhaps with the priests. He looked across the table. On the other side of Bast's chair there was a very short platform about six inches high and about two feet square. "Wonder what that's for?" he whispered to Mazu as they both sat down.

"We'll find out soon enough," she replied. Servants came up and filled their goblets with wine and they engaged in idle chitchat with the three priests already at the table.

A few minutes later the Nubian guard stepped forward again. This time he held a tall golden staff, topped by the same cat symbol as was on the barge's sail. He tapped the staff on the wooden floor and called out in a loud voice. "All rise for Bast, Lady of Flame, keeper of beauty, perfumed protector and daughter of Sekhmet!" As soon as he had tapped the staff, the priests at the table stood at attention, Mazu and D'Molay quickly followed suit.

Bast entered the galley, her retinue lined up behind her in single file. She wore a tight-fitting turquoise dress of shimmering, iridescent fabric. On her head a matching blue headdress with her cat symbol upon it had been placed. Around her neck and shoulders she wore an elaborate necklace made from semi-precious stones with a large silver hawk, its wings spread, in the center. It was the symbol of Horus and she probably wore it to honor him for the use of the barge. Bast nodded to the assembled guests. "Let us feast in honor of RA, who surrendered his very essence so that we would remain strong, and give thanks to Horus for the use of his barge." She made the arched sign of RA with her hands then walked over to her chair of honor.

"Be seated," commanded the Nubian in his deep voice. D'Molay froze halfway down to his chair as he saw what was revealed behind Bast as she walked over to her throne-like chair.

It was a sphinx, a creature with the body of a lion with the head of a woman. She had the same colored fur as a lion, but was smaller, perhaps the size of a large dog. She wore an Egyptos headdress and a gold necklace with a red stone. When she stepped up on the platform and sat down on her haunches just as a cat might do, D'Molay realized the platform was placed there so that she could easily eat off the table. He had a difficult time taking his eyes off her, as sphinxes were not commonly seen. He finished lowering his body into his chair. The rest of Bast's retinue consisted of priests and more advisors of one sort or another.

As everyone sat, D'Molay made a silent prayer to the One God in thanks for the benefit of the barge and the meal. It reminded him of the stories of early Christians who must have done similar 'subversive' prayer acts while living among the Romans. He had only resumed praying in the last few months, so the feeling of praying to a god other than the ones accepted in the realms was new to him.

Once everyone was seated, servants entered the galley carrying platters of meats, bread and fruits. The smell was sumptuous, and despite his snacking in the cabin D'Molay was very hungry.

Bast addressed her assembled guests. "Joining us on our return to Bubastis is the water goddess Mazu, and Hetepheres, one of my friends since childhood." Bast turned to the sphinx as the two of them exchanged cat-like smiles. "I hope you enjoy today's meal. We have grilled zebra, fresh squid, seasoned cyllestis bread and a variety of fruits. There is wine and ale as well, so enjoy." Once she finished speaking, the servants started to offer everyone servings of the foods and then retreated, standing nearby to give more to whoever wanted it.

"This is a most beautiful luncheon. We are honored to be invited to dine with you," Mazu said gracefully after sipping some of the wine.

"You are a goddess and D'Molay is favored by my mother. I could do no less. I admit I have my doubts about you both, but while you are on board, you are esteemed guests," Bast said just before picking up a bite-sized piece of meat and popping it in her mouth. "Mmm . . . the zebra is delicious today."

Instead of a plate, the sphinx was given a broad platter that was like a shallow bowl. Another smaller bowl was placed next to it which the servants filled with Egyptos ale. Unable to pick up the food with her paws, the sphinx ate just like a cat would, by taking bites and lapping up the food and ale directly into her mouth. After she had eaten for a moment, she turned to Mazu. "So, why does an Asian water goddess travel to the deep

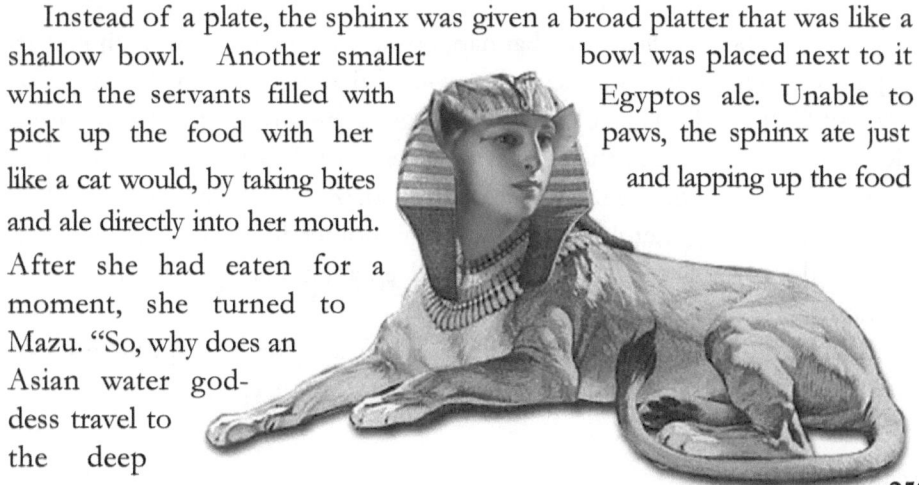

deserts of Egyptos? Wouldn't that be the last place you would want to go?"

Mazu smiled in agreement. "You would be correct, Hetepheres, but for the fact that we are travelling to the Lost Realm to rescue someone."

"Really? It sounds rather exciting don't you think?" she asked Bast.

"Didn't I tell you their story? These two and their man-servant want to go into the Lost Realm on their own, with no troops to back them up."

"Are you foolhardy or just very determined?" Hetepheres asked.

"Perhaps we are a bit of both," Mazu admitted, "but we are in no position to obtain troops, so we'll just have to carry on as best we can."

Bast ate some of the bread as she added in a slightly muffled tone, "We are to play a part in all this, Hetepheres. Mother has volunteered me to open the barrier for them. I'm sure you'll want to see that."

"I can go? But wait, we aren't going through the barrier are we?"

"No. We aren't going in, but they are. All I have to do is open the barrier for them once or twice. Of all the favors this man might have asked, that was his choice."

Hetepheres turned her eyes to D'Molay and studied him. Becoming a little uncomfortable under her scrutiny, he felt compelled to speak. "Yes, it was my choice. I do it to save the life of a helpless person."

The sphinx looked at him as if she were reading a book. "Ahh, but isn't the bond you have upon you also a reason?"

D'Molay was surprised by the insight demonstrated by her question. "Yes, there is that, but we took this bond willingly to help two women in distress."

"We?" Hetepheres asked as she turned to Mazu.

Mazu put down her goblet. "Yes, I too have the same bond."

Bast added her own comment, "Well, you both have my sympathies. I know what a bond is like and what happens if you don't comply with it. This explains much. The good news for you is that we are going straight to Bubastis, but it will still take two weeks to get there. My temple compound is deep inland, away from the Western shores, so it is a longer journey than most. Just be glad you are not travelling by land, or it would take you months."

"We are truly grateful to you and your mother for helping us like this. Words do not convey those feelings deeply enough," D'Molay replied earnestly.

Bast nodded her acceptance of his gratitude. "We will speak more of this mission you have, but for now let us enjoy our feast."

And they did.

Chapter 19 - Voyage on a Royal Barge

"So, what do you think of our guests?" Bast asked Hetepheres as she eased back on her divan. The two of them had retreated to the royal stateroom after the meal. This was undoubtedly the finest room on the barge, with exquisite draperies and furnishings made from rare woods and semi-precious stones. One wall had a large window with a wondrous view of the lands far below them, the nearby clouds drifting past as the two spoke.

"Do you really want to know?"

Bast had long ago gotten used to her friend's sometimes annoying manner of always speaking in questions, but she knew that was the way of all sphinxes. "What do you mean, Hetepheres?"

The sphinx paced around the room and her tail swished back and forth as she gathered her thoughts. Bast couldn't help getting a little irritated. "Oh for Ra's sake, just say it. What are you fretting about?"

"Is the male alone? Or not alone? Why do I sense another presence near him sometimes, but not at all times? Do you know what I mean?" Hetepheres gave her old friend and goddess a frustrated gaze.

"No, I don't know what you mean. Do you think he's possessed or hiding something?" Bast queried, trying to get a better idea of the sphinx's impressions.

"That would be easy to discern, wouldn't it? Could it be he's being followed, but by something very far away or so small it can't be seen? Isn't it strange that I can't be certain?"

"We'd better keep a close eye on him. I've found mortal men to be untrustworthy for the most part, so I suppose I shouldn't be surprised. What about Mazu, did you sense anything from her?"

"Have you forgotten my abilities around deities are limited?" Hetepheres reminded.

"I remember, but I hoped you'd sense something anyway. Perhaps you can get something out of her servant during the journey. He might be the weak link in the chain."

Hetepheres nodded in agreement. "Might he? Why are you so concerned about them, if I may ask?"

Suspicion played over Bast's face as she leaned in close. "It's just that he showed up right after mother was nominated to the Council. It just seemed too . . . coincidental. I had to go in her place on this favor, and I can't be in the City to help her when she might need me most. And I still can't believe that the three of them just plan to march into the Lost

Realm. There must be something more to it. Maybe Ptah was just trying to get me out of the way."

"Does not Ptah hold you in high regard? Besides, wasn't your original plan to leave for Bubastis anyway?"

"I was going to cancel the journey once I heard mother was nominated. I just hadn't told her yet."

"Shall I cross paths with the servant during one of my strolls up on deck?" Hetepheres said with a sly smile.

Bast nodded her agreement. "Yes, I'll have the guards let us know when he is about and you can meet then."

"Are we really going to get the key?"

"That's the plan, assuming they really do want to go to the barrier. I knew you'd love to return."

"Do you remember when I was last there?" Hetepheres asked.

"It's been years, but I don't know how many. Just keep an eye on those three, and let me know if you sense anything else unusual."

"Do you doubt that I would?"

Hetepheres' question needed no answer. Bast just leaned her head back on the divan and closed her eyes. Hetepheres walked over to the rug near Bast and curled up in a ball at her feet as the two of them took an afternoon nap.

Chapter 19 - Voyage on a Royal Barge

The new amphitheater of recreated Mt. Olympus looked exactly like the original, but Hera could still sense its differences. In days of old, Hera, as queen of the Greek gods, could feel the immortal threads of every deity in her pantheon when she visited this place. The amphitheater, the gods' gathering place, was then a buzzing hive of vitality. Now, with so many of her kindred diminished or entirely gone, the theater was more like a slowly boiling pot.

The amphitheater was ringed with statues of gods. Some, those who were missing or known dead, were shrouded out of respect. Hera walked slowly over to the image of Ares, studying the lifelike recreation of her son. The statue was gigantic and almost as intimidating as the god himself. The last time they had spoken, she had chided him about his choice to appear so often over the City in his aspect of Mars. She found his penchant for hiding in a ball of fire distasteful. The Greek form was perfect, and should not be changed. But he had continued to burn in the sky, for what son took his mother's advice? Pushing that issue aside, Hera touched the base of Ares' statue and spoke a line from one of his ancient hymns of praise.

"Thee human blood, and swords, and spears delight, and the dire ruin of mad savage fight."

Soon, Ares would come in response to her summons. Hera waited, turning away from his statue to survey the room. Her eyes landed on a newly draped image. Unable to remember who the statue represented, Hera went to it, the pain of disappointment gnawing at her heart as she approached. She lifted the veil and gazed upon the name inscribed on the figure's pedestal.

"You needn't worry about ever finding a rag thrown over me."

Hera dropped the covering and turned. Ares stood there, mighty and confident as ever, holding out his hand to escort her to a nearby bench. They sat together on an exquisitely hewn marble seat, decorated with cavorting satyrs and nymphs.

"I worry about all of us," Hera admitted. "The Realms spin out of our hands. There are too many gods prying into our business."

Ares smiled broadly. "That is why I hunt them. And catch them." He gave his mother a wink.

Hera looked around quickly to make sure none of the other gods visiting the amphitheater were close enough to listen to their conversation. When she was satisfied, she looked down at her lap, smoothing the folds of her gown. "And what have you done to him?' she asked, knowing Ares would understand exactly whom she meant.

Ares folded his arms across his chest. "He's enjoying a stay in the old Titan prison, chained to one of the Chairs of Parrhesia. As far as his kinsmen know, he's still a criminal at large."

Hera relaxed somewhat. Ares had done nothing rash, yet. "Who else knows this?"

"Deimos, Phobos, one of my squads. And Ioke was a great help in his capture," Ares nodded, remembering her skills. "I like that girl."

"Don't let Eros hear you say that or he'll play with his arrows," Hera warned with a smile. "He's due to cause some mischief. The only reason he hasn't is because Zeus has kept him busy running Council errands."

Ares shook his head in disgust. "Don't bring up the Council to me. Useless talkers they are. If anyone is ever to be punished for invading our realm it will be up to me to do it."

Hera sighed, realizing the time had come to drive to the point of her visit. "Zeus is firmly against any new trouble with Egyptos. He has even sponsored one of their goddesses for the vacant Council seat. If we do anything to upset the tenuous peace - "

Ares interrupted. "What is he thinking? Why does he elevate our enemy?"

"He has a plan, Ares," Hera said, deceptively. She knew Zeus was only thinking of matters in the short term, playing politics against Quetzalcoatl. But if she succeeded in convincing Ares there was some point to staying his hand, things could be left exactly as they stood. This seemed an acceptable compromise. "You will see Egyptos fall in a very

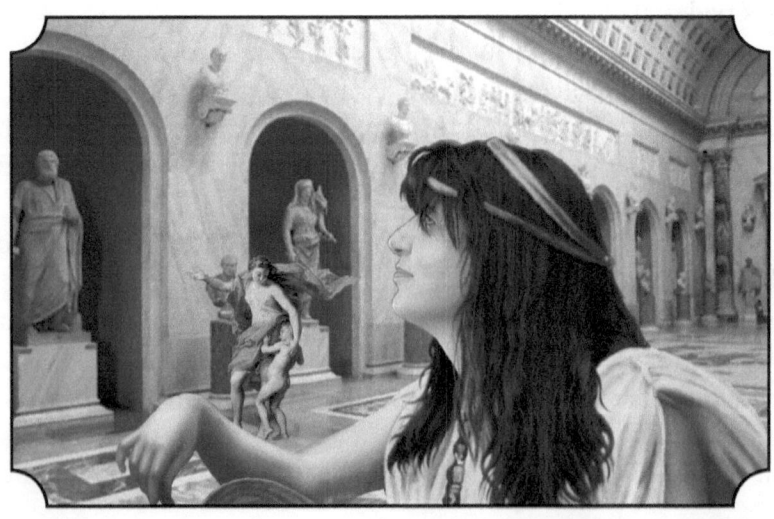

short time. And then, we shall treat them as we did on Earth."

Hera carefully watched her son's face as it shifted from anger to determination. "The time Alexander put his foot on Egypt bears repeating," he said. "If that is father's plan, I will let it play out."

"Good. Keep a close watch on your prisoner. He may prove a useful pawn in the greater game." Hera stood, placing her hand on her son's shoulder fondly.

"I'll check on him right now," Ares promised. "By the way, whose statue were you looking at?"

Hera glanced back over her shoulder at the shrouded goddess. "Circe's."

Ares responded with a vague grunt. Hera suspected he wasn't sure who Circe was. Ares never did pay much attention to their pantheon beyond the twelve Olympians and those who helped him in his acts of war. She watched him march back to his own statue and disappear into it. Hera prayed she would never have to lift a cloth to look upon her son.

For his part, fading away or being destroyed were ridiculous fantasies. He was too strong for such worries. Worry was the lot of the oppressed. He decided to enjoy that oppression by paying Set another visit. Besides, he'd thought of a few more questions that needed asking.

Taking to the sky as Mars was the fastest way to return to the outskirts of the Lost Realm, where he entered the secret mountain tunnel. By allowing his power to coat his body in a red glow, he generated enough light to show him the way through the corridors that led to Set's cell. When he reached it, the door stood open. The chair was empty.

Wonder briefly crossed Ares' face, soon replaced by fury, but ultimately erased by bloodlust. The chase was on again.

⚜

*L*ate the next day, the sun hung low in the sky behind the barge as it continued its journey. Quan and D'Molay were up on deck, leaning at the railing and watching the sunset. "Enjoy it Quan, You don't get a view like this too often."

"Yes. Now I've seen the clouds from the top. The way the sunlight hits them - they look like they're made of spun gold," he said contentedly.

A soothing voice came from behind the two men. "Yes, it is lovely, is it not?" As they turned, D'Molay and Quan saw Hetepheres just a few feet away. Quan's eyes grew wide as he saw her for the first time. D'Molay wondered how long she'd been standing there, and more importantly, what she might have learned by means of the same power she'd used on him the day before.

"I don't think you've met Quan, He's one of Mazu's servants," D'Molay said, hoping to avoid having to say the sphinx's name, which at this point he'd completely forgotten.

Her eyes darted to Quan and she looked at him the way one might stare at a moth trapped in a glass jar. "Quan, you are a servant too? Is this how we are alike, in that I, Hetepheres, serve Bast?" Her tail swished slowly back and forth as if dancing to some unheard melody.

Quan was clearly stunned that such an odd creature was talking to him. "Heet-efer-us," he stuttered out. "You are the first sphinx I've ever met."

"Does your land consider meeting a sphinx to be a great honor or a sign of dread times?" she asked enigmatically.

Quan stared at her blankly until D'Molay felt compelled to speak up. "Let's hope that you are a sign of honor and great luck for us, Hetepheres."

Her knowing gaze moved from Quan to D'Molay. She gave him a sideways smile. "May I give you my blessing? Ask the gods to make your journey successful?"

"We'll take all the help we can get." D'Molay wondered what the sphinx had in mind. They watched as Hetepheres lay down on the deck, her front paws stretched straight out before her. She became completely still and silent. Her mouth opened and an odd purring hum, mixed with faint words, came out. D'Molay strained his ears, but he could not pick out what was said. Quan began to inch away in fear, but D'Molay grabbed his arm and held him in place, lest he offend. Hetepheres ceased her vocalization and stretched.

"Could I have said it better?" she asked, returning to a more casual pose.

"I doubt it," D'Molay said. He nudged Quan.

Quan bowed. "Thank you for your blessing," he stammered out.

Hetepheres walked to the railing and sat beside Quan, looking out over the waters of the great lake below them and the golden clouds that drifted nearby, she sighed. "Wouldn't it be fun to walk upon the clouds?"

"A long walk is the same, no matter the pavement of the road," D'Molay replied. Although he knew that riding the barge through the sky was much quicker than sailing to Egyptos, it sometimes felt like they weren't moving at all, especially when he couldn't see the land inching by far below.

"Ah, that's not true," Quan objected. "It's the scenery that makes a road short or long."

Hetepheres laughed softly and turned away from the rail. "Two very different opinions, aren't they?" She walked away without revealing which outlook on travel she preferred.

D'Molay turned to Quan. "That sphinx," he said softly. "She can look inside a man, see his secrets. I think she just did it to both of us."

"Really?" Quan tapped the rail nervously. "But she blessed us, so whatever she saw in you must not be too bad," he reasoned. "Or, she was greatly impressed by me."

D'Molay had a strong urge to pitch Quan over the rail, and test for certain whether a man could walk on the clouds.

On the fourth afternoon of their journey, those same clouds grew thick and tall. In the distance, D'Molay could see flashes of lightning bursting in the sky. As louder rumbles of thunder announced that the storm was drawing near, all but the most essential of Bast's crew headed below deck to wait it out. D'Molay joined them, and was invited by several scribes to play a game. He sat around a table inlaid with a pattern of squares, listening as his hosts described how he was supposed to move the game pieces around the board. After several turns, he began to understand the strategy. He picked up the knucklebones to roll for his move and the room suddenly tipped violently to the right.

The game, the priests, and D'Molay too were thrown across the deck. All around him cries went up. Some were orders to set the ship to rights, others plain exclamations of fear. Above his head, thumping noises were heard from the top deck, as if many people were running about. It might be the sound of the crew getting the barge under control, but his gut told him chances were just as good that it was something else entirely.

D'Molay put one hand against the leaning wall of the chamber and edged out into the hall. He scaled a ladder, now tilted at a sharp angle, and made his way to the deck. Crawling out of the ladder hatch, he was forced to shield his eyes from a burning, red light. Then the shadow of a wing fell over him, and he thought it was Aavi. He twisted toward the source of the shadow and found himself staring up at a pegasus. Its wings gently stirred the air just enough to keep its hooves near the boards of the canted deck. The rider on its back wore light but exquisitely formed armor in the Greek style. D'Molay had never seen a pegasus rider this close, though he had watched them fighting in the sky during the war. They had fought then for Ares, but why had they attacked this ship?

When his eyes adjusted to the brightness, D'Molay saw that the heavy main sail and its rigging had been cut from its mast. It dangled precari-

ously over the rail, its weight contributing to the cockeyed position of the ship. Bast's crew had been herded toward her platform by more of the armored pegasus riders. The one near him raised his sword and pointed toward the group of prisoners. D'Molay raised his hands in surrender and carefully made his way over to the others. He arrived just as Bast burst out of the room behind the platform, a bitter snarl on her face, hands raised to attack. Hetepheres was close behind.

The red glow that pervaded the atmosphere flared. Even Bast had to cover her eyes as a fiery ball bigger than the barge burned through a near-by cloudbank. Smoke, thunder, and lightning churned around the sphere. D'Molay expected it to hit and obliterate them, but it stopped just beyond the deck rail. A tongue of flame licked out, and a god D'Molay recognized from the recent war strode down it as if it were a gangplank, boarding the barge. The god extended his left hand, and the giant orb compressed as its energy flowed back from whence it had come, back into the body of Ares. As everyone blinked in confusion, Ares made an announcement.

"This ship will be searched for the traitor Set. Cooperate fully, and we will reverse the measures we have taken to control this asset, and you may go on your way." He strode toward Bast, who glared at him in open fury.

"Set is not here," she hissed.

Ares merely looked her up and down. "This cat has been known to be friends with a dog."

D'Molay noticed that Bast was taken aback by that remark, as if Ares had struck a nerve. She fell sullenly silent as Ares stepped closer to her.

"Do you blame me for stopping you? Isn't Set your brother? He's rumored to be out in the Lost Realm. Is it just coincidence that here you come, in that very direction? I don't believe in coincidence, and until I've searched this barge, you're not going anywhere," Ares said.

"Are you Ares, the Greek god of War?" Hetepheres asked.

"I am, sphinx. And leave the questions to me." The god tipped his head and two of his riders headed to the lower decks. Shortly afterwards, the rest of the ship's complement had been marched up to join D'Molay at the platform, including Quan. But Mazu was nowhere to be seen.

"She's in a barrel," Quan whispered to him, sidling over. "We thought Quetzalcoatl . . . "

D'Molay nodded as he watched Ares' men report that they had finished searching the barge. Ares took their whispered counsel. The riders stepped away as he paced the deck, staring into the palm of his sword hand and toying with sparks he generated by flipping his fingernails against the pad of his thumb. Bast endured a tense wait before he finally turned to address her.

"An old warrior's instinct tells me there is something hidden on this ship," he said. "And I will find out what it is."

Bast found her voice again. She drew herself up regally and again declared, "Set is not here and I have not seen that traitorous dog in many years."

Ares was not intimidated. "Pull in your claws, cat. I never said he was."

"Then fix my ship and go," she demanded.

D'Molay suspected Ares had somehow sensed Mazu. He could expose her, but he knew little about Ares and where his allegiances might lie. Yet if Mazu remained hidden, this standoff could turn ugly very quickly. He had to risk it.

"Great Ares," D'Molay called out. "You are right. There is a goddess in the hold."

Quan wheeled on him, a look of abject betrayal on his face. Ares walked over to them.

"I knew it. Explain this, before I cleave you in two."

D'Molay started to speak, but to his horror, the words he wanted to say would not come out. He had intended to reveal that he had fought for Ares in the war for the angel and the beast, and that Mazu had nursed his men; that she was hiding because those same enemies who had attacked Ares' Fortress were still at large. But too much of that story was tied up in the spell of secrecy laid on him by the Council, and he merely gaped like a landed fish as Ares watched him. The god's expression turned grim.

He grabbed D'Molay, shoving him against the ship's mast. Ares pulled his sword and held it at D'Molay's neck. "Enough! I'll just kill everyone on board and burn this ship out of the sky. And I'll start with you!" Ares pulled back and swung for D'Molay's head, but at the last possible second, D'Molay seemed to slide down at an inhuman speed, landing in a sitting position at Ares feet. A chunk of wood flew from the mast as the blade struck it.

Suddenly Quan threw himself on his knees in front of Ares.

"Please! He cannot speak as the Council has stilled his tongue! Hidden below is an ancient water goddess and you are the master of fire!" he chattered. "She turned herself to water and hid in a barrel lest you burn her essence away. Please don't kill my mistress! Please!"

Ares stared down at Quan as he bobbed up and down, prostrating himself at his feet. He gave Quan a disgusted look. "Tell your water goddess I have better things to worry about then the likes of her." Then he looked at D'Molay. "And you? You may be a mortal, but I've only seen Hermes move like that. I could have used you at my fortress last season."

D'Molay smiled. "I was there Lord Ares. I fought alongside your men against the jackal hordes of Set."

The war god nodded. "Very well. I've wasted enough time here. We have a foul dog to hunt."

Quan and D'Molay's performance was enough to allay the god's suspicions, as a moment later Ares told his riders to reattach the sail. They grabbed the lines and flew up to set everything right. The barge gently shifted into its normal position. Without any apologies or polite farewells, Ares returned to his fiery aspect of Mars and his pegasus riders followed his orb away as it again disappeared into the thick clouds.

D'Molay noticed Bast wore a slight smile. The goddess nodded approvingly in their direction as she turned and reentered the galley.

"Look what you made me do." Quan frowned at D'Molay. "I had to make Lady Mazu sound like a coward."

"Don't blame me for what you thought of," D'Molay said testily. "But it worked, so be proud of that."

Quan considered this for a moment. "You're right! I saved Bast from Ares! I am truly a blessed one!" His grin was wide and ridiculous, and D'Molay was surprised at how much it cheered the man.

Chapter 20

The Key to Adventure

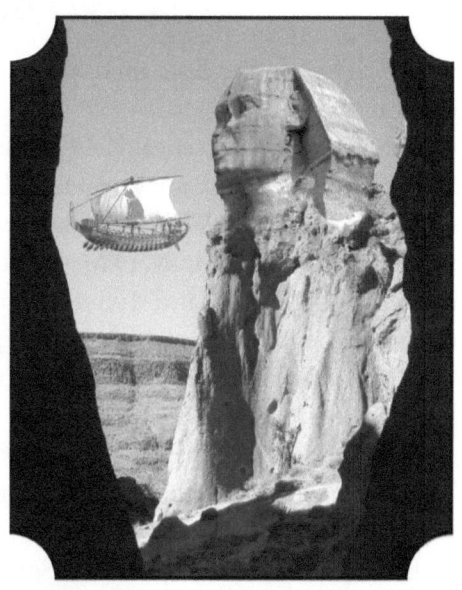

The royal barge began a descent into the rugged canyons of the western desert. It was a difficult maneuver, but there was almost no wind and they landed neatly in one of the wider canyons. As D'Molay looked over the rail, he could see that the bottom of the canyon was an old, dry riverbed that was now not much more than sand. The chief navigator had chosen this spot for that very reason. The ship seemed to hover just a few feet off the ground as many of the crew jumped off the ship, each holding long ropes which were attached to the barge. Orders were barked out and the men with the ropes secured them to boulders, logs and anything else that was heavy enough to stay on the ground. Shortly after the barge was secure, the ramp was placed so that Bast and her guests could disembark.

The priests were in charge of unloading the passengers. As they arranged a line, D'Molay waited to see where he and Mazu would be placed. At the front were four armored guards carrying spears. The shafts of their weapons also flew turquoise banners with Bast's black hieroglyph symbol of a cat's head. Behind them stood the Nubian guard carrying his scimitar, followed by Bast, who was dressed in a brilliant blue robe and matching headdress. Close behind was Hetepheres, also wearing an Egyptos headdress, then a bald priest carrying a papyrus scroll. Behind him, four more guards carried a large decorated chest, each one holding a handle at its corner. As a priest began to guide the two of them to a position behind the chest, Bast intervened. She glanced regally at D'Molay and Mazu. "You two - behind Hetepheres."

Mazu nodded her agreement. They quickly complied as more attendants and scribes were arranged at the end of the line. As they stood there, one of the priests raised his arms and recited a prayer. Once he was finished, Bast called out. "Let the blessed procession move forward!" The entire line then proceeded down the ramp and into the canyon ahead.

"Are we allowed to speak?" D'Molay asked Mazu as she walked at his side.

Before she could answer Hetepheres interrupted them. She looked over her shoulder. "Why shouldn't you? Haven't you been in one of these before?" she said happily. D'Molay got the impression that the sphinx was excited to be in this land. Even he enjoyed the warm breeze sweeping the canyon. The wind almost seemed as if it were welcoming them in.

Mazu turned her gaze back to him. "What was it you wished to ask?"

"Is it like this when you open the Asian Barrier?"

"You mean with the procession and prayers? No, but the gods of Egyptos are the masters of pageantry. They excel at it. Although I did need a priest with me to get the key from the dragon."

D'Molay raised an eyebrow "Sorry I missed that expedition."

"Was it exciting?" Hetepheres asked.

D'Molay wasn't a bit surprised that the canny creature had been listening. "Is that why you're here Hetepheres? Are you a seeker of adventure?"

Hetepheres gave him an unreadable smile that was both cloying and sarcastic at the same time. "Ha - who are you to ask such a question? D'Molay, the man who has spent his entire life chasing adventure to the exclusion of all else… Have you not?"

"Obviously you have great insight, Hetepheres. I can't deny your description of me, but you didn't answer my question. Is that why you are here?"

"Should not a friend help another?" she said, before turning away.

D'Molay gave up any hope of getting answers from the sphinx as the procession walked on. They entered a narrower canyon with walls that towered high overhead. D'Molay felt surrounded and constrained by the shadowed cliffs on either side of the trail. He had grown used to the bright cloud scattered vistas that five days in the barge had provided them. Missing that experience already, he glanced up at the sky. The silhouette of something ducked out of sight. He heard a whisper in his ear, "Beware the clifftops…" He was certain it was a warning from Aavi.

Hackles rose at the back of his neck. "There's someone up there," he blurted out. Mazu paused and looked up, seeing nothing. "Was it Aavi?"

Realizing no one else was stopping, the two of them moved forward again. "No, but she is near."

"Perhaps it is just some animal that lives here," Mazu reasoned. "This is Bast's expedition. She should know the dangers. We'll have to follow her lead, but let us be ready for something from above."

"Agreed," he whispered back.

The procession continued along the twisted trail, which grew narrower as they got deeper in. Every so often D'Molay would glance up, scanning the top of the cliffs for any additional movement. One other time he thought he saw something jump out of sight again. "There's someone up there all right," he told Mazu.

"But who, and why? It could be a guard of the keeper of the key."

"I hadn't - "

Just then a fair-sized rock fell out of the wall of the canyon and hit the ground near the front of Bast's procession, barely missing her priest with the scroll. Everyone froze for a second; then another rock fell, and another. D'Molay pulled Mazu back under an outcropping, safe from danger. "Everyone against the wall - NOW!" he shouted.

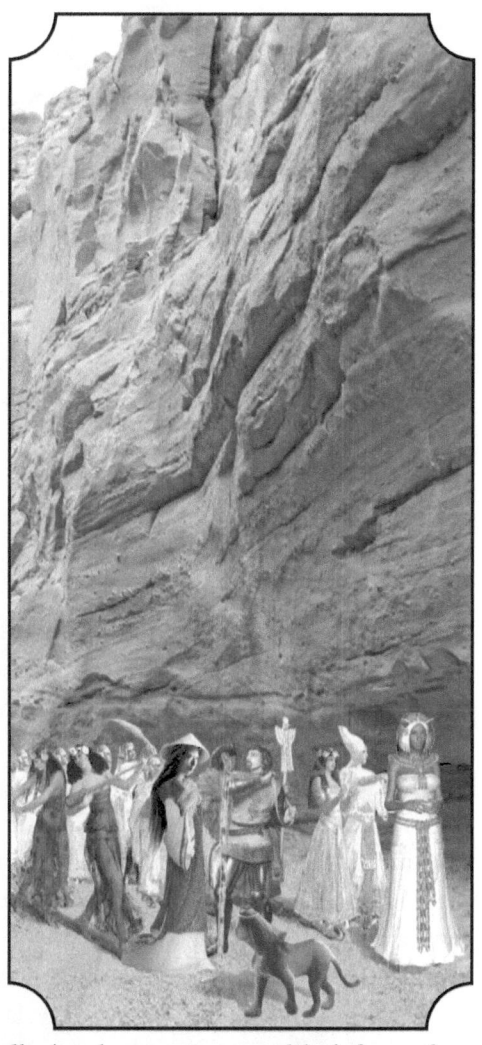

A guard up front echoed the call. As the party scrambled for safety, more rocks broke loose with loud cracks and struck with solid thumps, shaking the ground. As D'Molay looked past the falling boulders, he could see that everyone else was either close up against the wall or lying on the canyon floor, either knocked out, pinned by a large rock or worse. Bast stood at the far end of the trail, seemingly unafraid of the danger. She raised her hands high over her head and called out something that D'Molay couldn't hear over the noise of the rocks and the screams of the injured.

He watched Bast clap her hands. All the rocks stopped exactly where they were. Most of them were still in mid-air at eye level, while others floated mere inches above the ground. Looking up, D'Molay could see that all the rocks above them had also halted their descent. They hung suspended, like silent wind chimes. Bast wasted no time in getting everyone under her command. "It's safe now. You can all come forward. Gather up the wounded," she said imperiously.

Avoiding the strange floating boulders, everyone went towards Bast, stopping to tend to the wounded and unconscious.

D'Molay realized Mazu had hurried over to a large rock. "Be still, we'll get help," she said, kneeling next to it. Quickly approaching, he saw that Hetepheres was pinned under the stone.

"Hetepheres!" he crouched down, gently placing his hand on her front paw.

The sphinx looked up at him. "Can you get this rock off me?" she asked meekly.

D'Molay tried to smile. "I'm sure we can." He turned towards Bast. "Your Sphinx, she's trapped!"

Bast and two guards rushed over. "Get that boulder off her, but be careful about it," she ordered. The guards complied, and as they picked up the boulder, D'Molay carefully slid Hetepheres out of harm's way. Bast stood over her friend, deep concern etched on her face.

"My leg . . . is it broken?" Hetepheres quivered in pain.

Mazu placed her hand on her back haunch. "Yes. I'm afraid so. I don't have the power to heal." She looked up at Bast. "Do you?"

"Healing's not in my repertoire. I'm sorry Hetepheres, you'll have to go back to the barge with the rest of the wounded."

"Please? I've come so far and don't you need me?" Hetepheres winced as she pleaded.

"But you can't walk. Why make me watch you suffer if you don't have to."

"Maybe we can carry her," D'Molay suggested.

Bast looked off in the direction they needed to go. "We're not too far from the entrance, but still . . ."

"Bast?" Hetepheres begged.

"All right then. But let's get going, my spell won't hold these rocks forever." Bast turned her attention to the rest of the group. "Guards, take these four back to the barge." She pointed at an unconscious scribe, the scroll priest, and two other guards, all of whom were too injured to continue. "Our healer has work to do. If you don't hear from us in a day, send a rescue party."

Hetepheres looked up at D'Molay. "Will you carry me, Tracker?"

D'Molay smiled. "I'll do my best."

Soon the injured were on their way back to the barge and the rest of the party made their way past the strangely floating rocks and boulders. Bast paused, looking back to see that everyone was safely away from the rocks. She clapped her hands together and called out, "Vah-Tumn Ma!" All the rocks fell to the ground with huge crash. D'Molay felt the ground shake as he cradled Hetepheres in his arms.

"That's a handy power to have," he observed.

Mazu smiled, "Indeed. I'm afraid all you have is a water goddess."

"And a sphinx?" added Hetepheres.

And a guardian angel, he thought to himself. "That's plenty for any man."

Bast's procession continued though the winding canyon with no other incidents. D'Molay, taking turns with one of the strongest guards, continued to carry the wounded sphinx. They finally arrived at their destination, a huge set of ancient double doors at the very end of the canyon. They looked like they were made of solid bronze and were covered with intricate geometric designs. D'Molay couldn't miss the giant Council symbol   at the center of the two doors.

"This must be the right place. I'd recognize that flying eye anywhere," he said to Hetepheres.

"Is that what you call the great symbol?" she asked with a wince of pain.

Before D'Molay could answer, Bast ordered, "Bring Hetepheres forward."

Mazu stepped aside as the guard carried the sphinx to the front of the line.

Bast looked down upon her friend, "How are you feeling?"

"Do I look to be in great pain? Am I presentable?"

Bast smiled. "You're always presentable."

Hetepheres looked at the man carrying her. "Would you put me down? I'll walk from here, I hope?"

He complied and the sphinx carefully tried to stand up. She was able to, but had to keep her back leg off the ground as she stood. "That will do, perhaps?" she said with a wince. Hetepheres moved in an awkward three-legged hop to stand beside Bast. The two of them exchanged glances.

"All right then, can you still open the door?" Bast asked.

She nodded her affirmation then limped up to the doors and bowed her head. Bast stood directly behind her in a formal pose, holding the banner of Egyptos. Everyone grew silent. D'Molay realized that a ceremony was about to take place.

Bast began to chant. "Muui urek aq her sba pen en useyt ten Horus au-k rey-oa-n ta-aa aq-k an Bast . . ."

D'Molay didn't know the Egyptos tongue, but he recognized three words: 'Horus,' 'Bast' and 'sba.' The deities' names were obvious, and he had learned 'sba' meant door while he was on a mission for the Egyptos feline deities; it had been the password they'd given him.

"Taex en bu maa ren-t an ta-u aq-k her-a an Sekhmet . . ."

Mazu moved up to stand beside D'Molay as they watched. As Bast chanted, D'Molay noticed that Hetepheres started to glow a faint pale blue. The glow brightened, the color deepened, then -

D'Molay heard an outburst of warlike cries. Swiveling, he saw at least a dozen jackal-headed men charging toward them. Instinctively, he reached for his bow, but realized he had left it on the barge. "Jackals!" he called out.

"Defend Bast!" called out one of the guards as they all moved into defensive positions, their spears at the ready.

But Bast and Hetepheres seemed oblivious to the oncoming attack, apparently too deep into their opening spell to stop now. "Arit unem ent sba pen ann-uch fet nek ren-a henku!" Bast intoned, her gaze transfixed upon the huge doors.

As the jackals rushed forward, the guards used their spears to pierce the vicious creatures and keep them at bay. D'Molay drew his knife and slashed at any he could get close to. Unlike the jackals he'd fought at Ares' Fortress, these did not carry any weapons. They struck only with their claws and gnashing teeth.

An unlucky guard was overwhelmed and dragged into the mass of snarling creatures. There was no way to save him, but Mazu stepped into the gap he left and blasted some of the jackals with jets of water from her hands, providing a final defense for the remaining priests who stood in a semi-circle around Bast and Hetepheres. A jackal locked its jaws around the arm of another guard. D'Molay slit the neck of the hideous creature almost to the bone and it released its grip, wheeling away with a howl.

Suddenly there was a flash. Both Bast and Hetepheres became stiff, frozen in place. Two bright beams of light projected from Hetepheres' eyes and struck the large Council symbol on the doors. D'Molay felt the ground under his feet rumble as the two large doors began to open. A cloud of dust grew as sand fell. "Is it supposed to happen like this?" he shouted to Mazu as he tried to slice another jackal.

In response to the noise and light, the jackals turned and ran back into the canyon, away from the large doors as they opened. Mazu put her hand on D'Molay's shoulder as she answered over the rumble. "The battle is over. We held them at bay long enough."

The priests rushed forward to attend Bast and Hetepheres, while D'Molay and the rest encircled them warily, ready should the jackals return or something unpleasant emerge from the opened doors. Bast leaned close to her companion.

"Hetepheres, speak! Ask a question; say something, if you can."

Slowly the sphinx opened her eyes. "Did we . . . open the door?"

"Yes. Yes, you silly thing. It's open."

Hetepheres smiled as she closed her eyes, while a priest checked her leg and gave her some nectar to sip.

Bast stood up and surveyed the scene, seeing one of her guards dead and others bloody. She addressed the nearest. "What happened here?"

"A group of jackals attacked us, mistress Bast."

"Bast, I am sorry this has brought such difficulty. We would never have asked this of you had we known it would cause such loss," Mazu said, a look of pained sorrow etched across her features.

Bast sighed. "No one knows what dangers the future holds. At least we can be prepared for an attack next time. Let's get inside before those jackals attack again."

Mazu stepped back and returned to D'Molay's side. "We have cost Bast more than we should have. Be certain to tread carefully, ere we wear out our welcome," she warned him.

D'Molay stared at the dead guard and the other injured people around them. "Understood. Those jackals were just like the ones I fought at Ares' Fort. Do you think they followed us here?"

"I don't see how they could have. We flew here, and besides, aren't these jackal creatures native to Egyptos?"

"Yes, I see your point." Yet he still wondered if Set had found some way to mystically pursue them.

A moment later, Hetepheres sat up. Though her leg was still injured, the sphinx seemed to have recovered from the efforts of opening the doors. Bast had completely recovered and was ready to proceed into the entrance. Only her concern for Hetepheres kept her from immediately ordering everyone forward.

Hetepheres took a few tentative hops and looked towards the opening. "Now, aren't you glad I came along despite this injury?" she asked Bast.

"I'm just glad you're all right. Are you ready to go in?"

"Let's go, shall we?" Hetepheres replied as she hobbled over to Bast.

D'Molay couldn't resist speaking out. "Do you want us to carry you in? It's not a burden."

The sphinx looked back over her shoulder. "Is it wrong to want to walk into my family home on my own paws?" she replied.

"No, not at all." Hetepheres had revealed more to D'Molay about her reason for making this journey in that one sentence than she had in all their exchanges during the past week on the air barge.

Bast took a formal stance as she began to lead the procession. The group marched past the doors and into the shadows beyond.

D'Molay could see that they were in a tall hallway perhaps thirty feet across and forty feet high. The walls were smooth and the floor was flat. Every surface was so neatly finished he felt like he was in a corridor in a huge temple rather than walking through a carved tunnel. However, there was a layer of dust upon everything as if no one had been there in some time. After a moment or two, D'Molay thought he heard a faint booming sound in the distance. Soon they all saw a very large creature approaching from the darkness. D'Molay pulled his knife, but Mazu gave him a look that obviously meant he should not take any aggressive action. As the creature got closer, they realized it was another sphinx.

This male was huge in comparison to Hetepheres, being at least twenty feet tall as it marched along the passage. It had a long aquiline face and wore a headdress similar to those of the pharaohs. When it got about twenty feet away from the procession, it sat on its haunches, blocking the way. It looked down upon the party with a suspicious eye. Its deep voice boomed forth and echoed all around them. "You have entered the Keep, but if you wish to pass further can you answer my riddle?"

Bast stepped forward, with Hetepheres at her side. "We can. You have but to ask it of us, Guardian."

"Have you heard of two sisters, one who gives birth to the other and she, in turn, gives birth to the first? Who are these two sisters?"

D'Molay and Mazu exchanged uncertain glances. He was glad he didn't have to face such a question, for he had no idea what the answer might be.

Hetepheres nodded and Bast stepped forward. "The answer is day and night, oh Guardian. For surely day gives birth to the night as the night does to the day." Bast bowed, a sign of great respect.

The huge creature almost smiled. "They do, don't they? Do my old eyes deceive me, or have you returned to us my daughter?" He turned his gaze from Bast to Hetepheres.

The smaller sphinx bowed her head. "Did you miss me, father?"

"What do you think, little one?"

Hetepheres said nothing, but smiled broadly.

The larger sphinx addressed the group as a whole. "Do you wish to accompany me and obtain what you have come here for?"

"Lead on, Guardian," Bast affirmed. They followed the sphinx down the hall and into a huge chamber lit by a faint orange glow from above, though no light source was obvious. D'Molay could not even see the ceiling in this room as it disappeared into the amber mists above. The circular chamber must have been several hundred feet across. The large sphinx strolled to the center and sat down, looking very much like a masculine version of the giant statue near the great pyramids back on Earth.

"Why are you limping?" he asked Hetepheres.

She looked up. "Have you heard of the jackals striking in our land?"

"Jackals? They dare to intrude upon this sacred place?"

"I'm afraid they dare," Bast said. "Set released hundreds of them for an attack recently. There are probably strays that wandered from the main group. You know how mindless such creatures are. They killed at least one of my guards and sent several others back to the barge. Hopefully they survived the trek back."

The Guardian stalked away from his daughter and lifted his face toward the heights, bellowing in anger. "Where are my protectors?"

Down from the misty cloud flew dozens of the Guardian's warriors. They too were sphinxes, the size of Hetepheres, but with powerful wings. They circled then landed before the Guardian, each bowing a dutiful

head with the face of a man.

"Guardian, you have called upon us?" The leader of the protectors had old scars on his shoulders and flanks. D'Molay imagined he was a veteran of many battles.

The Guardian glared at them. "Can we not protect our own people from encroaching jackals? Will you do your duty and destroy them?"

The leader silently nodded in agreement as the others lifted their heads, ready to set out. Following the lead of their commander, the protectors leapt into the air and flew off down the tunnel, the way that Bast's procession had come.

Hetepheres watched them depart with sadness. "Will they return safely?"

"Should they not do their duty?" the Guardian asked. "And now, don't you think we should get you fixed up, little one? Do you still remember the way to the healer?"

D'Molay found listening to one sphinx confounding enough, but hearing both of them only ask each other questions was almost maddening. He wanted to jump in between them and demand that they actually answer each other's constant, queries, but he knew better. He turned to Bast. "It's a hell of a way to communicate. I don't know how they keep it up."

"It has always been thus with the Sphinx. They know what the other truly means by understanding the subtleties of the next question. You get used to it after a while." She barely looked at him as she answered. Her eyes were fixed on Hetepheres. D'Molay realized that she was still worried for her companion and probably blamed him for her injury. He already blamed himself, for he knew that if they had not gone on this journey Hetepheres would still be lounging somewhere, being feed grapes, or whatever sphinxes usually ate.

Hetepheres and her father finally finished their discussion and the smaller sphinx started to limp away. Bast immediately reacted. "Guards, carry her to wherever she wishes to go. I'll not see her in pain any longer." She then turned to address the Guardian. "Please know, we carried her through the canyon after the attack, but she insisted upon walking in here on her own."

The large sphinx considered her words. "Would my Hetepheres do anything else? She is a strong-headed one, is she not?"

Bast couldn't help but smile. "Yes, she is indeed. Will she be all right?"

"Do you doubt the skills of a high-priestess of Hathor?"

Bast's guards carried Hetepheres away. The Guardian settled down into a cat's pose, lying on his stomach with his great front paws stretched before him. D'Molay considered his immense feet and wondered if they had ever crushed a man. He smiled, realizing he could soon converse with the sphinx in questions of his own if such queries kept springing into his mind.

Bast, too, adopted a more casual stance as she and the Guardian began to converse. The great sphinx cocked his head and spoke openly.

"Now, Bast, shall we discuss your reason for being here? You wish the key to one of the locked realms, do you not?"

"Yes, Guardian. I . . .we . . . have need of the key to the Lost Realm." Her eyes quickly darted over to D'Molay and Mazu.

"So, you two are involved in this request?"

Mazu stepped forward. "We are, Guardian. Bast makes this request for us. We are the ones who wish to pass into the Lost Realm."

"You know of its dangers?"

"We do."

"Do you know where the Egyptos gate to the Lost Realm lies?" he asked Bast.

"Yes, I've been there once or twice. It's between the two great statues on the banks of the Heavenly Nile."

"Shall I show you how to use the key Bast?"

"Yes, please I've never actually used its power myself, though I have seen it open the gate."

"May I instruct you later? Perhaps your friends might like refreshments?"

Bast agreed to all of the Guardian's offers and graciously bowed as she retreated from the huge cavernous chamber. "Come with me," she told Mazu and D'Molay.

They proceeded along the way that her guards had carried Hetepheres. That hallway opened to a chamber of water fountains and a wading pool, then into an immensely tall room that reminded D'Molay of the inside of Notre Dame cathedral. It featured a large, round opening near the top that allowed the winged sphinxes to fly in and out. Along the walls on all sides were hundreds of carved alcoves which seemed to be used as homes for them. D'Molay watched several land, each in a different niche.

The group walked out of the chamber of alcoves and down another hallway. D'Molay noticed that none of these entrances had doors. Instead, curtains gave the inhabitants their privacy. He realized that without hands, a sphinx would find a curtain far easier to use then a typical door. "This place is huge, it must run for miles," D'Molay said to Bast and Mazu.

"Yes, the Sphinx established this home when the realms were founded eons ago. They've had ample time to tunnel all this out," said Bast.

"Do all the sphinx live here?" Mazu asked.

Bast smiled. "No, this is just the main aerie of the Egyptos Sphinx. I would imagine Olympia and Babylos have similar aeries, though I've never seen them." Bast stopped at a doorway covered by curtain marked with the hieroglyph of Hathor. "Hetepheres must be in here."

D'Molay parted the curtain, letting Bast and Mazu in first. Hetepheres was lying on a bed as a woman stood beside her wrapping her back leg in a bandage. Bast's guards stood lined against one wall in the room, and bowed as their goddess entered.

"Ah, you found me?" Hetepheres asked.

"Of course. Healer, what is her condition?" Bast asked.

D'Molay noticed coldness in Bast's eyes; he would not want to be in the healer's robes if the answer was going to be bad news.

The healer looked up from her work. "I believe the leg will be fine, if given a month or two of rest. I have reset the broken bone and this splint should keep it in place, as long as she doesn't move too much."

Bast folded her arms and smiled slightly. "Easier said than done, I suspect. Still, I am pleased to hear this good news. I feared amputation. A three-legged sphinx would be quite unseemly in the royal court." Bast approached and stood beside Hetepheres. The sphinx made a mock-frown.

"Why are you so cruel? Do you like to see me suffering like this?"

"Of course not. Now what shall I do with you? If you leave with me, you'll have to be carried out, very carefully, while jackals wait outside to attack us. Or you can stay here, safe and secure among your people while you recover. They'll take far better care of you here then we can on the barge."

Hetepheres tilted her head back and looked at the ceiling. "That's not really much a choice, is it?"

"You did say you wanted to visit for a while. Now you have an excuse. I'm leaving you here, but I'll be back this way in a month or so when I head back to the City of the Gods. I'll pick you up then."

"A month? What about your mother and the Council election?"

Bast sighed. "Truthfully, I don't know what I could actually do for her even if I was at her side." Bast reached out and gently placed her hand on the sphinx's arm. The two of them exchanged glances.

"You do know I'll miss you?" Hetepheres asked.

"Yes, and I'll miss your constant questions. Now, I'm sure you need some rest, so we'll get out of the way and let the healer do her work. I expect you to be scurrying around on all fours when I return." Bast turned to her guards and ordered them out into the hallway.

"D'Molay, please stay a moment?" Hetepheres wiggled around to face him as the healer made an adjustment to her bandages.

"Of course," D'Molay said, approaching the bed.

"Did you notice me watching you? Do you know something pursues you?"

"I know." D'Molay felt a coldness tickle the base of his spine as he was reminded of the dire pronouncement of doom laid upon him after falling in the Styx. Was some death shade truly waiting for a chance to pounce? He shook off his fear and forced himself to give Hetepheres a look of confidence. "But someone else is also watching over me, so I hope I'll remain safe."

"Will that be enough? Will you be prepared for the terrible thing that will happen? Are you ready for betrayal?"

D'Molay patted her paw. "I can only do my best to deal with whatever comes my way. Thank you for the warning. You take care too." D'Molay left and joined the others out in the hallway. As they were escorted back to the main chamber, Mazu quietly asked, "What did she tell you?"

He gave her a grim look. "It was a warning. She told me I'm going to be betrayed."

<hr />

*T*he march back to the air barge was mercifully free of jackal attacks. The Guardian's protectors could be seen circling in the skies, and the party felt very safe as they traveled, despite their reduced numbers. Quan was overjoyed to see Mazu again, and listened raptly as she told him of their battle with the jackals and the opening of the gate. The barge took them next to Bubastis, the place in Egyptos that Bast called home. Leaving the airship behind, D'Molay, Mazu, Quan, Bast and two dozen of her guards set off across the sand on camels. Bast brought no other priests or servants on this journey, wanting to travel quickly. At the beginning of the second day she directed D'Molay to scout ahead for any trouble.

As D'Molay rode over a dune, he saw two ancient Egyptos statues of a male and female seated on thrones. They sat side by side in the desert, facing a river. He estimated they were at least forty feet tall and carved of some kind of opaque, pink quartz. He returned to the party to report this wonder.

"Good," Bast said. "We have arrived. That is the gate."

The party gathered at the foot of the male statue. D'Molay ran his hand over the rough surface of the weathered monument as Mazu and Quan stood beside him. "Arrow and sword marks. There have been many battles fought here."

"The realm gates were some of the first things built after the borders were decided by the first council, thousands of years ago," Mazu replied. "And not all attempts to pass through them involved having the proper key."

Bast retrieved the key from her pack. It was a small crystal pyramid, about the size of a pomegranate. She placed it exactly twenty-four paces in front of the statues, at the midpoint between the two of them. "Lady Mazu, I would speak with you, before I open the gate."

"Of course."

Quan and D'Molay watched them walk out of hearing. "What do you think she is telling our mistress this time?" Quan asked.

D'Molay smiled slightly. "Maybe she's trying to talk Mazu out of taking you with us."

Quan grimaced. "Hah, you would be dead by now if I had not been on this journey."

"Sometimes I wish I was." D'Molay mentally kicked himself for this lie. Ever since the Styx, he seemed haunted by talk of his own demise. A moment later, Mazu returned. "Everything all right?"

Mazu nodded. "Yes. She gave me details on how to return when the time comes."

"Well, that might be useful to know." D'Molay watched as Bast moved to kneel before the crystal key. She ran her hands over it and began to chant.

"Maui arekaq her sba pen useyt reyoa-n Bast. Ta-u fet-nek sba!" The crystal began to emit a faint blue light. The goddess stood up. Outstretching both her arms, one towards each statue, she began to sing. "Henku-nef faat ren-a enen arit."

D'Molay noticed the pyramid's glow strengthen as if it were absorbing the power of her song. Bast sang louder and faster until she seemed to be no longer voicing words, but merely singing notes. The pyramid grew even brighter as Bast hit one final high note. A bolt of bright blue energy shot forth from the crystal and struck her. It ran up her body and out from her arms straight into the two statues. D'Molay saw blue energy swirling in the air between the two statues. A whirlpool formed, which morphed into an opening. Mazu moved forward.

"The gate is open, we must go though quickly." Walking forward, Mazu lead her camel. Quan hurried right after her and D'Molay followed. As they moved into the vortex, they fought against a strong wind. Dust and small bits of debris assaulted them.

"The wind is too strong!" Quan cried out.

"Damn the wind! Keep moving!" D'Molay urged. They dragged their camels forward as the wind whipped sand against their skin, stinging like tiny arrows thrown by a thousand ants. As they came to the end of the strange storm, D'Molay took one look back and saw Bast fall to her knees before the gate closed; then she and the two statues vanished.

Mazu, Quan and D'Molay now stood alone in the middle of a desolate wasteland, uncertain of their path or their prospects.

Chapter 21

Rivalry and Brotherhood

As they rode in the golden carriage though the streets of the City, Sekhmet felt even more excited and nervous than she had on the day her banishment from the realms had been lifted. Tenh-Mer sat at her side, attired as an Egyptos handmaiden. Her usually loose hair had been carefully braided into hundreds of small long strands just for the occasion. Sekhmet could not stop looking at her companion's makeover. "You are simply beautiful today, Tenh-Mer."

The demoness smiled. "Me? What about you? With that gold dress and all the jewelry and turquoise headdress - you really look like a goddess! But all these clothes and braids are itchy! How do you wear them all the time?"

"You get used to it," Sekhmet smiled. She looked off into the distance wistfully. "I wish Bast could have returned to the City in time for this."

"She'll be back soon. I'm sure she'd be here if she could." Something about the carriage suddenly captured Tenh-Mer's attention, and she squirmed around, stretching to examine the seats, the floor, and the other appointments. "Hey, is this the same carriage we rode in when we first came to the City of the Gods?"

Sekhmet was pleased by her companion's keen observation. "Yes, I asked for it. It brought us good luck last time we rode in it, and I feel like we could use some more now."

"You don't need any luck, everyone will vote for you. You're the smartest, the kindest and the prettiest goddess ever." Tenh-Mer crossed her arms and nodded, as if her belief in Sekhmet was all it took to ensure her victory. The cat goddess laughed.

"There is more to it than that, but I appreciate your heartfelt convictions."

"Well, you'll get my vote anyway."

Sekhmet let her fingers run through Tenh-Mer's new braids and gazed into her eyes, immediately feeling the romantic effect of the demoness's power. "Too bad for me you don't get to vote. Only Pantheon leaders have that privilege."

"Hmph. But aren't there only like . . . nine of them?"

"There are nine main realms, but hundreds of Pantheon leaders. Many smaller Pantheons sit within the larger realms. They all get a vote too."

Tenh-Mer was a little confused. "Even Egyptos has other Pantheons in it?"

"Yes. There's the cult of Aten the sun god, and the Elders of the Necropolis, along with a few more. Each of them has their own leader and worshippers. There are dozens of different Pantheons in the Mayan Realm: Incas, Aztecs, Sioux and Navajo, just to name a few. All their leaders get a vote. And that's a problem for me. They don't know me at all. I have to try to meet as many as I can, if I am to win. That's where you can be helpful."

"Me?"

"Yes. Ptah says I need to use every asset I have, if we are to convince strangers to vote for me. I want you to be at my side to help make a good impression upon them. Especially the male deities." Sekhmet gave Tenh-Mer a conspiratorial wink.

Tenh-Mer smiled mischievously. "Oh, I see. Should I do anything special?"

"No. In fact, I want you to be very quiet and regal. Today you are my handmaiden. So after the ceremony stay at my side and be silent. Do you think you can do that?"

"Well . . . It won't be easy, but I'll do it for you."

She gave Tenh-Mer a hug. "Good. Then we are as ready as we can be."

The carriage took them to the main entrance of the huge Council building. Several guards and a priest stood by to greet them. They all bowed as the cat goddess stepped out of the carriage. "Lady Sekhmet, welcome. We're here to escort you to the opening ceremony."

"Then proceed." She was pleased to see that Tenh-Mer had, as ordered, stayed silent and close.

The escorts led them through a labyrinth of hallways and up a dozen sets of stairs. As they walked along, Tenh-Mer's tail began to nervously twitch. After trying not to fidget for a few moments, she anxiously gripped Sekhmet's arm. "Something's not right. I feel - Look out!"

Suddenly a deep, red cloud - a gaseous apparition with a hideous gaping maw - formed in front of the escorts and swallowed them with one forward surge. The floating creature headed towards Sekhmet, its mouth open to consume her next.

"Hutep sba An-ankra!" Sekhmet cast a shield spell which halted the thing for a few seconds, but it flowed around the spell like a red octopus might clamber over a glass bowl. Its dark tendrils reached out for the goddess.

An angry hiss and a flash of pink

streaked across the floor and grappled with the oncoming red thing. Tenh-Mer tore into the monstrosity, slashing and tearing, her wings beating wildly like an insane bat attacking an over-ripe fruit.

"Tenh-Mer!" Sekhmet shouted in alarm, but her fear was soon allayed. Shreds of gore flew about the hallway until there was nothing left but a pile of oozing red goo and a hyper-ventilating pink demoness, her eyes burning with wild-eyed fury. Tenh-Mer crouched, her chest heaving, like a rabid dog on a hot day.

Sekhmet ran forward to embrace her protector. "It's gone, you killed it, you killed it!" Tenh-Mer gave no response. Only the raspy, heavy breathing of an animal crossed her lips. Sekhmet waited patiently. It was rare to see this aspect of her companion's nature, but there was no telling what the cloud creature might have done had the demoness not acted from pure instinct. When she wiped a clot of gore from Tenh-Mer's cheek, it dissipated like smoke as soon as it was touched.

The sound of footsteps ran up from behind. "What's going on?" came a male voice.

"We were attacked." Still crouched around her companion, Sekhmet turned to angrily face the man, who paled when he saw who she was.

"Lady Sekhmet - attacked? That's not possible!"

He appeared to be one of the many high priests who worked in the Council halls, though she did not recognize him. "Look around! How do you explain - " Sekhmet's accusation stalled as she realized the area was clear of any sign that a struggle had taken place. The walls that had been splattered with blood and gore were now completely clean. She stood, scanning the hallway. "It's all gone. Even our escorts have vanished. There was a creature and it attacked us. My companion killed it."

The priest shifted uncomfortably and bowed. "That is well, then. I was sent to find you. We feared you got lost in the building when you did not arrive in the hall. The ceremony will take place in less than an hour. You must meet the other candidates, and be placed in the proper order for the procession."

Ignoring the tedious man, Sekhmet reached out to stroke her friend's hair. "Tenh-Mer?"

Slowly, Tenh-Mer looked up. She was shaking, but her vicious demeanor had faded away, replaced once again by the personality of a young girl. "I-is it g-gone?"

"Yes, we're safe now, thanks to you. Can you stand? Let me help." She got Tenh-Mer to her feet. "Which way, priest?"

"This way."

The three of them, Tenh-Mer still being supported by Sekhmet, walked down several hallways and flights of stairs. The priest led them to a large pair of wooden doors incised with intricate symbols from different Pantheons. Numerous gods and their servants were going in.

"This is the main auditorium. Your servant must wait here. You have to go to the back so they can bring you in with the procession."

Searching the area, Sekhmet recognized a deity and quickly motioned her over. "Tara. It's so good to see you again."

The blue-skinned Hindu goddess put her hands together as if in prayer and bowed her head. "Indeed. I'd heard of your nomination, and I didn't want to miss it. I see you brought Tenh-Mer as well. Hello, little pink one. My pixies often ask about you."

"Ooo! Tell them I say hi. Isn't it amazing that Sekhmet could be on the Council?" Tenh-Mer said brightly, remembering old adventures she had enjoyed with Tara's impish friends.

"Even I find it hard to believe I've been nominated," Sekhmet admitted. "It was a complete surprise. I would stay and talk, but I have to go. Can you take Tenh-Mer in and sit with her? Ptah is in there somewhere, but I don't have time to find him."

"Of course, it would be my honor," Tara said.

"Thank you. I'll see you both after the ceremony. Tenh-Mer, listen to Tara and stay out of trouble, all right?"

"I promise."

"Come along then, Tenh-Mer. Let's find a good seat."

As Sekhmet left with the priest, she couldn't stop thinking about the creature. *What was that thing and who had sent it?* She realized that the stakes in this game were very high, and clearly someone would go to any lengths to win.

She was led to an antechamber behind the auditorium. Seated casually in one of several plush chairs was a striking woman with long red curly hair and a dark blue dress. She was busily munching on a pear that had come from an overflowing basket of fruit on the polished table that sat in the center of the room.

"I was beginning ta wonder if any of the rest of ya were gon'ta show up. By the look of ya, I'd have ta guess you're Sek-Met, the cat-goddess," she said, with her mouth half-full.

Sekhmet noted how casually her fellow candidate seemed to be taking the proceedings. She couldn't imagine gorging herself in such a carefree way right before a serious ceremony. She inclined her head, ever so slightly. "You are correct. I give greetings to a fellow goddess."

"Ceridwen. I'm the Celtic goddess of transformation, among other things." She took another large bite of the pear. It immediately reminded

Sekhmet of the thing that had just tried to eat her a few moments ago. Could she have had something to do with that?

Ceridwen noticed the odd way Sekhmet was staring at her. "What? They left the fruit here in that bowl - aren't we allowed ta eat it? Is this some kind of a test?" Ceridwen shifted her attention to the half-eaten pear, turning it back and forth in her hand as if to discover something wrong with it.

Sekhmet turned her gaze away. "No, no. Just nerves before the ceremony."

"Then settle in and have a pear. We don't get many pears in the Celtic Realm, They're a delicacy. I couldn't resist." She took another bite as she stood up.

"Have you ever been nominated before?" Sekhmet asked, hoping to get some information that might be useful.

"Me? Nah - I've never even thought about bein' on the Council ta be honest. It just sorta happened. And you?"

"No, and being nominated was unexpected for me as well."

"Well there ya are - We're two pigs in a poke."

"Two what?"

Before Ceridwen could explain, the door opened. A green-skinned, very tall goddess with glowing yellow eyes stepped in. Her dress of gold and semi-precious gems kept a classic, stiffened shape as she moved.

"You two must be the other nominees," the new-comer said haughtily.

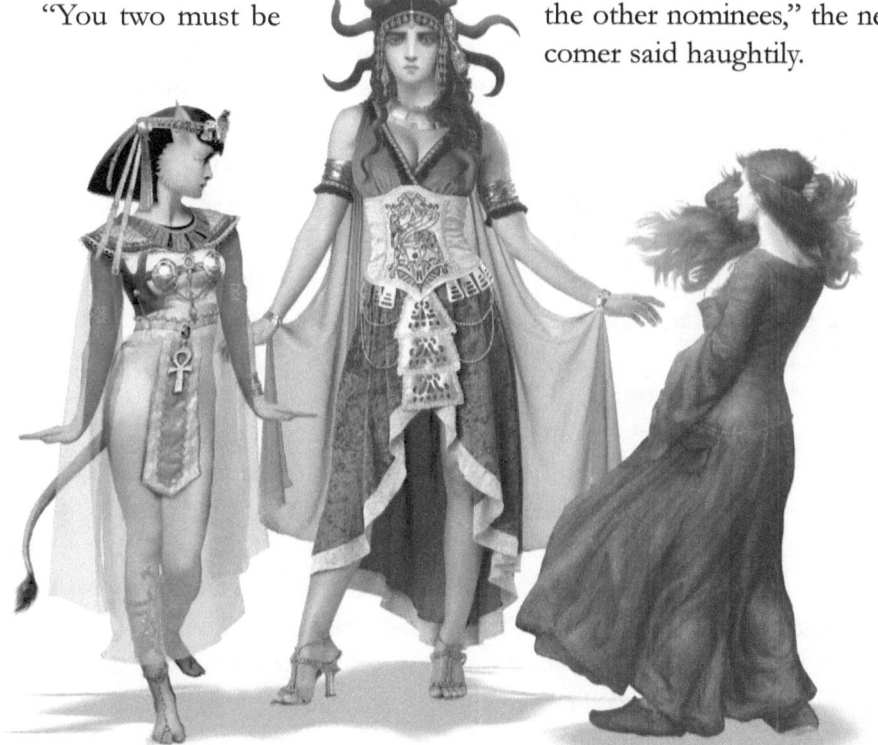

"I am Sekhmet and you are . . ."

"Lamasthu. Didn't anyone tell you?"

"Hello, I'm Ceridwen, My, you're a tall one."

"Perhaps you are just . . . a short one." Lamasthu looked down her nose at the red-haired goddess. Ceridwen shrugged off her scorn.

"Or, perhaps you're just trying ta appear more impressive. Didn't the priests tell you we're supposed ta all be the same height during this campaign?"

"The campaign hasn't started yet, so those rules are not in effect," Lamasthu replied tersely.

Sekhmet interjected. "But it is about to start, so perhaps we can all settle on a height. Shall we say seven feet?" Sekhmet and Ceridwen both grew to a seven foot height.

"Very well." Lamasthu shrank until she was only an inch or two taller than they were.

Ceridwen rolled her eyes, whispering to Sekhmet. "Talk about petty. She's still taller than we are, as if that's going to make a difference."

The room fell into an uncomfortable silence.

One of the high priests opened the door. He carried a banner with the Council symbol emblazoned upon it. "They are ready for you. Please follow, esteemed goddesses."

The three deities stepped through the door and into the auditorium. The midday sun sparkled in through a beautiful crystal dome far above their heads. From the far side of the room, a band was playing an inspiring march. There were hundreds of spectators seated on long semi circular benches with a wide path in their midst leading from the assembly room to the stage. Side by side, Sekhmet, Ceridwen, and Lamasthu entered. Behind each, a line of priests followed, the first of each line carrying a banner that represented the realm of the goddess that led them forward, Egyptos, Celtic and Babylos. Behind these lines, a massed group of priests carried banners of the nine main realms. Those in the crowd cheered as their lands' symbols passed by.

As they approached the front of the auditorium, Sekhmet spotted Tenh-Mer waving frantically from the crowd. Tara sat on one side of the demoness, while Ptah rested solemnly on the other. Sekhmet suppressed a smile as Tenh-Mer's elbow bumped Ptah's ribs, causing him to flinch away in annoyance.

They marched up to the stage, where the Council members, dressed in their finest attire, awaited. The three goddesses came to a halt at the bottom of the stairs that led to the stage. Konohana stepped over to the marble podium at its center. The room grew silent as her voice echoed in the chamber.

"Welcome, nominees. With the cycle ending, my time on this Council will soon end, and another must take my place. Since the day we left Earth, this method of succession has been honored. Its ways are set in stone. One of the three nominees who stand before me will join this august body. I wish you all good tidings and look forward to getting to know each of you before the final vote."

The three nominees bowed respectfully as she stepped off the dais. Zeus took her place. He looked each of them in the eyes, his voice a deep baritone.

"Greetings, candidates. Rules govern our realms. To serve on the Council means you will be subject to rules within rules. As a candidate, you already have new responsibilities that you must take heed of as you campaign. You or your agents are not permitted to attempt to eliminate any nominee. This includes kidnapping, teleportation, disablement or murder. While this may have occurred in the past, it is no longer tolerated. Anyone caught committing such acts will be immediately disqualified."

"Shocking," Ceridwen gasped to Sekhmet. "Did they really carry on like that?"

Lamasthu glared at her two rivals, but remained silent.

Zeus continued. "You must also accept the secrecy bond before you can proceed to the next part of the process. There are many issues of a delicate nature we deal with, and thus privacy and security must be maintained at all costs. You will be required to sign a bonded agreement to that effect. If any of you are unwilling to do so, you should withdraw from the contest now." Zeus paused to see if any of them would leave. "Very well. Ascend the stage to sign, and let the campaign begin!"

Lamasthu surged forward to make sure she was the first to undertake the bond. As Sekhmet waited her turn, she noticed Ceridwen staring off toward the left side of the stage. Following her line of sight, her eyes tracked Shiva. She wondered if the Celt had ever seen a Hindu god before. Ceridwen seemed quite rough around the edges, as though she had no concept of the tact required to interact with foreign gods. Sekhmet judged the goddess would make enough diplomatic mistakes to be no competition at all. Lamasthu, however, was another story. Sekhmet stepped forward, said the sacred vows, signed her name, and accepted the bond. Despite her misgivings, there was no turning back now.

Zeus had detoured through Afrik to reach the Cold Realms. Traveling through Quetzalcoatl's lands would have been a shorter journey, if one considered only the distance. But he could not have crossed the Mayan Realm without being delayed. Invitations to accept the hospitality of every scattered temple along his route would have been extended. As a Council member, he would have been forced by convention to accept them, and by doing so endure no end of oblique questioning regarding why he was visiting those lands.

The lords of Afrik, as he expected, had no concern about his comings and goings. They ruled their realm as if the Council and its politics did not exist. Afrik sated its desire for military glory by local intertribal sparring and remained neutral in most conflicts to protect its extensive trade-based economy. Zeus knew more of their lovely women than he did of their leaders' likely allegiance to candidates for the empty Council seat; but their votes did not matter to him. As he moved within a bolt of lightning over their realm, he supposed they would most likely support the candidate from their neighboring land, Egyptos: Sekhmet.

Zeus moved with great speed and soon the lush jungles, sweeping plains and dune-ridged deserts of Afrik were left behind. He had come to colder terrain. As his lightning crackled over a grand stone tower, Zeus descended in a shower of sparks, reforming and dressing himself in a heavily ornamented cloak. His estranged brother would not be impressed by the garb, but his guards and servants would. Several of those rapidly emerged from a stairway access door to the tower platform. Four guards gave him the barest of bows that seemed to serve for Norse hospitality while a beardless youth, likely a scribe or poet of some ilk, groveled more appropriately as he took the lead, escorting Zeus down winding steps to an intimate hall. It was barely warmer than the top of the tower, thanks to windows in the walls that lacked any shutter or curtain. A rime of frost had etched the rectangles in white. Their lack of cover had allowed small drifts of snow to powder the floor beneath them. Zeus moved to stand in the center of the room, away from the intruding weather.

Several sturdy wooden chairs with massive backs ringed him as he approached a round table gracing the chamber's center. The young man collected two large goblets from the table and crossed to a small hearth built into the wall. He stirred an untended pot, left hanging to heat over embers, then ladled a portion of a steaming mixture into each cup. He stood, waiting with hot drinks in hand, as one of the guards knelt before the most intricately designed chair and inserted the butt of his sword into a depression within one of the legs. Upon this signal, the seat began to glow with a dim light. A god soon appeared upon it. He was kingly, the socket of one missing eye seeming as perceptive as the present one that fixed on Zeus. Dressed for hunting, in clothing fitted perfectly to his body, the lord of the tower stomped one booted foot to dislodge a clot of ice. Zeus watched it scatter across the floor as the leader of the guard bellowed, "Odin has come!"

"To my dear brother," Zeus said with a forced smile, lifting his goblet for a toast, "whose heart toward me is cold but whose hospitality is always warm." He eyed Odin over the rim of his cup as he took a drink of thick, hot mead.

Odin leaned forward and took up his own drinking vessel. "Is this another 'let's be friends' visit, Zeus?" he asked. "Or is it a complaint? Has one of my sons stolen one of your women? Or perhaps you want something of me. Has the Council kitchen run out of ice?" Odin smirked as he took a drink. "You only visit on occasions of dire need, so my curiosity is aroused. Why come to me?"

Zeus strolled over to the hearth, noting the runic inscriptions in the stone that surrounded it. "Actually, I don't have a request. Merely a question."

"A question? Well, I am an expert on building a pantheon from scratch with the spare parts of forgotten things trapped in frozen tundra - so if your query is pertinent to that area of knowledge . . ." Odin snorted and lifted the goblet to his lips. He swallowed slowly and at length before settling back into his chair. "Or do you need advice on the latest styles of winter cloaks. You would profit by it."

Zeus sighed, resolving not to react to Odin's witty little barbs. He was no match for his brother when it came to making words bite as sharply as a harpy's claws, so he tried to move the conversation along quickly. "Yes, yes, I know. Fate cheated you just as much as it cheated Hades. I thought we were past all this. You've done well for yourself, Odin. We're seen as equals now that all we gods must live together. In fact, I'd venture to say that the realms have a far better opinion of you than of me."

Zeus hoped his flattery would put enough salve on the old wound to allow him to have a productive meeting with Odin. There were few who knew the truth, that along with Hades and Poseidon, Zeus had another sibling who gambled with them for control of segments of old Earth. Zeus had gained the sky, Poseidon the sea, Hades the underworld, and Odin the cold and icy wastelands. As the oldest gods faded from mortal

memory, it had been easy to manipulate the tales of scribes and poets to erase Odin, at his own request, from the Olympian records. Odin hated the portion that his bad luck had dealt him, but chose to view it as a fresh start. He boasted he would make his lands great by his own efforts, to raise them to an equal or greater fame than the Greek kingdoms of his brothers. He had been true to his word.

"If they think better of me than of you," Odin said, relaxing, "then not all gods are fools." He gestured for Zeus to take one of the chairs. "Sit. You're blocking the fire."

Zeus picked a seat, arranging his cloak around his knees to keep the cold breeze from his legs as Odin dismissed his guards and sent the boy off on some errand. Zeus tapped the rim of his goblet with a nervous finger. "I suppose you've heard there's to be an election. I wonder whom you and your court will support."

"I don't have a court, Zeus," Odin laughed. "I have several large halls filled with miscreant godlings I've begotten who suck up my food and mead faster than it can be sledded over the snow. If more than two of them are sober enough to show up for a Council election, I would be pleasantly surprised." Odin leaned forward in his chair. "But I have made up my mind, and I suspect it's my vote that you're truly curious about."

"It is," Zeus admitted. "I hope to hear that you will endorse Sekhmet."

"Sekhmet? You're joking, Zeus. A cat? We might as well be ruled by the kits that pull Freyja's chariot." Odin laughed heartily. Zeus stewed in his chair, wondering if it would be possible to change Odin's mind. The wind whipped up outside the tower, forcing a new blast of cold down upon the gods. Carried upon the wind was a falcon feather. It danced and spun over the table - and put an end to Odin's mirth.

"Freyja," Odin said apologetically to the feather. "I meant no insult."

Zeus watched as the single feather split into many and continued to multiply until a great heap of plumes mounded on the table. Then a female form pushed up from beneath them, revealing the goddess Freyja, who gazed at Odin with gentle rebuke in her eyes. The falcon feather cloak stirred gracefully over her shoulders as she lightly stepped down from the table, walking upon the air as easily as Zeus had tread upon the stone stairs.

"The cat goddess is a good candidate," she said, brushing a long tress of golden hair away from her right eye. "Cats are loyal and strong." Freyja gave Zeus a welcoming nod as she moved to stand next to Odin's chair, laying a delicate hand upon his shoulder to show him she was not angry.

"This is true," Odin said. "But we have already agreed to vote for the Celtic witch, Freyja. Remember, you made me promise this." Odin grinned at Zeus, much like a cat who had stolen the cream. Freyja nodded in approval.

"Yes, we shall vote for Ceridwen. I know her. Her magic is harmonious with mine and I sense that a time of a power for us sorceresses has come with this cycle." Freyja turned toward the hearth, pursed her lips, and breathed toward the flames. Multicolored smoke was drawn from the heat, taking the shape of beautiful mountain flowers. "It is you who should change your vote," she teased. A shower of ethereal petals floated from the hearth to form a crown around Zeus' head.

Odin laughed again. "Quench your hopes, Freyja. This is Zeus before you, notorious for bending women to his will, not the other way round."

His disappointment slightly muted by the presence of beautiful Freyja, Zeus placed his palms on the tabletop and rose to his feet, shaking his head. "At least it will be a good race, then," he conceded, calculating aloud. "Olympus supports Sekhmet, as does Egyptos. Celts and Norse, Ceridwen, while the Babylonians and Mayans are in the camp of Lamasthu."

"So it seems you have business in the other realms," Odin suggested firmly, as he noticed Zeus' eye lingering upon Freyja's thighs. "See if you can sway the Asians or the Hindu to vote with you."

Zeus pried his eyes from the goddess, realizing Odin was right. "Indeed. There is work for me to do, much as I despise such exercise." He moved toward the windowed wall, drawing out a bolt of lightning on which to fly away.

"Farewell, Zeus," Freyja called after him as he flashed away in a boom of thunder. "And if your cat wins, I will be watching to make sure she is treated with the respect all cats deserve!"

On his way back to the City, Zeus weighed Odin's refusal to support Sekhmet and decided it was a mere featherweight of disappointment. If Odin had been willing to vote as Zeus wished, he would certainly have asked for some favor in return. Zeus did not want to incur any new debts. He already felt as if he was making far too many compromises at a time when his power base was uncertain.

He frowned as he flashed through the sky. Hermes had still not found Circe. Olympia's storehouses of nectar would soon have to be unlocked to meet the needs of the gods in his realm. Worst of all, Helios was agitating for vengeance at a time when Zeus could not even determine whom he should avenge. Another realm? One of his own kinsman? Zeus had inquired of the Fates who was to blame for the flooding of the king's palace, but they denied weaving any such thread into Helios' destiny. As for Circe, the three women claimed that someone had stolen her tapestry from its loom, so they were unable to check if she still lived. His entire visit to their cave had been an utter waste of time. If he did secure a new nectar supply, he was tempted to severely cut back their allocation.

Pleased with his decision to punish the Fates, Zeus focused his judgment on Helios. He and a few of his courtiers, who had the good fortune to be boating at the time of the flood, had relocated to the City. It had been less than a day before they had insulted Apollo and been chased out of the Olympian District. Then Helios had discovered that there were loans to be had from the bankers of Babylos and foolishly ran to them for support. Zeus chafed at the idea of the fickle king in their pocket, both financially and politically. But in all honesty, he was glad that Helios was out of his way for the moment. Babylos could deal with him when his debts, which he had no means to repay, came due.

All these troubling thoughts eased as Zeus descended as golden light into the Council Hall. The sight of his lovely attendants and the normal bustle of priests keeping the City running calmed him. He accepted a cup of nectar one of the chamber servants hurried to offer him, drinking of it deeply. His tongue retreated from an unexpected flavor.

"This cup is befouled," he complained, dropping it back on the servant's tray. "Bring another." An attendant rushed up with a different platter and Zeus grabbed another goblet, sniffing it suspiciously. It, too, was not his usual brew. He growled with the sound of distant thunder as Quetzalcoatl strolled casually into the room. He also had a cup in his hand.

"So, what do you think?" he asked. "This nectar of Babylos has a bitter taste, but its repowering strength seems adequate." Quetzalcoatl took a sip. "I do miss the sweetness of Circe's brew, but I don't suppose we'll taste that again."

Zeus forced a swallow of the life water down his throat, trying not to taste it. The experience confirmed Quetzalcoatl's observation that it provided strength at the expense of flavor. "Circe will be found," he said with more confidence than he felt. "But I suppose in the short term we will have to make do with this swill."

Quetzalcoatl laughed. "Best not to say that in the presence of Lamasthu. She feels very strongly about the quality of the nectar mills of Babylos. And in light of the secret that we all must keep, a secret she knows . . ."

Zeus waved a hand at Quetzalcoatl to stop him talking. "You don't need to say any more."

"Do you think me foolish enough to go on? I will only point out one practical thing, Zeus. Think of the needs of the realms when you ask support of the Pantheon leaders. It is within the rights of Babylos to withhold their nectar supplies entirely for their own gods if Lamasthu is not elected. The rest of us would weaken while their realm would grow powerful."

Zeus stubbornly slapped his cup down on a table. "I'm sure you would find a way to stay strong," he said.

"As would you. It's just something to think about if you cannot get round this problem."

Zeus released a heavy sigh. "Konohana is lucky. She'll soon be under the enchantment of forgetfulness and free of these burdens."

"Ignorance is bliss, some say."

Quetzalcoatl smiled into his cup as he tipped it to his lips and drank deeply. He was confident the nectar problem was enough to push Zeus into his court. Now, there was only Shiva to dispense with.

Bast walked wearily, but gratefully, into her pyramid palace in Bubastis upon returning from opening the Lost Realm gate. In the atrium, a dozen servants who tended the palace in her absence were gathered to greet her. They bowed deeply as she approached.

"Welcome home Goddess," they recited in unison. "We greet thee with devotion eternal."

"You have my blessings. Bring a meal to my antechamber. I've been on a barge with far too many people for weeks. I require privacy."

Several servants immediately moved to attend to her request as she climbed the long, dark stairway to her private room near the top of the pyramid. Her pyramid had been sealed by her mother while Bast had been entombed for a decade. Now she felt comforted that her room had been preserved perfectly, waiting for her all this time. Unwilling to wait for the servants, she removed some of the sheets that had been draped over the furnishings to keep out the dust. While pulling one back, she noticed a movement in the corner of her eye.

"Hello, sister," came a male voice that was all too familiar.

Bast whirled around. "H-How dare you come here!"

"Where else might I go in my hour of need?" Set approached her slowly.

"To Hades for all I care. Haven't I suffered enough for my . . . association with you? You killed our father!" she hissed.

"And you helped me do it, dear sister. Never forget that."

"Killing Geb was never part of the plan. You said we would usurp our parents, you never spoke of murdering them." Bast could feel the hair all over her body prickling. She wanted to strike and tear out his eyes, but knew that in a fight Set would have the upper hand. He was far more powerful than she. Bast desperately tried to think of what she should or could do, but nothing came to mind other than trying to escape. She edged toward the door, but Set moved in the same direction to maintain his proximity.

"How else did you think we could replace them? They weren't going to willingly step down. Besides, it worked for a long time, did it not? Both you and I ruled for several millennia before your mother returned and pushed you out." Set offered her a toothy smile. "I visited your prison several times while you were entombed, you know. I missed you." He reached out to stroke her cheek.

"Don't touch me!" Bast pulled away, a look of disgust and guilt etched on her perfect feline visage.

"Really, is that any way to treat your brother . . . your lover?"

She closed her eyes and tried to block him out of her sight, but it only made things worse. Visions of their carnal relationship flashed though her mind like a rapid flooding of the Nile. She almost retched, remembering how they had behaved and the degeneracy of their times together. These were deep, personal memories she had managed to suppress, until now. Silent, she stood, trying to keep herself under control. Finally she turned to him.

"That time has long passed. I was a foolish child then. Now I am a woman. I reject you and all you stand for. Leave me, and do not return."

Suddenly his hand was on her throat and she felt his breath on her face.

"Oh, it's not as easy as that, sister. I am not some priest you can dismiss with a wave of your hand. I need a place to stay."

She stiffened in his grasp, trying to pull away. "You dare come to me now, just because you are lonely and need a bed for the night? Let me go!" She was a bit surprised when he did, but he was ever unpredictable. Her hand flew to her neck, as if she could brush the memory of his grip from her fur. "You can't stay here. You're mother's worst enemy. I spent years trying to prove myself worthy to her. I'll not throw that all away. Now leave, before I have a Council guard haul you away like the trash you are!"

Set's red eyes started to glow as he glared at her. "I don't think you realize the delicacy of your situation, dear sister. You helped me kill Geb by drugging Sekhmet. You are as much to blame for his death as I. The only difference is that no one is aware of your complicity in his untimely demise."

"That's not how it happened and you know it. You lied to me."

Set smirked and waved a cavalier hand. "It doesn't matter what really happened, only what everyone believes happened. Call the Council, I dare you. Shall I tell them what you did, or shall we leave things the way they are?"

"I won't help you. I won't!" Yet she knew, even as she said the words, she had no choice.

"You don't have to help me. Just let me have a place to stay while I make arrangements to stay elsewhere. Is that too much to ask from your own brother?"

"Step-brother," she corrected dejectedly. Somehow that fact made their earlier relationship more acceptable to her now. She felt completely helpless. It always seemed that Set held all the advantage in their dealings, no matter how hard she tried to untangle herself from his machinations. "You can remain, but stay out of my sight and of any others, even the servants. No one must know you are here."

"At last we agree on something. Don't worry. I'm sure you'll come to enjoy my company yet again."

"The sun in the sky will burn out before I enjoy anything with you. This room is yours, then. Do not leave it."

"Very well. I knew you'd see reason," he said, an unpleasant smile upon his face.

"I'm returning to the City of the Gods in a few days. Mother will be expecting me. I hope before then you'll be out of my sight."

"Don't be so quick to leave, dear sister. You just returned home. Try to enjoy your stay here. The City of the Gods can wait until I am safely away from here."

Giving no reply, she turned away and stared at the tapestry on the wall. It portrayed a mother and daughter embracing. Sekhmet had given it to her when she was child. A tear ran down her cheek as she walked out of the room, feeling as powerless as a serving maid in a brothel.

Chapter 22

The Lost City

From the top of the dune, D'Molay could see a shape in the distance. "There's something ahead. Could be a palace, maybe a city," he called down to the others.

"Then we should visit and hope they welcome guests," Mazu said as her camel caught up with his. Close behind her came Quan, perched proudly upon his animal like a satrap.

As he did at every stop, Quan took the opportunity to voice his opinion about what to do next. He prodded his camel to a stop next to Mazu's and leaned slowly toward her, taking care not to slip from his mount."Or we should avoid it, and escape a trap," he added.

D'Molay had come to accept the man's inflated ego and contrariness, but had not yet completely schooled himself to ignore it. "We'll never find Scylla if we don't look," he said, mild irritation evident in his voice. "We can get there before nightfall, so let's make for it. I'll keep the lead." D'Molay immediately started down the side of the dune, heading for a flatter run of desert.

"He wants to die first," Quan said, unwinding the colorful scarf wrapped around his head and beating out the dust that had collected on it.

Mazu smiled at her devotee. She enjoyed his personality. She'd never confess it to D'Molay, but she was vastly entertained by Quan's remarks. They distracted her from many of the depressing revelations she was still hiding from D'Molay. However, Quan was wrong in this case. "No, D'Molay's days of wanting to die are behind him," she said. In light of his recent swim in the Styx, she believed this to be doubly true.

"If you say so, Lady Mazu," Quan acquiesced. "But if he stirs up a sand beast or a lair of bandits . . . " His worries trailed off as they hurried to catch up with their leader.

After an hour of riding, they could see more of their destination.

Carved stone columns stuck out of the sand among crumbled walls and statues, some canted at odd angles. When they reached several intact buildings on the outskirts of the deserted place, they discovered them to be empty shells. D'Molay's slumped shoulders made his disappointment clear.

"Maybe there are people living in the central region. That's often the case when a city is in retreat," Mazu said, hoping to instill some optimism in the men. D'Molay said nothing, merely urging his camel to continue on, leaving Mazu and Quan to converse about the styling of the abandoned plaza and the obscure designs etched in its paving stones.

The wind blew gusts of sand before them as they traversed the central street of the forgotten town. There was no sign of habitation. As they passed the remains of some larger ruined buildings, they saw a huge crater hundreds of yards across and hundreds of feet deep. Everything within and around the crater looked as if it had been melted by some unimaginable heat, leaving crumbling buildings and debris half-buried in the ever-shifting sands.

"Fire dragon nest!" Quan chirped in alarm.

Mazu smiled. "Don't worry. If we meet a fire dragon, I can put him out."

D'Molay began to dismount his camel. "I want to see what's down there." The animal grumbled as it knelt.

"Even the camel thinks he's crazy," Quan muttered. Ignoring him, D'Molay walked on towards the crater's edge as Quan turned to Mazu. "What made that hole?"

"In the early days of the realms, there were many battles. Few pantheons were satisfied with what the Council gave them and often attacked the cities given to others. When peace came, this area was so badly damaged that it was sealed off to use as a place to keep things too dangerous or unwanted. That's why it's called the Lost Realm."

"Ah, we shouldn't let him go alone then," Quan said.

"More curious now that I've convinced you it's not a dragon's nest?" Mazu teased. "Very well, let's get off and give our camels a rest."

The camels sat languidly in the heat as the goddess and the fisherman joined the tracker. He stood at the lip of the crater, gazing down at what was once the stairway of some grand building. He was able to descend a section of the broken steps, moving down to where the remains of a partially destroyed statue of a woman lay. The image of Aavi turned into salt flashed through his mind. *I wonder if she was able to follow us into this realm?*

Quan broke D'Molay's train of thought. "What are you doing down there?"

D'Molay looked up to see Mazu and Quan looming above him. "I was considering camping in here out of sight for the night, but it's too unstable. One loud snore from Quan and we'd be buried in an avalanche of stone."

Quan folded his arms and lifted his chin high. "I do not snore."

"Yes . . . " Mazu grinned, ambiguous toward which man's statement it affirmed. "I think the buildings we saw as we came into this town seemed safer. Perhaps we can find a place to rest more like them." They moved on.

A short while later they found a crumbling temple that still had walls and a roof. It was large enough for the three of them - and the camels - and even had an old cooking pit in the center of the floor. D'Molay converted that into a campfire and found two toppled benches that allowed them to sit around it. Quan began to prepare a meal while Mazu used her power to make sure the camels had something to drink. She made water appear in her cupped hands and the animals drank eagerly.

They shared warm tea, dried meat and the last of the crumbled Egyptos sweet cake Bast had added to their provisions. After dinner, D'Molay kept one eye and ear alertly pointed toward the door while Quan began to nod from the seductive warmth of the fire. Mazu, less paranoid and in no need of mortal rest, preferred to talk.

"Do you sense something out there, D'Molay?"

He downed the last of his now cold tea. "I don't know. With the things we've seen lately everything seems threatening. I still want to know what Circe was doing with all those urns filled with blood."

Mazu dropped her head, tossing a small twig into the fire. "There are some things that are better not to know. You have the antidote and we escaped Hades with our lives. We should be thankful for that."

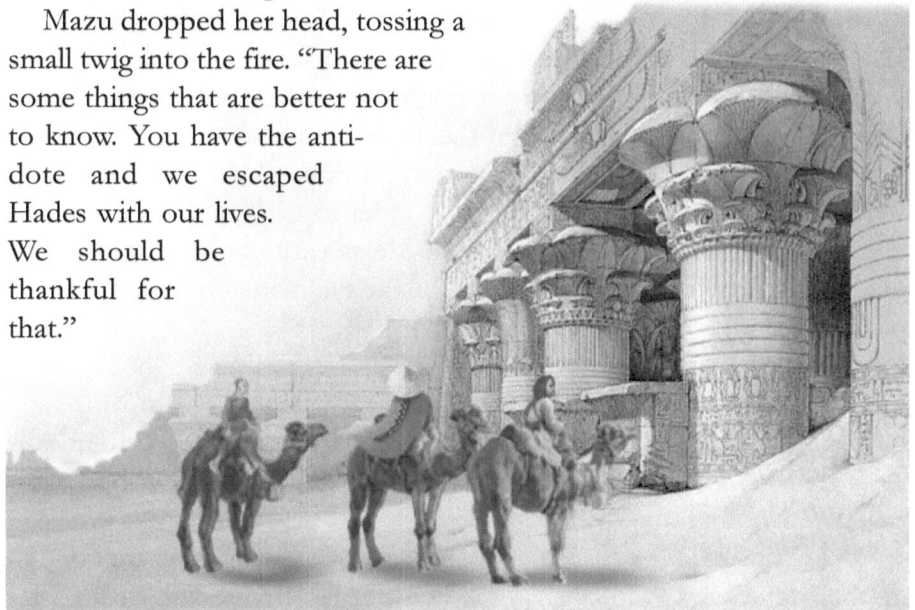

"I know. It's just hard to forget. She had so many urns. Hundreds, thousands of them."

"Millions," Quan interjected awkwardly in an attempt to pretend that he hadn't nodded off and was part of the conversation, his head jerking up from where his chin had rested upon his chest.

Mazu picked up the kettle and warmed D'Molay's cup. "However many, there is nothing to be done tonight. Circe's lair is on the other side of the realms. We need to concern ourselves with our current situation."

"Sorry. I know you're right. I just can't stop thinking about it. Where did all that blood come from and what is she doing with it?" Despite his unanswered question, D'Molay went over to his traveling bag and got out his map of the realms, returning and unfolding it to consult with Mazu. "As for our current journey, we don't have much to go on as far as my map is concerned. Based on where we entered, I think we are about here." He pointed to an area of the map beyond the barrier they had passed through and studied the lands nearby. "Isn't Scylla supposed to live along the shoreline of a lake?"

"The dryad didn't mention a lake, just the Anagar swamp. But water clings to water, so it could be near one," Mazu said.

Quan stretched and slapped his thighs in an attempt to wake himself fully. His next words came out in the company of a yawn. "You had to talk of water, didn't you? Now I have to go rid myself of my own."

Mazu smiled at Quan's simple needs as he walked out. She wished she and D'Molay could set their anxiety aside as easily as he. She eyed the map. "Could the swamp on your map be the same one we seek, but called by a different name?"

"Possibly. I got my information from the camel trainer in Bubastis. Maybe Anagar is the word for it in another language."

Suddenly Quan rushed back into the room, arms gesturing frantically toward the darkness outside. "I saw something," he hissed in a loud whisper. "Someone's found us!"

"Who, Quan?" Mazu asked, extending a calming hand to catch one of his flailing arms. D'Molay shot to the door-less frame and melded his body to the wall, peering into the night, listening. He heard nothing, other than the sound of the night wind.

"I'm sure there are men out there!" Quan insisted.

"One way to find out," D'Molay said. He took one step outside but immediately everything felt wrong. He fell into a defensive crouch just in time to miss being hit by a spear that flew into the temple and slammed against the back wall. He wondered if it was Aavi or his own instincts that forced him to the floor, but he had no time to evaluate which was the case.

"Away from the doorway!" D'Molay commanded. Quan and Mazu quickly complied, with Quan being visibly shaken. Mazu, as usual, wore a mask of calm concern.

"You were right, Quan. I wonder what they want," she said as two more spears thudded into the wall and a shout went up from the warriors outside.

"Based on those spears, they want us dead!" Quan said, trying not to hide too obviously behind Mazu's robes.

"Then I will try to change their minds," she decided. Before D'Molay could object, Mazu quickly stepped into the opening. "Cease this saber rattling, we mean you no harm," she said in a loud, strong voice. This offer was met with a new volley of spears.

Quan screamed in horror as their points pierced Mazu and their shafts continued through her body, splattering dark liquid in their wake. Every instinct and experience told D'Molay that Mazu ought to be dead, but still Mazu stood, unaffected by the attack. "Mazu!" he cried out.

She glanced at him for just a second before again addressing whatever waited outside. "Now that we've gotten that out of the way, perhaps we can discuss this reasonably." She took a few more steps forward and moved out of D'Molay's view.

He stared at the spot where Mazu had just stood, seeing only the dark puddles on the floor. Then he came to a sudden realization. "It's not her blood. It's water!" Two more spears flew through the entrance as a spray of additional water followed them in.

"W-water?" Quan sheepishly asked, still in shock from the attack on his beloved Mazu. But the goddess seemed to be fine. D'Molay and Quan could hear her berating their unknown enemies.

"I am not certain which will run out first, my patience or your spears. Where is your leader? Let me speak to him ere I'm forced to drown you all."

D'Molay couldn't resist the urge to lean over and take a peek out the arched entry. It was almost pitch black outside as the moons had set in the sky, but he could see Mazu in the light from their campfire. Though she was still in the shape of a woman, she had turned completely into clear swirling water, the flicker of the fire making her form glow and shimmer.

"Kill that thing!" came a call from the darkness. At the same time, D'Molay was again inexplicably shoved away from the door into a safer area of the room. Certain he had not imagined the effect twice, he had faith that Aavi was the cause of it. He was grateful for her efforts as more spears flew through Mazu to harmlessly bounce off the back wall.

"Thing?" Mazu was yelling. "You dare call me a thing?" D'Molay had rarely seen her so angry, but now, like a churning sea during a storm, she was roiling. Mazu outstretched her liquid arms and they turned into flexible whip-like geysers. The attackers who were charging toward her were blasted off their feet back into the darkness, except for one. He managed to hurtle past Mazu and throw himself through the doorway. The warrior slid along the wet floor, grabbing one of the spears that had been thrown inside.

D'Molay lunged at the large figure before he even realized it was a minotaur, with a massive bull's head, bulky muscular body and large cloven hooves. D'Molay moved quickly, grabbing the shaft of the man-thing's spear while thrusting in with his knife. The minotaur grabbed D'Molay's hand, stopping the advance of the knife. D'Molay felt painful pressure as the creature tried to force him to drop his blade. Unable to bear it, he let go, and the knife hit the floor. The minotaur then threw D'Molay off as if he were no more than a bag of laundry.

D'Molay flew head first towards the nearby wall, but instead of crashing into it, his progress was supernaturally slowed, allowing him to lightly thud against the wall and slide down to the floor. Wasting no time, he rolled up on his feet, grabbing a spear in the process, and readied himself once again for an attack.

The minotaur grunted at him and charged, spear at the ready, like a knight at a joust. D'Molay followed in kind, running to meet him, but at the last second he dropped to the floor and slid, shoving the spear up into the minotaur's gut, as he collided with its leg. The minotaur's spear missed D'Molay, scraping the ground and falling out of the creature's grasp. Immediately D'Molay rolled out of the way and got his back against the opposite wall. But the minotaur wasn't done, despite having a spear sticking in its torso. The creature spun to face D'Molay again. It grabbed the spear with one hand, pulling it out and pointing it back at him. It started to move towards him as blood poured out of its wound.

D'Molay tried to get to one of the other spears lying on the floor, but they were out of reach. The man-beast closed the gap between them and swung out with its massive fist. He dodged the blow, but the creature grabbed him with its other hand. Just then, the creature bellowed in pain. Quan had picked up a spear and run it though the creature's gut from the side. The minotaur dropped D'Molay, turning on Quan and knocking the man off his feet with the shaft of the embedded spear as it swung around. It bellowed again, taking several staggering steps forward. Quan was frantically crawling away, but before he got too far, the creature stopped moving and fell face forward onto the ground, missing Quan by mere inches and crashing to its death on top of D'Molay's traveling pack.

Seeing Quan was all right, D'Molay lurched across the room to retrieve his knife and headed for the door to see how Mazu was faring. He watched as she continued to drive back any warriors foolish enough to cross her path. She struck them with powerful blasts of water, which looked like a whips made out of liquid crystal. The long coils defied gravity as they swung in the air, striking opponents right and left. Finally the attackers withdrew and the night fell silent. D'Molay walked outside to praise Mazu for her victory. As he approached, she resumed her human form, leaning on her wooden staff. He was shocked to see she looked very old once again, her youthful appearance having vanished.

"That was amazing," he congratulated, but putting his hand on her shoulder he could feel she was shaking. "Do you need help?"

"Yes. Get me back inside," she said in a strained voice. As she turned he could tell she was unsteady on her feet. Putting his arm around her waist, D'Molay helped her back inside. Mazu seemed older, thinner, and more fragile then she'd been in months.

"What's the matter? Did they cast some spell on you?" There was deep concern in his voice as they got inside the battered temple, out of sight from any who still might be watching.

"My Lady, you saved us!" Quan exclaimed as he came over to them.

"L-let us hope that is the case," she responded weakly as D'Molay helped her sit down by the fire. She looked tired and worn out; the lines on her face had all returned. She had been much younger and powerful in the last month, and he'd gotten used to her that way.

"Mazu?" D'Molay asked again.

She gave him a sidelong glance and tried to swallow. "They did nothing, other than force me to use my reserves to keep them back. The effort has drained my life force. I'll recover, but it will take some time." She closed her eyes as though even the effort of answering had taken a toll on her.

"But I've seen you use your powers many times before. Why has this attack weakened you so much?" D'Molay sometimes felt he would never understand the way gods worked. He'd always assumed Mazu was immortal and invulnerable. She gave him a weary look.

"We are in a desert and I am a water goddess. I have been away from life-giving waters for too long. Now I am paying the price." Her voice faded off.

"We need to get you to water as soon as we can!" Quan insisted. "You never should have gone out to fight them," he chided her, the concern in his voice obvious. He then fumbled with the pockets of his coat, retrieving something. "Mistress, I saved a bottle of the life water. Using it would restore you, as it has in the past," he said.

Despite her condition, Mazu gave Quan a harsh glare. "I told you to give all my water to Charon and you disobeyed me?"

Quan was crestfallen, unable to hold her disapproving gaze. "I - I am sorry my goddess. But please, I beg you, for your own sake, please partake of it." Quan prostrated himself before her, his head touching the floor as he slid a blue glass vial topped with a cork toward her. Mazu stared at it disdainfully.

For a change D'Molay tried to defend Quan. "I understand why you're angry, but isn't it good that he didn't do as you asked?"

Mazu's gaze turned from her disobedient servant to D'Molay. "Good has nothing to do with this, I assure you." He noted a look in her eyes that reminded him that she had lived far longer and knew far more than he might ever learn.

"Please Lady Mazu, you must," Quan added, still not daring to look up from the floor.

D'Molay reached over and picked up the small blue vial, holding it close to his face to see it in detail. The liquid looked clear, perhaps with a trace of lavender and small golden flecks shimmering within it. It seemed more like an oil extract or syrup than water, as it moved slowly when he tilted the vial. "What is this?" he asked.

"It is the nectar of the gods. It is used as . . . medicine when needed."

"Well it is needed. You need it. If we are to continue on this journey, you must take it." D'Molay took the vial and placed it in her hand.

She held the vial tightly. "Should I?" She looked at the two men in front of her, and realizing her responsibility to both of them in this dangerous realm, came to a decision. "Very well. I will take it once again." She opened the vial and drank down its entire contents.

D'Molay saw her hollow cheeks fill out, the color return to her face, and the lines on her face vanish. The age spots on her hands faded and the veins retreated back under her skin, which became smooth once again. Even her hair seemed to become fuller and slightly darker. She frowned when she realized D'Molay was gawking at her.

"I am not a circus attraction. Let me rest now and the nectar will finish its work while I sleep," she said waving the two of them off.

"All right, Mazu. Rest well." D'Molay got up, took a spear and stood near the doorway, keeping watch for any other threats. Looking out at the ruins in the darkness, he wondered why Mazu had been so hesitant to drink the nectar and what untold cost she might be enduring by doing so. Mazu was not one to reveal her personal secrets, so it was unlikely he would find out anytime soon.

"Quan, you're half asleep already," D'Molay said, dragging one of the benches to face the door to watch for more trouble. "I'll watch over

Mazu. You can have a turn later." Perhaps subdued by being out of Mazu's favor over the vial, Quan obeyed D'Molay without comment. He lay down near the fire and closed his eyes, eventually filling the chamber with soft snoring. D'Molay stared out into the night and tried to ignore the presence, and the stench, of the dead minotaur in their company.

"Aavi," he whispered after sitting for some time. "Are you with me?"

D'Molay felt a soft, invisible hand touch his.

A few hours later, Quan took his place as lookout and D'Molay managed to get some sleep. Fortunately for both of them, there were no further attacks. At dawn, Quan returned to awaken him so they could prepare to leave.

D'Molay checked on Mazu. Whatever had been in that vial had made a tremendous difference. As she lay there asleep, she looked more like a woman of forty than the ancient shell he had seen last night after the battle. He gently shook her shoulder and she sat up.

"So how are you feeling?" he asked. "You look almost as well as I've ever seen you."

She brought her knees up, resting her arms and head on them as she spoke. "I am quite well, though I still need to merge with fresh water sometime soon to fully recharge my powers."

"Let's see if we can get past these ruins and find you some water while we're at it." D'Molay looked on in approval as Quan busily packed his and Mazu's camel. To do the same with his was going to require a little more effort. "Quan, help me shift that minotaur off my pack."

Quan let out a disgusted groan, clearly unenthused about the task. D'Molay gave him a no nonsense glare and he eventually joined him beside the dead thing. "Why bother?" scoffed Quan. "Anything in your bag is smashed flat now. Good thing we ate all the cake last night."

D'Molay froze. *Smashed?* He quickly knelt by the minotaur. The strap and a section of his bag could be seen sticking out from under the beast's armpit. D'Molay grabbed its heavy arm and lifted it high. "Slide the bag out," he ordered as the body lifted just enough to expose the whole bag. Quan gave the pack a yank and D'Molay let the dead meat fall to the floor.

"Flat as a rice cake," Quan pronounced. "I told you."

D'Molay stared at the wet stain that hadn't marred his bag the night before. "No," he muttered as he opened the sack and began to dig, narrowly avoiding cutting his fingers on the shards of glass inside. "Damn!"

"What's the matter?" Mazu asked.

"The bottle, Circe's antidote. It's destroyed." D'Molay dumped out the bag and the three of them stared at the shards of glass as he picked them out of his other belongings.

Thus, the day's ride began on a somber note of disappointment framed by dread. They rode out into the dry morning still perplexed over the night's attack, and wondering if their enemies were still nearby. The answer to that question came soon. After a short ride, they entered an area of rocks and debris. And from its cover, dozens of creatures stepped out to block their way. Almost all of them had long bronze spears like the ones that had been thrown at them last night. These enemies ran forward, surrounding the camels and pointing a dozen spears at each one of them.

A half-man, half-snake carrying a large scimitar slithered up the highest rock in front of them. "Halt and sssurrender, or die on your camelsss," it hissed. D'Molay recalled such creatures were called nagas, and their reputation was a vicious one. They were well suited for exile in the Lost Realm. Mazu and D'Molay exchanged glances. Outnumbered and surrounded, there was little they could do. D'Molay answered them, his voice flat and tired. "We mean you no harm. We surrender." The whole situation reminded him of his life long ago on Earth, escorting pilgrims through the Holy Land where Muslim raiders would demand payment or outright kill those who traveled through their lands.

"A wissse choice. Drop your weaponsss on the ground," the naga ordered in its sibilant voice.

"Why did you attack us last night? We are just travelers passing through this place," Mazu said, as Quan and D'Molay dropped their weapons.

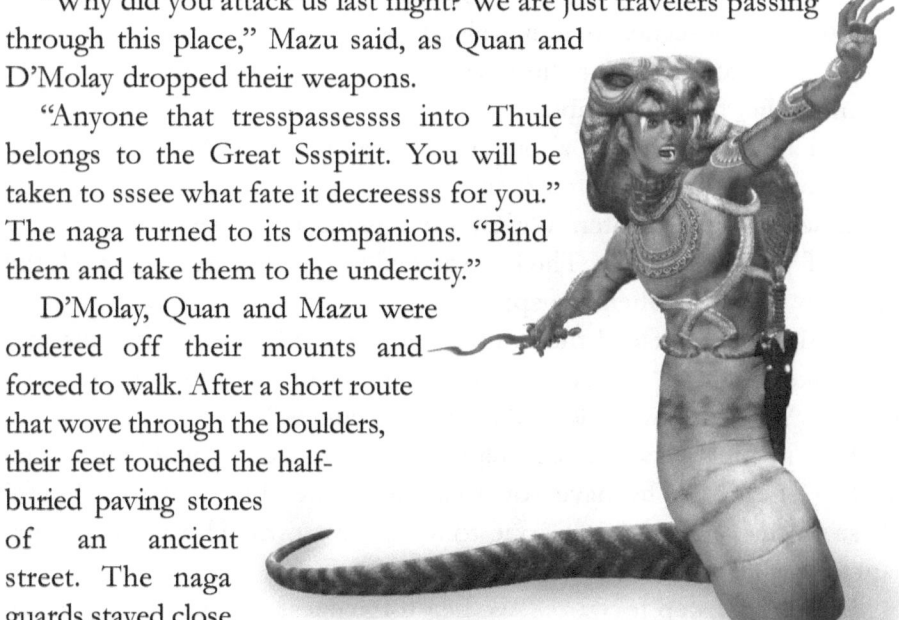

"Anyone that tresspassessss into Thule belongs to the Great Ssspirit. You will be taken to sssee what fate it decreesss for you." The naga turned to its companions. "Bind them and take them to the undercity."

D'Molay, Quan and Mazu were ordered off their mounts and forced to walk. After a short route that wove through the boulders, their feet touched the half-buried paving stones of an ancient street. The naga guards stayed close by, their spears discouraging any thought of escape. Quan was visibly shaking, in fear of his life, while Mazu maintained her usual dignity. D'Molay wondered if he was on his way to the death his dunking in the Styx foretold.

They continued down the broken street toward another section of ruined town. Another crumbling building, that still had its roof and walls, was the destination. A palace or government station at one time, it now maintained only a hint of past grandeur. Prisoners, camels and the nagas marched under a weathered archway and headed for a dark expanse near the back of the building. As they came closer, D'Molay could see an entrance leading down into the ground. Soon they were descending down a dark shaft lined with stone and marble. There were elaborately carved statues of male and female naga along the sides of the tunnel. Their headdresses and outfits marked them as rulers or deities. Though the statues were in better shape than the ruins above ground, they were very old and mostly neglected. Lichen had encroached on the marble and the smell of mold and decay was strong.

At the end of this tunnel they came to two large bronze doors that opened as they approached. The guards herded them into a large round room, perhaps fifty feet across and a hundred feet long. Twelve large entrances were evenly spaced around the chamber, which seemed very ancient and overgrown with the roots of long-dead trees.. The chamber was dark, save for a strange glowing ball of light at the far end, the only thing that lit the scene. As they walked forward, D'Molay noticed minotaur guards stationed near the glowing ball and at several of the other entrances that to the chamber.

The ball of energy was about fifteen feet across. D'Molay wondered what powered it as he watched silent bolts of electricity writhe over its bright whitish-blue center. Within the ball he could see other colors, swirls of pink and purple. The ball seemed to hover in mid air, much the same way Aavi did when she appeared.

The naga leader faced the brightly glowing ball, raising his arms in a praise-like gesture. "Great Ssspirit, we have brought you more trespasssers. With your wisssdom, decide their fatesss."

D'Molay flinched and Quan yelped as a loud voice boomed out of the swirling energy. "Why have you trespassed into the Land of Thule?" These words came not from one tongue, but from a chorus of discordant voices all speaking at once.

Mazu took a step forward. "We beg forgiveness, for we did not know the name of this place or that any still dwelled here. We were seeking only shelter and water as we journeyed across these lands."

"Many have told that lie," the multi-voice chorused. "We have no resources for outsiders in this harsh land of dust and heat. Once long ago, this land was fertile, but that time has passed. You warring gods saw to that." The electric ball pulsed. "Prepare them for execution."

The guards moved in, ready to drag the three away to their fate.

"Wait, I have something that will be of far more value to your people than our deaths. Please, let me explain."

D'Molay seized on Mazu's words with hope. In recent days, it certainly seemed she had been hiding something from him. Perhaps he was about to find out just what it was. They waited tensely as the ball continued to pulse, the pink and purple undertones dancing across its surface.

"I will hear your offer," it said. "Speak it."

"I have the ability to bring water to your people. Your warriors have seen my powers for themselves. Surely water is something that would be of value in this desert. I will bring you life-giving water if you spare our lives and allow us to safely leave your land."

A faint whispering came from the glowing ball, as if all the voices within it were discussing the matter. There were so many voices; it was impossible to distinguish what was being said. After a moment, questions emerged. "How would you do this? And how long would such a task take?"

"If you can take me to a water source like a well, a stream or a reservoir, my powers can ensure that you would have ample water for years to come. Surely there is some small spring that keeps you all alive even in these lean days." Mazu bowed, awaiting the reply as the voices in the ball started another discussion.

"Mazu," D'Molay whispered, "are you strong enough to do that?"

One of the guards objected to D'Molay speaking, and struck him in the stomach with the butt of his spear. D'Molay crumpled, his breath knocked out of him. Mazu moved quickly to stand between him and another strike from the naga.

"Please," she said, "he meant no disrespect."

The leader of the serpent-men turned on all of them. "Quiet!" he hissed.

The ball spoke again. "What guarantee do we have that you would not just escape?"

"You could hold my companions until I have completed the task. When I have brought you the water, you will release us all, with our animals and supplies, and allow us to pass through your lands with no further interference."

The unearthly whispering resumed again, but it was very brief this time. "You have just shown you care for your companions by how you reacted when one was punished, so your offer is sound. There is indeed a well our people use, but it has become all but empty. If you can make your magic refill our well, we will agree to your terms. If you fail, or attempt any trickery, we will kill you all, slowly and painfully."

"I understand. I will not fail you or my friends," she added as she exchanged a glance with D'Molay and Quan.

"Escort her to the well," pronounced the orb. "Watch her carefully, but allow her to work her magic. Lock the others in a holding pen. Bring all back for judgment when the task is done. Those are the orders of the Great Spirit."

The leader of the naga bowed. "It will be done Great Ssspirit." He waved his hand, and six guards marched Mazu out of the room through one of the other doors. The rest of them forced D'Molay, Quan, and the camels back the way they had come and locked them all together in the same cell. It was a dark, square room with one bronze door, a sputtering torch on the wall and nothing else at all within.

"What will become of us now? Quan asked, fear evident in his tone.

"We wait and hope that Mazu can give them what they want."

"Those are hardly words of comfort, D'Molay," Quan grouched.

"Things could be worse. At least we have our supplies with us. Let's see what we have to make our accommodations a bit more livable."

While her two friends came to terms with life in a cell, Mazu and her escorts descended down another long series of tunnels. Some of them passed through living quarters for the Naga residents of this underground refuge. The inhabitants seemed just as intimidated by the guards as Mazu was. They slithered into doorways and generally made themselves scarce as she was marched by. Mazu caught the eye of one young one peeking at her from behind a statue. Hunger and thirst were etched on her face.

At the end of a long winding staircase that got narrower and narrower until there was only enough room for one person at time, stood another bronze door. There were runes painted on it, in a language she did not recognize. The guard in the front opened the door and they entered another round chamber about forty feet across. In the center of it was a large opening about twenty feet wide. Extending from this pit and rising beyond the ceiling and down into the darkness were two very thick ropes. Large buckets were attached every three feet or so. The guards nudged her to the edge of the abyss, without giving her any further information about the structure. The first thing she noticed was that the buckets were empty, and the ropes were dry. This well was not doing the naga any good.

She stood at the edge, peering down into the impenetrable darkness to see if she could sense water. "Yes," she announced. "There is water in the depths. I will have to merge with it to see if I can coax it up to a higher level. It may take a few hours to seek out other sources to add to what is left." She turned back to the Naga. "Is this agreeable to you?"

The guards looked at each other as if they weren't really sure which one of them was in charge. Finally, one decided to answer. "Do whatever you wisssh, but know that if you fail to return, your companionsss will die."

"I will return for my friends, do not doubt it," Mazu said. She jumped into the well, turning to water as she fell.

Chapter 23

Campaigns in the Realms

Sekhmet stepped out of the Pantheon Halls into the warm afternoon. The heat immediately refreshed her. Several hours spent visiting the embassies of pan-theon leaders had worn her patience thin. She was not accustomed to political chattering and found it difficult to remember all the names and origins of the gods of the more minor sub-realms. However, she knew that any of her faults would likely go unnoticed in the shadow of Tenh-Mer's aura of attraction. Judging from the enthusiastic support that most of the leaders she'd just visited displayed, her demon companion was a most effective campaigner. Sekhmet left the building assured of many votes. It was a shame the demoness was not divine. She would certainly liven up things in the City if she herself could be elected to the Council.

"I'm hungry," Tenh-Mer complained the moment they arrived on the lawn surrounding the Meditation Shrine. More dignitaries from the realms would be entering through the North Gate soon, and Sekhmet hoped to greet them there before they dispersed throughout the City. "I smell food," the demoness said.

Sekhmet also noticed the aroma of frying meat. She turned toward the Asian District, whose cooking schools were famous for their delectable menus. Their proximity to the Meditation Shrine had to be an incredible distraction to anyone trying to reach a higher plane of consciousness. Mouth-watering temptation was just a short walk away.

"Go eat," Sekhmet said. "But fly quickly, I still need you." Tenh-Mer responded with a happy squeal and darted briefly across the lawn before taking flight. "And don't come back with noodles in your hair!" Sekhmet called after her.

All Tenh-Mer heard was 'noodles.' Her stomach rumbled as she glid-ed down to a row of food carts that lined the space between the north-ern walls of the City and the Asian District. She hurried to a large cart that had long rows of drying noodles hanging from racks. A bubbling pan of sweet, orange sauce steamed over hot coals. She asked for a bowl. A besotted boy grabbed one and stuffed it with as many noodles and nuggets of fried meat as it could hold. He poured a generous amount of the sauce on top and handed it to Tenh-Mer. She smiled at him and made him take the coin she offered. He looked like he was going to faint when she touched his hand.

Looking for a place to eat, she saw no tables near the carts. She decided to fly up to the nearest comfortable rooftop, choosing one that overlooked a graveyard. It was actually a pretty scene, with miniature shrines and interesting statues marking the many burial sites. People were visiting the graves and setting little sticks on fire that billowed tiny plumes of smoke. Tenh-Mer watched everything while she devoured her lunch, slurping the noodles straight from the bowl and tearing into the fried meat pieces with her sharp teeth.

As she tipped the bowl to her lips to drink up the last of the delicious orange sauce, she noticed something jump behind a tombstone. She swallowed quickly and peered into the graveyard. Tenh-Mer wondered if she'd just seen a ghost and thought of a story she'd heard that Asian ghosts were always hungry. Glancing into her bowl, she spied a few noodles sticking to the bottom. Smiling, she decided to offer the scrap to the spirit, if she could find it.

Tenh-Mer launched off the roof and landed gracefully behind a small pagoda shrine. She leaned out to check if any people were nearby. She didn't really want to disturb anyone who had come to light the pretty sticks. Some of them looked very sad and Tenh-Mer felt sorry for them, but she was only interested in the ghost. Seeing no one about, Tenh-Mer came out of hiding and slowly walked over to the stone where she thought she'd seen something. She held the noodle bowl out in front of her.

"Are you hungry?" she whispered, waving the dish around. She heard a giggle from behind the monument and took another step closer. "Would you like a noodle?"

A tiny face popped up over the top of the stone. It stuck out a green tongue and winked at Tenh-Mer. Then a little arm reached up and threw a chewed-on poppy flower at her face. She hadn't seen a ghost; she'd found a fairy.

"Hey! Be nice!" Tenh-Mer complained. "Do you want this noodle or not?" But the fairy merely laughed at her and took to the air.

"You won't catch Ellidol!" the dark-haired fairy called out as it flew away.

"Wait a minute!" Tenh-Mer cried, dropping the bowl and flying after the rude little creature.

She chased it through the streets of the Asian District, in and out of pavilions and across rooftops. They raced over courtyards where men were drilling with swords and disrupted classrooms where students labored with inky brushes. Soon she was having so much fun she completely forgot her promise to Sekhmet to return quickly. Their mischief continued until a man began to beat upon a gong to summon a City guardian to catch them. As the gong's ring echoed through the street, the fairy turned back and motioned to Tenh-Mer. Following it, Tenh-Mer flew over the district wall and headed into a forested park. The fairy dove down into the dark mystery of the wood, but Tenh-Mer easily followed, led by its bright glow. They came to a large, ancient tree stump. The fairy grabbed Tenh-Mer by a braid of her hair and pulled her over to it.

"Oww! Quit it!" Tenh-Mer protested, but the fairy was persistent. Tenh-Mer allowed herself to be positioned on top of the stump and a strange thing happened. Suddenly she wasn't in the woods anymore. She and the fairy were in an underground world that shimmered with rainbow light.

Flower-lined pathways curved around grassy mounds. The fairy buzzed down one of those lanes. Tenh-Mer lingered by the thick roots of the stump, entranced by the beautiful scene. Looking up, she saw that the top of the stump's roots extended into a portal, explaining how she had dropped into the hidden world.

Tenh-Mer started down the path that the fairy had taken, but the little pest was nowhere to be seen. Then she heard soft voices ahead. They sounded happy and kind, so she decided to find out if they knew where the fairy had gone. She pushed into the branches of a bush dotted with purple flowers and peeked through the leaves, staying hidden. Tenh-Mer knew that even though someone sounded nice, they could really be dangerous. But she relaxed when she recognized the two gods. She'd seen them when she sat with Tara at the Council auditorium, and Tara had even told her their names. The blue one was Shiva and the other was Ceridwen. Tenh-Mer's eyes grew wide as she watched them embrace and kiss. Their desire for one another became even more obvious as Tenh-Mer watched. Worried she might be influencing them, she quickly snuck out of the bush and ran back to the stump. Even worse, seeing the familiar gods had reminded her of Sekhmet, reminded her that she had been gone far too long.

The fairy forgotten, Tenh-Mer jumped through the portal and flew as fast as she could back to the Meditation Shrine. There, Sekhmet was surrounded by a small crowd of deities. She gave Tenh-Mer an irritated glance as she hurried up to her.

"And this is my companion and protector, Tenh-Mer," Sekhmet told them. As the gods and goddesses were drawn to the demoness, Sekhmet gave Tenh-Mer a sharp tap on the head for being late. Fortunately, no noodles fell out of her finely braided tresses.

Back in the graveyard, a hungry ghost found a few stray noodles.

---

*T*he earth beneath Thule guarded jealously the little water it retained. Mazu's liquid form was much larger than the trickling spring she traced. She felt like a fat fish trying to swim in a shallow saucer. Still, she was encouraged that there was a steady stream to follow, no matter its size. She moved against its gentle current, determined to discover why the flow was so diminished.

There was nothing to interrupt her journey in darkness. At times her essence was stretched for tens of feet as she seeped along the narrowest of crevasses. No tiny creatures clung to the rocks. There was no sign that anything had ever lived in these waters; no abandoned shells, not a single fishbone. Mazu wistfully remembered other underground rivers she had explored that held entertaining wonders. She'd seen the swallowed ships of ill-fated heroes, hunted for the little treasure troves of canny octopi, and enjoyed the hospitable palaces of other water gods. This trip, so far, was pure tedium. Were it not for her hostage friends, she would abandon it gladly.

The stream led her to a tall wall which stood like a partial dam. Mazu inched up along the wet rock, fighting gravity and the downward flow of the water. She reached the lip of the wall, which brought her to the edge of a wide, deep pool. Sinking into it gratefully, Mazu drew her extended body back into a reasonably human shape and floated comfortably for a few moments, enjoying the rest. But she could not dally long, for she was no nearer a solution to the naga's water problem than when she began. The tiny waterway she had traced could never have been the main feeder for their well. There had to be another watercourse that had failed. Mazu hoped the gods of luck would allow her to find it quickly.

She began her search anew, examining the irregular sides of the pool beneath its waters, as well as the low ceiling that her head frequently brushed with a quiet splash. Little by little, the rock dome above her rose away from the pool, and the next time she heard splashing she knew that her head was no longer the cause. There was something else in the water.

Mazu gently sunk beneath the surface, becoming solid for a brief moment to more easily pull a charm from her robes. It was a lead fisherman's weight, carved in the shape of a man that Quan had once given her as a gift. She remembered his words at the time. *It is a magic thing I found inside a fish*, he'd said reverently, as he dropped it into her hand. And so it was. The little figure held no great sorcery, but, perhaps due to her silent prayer for good fortune, it possessed the perfect small enchantment to introduce her to those who shared these waters. Mazu released it from her fingers.

The weight did not fall to the depths, but floated steadily where she let it go. She knew this because the little man had begun to glow brightly. After another moment, he came to life, his tiny limbs propelling him about in a small circle as he backstroked comically. Mazu fought not to laugh aloud as she eased back into more shadowy depths to see what the lure would attract.

Her wait was short. Almost immediately she felt the current stir as something began to swim toward the light. Three small shapes appeared before her. The lure's glow teased her with glimpses of a fin, a claw, perhaps a tentacle. Mazu tensed, remembering the ketos in the Styx. Were these as dangerous? When a skinny tongue from one creature reached out and playfully batted at the swimming figure, and the head fin of a second batted it toward the waving paw of a third, Mazu realized the things were playing, not feeding or attacking. She watched them frolic for a few moments more before revealing herself.

Gently, Mazu joined them and took her turn at play, batting the figure with the back of her hand up toward the surface of the pool. As if it were sentient enough to take the hint, the little lead man breast-stroked upward. The momentary surprise of the creatures at her appearance vanished as they chased after the toy. Soon the entire watery party had their heads out of the pool. Mazu wondered if she looked as strange to the creatures as they looked to her.

"We ran away!" one of them declared cheerfully, slapping the water enthusiastically with its tail. "Is this your pond?"

"Can we live here?" a second asked. "We'll play with you all you want!"

Mazu was surprised to hear the creatures speak and even more intrigued that she understood them. These odd beings must have sprung from a very intelligent source, in spite of their primitive appearance. Mazu recovered from her shock, smiled reassuringly, and addressed their remarks in turn. "Did you? No. I suppose, and thank you." Then she noticed the third animal was backing away. Taking a guess that this one was female, for its head fin was smaller and its snout more slender, she pointed out its reticence. "Why is your sister afraid?"

"She thinks we're lost," the tail-slapper said with a roll of one eye.

"Never said that," the female monster muttered. "You're both so stupid. Don't you see what it looks like?"

Her brothers swam closer to Mazu and studied her face. Mazu looked deeply into their green eyes and admired the way their iridescent scales sparkled mutedly from the lure's glow. "I look a bit like a human, don't I?" Mazu admitted. "It's wise to be careful around men. But I am not one, so do not worry."

"It does look like the one that was chasing us, just a little," one of the brothers begrudgingly admitted to his suspicious sister. Mazu made her-

self a bit more diffuse and liquid to further prove that she was different.

"Ah. I thought that might be the case. But as I said, I am not like that," she emphasized. This was good enough for the brothers, who immediately resumed chasing the animated man. After a few moments, their sister came closer.

"If this isn't your pool, why are you swimming here?" she asked.

"I could ask you the same thing," Mazu gently teased back.

"Because we're hiding!" the brothers chimed in. Their sister snorted a stream of gurgling bubbles in annoyance.

"Maybe you are. But I'm looking for mom," she said.

"Perhaps I can help you find her," Mazu offered. If she could assist these young ones, they might be more willing to help her in return. "I have some experience in seeking for lost people."

"Really?" one of the boys asked. "Are you looking for somebody right now?"

Mazu decided to tell the creatures a simplified version of the truth. "No. I'm here because I'm looking for the place where the water stops. My friends live in a deep, deep well that is drying up. I have to find out what is blocking or diverting the water, or my friends will die."

"That's awful," the other male monster said. "I'm glad there's plenty of water in our swamp."

Mazu immediately seized on this clue. "I like swamps. So wet and green. What's your swamp called?"

"Home," said the sister, with a shrug.

This disappointed Mazu, but she realized that interrogating children might result in misinformation. "I'd like to see your home," Mazu said. "Maybe we can find both your mother and the source of my water problem on the way."

"Okay! Follow us!" said the boys. They began to swim toward the far side of the pool. Their sister slowly turned and set out after them. Mazu retrieved the magic weight, tucked it safely on her person, and flowed after them. Its glow slowly faded away as she crossed the pool.

The trio ducked into an underwater tunnel. Like all the underground passages, this one was pitch black. Mazu could sense which way to turn from the slight currents, but she wondered how the monsters found their way. Perhaps they used some sort of echo technique, like bats did. Mazu stretched out her liquid arms to judge the size of the passage. The fingers on her left hand traced along a smooth, slightly slimy wall. They swam on.

Soon Mazu could see a dim green tint breaking through the black.

They were nearing a passage that opened on the children's swamp. The monsters twisted up to the left, but as Mazu followed them she sensed another branch to her right. She hurried after the creatures, all of them breaking the murky surface of the swamp almost together.

"Will you please wait for me?" she asked. "I thought I saw something just inside that tunnel."

"Yeah, but hurry," the sister said wearily. "We still have to find our mother."

Mazu promised to be quick, and ducked back into the hole.

*D'*Molay tried to sleep, but between the camels ruminating and Quan fidgeting, he was having little success. At least the cell they'd been locked in was comfortably warm, well-insulated by the desert sands. In fact, it was luxurious compared to many prisons D'Molay had been held in.

"Snake men," Quan was muttering. "Not to be trusted... Even if Lady Mazu succeeds - "

"She will," D'Molay interrupted.

"Oh, that's right. You know everything." Quan sighed and clapped a frustrated hand on the top of his head as he paced. "Except how to choose roads that aren't infested with trouble."

"Sit down and go to sleep Quan. Time will pass quicker and Mazu will return all the sooner." D'Molay expected another sullen protest but Mazu's devotee seemed placated by the prospect of her speedier return. Quan yanked a bedroll from his camel's assorted burdens and spread it out along the wall.

"You be quiet, too," he chastised D'Molay. "Keep that lady you think you see inside your dreams."

"She's not a hallucination." D'Molay's words were low and certain, and carried within them a quiet force which Quan wisely chose not to dispute. He replied only with a grunt that sounded like his camel was adding her opinion on the matter. Minutes later he was snoring softly. But D'Molay, roused to full wakefulness by Quan's taunt, now could not get that lady off his mind. He rose to his feet, stretched, and leaned against the wall of the cell, thinking.

Even though he hadn't been able to see Aavi, as he had while they fled the harpies, he knew she had been there for him during the fight with the minotaur. He truly had a guardian angel. Mazu and Quan had no invisible protectors. The goddess was struck repeatedly in the fight and Quan avoided injury thanks mainly to his practice in self-preservation. But he had been specifically nudged out of the path of spears and cushioned when he should have impacted the wall with stunning force. Had these things happened to him on Earth, the tracker would have believed with certainty that his role as a Knight Templar granted him God's protection. But here in the realms, his deity was silent. D'Molay's renewed faith seemed the only evidence that His power still existed. But Aavi had come to the City of the Gods. She had breached the barrier that kept her angelic world separate from the lands in which he was trapped, yet it seemed that barrier still had an effect on how completely she could manifest here in the realms. D'Molay quieted his thoughts and alertly attuned his senses to the prison cell. If he concentrated, if he strove to be sensitive to every nuance, he felt sure he could see her, perhaps even touch her again. Barely breathing, he waited.

Quan rustled, turning over in his bedroll. One of the camels pissed on the floor. His own stomach rumbled. D'Molay's temper flared.

"Damn this place!" he growled, discarding his dusty cloak and slamming it to the ground. He was no seer. He had no insight into unseen worlds. He wished he were crazy; perhaps then he could see Aavi any time he wanted. Roused by the noise, Quan sleepily levered himself halfway up with his elbows.

"Is Mazu back?" he asked, blinking.

"No," D'Molay said, bitter frustration in his voice. "There's no one here."

❧⚬✦⚬☙

Mazu floated before the obstruction, studying it. An artist would have appreciated its beauty, had there been light enough to bring it to view. But pretty as it was, it had to move. Now that she had discovered the problem, Mazu understood why the naga's well had dried to almost nothing.

The underground channel that fed Thule had been almost completely blocked. Not suddenly, from a rock fall, but bit by bit over hundreds of years. Mazu stood before a massive colony of ladder barnacles, a type of crustacean peculiar to the realms. Unmolested, they would grow to amazing heights. Thousands of gently rounded, petal-like shells were concreted one upon another. Colorful frills spilled from their mouths to feed on the choice tidbits that floated down from the swamp. The colony could have begun on just one rock situated unfortunately at the channel's mouth. Over time, the population had grown upon its own dead layers to become as wide and as tall as the channel.

Mazu was relieved to find that the drought had a natural cause. She had enough troubles without initiating a new conflict with some other god. However, how was she going to unblock the watercourse? She carefully examined the size of the colony, pondering what to do, as the monstrous children swam back to see what was keeping her.

"You're taking too long," one of the boys complained, nudging her with a frill on his tail.

"Be patient. I've only been here a few minutes," she said. Mazu took the complaining brother by a side fin and pulled him toward the barnacles to show him the problem. "This is what blocked the water from getting to my well."

"Oh. Did you ask it to move?"

Mazu was surprised that the children knew so little about barnacles. "I don't think they can," she said.

The sister shot a stream of bubbles at the colony which caused a dozen frills to retreat within the safety of their shells. "They don't have any choice. They have to move when he does."

Mazu followed the female as she dove down to the very bottom of the colony. The child swam back and forth in front of it. Mazu had assumed the barnacles had built on stone. But looking closer, she could see fish scales.

"They live on a fish?" she asked. The children voiced their affirmation.

"Mother told us that some very old fish have shells on their backs, like turtles," said the sister. "She said that sometimes a fish can go to sleep for ages and wake up with all kinds of things stuck to it."

"It's gross," giggled one of the brothers.

Mazu was again impressed with the knowledge of the small monsters. "Your mother has taught you well."

"She knows about everything in the water," the sister said proudly. Then she sobered. "Do we have to wake up the fish before we can look for her?"

"Yes, I'm afraid so. But it shouldn't take long if you help." Mazu was about to tell the siblings how to proceed when they started without her. Before she could stop them, they darted in to nip at the barnacle-covered fish. They prodded beneath it with their spiny snouts and bombarded it with bubbles as they barked snapping sounds in its direction. Mazu dropped down to corral their enthusiasm but their efforts quickly had the intended effect. The great fish came suddenly and violently awake, lurching away from the channel mouth in a shower of dislodged and broken barnacles. It powered back down the passage toward the pool where Mazu had met her new friends. The waters, as if they too had been rudely awakened, rushed into the opened tunnel.

"Get back!" she exclaimed as she felt the strength of the flood. But even as she cried out, she saw the current sweep the monsters away with it. She threw herself after them, hoping that the small beings would not be injured if the force of the water threw them against the channel walls. Those walls flashed by Mazu in a blur as she sped with the current. Just ahead, she could see one of the creatures' tails wiggling. Several trails of bubbles streaming back toward her indicated that the little ones were still alive. With relief, she realized that the diameter of the channel was growing; they had to be in the main aquifer that led to Thule. That was good news for D'Molay and Quan, but bad news for these children. Without a doubt, they were now even further away from their mother.

As the channel continued to open, the water lost some of its force. Mazu was able to catch up with the three monsters. They seemed none the worse for the unexpected ride. She admired their resilience as they splashed along.

"Are we going to your well?" one of the boys asked.

"Indeed we are," Mazu said. "I'm sorry if you didn't want to come. But we'll look for your mother along the way." Mazu extended the sleeves of her watery robe and swept the children into a loose embrace so that they would not be separated again as they traveled. "What can you tell me about your mother? Does she look like you?" Mazu theorized that these odd children were birthed by a god, but the shocking answer she received proved this was not the case.

"Scylla looks just like us, but bigger," the sister said as they spun around a bend in the channel.

Chapter 24

To the Dead
Sea Swamp

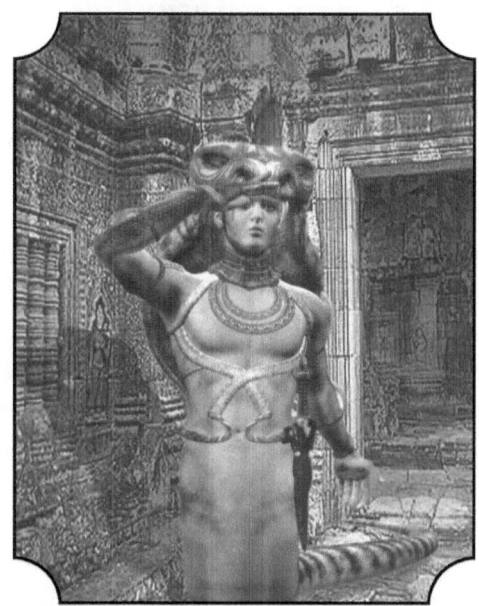

When a naga threw open the door to the cell, D'Molay feared he was in for a fight. However, the guard made no threatening move.

"Gather your thingsss," he said. "Your goddesss has kept her word."

"You heard him, Quan," D'Molay picked up his cloak and prodded his camel to its feet. "Let's get out of here."

"With pleasure!" Quan scrambled about the cell, picking up various items he had strewn about in attempts to be comfortable and amused.

"Only you could make a prison cell look sloppier than it already is," D'Molay criticized mildly. "Hurry up."

A few minutes later he, Quan, and the camels followed the guard back to the hall of the Great Spirit. Amid a bustle of snake men who were organizing work parties to tend to the revitalized well, Mazu waited for them. She stood posed in a strange position with her arms held out in a wide circle. As he came closer, D'Molay realized she was holding a small pool of water inside her arms.

"When you promised to bring them water, I didn't think you meant an armful at a time," he said.

"I'm not just carrying water," Mazu smiled back at him. "We have three new traveling companions."

Quan rubbernecked from behind D'Molay. "What do you mean? I don't see any -" Quan balked and retreated as one of the creatures cautiously poked its head up.

"That's . . . a bit inconvenient," D'Molay said, trying to guess why Mazu had added another layer of complexity to their quest.

"Not at all," she corrected. "We aren't the only ones looking for Scylla. These are her children."

"Her children?" D'Molay repeated, trying to piece things together.

Mazu explained how she'd met the creatures and described the way they were swept back to Thule. "I think it's very likely that Scylla is still in their swamp. Once we arrive, what better guides could we have than her children?"

"I can how see returning them would make her more willing to talk to us," D'Molay said. "But won't it be hard for you to carry them so far?"

"Would you rather do it?" Mazu scoffed. "Really, D'Molay, you need to give me some benefit of your extensive doubt."

"Alright, no offense intended," he laughed as they exited, making their way back up to the outside lands past the deteriorating walls and their neglected carvings. Apparently the price for their passage through the Naga's lands had been paid in full, for the snake men they passed did not hinder them in any way.

When they emerged from the ruins, Quan helped Mazu mount her camel. She had an awkward time of it, juggling the watery cargo of small swimming monsters in her arms, but after a minute or two she settled in. Quan scrambled aboard his camel and took up the lead rope of Mazu's animal since her hands were full. He looked askance at the creatures in her arms.

"They aren't going to jump out and bite you," Mazu promised.

"Unless we want to!" giggled one of the boys, who used his tail to flick a stream of water at Quan. It missed the man, hitting his camel in the face. The beast grumbled and took a few steps sideways towards D'Molay, who put a firm hand on its neck to settle it.

"So they can speak," D'Molay noted with interest.

"And bite," Quan chimed in. "They're dangerous! And we're going to take them to their mother, who is bigger and more dangerous?" He sighed dramatically so the others would know how put-upon he felt.

"Stop complaining, fisherman," D'Molay smirked. "You're protected by a goddess and a hero." *And an angel.* He climbed aboard his camel, remembering what a pleasant traveling companion Aavi had been in contrast to Quan. As he glanced back toward the ruins, he imagined the questions she would have asked about the intricate carvings. His eyes were drawn to a solitary pink desert flower forcing itself gently toward the sun from a crack between two stones. Resentful of its gentle beauty in light of his own struggles, he turned abruptly away and nudged his camel after Mazu and Quan, who had set off in the direction of the swamp. Out of his view, the flower petals stirred as if stroked by the touch of an unseen hand.

The next few days of their journey passed safely thanks to Aavi.

D'Molay was warned of any dangers, creatures or obstacles that were ahead. He heard her voice in his ear as they avoided a huge flock of murderous bats, a Cyclops, and even the passage of an insane Titan, any of which could have easily killed them. However, Aavi said nothing other than the warnings, despite his efforts to communicate with her. *Is she still mad at me for killing the harpies as we escaped Circe, or is there some other heavenly reason, beyond my understanding?*

As they hid at a cave entrance, watching the huge scaled feet of a Titan pass by, D'Molay said, "I can see why Bast thought us mad to enter this realm. Death seems to wait around every corner."

His companions were in complete agreement.

Their trek continued, Mazu and the children using their keen sense of water to return to the swamp. Winds blowing from the region of the distant swamp sent them tantalizingly cool breezes from time to time. As they rode, Mazu spoke of the great old fish blocking the well and the small monsters told them other stories of the place D'Molay called Anagar. Still wistful over thoughts of Aavi, D'Molay only half listened to their childish chatter, but was grateful for it. Their amazing tales were keeping Quan from voicing his usual mundane complaints.

Two more days passed before they could actually see the green edge of the Anagar Swamp. D'Molay, with the goal in sight, no longer needed to follow Mazu. Once again he took the lead, keeping an eye on the ground to make sure no quicksand lay in wait. The earth beneath them became muddier and more plant-covered as they moved on, but fortunately no bogs appeared to mire them. After another quarter mile, however, it was clear that they would have to continue on foot.

"This is as far as these camels can go," D'Molay said to Mazu. "We'll leave them here with Quan to watch them."

"Yes," Mazu agreed, before Quan could object to being left alone among both real and imagined dangers. She turned to him. "You should be safe enough while we're gone. Take the camels and hide at the water's edge in that stand of trees."

D'Molay could not resist a goad. "And if something comes after you, you can climb up one of them. Watch out for tree snakes."

Mazu suppressed a smile as Quan paled slightly. "More snakes?"

"Just stay alert," D'Molay said. "We're counting on you."

Quan helped Mazu slide off her camel. After D'Molay slung a water skin and a small satchel of traveling supplies over his shoulder, Quan led all the animals off as ordered. When Mazu reached D'Molay's side, he glanced at the pool of water suspended between her arms.

"They've gone quiet," he observed. Scylla's children were floating gently just beneath the surface, napping.

"Count it good fortune," she said. "Most children are troublesome on a journey. Even Aavi pestered us with many questions."

What she said was merely the truth, but D'Molay did not like being reminded of Aavi's faults. Thinking of her weaknesses only led to brooding about his own, reminding him of his failures. He ignored Mazu's remark and focused his attention on finding the driest points upon which to set his feet. There were few footsteps that did not present the soles of his boots with a muddy kiss. Next to him, he noticed Mazu skimming easily over the soggy earth.

"Wish I could work that trick," he said as the murk continued to deepen. He shook a clinging clump of wet grass from his right foot. "My boots may not survive this." Then his thoughts turned to more a serious problem, "What are we going to do without the antidote for Scylla?"

"As you told Quan, you have a goddess looking after you."

"So you have an idea?" he asked expectantly.

"I have hope. Hope that we will find a way to change her back or perhaps use her children to lure her out of this realm or even capture her."

"Thats's a lot of hope, Mazu."

"It's all we have at the moment."

A few steps later a waterfowl shot out of the undergrowth ahead of them, causing both D'Molay and Mazu to flinch. In response, the children began to stir. Heads popped up from the water and D'Molay saw several eyeballs scan the area. Since the things could talk, he felt it time to get some information. He squelched across the swamp and peered down at them.

"So, about your mother. Where did you last see her?"

"We were playing by the big tree," one of them volunteered. "But when we came up from the water she was gone, and there was a scary thing that looked like you there."

"A big tree, you say?" D'Molay looked around them. There was no shortage of trees. Many, hung ominously with mossy overgrowth, loomed over the swamp, blocking out anything too far in the distance. "Trees like these?"

"No, bigger," the child insisted.

"These aren't big at all," one of its siblings said.

"Then it shouldn't be too hard to find, should it?" D'Molay posed his next question to Mazu. "You didn't happen to see any giant roots under the ground, did you?"

She shook her head in the negative then looked down at the creatures. "Did you live in this tree, or were you just swimming near it?"

"We can't live in that tree," the sister said in an exasperated tone. "It's full of spiders."

"Good news at last," D'Molay snorted. "I suppose they're water spiders, too."

"Nope. They can't swim. They catch the birds and other things."

Mazu flexed her arms, which were getting a bit stiff from carrying the children. "If I put you down, do you promise not to swim away?"

"What are you going to do?" D'Molay asked.

As the creatures gave their word to stay nearby, Mazu set them down in the shallows to her left. "We can't wander around hoping to trip over this tree. I need to look for it."

"I thought that's what we were doing."

"It was. But now I need to look for it my way."

From D'Molay's point of view, Mazu slowly became taller and thinner. She stretched her watery form into a thin stream which reached up and through the drooping vegetation that hid the horizon. The children chattered with amazement and even D'Molay, who had seen Mazu perform many amazing feats, was impressed. He was eager to ask what she could see, but suppressed his impatience. Noise could draw unwelcome attention. Gazing up to the heights, he hoped that the goddess would quickly find the spider-infested tree. After only a minute, she descended and took her normal shape.

"It's not far," she told him before picking up the little creatures again. She settled them within her arms with a reassurance. "We'll have you home very soon. Let's hope your mother is waiting there for you."

"Which way now?"

Mazu pointed to their right. D'Molay peered at the thick vegetation, seeking an easy path. He spotted a line of tree trunks that had fallen end to end like dominoes, victims perhaps of a storm or some god's petulance. Whatever had toppled them had created a makeshift road that provided the tracker more sure footing than the watery swamp. He hopped onto the first trunk, testing its strength. All seemed solid. With Mazu skimming along nearby, he trod on. A smile crossed his face as he remembered a similar instance of crossing timber, one that had pitched Sergius into a river. His old friend had many talents, but balance was not foremost among them.

D'Molay jumped a short distance to land safely on the next trunk. This one had dead, scraggly branches to skirt, but he still made speedy progress. By the time he used one of its larger limbs to swing himself over to the third fallen tree, he noticed that they were moving into deep shadow. The great tree, its cause, was in sight. The others saw it too. He heard splashing and the voices of the monstrous children calling loudly for their mother.

D'Molay whirled about, gesturing to Mazu. "Can you keep them quiet?"

"I suppose I could. But we may find Scylla sooner if we let them cry." Mazu glided closer to the tree with them as D'Molay surveyed the swamp. A pervasive feeling of unease had settled in his gut. He expected that the hair on the back of his neck would be standing up were it not drenched in sweat from his exertions. Around them, he knew living things were stirring. Amphibians croaked. Disturbed wings flapped. A woman screamed.

The sound came from far above his head. D'Molay drew his knife, hoping its special attributes would prove helpful if an attack came down from the tangled branches of the giant tree. He looked up at its bulky limbs that twined upon themselves in thick knots. His eyes darted from one section of the tree's canopy to the next, searching for movement. "Where did that scream come from?"

"I don't know," Mazu said. "I'm going to safely hide the little ones until we sort out this trouble."

As Mazu glided off through the marsh ushering the triplets, D'Molay began to walk around the great tree's trunk, stepping carefully across tangled roots that stood exposed above the level of the swamp. He was beginning to think that the scream had been the unfortunate woman's last when he heard another, weaker this time, from the heights. D'Molay's brow furrowed as he squinted at the branches above his head. He angrily brushed away a fly that tickled his neck. He could see nothing suspicious, but was sure the sound had come from the upper branches. Another bug skimmed just under his nose and he swiped at his face with the back of his hand. Several more flying pests landed on him, but, having resolved to climb the tree and investigate, he ignored them.

The torment of insects was to be expected, in a swamp. He reached up, taking a grip on a stubby handhold, testing it for purchase. One of the small bugs landed on the back of his hand. It looked like a spider. With wings. What the children had said about the spiders that lived in the tree flashed into his mind.

"Mazu, the tree spiders can fly. But they're small," he called back.

The words were barely out of his mouth when an entire swarm of flying spiders caught up with their earlier scouts. D'Molay found himself enveloped in a tornado of buzzing wings and skittering legs. He felt the first threads of sticky webbing shoot across his face. He barked out Mazu's name, but the spiders were so adept at their spinning his mouth was already half covered, mostly muffling his cry. Within seconds his arms were pinned at his sides and his legs were swathed in webbing from the knees up. He managed to crush dozens of the tree spiders under his boots, but those losses seemed no deterrent to the army that had seized him. After another frantic moment of struggling he felt all the tiny,

prickly legs of the spiders grab hold of his cocoon. A thousand wings beat in unison and he was lifted up into the canopy. He watched the ground recede beneath him, and wondered two things. Would Mazu find him, and why hadn't the spiders webbed over his eyes?

Up, up they went. D'Molay still had his knife at the ready. He wiggled it a bit and judged there was just enough play for him to cut through his bonds. He couldn't try to escape yet, however. Until the spiders stashed him somewhere, freeing himself would only result in a plummet to his death. The world tilted around him and he fought a wave of dizziness as his captors tipped him sideways and wedged him between two worn limbs. He could see dark stains of blood and imagined the smell of old entrails lingering on the bark.

Their work of carrying him done, the spiders' hold on him loosened along with the itchy sensation it caused. D'Molay could still feel a few of them crawling near his feet. They were either finishing their webs or removing their dead that were wedged between the treads of his shoe soles. As they worked, he wiggled weakly in pretense of appearing just another helpless captive. He even groaned in faux fear.

A matching mewl responded to his distress cry, kindling a satisfying spark of hope in the tracker. He now knew he wasn't the only one tucked in the tree spiders' pantry. With no little impatience, he waited long minutes until he could no longer feel the spiders working on him. Swiftly he sliced through the webs with ease, emerging from his cocoon. The spun shreds, silver in color, had turned black where his knife had touched them.

Treading carefully on the remains of webbing, he braced himself against the tree while he removed a rope from his pack. He tried not to look down as he securely tied one end of it to a sturdy branch and harnessed his chest with the other. Having taken steps to preserve his life if he slipped, D'Molay began to seek for the owner of the other voice. Around him were dozens of knotty tree limbs, wound one upon the other to create a network of handy pigeonholes for victims. Here and there lay scattered bits of old clothing and browning bones, of undetermined age, stripped of their flesh.

"Make a sound," he commanded, as loudly as he dared. A high pitched squeal answered him. Moving in the direction of the sound, he spotted a trail of webbing dangling from one of the pockets. Playing out his rope, he headed toward it. "Again!"

The female tone repeated, assuring D'Molay that he was on the right track. Reaching the site of the trailing web, he leaned into the opening and found a human-sized cocoon. Putting his knife to work, he uncovered a woman. Shivering, she sat up, drawing her limbs into herself to cover her nudity, although she did not seem particularly embarrassed about it. D'Molay raised an eyebrow, trying to work out why anyone would have been caught naked in a swamp. Remembering a discarded

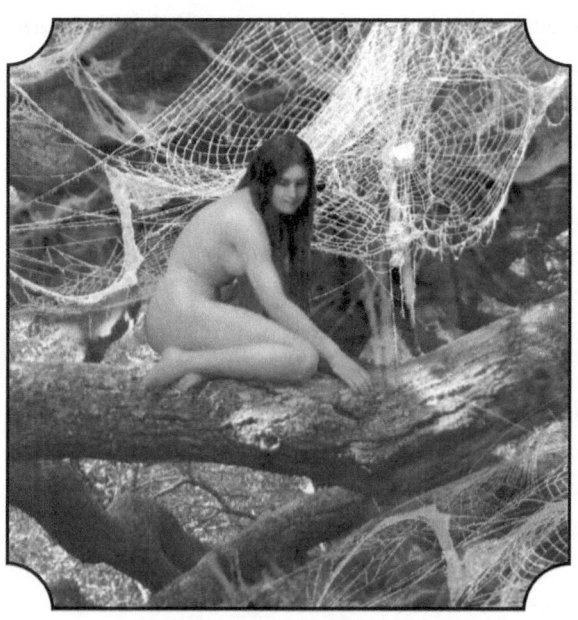

tunic he'd stepped over, he turned to retrieve it.

"Here. Put this on. Are you hurt?"

She quickly donned the tunic, her skill in dressing a contrast to that of Aavi, the last nude woman D'Molay had rescued. She flipped her shoulder-length, black hair free of the garment's neckline and spoke boldly. "No. Just frightened. And disgusted."

"I was hunting in the swamp and I heard you scream. When I followed, the spiders attacked me. Luckily they took me right to you. Is there anyone else here?"

"I don't know, we should look." She was on her feet now, craning her neck to see into some of the other compartments. Her initiative and bravery impressed D'Molay, who had been dreading descending the tree with a cringing damsel.

"Of course. But let me do that. I'm tethered to the tree."

"Go then," she nodded, tearing a length of vine from its run on the bark and cleverly fashioning it into belting to secure the billows of her tunic as D'Molay moved away. He visited all the nearby holes, leaning in and calling softly. There were old, dry webs and more bones, mostly animal this time, although many were too strangely formed for him to identify. When his rope no longer stretched far enough to reach more openings, he gave up the search and returned to the woman. He found her clinging tightly to a branch, leaning out slightly to peer down at the swamp far below.

"Nothing. If anyone else was caught, it's too late for them." D'Molay had been blunt, but was concerned about how much time they had before the spiders noticed their escape. The woman showed little emotion at his words, for which he was grateful. She eased back from the edge of the tree limbs toward him.

"Can you get me down?"

"No guarantees, but I'll do what I can. How good a climber are you?"

The woman bit her lip, looking doubtful. "Hard to say. But I'm a good swimmer, so if you have to drop me, aim for deep water."

D'Molay nodded. "I'll keep that in mind. Come. I'll rope us together." It took only a few moments for D'Molay to adjust his rope harness to hold two, the woman pressed tightly against him, her back to his chest. His plan was to lower them to a section of the tree that had more climbable limbs. Gauging distance, he convinced himself his rope was just long enough to get them there.

Foot by foot, they rappelled down through the tree. The starts and stops were jarring until D'Molay became accustomed to the cumbersome extra weight of his passenger. However, she had an agile grace that made the descent less dangerous than it could have been. Often, one of her feet would assist in bracing them at just the right moment, or a hand would reach out to steady them against a branch to prevent a spin. However, her skills could not mitigate the fact that D'Molay's rope turned out to be about twenty feet too short. They hung silently, considering the drop.

"Where's a flying spider when you need one?" the woman joked.

Several scenarios for reaching the ground flashed through D'Molay's mind, none of them pleasant. He settled on the only practical one. "The bark. It's tough and layered. If we use it as foot and handholds, we might be able to free climb the rest of the way down. Take the knife from my hip." As she reached behind her to extract the weapon, D'Molay grabbed tightly to protruding bark strips and settled the toes of his boots into sturdy indentations. "Now, you need to cut through the rope. And don't lose my knife."

The woman laughed nervously. "You're worried about your knife?"

"Do it."

She slid the blade beneath the rope. D'Molay tensed as she severed it, pressing her as tightly as he dared, hugging the tree. He reached down with his left hand to find a new hold and began to ease them down along the trunk each time a foot or hand came to rest in a safe haven. He imagined the woman was suffering some scratches from being pressed against the bark, but she did not complain, even when her makeshift dress snagged a pointed shard of wood and ripped. When they finally reached the platform of spreading limbs, D'Molay quickly shrugged both of them out of the harness. He turned the woman around to check her for injuries. As he expected, several pink scrapes were rising on her bare arms and legs. In spite of this, her brown eyes sparkled with excitement at their success. She handed him the knife.

"Here. Safe and sound."

"That we are. For the moment." D'Molay sheathed the weapon and warily scanned the surroundings as he caught his breath from the exertion of the descent. Seeing no spiders or other threatening creatures, he turned his back to his companion. "Get the water skin from my pack, would you?"

She laughed. "Do you ask all the girls to rummage through your pockets?"

D'Molay looked back over his shoulder with an intrigued grin. This one's saucy forwardness reminded him of the French court ladies of old. "Only the ones to whom I've not been properly introduced."

She reached into his pack, procuring the flask and handing it to him. "I don't know your name, either. Perhaps I'll call you Cutter, for freeing me from the webs."

"How about D'Molay?"

"As you wish, but Cutter has a far better ring to it."

"And what do I call you?" D'Molay asked, taking a deep draught of water.

"Scylla."

Choking and spitting, D'Molay coughed out his surprise. "We've been looking for you! But we thought you were . . ."

She crossed her arms and narrowed her eyes as he gaped at her. "What?"

"We were told you were a monster."

D'Molay noticed her expression change. Her previous bright and engaging demeanor retreated. Almost sullenly, she confronted him.

"At least a monster can be seen for what it is."

"I meant no insult," D'Molay said. "Trust me, I am more than happy just to find you." He spread his arms wide, hoping to appear respectful and supportive.

"Explain why you were looking for me," she challenged, placated, but still suspicious.

D'Molay had hoped that discussion would wait until they were safely on the ground. To be honest, he hadn't had time to frame a convincing argument that would ensure Scylla's cooperation with their quest. Should he spin a tale of Glaucus' love for her, or offer her revenge on Circe? His response took too long. She turned away with a huff and began to make her own way down along a limb.

"Never mind. Keep your secrets in exchange for saving me. I have to find my children."

He hurried after her, moving down the tree as quickly as he dared.

"We've already found them," he said. "But - "

"All three? A girl and two boys?"

"Yes, but they - " D'Molay clapped his mouth shut as he saw hope in her eyes. His heart warmed, but his spirit was unsettled. Did she know her children were monstrous? And the small creatures had been afraid of beings that looked human; something about the situation wasn't right. He decided it was best to simplify his response. "Yes."

That one word spurred Scylla to move even more quickly along the limbs. D'Molay was pressed to keep up. "How were you separated?" he asked, sliding along the bark.

"We were swimming, but suddenly I felt ill. I think I passed out for a moment. When I woke up I was floating in the reeds."

"And your children?"

Scylla paused to shirk aside a small branch that was clinging to her tunic. "I heard them splashing and crying, but they wouldn't come to me. They were frightened. It was as if something was chasing them."

D'Molay searched for something noncommittal to say, settling on, "Well, they're safe now." Scylla continued on through the tree.

The rest of their journey passed without conversation, allowing D'Molay to consider matters other than the uncertain upcoming reunion. He kept a wary eye out for the tree spiders, wondering if they would attack again. Fleeting thoughts of Circe's urns and Aavi's obsession with them skimmed through his mind. He even jealously conjured up a vision of Quan lazing about at the fringes of the swamp with the camels. He'd once had a ridiculous argument with Sergius about whether slaves had it easier than their masters. Maybe in Quan's case it was true.

When they reached the lowest limb, D'Molay jumped down first. Then Scylla hopped down into the haven of his outstretched arms. She quickly stepped away from his embrace, her bare feet squelching in the bog.

"Where is your friend?" she asked.

D'Molay did not relish yet another hunt for a missing person. "Mazu!" he yelled, hoping the goddess would hear him the first time so he did not have to risk another outburst.

"Over here, D'Molay," she responded. He led Scylla toward the sound, which had come from behind some of the tumbled trees over which he had traveled. They heard the gush of spraying water as they closed in.

Rounding the edge of an upended root ball, they saw Mazu. She stood like a sculpture in the middle of a fountain, water springing up from skyward palms to form a liquid dome over her and the three small creatures playing in the droplets showering at her feet. Scattered just beyond the rainy dome were the bodies of thousands of flying spiders. D'Molay's mouth curled a bit in disgust as he watched the children's tongues reach out to snack on them.

"I'm glad you're safe," Mazu said. "I was going to seek you out, but some insects attacked as I was moving the children to safety." After a few last spiders tried valiantly to pierce her water shield and drowned, she stopped the flow and nodded to the woman D'Molay had retrieved. "But it seems you didn't need my help."

D'Molay laid out the situation quickly, for Scylla was already falling down at Mazu's feet in joyous relief. "I've found their mother."

Scylla collapsed with a relieved sigh and reached for the nearest child. It was the girl, who squeaked and dodged away as her brothers also edged back to huddle at Mazu's feet. Then some squalling ensued as the youngsters competed for the best hiding place and Scylla, confused, reprimanded them for their odd behavior.

"Stop it! Come here! Why are you hiding?" Scylla turned a glare upon Mazu. "What have you done to make them afraid of me?"

Mazu stilled the protective fountain. The absence of the splattering water gave her voice more prominence. "We have done nothing but reunite you. The root of their fear is in you alone."

D'Molay crouched down to speak to the children. "Is she the one that chased you?" Three timid nods answered the question. "And you'd never seen her before that time?"

"This is ridiculous!" Scylla said. "What game are you playing? Purta, Trell, Wagen, stop it right now!"

"She knows our names!" the daughter gasped. Mazu, who had been observing Scylla silently during the exchange, decided it was time to move things forward.

"I'm afraid you have changed, not these youngsters. Haven't you noticed your own body? Look closely at it. What are you, Scylla?"

Scylla shot Mazu a fierce look before glancing down at herself, but her confidence vanished as she stared at her arm. "I am . . . I am . . ."

D'Molay rose to his feet and put a supportive hand on her shoulder. "You are a woman, now. But long ago, you were transformed into a creature like these, and before that, you were a water nymph."

It seemed too much for Scylla to process at first. She stared dully at her hands, turning them over and back, tracing the line of one finger with another from nail to knuckle. After a few still moments, she abruptly broke away and leaned against a mossy tree trunk, looking down into a pool of still water at the reflection of her face. When she turned back to D'Molay, tears streaked her cheeks. "The gods play with me, turning me from one thing to another," she said haltingly.

Mazu shooed the children away from her feet and approached Scylla. "Suffering has as much to do with one's attitude as one's torment. Despite what was done to you, you endured well. You created life. You came through this strong and ready to confront your enemies."

"Our enemies," D'Molay added.

"You think I care about your enemies?" Scylla spat back. "You want to use me for your own ends, like all the others!"

"In a way, you're absolutely right," D'Molay said. Scylla was surprised by his forthrightness, which was exactly the response he was hoping for. "We've been forced by a god to interfere with your destiny. In this we had no choice. But you can choose the next path of your life once we have completed our duty."

"I believe that if you let him explain why everything happened to you," Mazu added, "all of us will be free."

"What about my - where did they go?" Scylla pushed past D'Molay and scanned the undergrowth. "Wagen! Purta!"

Mazu held out an arm to keep Scylla from running deeper into the swamp. "Your children have gone. They are old enough to feed themselves, and from what I've observed, you have taught them how to survive. As with all children, the time comes when they no longer need their mother. I'm sorry, but there is nothing you can do for them now."

Scylla choked back a sob. D'Molay decided that keeping her moving would be the best course. "We have transportation and supplies at the edge of the swamp. Have you ever ridden a camel?" She shook her head, and took D'Molay's extended hand. "It isn't difficult. Even our idiotic servant quickly learned, and you won't have to ride alone."

"I suppose you want me to ride with you," she replied, a bit of her spark resurfacing. D'Molay smiled, already imagining the challenges Scylla's strong personality would pose on the trip back to Glaucus.

"No. I think I'll make you ride with Quan."

Scylla went, but broke down, crying for her lost children most of the way back.

D'Molay realized she was inconsolable for now and that there was little he or Mazu could do, other than move forward.

Chapter 25

The Wild Woman

Quan had tried to ignore the passing of hours since Mazu and D'Molay had left him to brave alone the thousand evils that could emerge from the swamp. But as the orbs that gave daylight to the realm shone mercilessly overhead, driving him under the shade of the trees at the water's edge, the lengthening of shadows forced him to acknowledge the time. He was well into fretting about how he would survive the coming darkness when he heard voices and the faint, sweeping sound of foliage being pushed aside.

"Lady Mazu?" he called softly, scurrying to the side of his resting camel and throwing one leg over it in preparation for a quick escape should the sounds not belong to his friends. He slouched in the ungainly position until he spotted D'Molay emerging from a stand of tall grass. Relieved, he tried to abandon his half-mount, but entangled his boot strap in some loose threads of the blanket that graced the camel's back.

D'Molay laughed as he found Quan squirming atop the irritated animal. One of Quan's hands was stretching to extricate his shoe and the other was clutching the camel's neck for balance.

"Are we interrupting something?"

"I'm stuck!" Quan complained.

"Good. That's probably kept you from running away," D'Molay said as he went to his aid. With a twist of his fingers, D'Molay loosed the stubborn run of woolen yarn that held Quan captive and turned toward the others. "You see, Scylla, if this one can ride a camel, you definitely can."

Upon hearing this, Quan surveyed the scene, expecting to see some kind of horrible creature. Instead, a very pretty woman stood next to Mazu. Quan hurried over to the goddess. "Well done, well done," he praised Mazu, bobbing respectfully and sneaking glances at Scylla as he did. "You have achieved the quest."

"Scylla, this is Quan, my chosen servant," Mazu said. Quan beamed at the new and attractive arrival.

"I am glad we found you! Now we can go back to the City and away from all the monsters in this realm." At the mention of monsters, Scylla looked away, unable to meet Quan's happy, eager face.

Noticing her discomfort, D'Molay broke in before Quan could blurt out any more unintentional insults. "Quan, help me with the camels. We can put miles behind us before it gets too dark." After a nod from Mazu spurred him to do as he was asked, Quan followed D'Molay.

Mazu observed Scylla as the men went to work. The formerly-cursed woman frequently looked back toward the swamp as if something was trying to draw her back into its deadly waters.

"You will feel better once we leave," the goddess counseled.

Scylla fixed her gaze on Mazu's face, forcing herself to concentrate on something other than her past. "How far must we go?" she asked.

"Across many sands. Then over the water to the shores of Olympia."

"How can we go so far? I don't remember everything, but I do know that crossing realms is dangerous," Scylla asked skeptically. Mazu tried to reassure her.

"D'Molay has important friends. He has permission to travel through many lands from the Council of the City. Our journey won't be quick, but it should be safe enough."

Scylla's focus on Mazu was broken by arguing voices as a mild spat broke out between D'Molay and Quan over how best to tie down the bag that held the servant's cooking kit. Their mutual frustration at not having their way amused the two women.

"I'm afraid you'll have to put up with more of that," Mazu warned her, chuckling.

"I can endure it," Scylla decided. "I owe D'Molay my life, and a debt to the rest of you for providing me a way out of this realm." She cast another glance over her shoulder. "I feel I don't belong here anymore."

"Change always comes," Mazu replied. "And with it, many choices."

"Choices," Scylla mused. "It would be nice to have them for a change."

D'Molay approached them. "Ready to ride?" He held out a hand to Scylla. She glanced at it, winked at Mazu, and walked right past D'Molay to Quan and his camel. Quan let out a vocalization halfway between shock and glee as she approached. Mazu quickly stepped toward her own camel to hide her smile at D'Molay's minor rejection. "Well that proves she was a nymph, they like playing these sorts of games," he said under his breath.

Scylla took her seat on her chosen camel with grace, impressing Quan.

"Ah, you are a skilled rider," he flattered as he clambered up in front of her. Scylla leaned back and away from him, but was soon tipped forward to smash against his back as the camel's rump rose before its front. Scylla was the only one who couldn't see Quan's broad grin at the contact.

"Gods," D'Molay muttered to Mazu, who was able to interpret the depth of the adventurer's frustration with her servant from one mere word.

"If you dislike the seating arrangements, I can ask Scylla to trade with you." Mazu laughed, imagining Quan and D'Molay on the same camel. D'Molay's disdainful look put that notion to a quick death.

The group set out across the sands. At first, Quan attempted a flirtatious banter with his passenger, but soon found that he needed to pay complete attention to keeping their camel moving quickly enough in the fading twilight to keep up with Mazu and D'Molay. Aside from answering a few of Scylla's questions about the terrain they were crossing, conversation was minimal.

As the first night stars appeared, the smooth sands began to give way to scattered rubble, signaling they were again nearing the ruined city. Quan launched into a story of Mazu's great bravery during the minotaur attack. He gave D'Molay his due in the battle, but couldn't help exaggerating his own role in the fight. As Quan was trying to convince Scylla that he had thrown a spear and hit a minotaur right between the eyes, D'Molay held up a hand signaling all the riders to stop.

"We'll camp here," he announced. "In early morning we'll move through the ruins as soon as there's enough light to see our way. With luck, we won't encounter any more of its residents."

"They do have a way of delaying one's travels," Mazu said.

Scylla leaned back to keep her balance as Quan made their camel kneel. "No hurry," she said. "I'm not that eager to be delivered."

"Don't worry," D'Molay said. "Glaucus has no authority to hold you against your will. We just have to bring you to him."

"What authority does he need?" she pointed out. "He's a god." Scylla slid off Quan's camel and stretched, working some of the aches from her legs.

"So is Mazu," Quan interjected, swinging his right leg over the camel's back to dismount. "She'll keep him honest. And if she needs any help, I can employ my fish hook!"

Scylla burst out laughing at the servant's bold assertion. "You fish for gods?"

"He's fishing for a punch in the face," D'Molay countered, suppressing a grin of his own. Quan wrinkled up his nose, folded his arms, and turned to Mazu.

"Yes, Quan, set up camp and prepare a small fire," the goddess directed, anticipating his question. "You can finish telling Scylla about our adventures after dinner." Quan nodded and set to work. One by one, he took the camels a short distance away and hobbled them to prevent them wandering away while he was busy with his work. Mazu called Scylla over to help her spread a large blanket over the sand. They sat down to talk as D'Molay took advantage of the uneventful moment to unpack his map. He settled close to the small campfire Quan had lit. By its light, he drew in the borderline of the Anagar swamp. He sketched one of the tiny flying spiders in the margin of the parchment.

Quan shuffled over with crocks filled with dinner. D'Molay set his map aside, took a bowl, and nodded his thanks. He had to admit he appreciated having a servant to cook and clean up after him, even one whose personality wasn't what he wanted in a bondsman. He watched Quan make a beeline for Scylla and present her meal to her with a flourish and a bow. D'Molay lifted his own bowl to his lips and tasted a spicy stew of fish and vegetables. As he ate, he noticed Mazu sitting serenely by herself. Since she had consumed the elixir after the fight with the minotaur, she seemed to need little sustenance. However, Mazu seemed to look a little older with each passing day.

An hour passed. During that time the party had drawn closer to D'Molay at the campfire and settled down to rest. D'Molay yawned, felt the urge to urinate, and took a short walk to relieve himself in private. As he buttoned up his trousers, he heard a low, guttural, growl from behind him.

He spun, hand moving efficiently to draw his knife as he peered into the darkness for the source of the sound. Something was crouched about halfway between where he stood and where the others slept. D'Molay awaited an attack, but the shape remained hunched on the ground, swaying from side to side and making random, unintelligible noises. Remaining at the ready with his knife, D'Molay attempted to communicate.

"What are you? What do you want?"

He took two steps closer. The thing grumbled out another utterance and crawled backwards, maintaining its distance. The move brought it a little closer to the campfire. D'Molay realized if he could herd it further in that direction, he could get a decent look at it. It was best to know what he was up against. He continued to speak to it.

"I don't want to fight you," he said firmly, again walking toward it. "Are you watching us?" His plan was working. The form kept its distance from him as he approached, scooting ever closer to the campfire. D'Molay could now see that it was human in shape. If he could make it move it a few more yards toward the fire he'd be able to identify how much of a threat it was.

"Can you speak, or merely groan?" D'Molay delivered this demand on the march, briskly advancing to close the gap between them. Startled, his quarry unsteadily rose to a standing position and turned to run. Taking full advantage of the intruder's fear of him, D'Molay charged toward it and grabbed its arm.

"Scylla?"

D'Molay stared dumbfounded at the hostile grimace on Scylla's face. Her eyes were half-vacant and her body shivered in his grip. Gulping in a breath, she spilled a string of gibberish at him before beginning to struggle. Squirming, kicking, and snapping like an irritated cat, she wrested herself free and started to run. Had she been an unknown monster, D'Molay would have thrown his knife and dropped her without a second thought. But she was not some chance encounter. She was their cargo.

"Mazu, Quan! Wake up!" D'Molay called out as he raced after Scylla. She ran toward the camels and hid behind one. D'Molay pulled up short, not wanting to drive her any further away from the camp. The camel huffed nervously, disturbed by the commotion.

"What's wrong?" Mazu had appeared at his side in the blink of an eye. She followed his pointing finger and noticed Scylla huddled by the camel.

"She's gone wild," D'Molay explained. "She crept up on me, growling. I think she's out of her mind."

Quan raced over, knuckling sleep out of his eyes. "What's happening?"

"Our guest did not sleep well," Mazu said. "You were resting next to her, Quan. Did you see her rise, touch anything in the camp, eat anything?"

"No, I saw nothing. I was sound asleep until I heard the tracker call for us."

D'Molay put his knife away. "Well, something made her change." He glanced upward, expecting to see a full moon or other cosmic portent of evil. But the night sky was calm and clear.

"I suggest we restrain her for the sake of her own safety as well as our own mission," Mazu proposed.

"Agreed," D'Molay said. "But I tried that already and missed my chance. Maybe you should do it, Mazu."

Mazu turned to face D'Molay with a familiar twinkle in her eye. "I have servants for tasks like this. Quan shall do it."

"What?" he blurted. "Me? I'm no match for a wild woman!"

"She's the same woman you were regaling with your heroic exploits as we travelled," Mazu chided. "I think it's only right you live up to your reputation."

"But my Lady - "

Any additional excuses were silenced by Mazu's frown.

"This should be interesting," D'Molay remarked to Mazu as he folded his arms to watch as Quan tentatively crept toward Scylla. He inched toward the camel, his bobbing and weaving reminding D'Molay of a pigeon enticed by crumbs of bread to enter a snare.

"Scylla," Quan squeaked out. "It's only me. Don't run away."

D'Molay laughed as Quan almost jumped out of his shoes when Scylla responded to his words with a loud growl. "Don't you run away either," D'Molay reminded Quan.

"Their fear is equal. That makes a good match," Mazu said cryptically.

D'Molay watched intently. Quan managed to get close. He and Scylla were now separated only by the camel. One of the servant's shaking hands reached out to grip the animal's bridle. The other, no more steady, Quan held out to Scylla. She considered it for a moment. Then she shot from her position, darting around the camel's head to tackle Quan.

In the squalling that ensued, it was difficult to separate the camel's bleating from Scylla's strange, guttural barks; but Quan's screeching was loud and clear.

"No! Don't kill me! Let me go!"

Scylla had wrestled Quan to the ground. She sat upon his chest, pinning down his arms. Her hair dangled in his face as she moved her mouth toward his neck, baring her teeth to bite. D'Molay immediately moved to save Quan, drawing his knife, but Mazu blocked his way with her staff.

"He is my responsibility."

Extending one finger, Mazu aimed a thin, concentrated stream of cold water at Scylla's hip. It struck with a sting that drew her attention away from ravaging Quan's throat. She rolled off him and snarled, rubbing her body where the water had left its mark. Quan wasted no time scrambling away like a bug.

"What's wrong with her?" he said, gulping for air and gesturing unsteadily at Scylla. "Did you see? She tried to eat me!"

Mazu pulled her staff out of D'Molay's path. "Please restrain her now."

"Quan, get my rope from the other camel's pack," D'Molay said, turning to Mazu. "It's only going to be harder now that he's agitated her."

"Perhaps. But I wanted to observe more of her behavior. We have to discover the cause of it."

Quan stomped off toward D'Molay's mount, grumbling about them risking his life. He cast several looks back over his shoulder to make sure Scylla wasn't coming after him. Returning with the coil, he thrust it out to D'Molay.

"Your turn," he said.

D'Molay laughed at his resentful demeanor. "I didn't make you go over there. Complain to your mistress."

Taking that as a suggestion, Quan began to chatter to Mazu, bombarding her with questions about why Scylla had changed and why she had thought sending him to her was a good idea. D'Molay abandoned them to their debate. Running the rope through his hands to remind himself of the feel of it, he cautiously circled the woman he was tasked to capture.

Over his years as a tracker for the Council of the Gods, D'Molay had stalked and trapped many men and beasts. Usually he relied on stealth, placing crafty snares or using the terrain to box them into a corner with no escape. Apprehending a target in the wide open world, one that was fully aware of his intentions, challenged his skills. He was more than slightly annoyed that the goddess refused to intervene. Would it have taken much of her power to douse Scylla, half-drown the fight out of her and leave her easy for the taking? D'Molay dismissed his question with a soft curse. He'd asked himself many times why the gods chose action or inaction. He accepted that he'd never know. Job after job, he had performed his assignments without the benefit of insight into their origins or consequences. He shifted into that mindset and focused on his current task.

Instinctively, he surveyed the surroundings, noting no convenient cover for the woman to hide in if she chose to flee. She had the disadvantage, too, of bare feet, to which the hard, rock strewn ground would not be kind. What he had observed of her before she took this strange turn had shown D'Molay that she was daring and athletic. However, considering his advantage in footwear and the confusion of her mind, he was fairly confident he could catch her if she ran. His hands ceased their play on the rope. He had created a lasso and was ready to employ it.

D'Molay inched closer. Scylla had not moved from the spot where she had landed when Mazu's strike knocked her off Quan. Her eyes bored into D'Molay's, but he was not certain that there was any intelligence behind the stare. Scylla's frozen posture and stricken appearance briefly reminded him of those who had ended their existence as salt statues during the last war. He took another step toward her. She cringed away, lips drooping open, a softer moan escaping them. A sound that was almost a word followed, then her eyes rolled upward into their sockets and a convulsion shook her. Scylla collapsed, twitching, as D'Molay took advantage of her fit to dart in and securely bind her ankles and wrists.

"That's got her," he called out, scooping her up and carrying her back to the campfire. He put her down on a blanket and examined her, checking the strength of her blood's flow at her throat and inspecting her exposed skin.

"What are you looking for?" Quan asked.

"Wounds. I've heard of reptiles and insects that can drive you to madness with their venom. But I don't see any bite marks."

Mazu stepped over and crouched down next to Scylla, extending a hand to touch her chest. It rose and fell rapidly from Scylla's shallow breathing. "I suspect this sickness is connected to her transformation from monster back to girl," Mazu said.

"An after-effect? Have you seen this happen before?" D'Molay stood up and watched as Mazu gently ran her hands over Scylla's body.

"Not specifically," Mazu admitted. "But magic powerful enough to change a being's fundamental nature opens the door to undesired consequences."

D'Molay adjusted his cloak which had twisted to the left as he'd carried

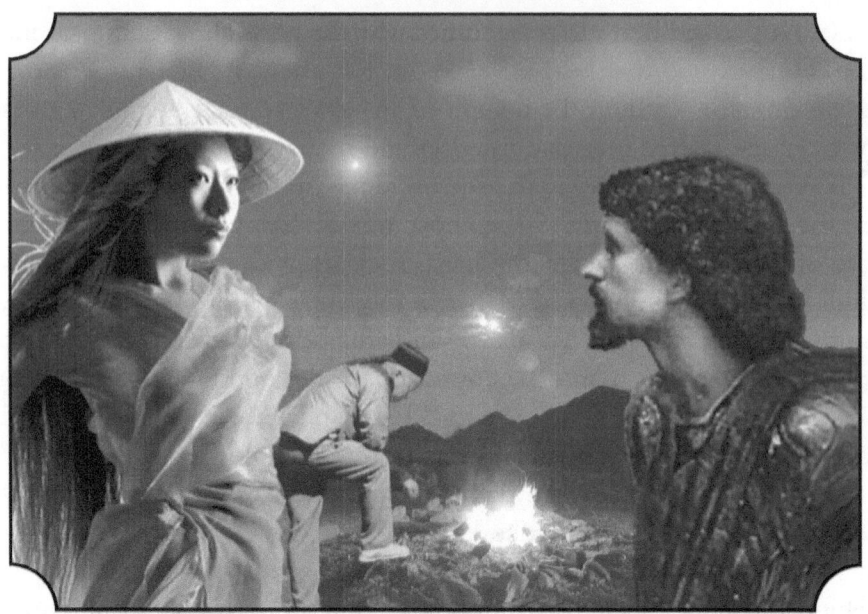

Scylla to the campfire. "Since we don't know how she was changed from monster to woman before we even found her," he said, "we might never discover a way to help her. And without an antidote, she may be lost."

"Maybe the monster part of the first spell just wore off," Quan speculated. "And maybe this part will stop too."

"I might entertain that idea if the witch who cursed her was anyone but Circe," D'Molay said. "I don't know much about sorcery, but I imagine her spells are stronger than most. Besides, it's too much to be a coincidence that the spell wore off just as we are looking for her. Maybe Aavi managed to change her back... I don't know. Maybe we'll never know."

Scylla twisted away from Mazu's touch. "She's waking up," the goddess said. Scylla opened her eyes, blinked several times, and tried to sit up.

"I'm tied. Why am I tied?"

"You turned wild," D'Molay told her. "How do you feel now?"

"Wild? What do you mean? I went to sleep, and - " Scylla's eyes darted from face to face. "I don't remember anything else."

"There's little to tell," Mazu said patting her hand in comfort. "You led D'Molay on a merry race and wrestled a bit with Quan."

Scylla's face flushed and she tried to hide her embarrassment by tilting her head down to look at her bound hands. "I'm sorry. I don't know what happened. Will you untie me?"

D'Molay gave her a hard look. "I honestly don't want to. If this happens again, you might not be caught as easily."

Scylla spent the night in her bonds, dreaming of the freedom of monsters.

An hour before dawn, D'Molay and the others resumed their journey. This time, Scylla rode with D'Molay, one wrist securely tethered to a rope around the tracker's waist. It wasn't the safest way to travel; if she jumped from the camel he was sure to be pulled with her. But it was easier to convey her as a prisoner than to watch her every moment along the way.

Scylla hadn't said much after her 'wild' episode; neither had Quan. D'Molay was grateful for the awkward silence between them. He was content to focus on completing the trip safely. The lack of chatter helped his concentration considerably.

Again with Aavi's whispered warnings, D'Molay was able to guide them safely past giant scorpions, a wild tribe of minotaurs, and away from the pyramid of an angry wizard-priest. They moved efficiently and passed the ruins of the naga without incident. As they left that place, Quan's tongue finally loosened.

"I'm glad to watch this realm disappear behind us," he said. "How much farther is it to the coast?"

"Half a day if we avoid more delays," D'Molay answered. He turned to address Scylla, wondering if the woman was feeling any the worse from her feral malady. "How are you doing?"

"I'm fine," she said flatly. "I haven't had the slightest urge to chew on you."

"Ah, you had to mention chewing; riding makes me hungrier than sailing," Quan lamented, rubbing his stomach.

"Eat some dried fish from your pack," D'Molay said. "We aren't stopping now, there's too much danger." He urged his camel to pick up the pace. Scylla's hand touched his shoulder.

"Wait," she said. "I'm hungry too."

D'Molay turned their camel back, angling toward Quan's. "Hand her some fish," he commanded. Quan managed to dig out a portion in time to place it in Scylla's hand as D'Molay rode by, keeping their mount on the move. D'Molay could hear Scylla ripping into the fish with her teeth as they continued on. He tried not to think about what her teeth might do to the back of his neck if the madness struck again.

"This is where we must turn to the west," Mazu announced. "Bast told me the secret of another gate. We must ride to the river."

"Whatever you say," D'Molay said. That at least sounded better than endless tracking across the desert. *Well at least now I know what they must have been talking about in secret.*

Much to his satisfaction, the rest of their ride was uneventful. They were treated to the sight of several bizarre but harmless creatures when they stopped at a waterhole. These were rabbit-like animals that sported feathery ears set upon almost human faces. D'Molay tossed a bit of fish to one, wondering if it had once been a man or woman. It grabbed the tidbit, running in circles with it playfully as the others gave chase, like a puppy with a bone. Its antics seemed so innocent he then fancied the animal might be a transformed child, but he would never be able to confirm that. The creatures were just one of many secrets in this realm of forgotten things.

The day's heat was strong upon them when they came in sight of the river. D'Molay speculated it was the Heavenly Nile, a great river that divided Egyptos from Afrik. He didn't realize it also extended into the Lost Realm. Ancient pilings of an abandoned pier stood straight ahead of them. Something was tied to one.

"Is that a boat?" D'Molay asked, squinting into the sun.

"It should be," Mazu said. "Bast promised she would make one available for us."

They rode in for a better look. It was indeed a boat, but it wasn't the most interesting thing at the old pier. A tremendous giant crab squatted on the shore. Its shell was bluish green, its claws, legs, and mouth parts mottled yellow-brown. The crab's claws fidgeted, opening and closing as the riders came closer.

"Look at that Pincher!" Quan exclaimed, calling the crustacean by the slang term used by many fishermen of Mazu's realm. "If we catch it, we can eat for days!"

"You need to look closer," Mazu suggested. "I think you will find it bears the same mark as the boat's sail."

"I see it," Scylla said, craning around D'Molay's shoulder. "A white symbol."

D'Molay sought what Scylla described. There it was, on the crab's right claw, a hieroglyph. It wasn't Bast's symbol, or Sekhmet's. Yet it looked familiar to D'Molay. As he tried to remember, he was struck by the real-

ization that the last time he had laid eyes on such a mark had been in his mortal lifetime. A recollection of interrogating an English alchemist brought the image of the glyph to sharp focus in his mind's eye. It had graced the cover of a forbidden book D'Molay had come to burn. Then, he had little interest in the tome's contents. Now, his time in the realms of the gods had allowed his mind to open to subjects once forbidden.

"Does anyone know what that symbol means?" D'Molay asked.

"Does anyone here look Egyptian?" Quan jabbed, spurring Mazu and Scylla to laugh. D'Molay was dissatisfied to have no answer, but let the remark pass for it seemed to lighten the mood.

They approached the boat and the crab cautiously. Once they were within ten feet of it, the creature's eyestalks flexed toward them and froze for a moment, as though it was studying them. Apparently satisfied with what it saw, the crab turned away and scuttled into the water, its shell quickly disappearing beneath the surface.

"It was guarding the boat for us," D'Molay said. "Another favor from the cats. I am truly in their debt."

Chapter 26

The Boat and a Mare

Quan was the first one off his camel. He hustled over to the small ship and began to inspect it. D'Molay half-listened to his commentary about the state of the boat's equipment and provisions as he and Scylla dismounted together. He glanced at the rope connecting them, annoyed at how it was restricting his actions now that he had something to do besides guide a camel. Scylla noticed him glaring at the rope which belted her to him.

"You might as well let me loose once we sail," she said. "I can't run across water."

"But I'm betting you can swim," D'Molay countered, the woman's recent past as a water creature not forgotten. Mazu cleared her throat.

"Release her. I will take responsibility for retrieving anything that goes overboard."

D'Molay reached for his knife and snipped the rope connecting them. "Good. That means I can get some sleep."

"Did you not rest last night?" Mazu asked. D'Molay noted the quizzical expression on her face and knew she had indeed observed him sleeping, for in truth he had managed to rest many hours despite the tension of Scylla's fit.

"Not well," he fibbed. "And I want to be sharp when we get back to Glaucus. I'm of little use as a sailor anyway."

"That's true," Quan said, extending a hand to help Scylla climb into the boat. "He's more like cargo."

"Then this cargo is going into the back," D'Molay declared, "where it's dark and quiet."

He boarded, brushing past Scylla who stood awkwardly on deck as Quan bustled about at Mazu's bidding. But the woman and her problems were of minor interest to him at the moment. She'd been trouble enough, and he needed a break. D'Molay made his way to one of the compartments just below the stern and found a comfortable spot against a short stack of grain sacks to rest in. He removed his cloak and brushed some of the desert grime from his shirt sleeves and trousers, wondering what disheveled state his hair and beard were in. He ran his hands over his head and face to smooth them down, just in case he had a visitor.

"Aavi," he whispered, "I'm alone now. Please come out."

D'Molay sat as still as possible, the sounds of his own nervous breathing mixing with the noises of footsteps on the deck above his head. As the

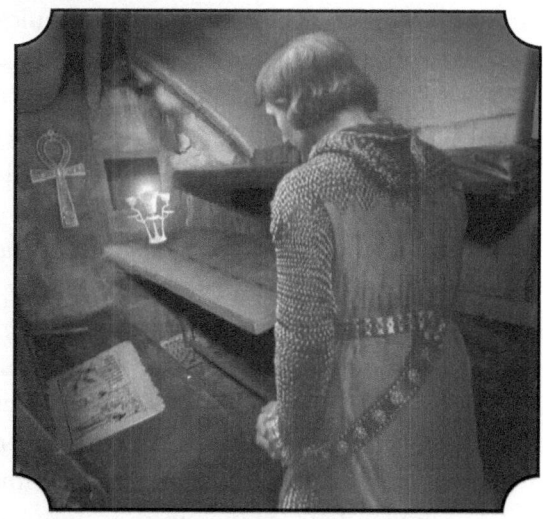

minutes passed, he continued to meditate and pray for her to appear. He had so many unanswered questions he wanted to ask her. With no sign of her, he wondered whether he had made a mistake in isolating himself in a dark place. D'Molay's mouth twisted in a sardonic grin as he surveyed the eerie shapes of hanging ropes and nets that seemed to hold up the shadows. Perhaps this place was better fit for meeting a devil than an angel.

The ship began to move. He felt it bank and turn. He heard the women's voices relax into muted conversation and the dull snap of the sails in the wind. The drone of it made him drowsy. But although that had been his excuse, he had not isolated himself in order to sleep. He roused himself, focusing on finding some way to interact with Aavi.

A scraping noise drew his attention upward. Quan was doing something on deck again, and D'Molay was momentarily irritated by the interruption. Then the room was suddenly illuminated by sunlight. D'Molay blinked up at a gridded hatch in the deck above his head. It must have been covered by a cancas that Quan had just removed for some purpose. Light slotted down into the compartment, motes of golden dust swimming in their space. Immediately, old teachings about expectant faith swelled in D'Molay's heart. He peered into the warm light and yearned for something to happen.

One small fleck of dust glittered. It drifted into another, causing it to sparkle just as brightly when they collided. D'Molay watched in breathless anticipation as the particles infected their neighbors with splendor. When a great many of them had taken on this glory, they began to vibrate and coalesce. The sparkling, delicate mass stretched and began to take on a human shape. D'Molay's heart leapt in his chest.

"Aavi?"

As the exclamation left his lips, a loud, distressed squall from one of the camels, followed by a yell from Quan, intruded on his wondrous interlude. This initial interruption was quickly enhanced by a feral, feminine screech and the thump of the butt of Mazu's staff on the deck. D'Molay joined in the ruckus with a vicious snarl of his own as the racket broke whatever spell the sunlight had tried to weave for him. The flecks of dust lost their sparkle and drifted apart; D'Molay surged to his feet and rushed out of the compartment.

"What in the nine levels of Hell is this?" he shouted as he emerged to see Mazu standing by a bleeding camel, offset by a struggling, feral Scylla whom Quan was restraining, both arms wrapped tightly around her from behind.

"The wild has taken her again," Mazu said.

"Don't bite the animals!" Quan was lecturing the thrashing girl. She flailed her head from side to side, baring her teeth and trying to reach any available part of Quan's body with her mouth. "Ahh, stop biting!"

"Enough!" D'Molay bellowed, furious. He had been so close to seeing Aavi and his chance had been ruined. It took all his restraint not to charge Quan and Scylla and throw both of them overboard. "I've had enough of this! Tie her up and sit on her until we get back to the City. I don't care if she eats half of you on the way."

Quan glared at D'Molay, clearly about to argue and complain to Mazu about his demands. Scylla went limp in his arms and started to weep, the fit passing.

"Quan, take her to the bow and do as he said, for now," Mazu said. As Quan guided Scylla to the other end of the boat, Mazu turned and inspected the wound on the camel's ear. The blood Scylla had drawn was already clotting. "This is nothing serious," she determined. "But I am concerned about what ails you, D'Molay."

"Which blight in particular?" he asked scathingly. "This mission, that crazy girl, or Quan?" D'Molay released an exasperated sigh, unable to suppress the resentment building up in his core. His companions seemed to do nothing but prevent him from making the breakthrough that he knew would reunite him with Aavi. "Do you know what they interrupted? She was coming back to me, she was almost here."

"D'Molay - "

"No! I'm not going to be talked out of it again." He met Mazu's eyes squarely, determined not to back down in his conviction. She returned his look firmly, equally secure in her assessment of his mental state.

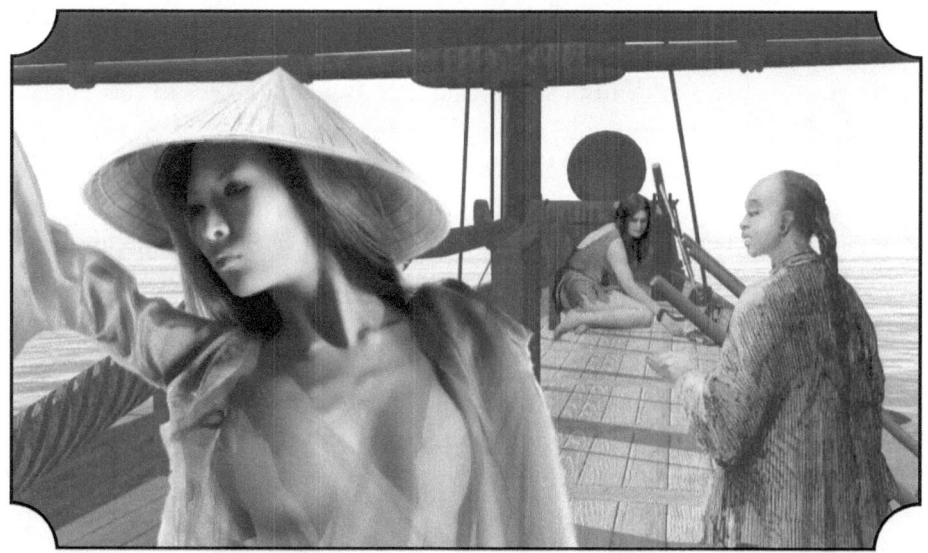

"Then I'll say only this. Beware of being tricked by seeing what you wish to see."

D'Molay glanced toward the other end of the boat, where Quan sat with a contrite Scylla, doing his best to cheer her up even as he tied her. "I know a hundred different knots," he was bragging. "See this one? It looks like a frog."

"Tie it tight," Scylla muttered. "I can't even feel the change coming. Stay away from me, for your own good."

Her desire for solitude matched D'Molay's. He retreated to the below-deck chamber hoping for another sign of Aavi. But like the deserts of the Lost Realm, the room gave him nothing but sun, dust, and loneliness.

<hr />

"There's so many people!" Tenh-Mer said to Sekhmet as they waited outside the Council Hall. She leaned in closer to Sekhmet as the crowd pushed past them to reach Ptah's display. Even though her goddess was about to make a speech, the spectators were more interested in the new model of the City that Ptah, who had designed and created many beautiful cities on Earth, was presenting as Sekhmet's signature public project should she be elected.

"I know," Sekhmet said, sliding an arm around Tenh-Mer to turn her away from a leering old priest who had come too close and was enchanted by her aura. "But this is very good. I need the support of the citizens. If they like me, they can influence their leaders to vote for me too."

Sekhmet let out a short self-deprecating laugh. "Besides, once I start speaking, the crowd will probably thin out."

Tenh-Mer had her doubts about that. From what she could see, everyone liked Sekhmet and would stay to hear her talk. Plus, there was a great deal of interest in the plan Ptah had devised to rebuild parts of the City that had fallen into disrepair, like the blocks of abandoned temples on the eastern side. Tenh-Mer longed to go look at the interesting tiny model of his ideas, and stood on her tiptoes in an attempt to see. But it was too far away, and Sekhmet would not allow her to go over to it until everyone else was done looking.

Sekhmet looked up to the sky, judging the time of day. "Come. Let's go to the podium before I forget what I planned to say."

"You'll win them over," Tenh-Mer said with confidence. "Your project is so much more fun than those other ones." She smiled brightly up at the goddess as the crowd parted to let them pass.

"I hope so," Sekhmet said. "But people don't always vote for good ideas."

Tenh-Mer found that statement very strange. "Why not?"

"Because they desire more the secret things they hold in their hearts."

Sekhmet and Tenh-Mer turned around at the sound of the new voice. It was one of the Olympians. He was winged, handsome, dark-haired, and as attractive to the crowd as Tenh-Mer was.

"Unfortunately, that is very true," Sekhmet said cautiously. "Aren't you Eros?" She'd seen this god in Zeus' company often during the campaign events.

"Yes. And you have my vote, and not just because Zeus is your sponsor."

"Thanks!" Tenh-Mer said brightly. "I'd vote too, but I'm not allowed." Eros looked down at her with an amused grin.

"Then perhaps I can vote twice," he joked. Tenh-Mer, not knowing this was impossible, nodded enthusiastically.

"May we speak at the podium?" Sekhmet suggested as the press of gawkers grew thick again. "Ptah's guards will give us room to breathe."

"Of course," Eros said, and they threaded through the crowd toward a squad of Egyptos guards, who parted their spears to let them ascend to a raised platform. Eros and Sekhmet settled on curule chairs to talk while they waited. Tenh-Mer wandered over to the edge of the stage, craning her neck toward Ptah's City model. She could see it a little better now, but it was still so far away.

"Your campaign promise to renew the City is proving to be popular," Eros said. "I think you'll secure most of the votes of the Pantheon

360

Leaders who have little land out in the realms. Not having to look out over blight from the windows of their embassies will be a positive for them."

Sekhmet nodded. "It was Ptah's idea, really, but I am fully behind it. He's a genius when it comes to architecture. Even craftsmen who don't care much for Egyptos in general respect his talents."

Eros tipped his left wing around Sekhmet, shielding them from any eavesdroppers. "Zeus is very pleased that you chose this project. He's wanted to clean out undesirables from those districts for years."

Sekhmet said nothing in response. She hadn't considered that consequence of rebuilding; the more she thought about it, the more uncomfortable she felt with those ramifications of her project. Eros pulled his wing back.

"Your approach will win," he went on. "Everyone's tired of hearing about law and order, like Lamasthu preaches. I saw all of the last war, and none of her rules protected Olympia. And Ceridwen's a good goddess, but there just aren't enough voters who care about rejuvenating the dead fringes of realms that no one even lives in anymore."

"You sound like Ptah," Sekhmet said, pushing doubts away. "I agree that keeping the City at its best is necessary to the eventual rebirth of our entire world."

"That's a great line," Eros smiled. "Use that in your speech." He looked up as the spears of the guards parted again and Ptah joined them. "Looks like your time has come. Good luck."

Eros stood up as Ptah drew near Sekhmet to give her some last-minute advice. He stepped over to the end of the platform where Tenh-Mer gazed longingly toward the display. His power to sense the yearnings of others made him smile when he realized what a simple thing Sekhmet's strange companion desired.

"I haven't seen it either," he said. "Shall we go together?"

Tenh-Mer already liked this god because he seemed so much like her, with wings and a body that everyone seemed to love. His invitation to do exactly what she wanted was completely irresistible. She happily took his outstretched hand and walked with him down the stairs, across the square, and over to the City model without even asking Sekhmet if she could go.

When they reached the table, Tenh-Mer let go of Eros' hand and tapped her fingers on edge of the transparent glass model's base. The model was a wonder. She could see into every tiny building. Each little room and balcony was detailed with doors and railings. Tenh-Mer imagined herself walking up the miniature stairways and sitting in front of the many hearths and fireplaces. She especially liked the spun glass trees and fountains that added a natural touch to the pristine streets.

"It's so pretty," she sighed. "I wish it could really be made of glass."

Eros laughed at this. "I think people need a little more privacy than that would provide," he said. "Although, they might behave better if we did it your way."

They walked around the table, pointing out more interesting details to each other. In the distance, Sekhmet was speaking, but neither really noticed.

"There's just one thing I wish this model had," Tenh-Mer said as they completed their circuit.

"What's that?"

"Secret tunnels! I was just in one and it was lots of fun," she said.

"Really? I know of a few. I use them in my work, you see," Eros said. "Sometimes I have to sneak into places and make couples fall in love." He smiled down at Tenh-Mer. "Which tunnel were you in?"

Tenh-Mer felt like she had found a kindred spirit. He even liked tunnels!

"It was under this stump in the woods by the Asian wall," she confided enthusiastically. "I followed a fairy through the tree and found all sorts of underground things. There were flowers and paths, and I bet lots more but I couldn't stay there very long."

Eros nodded. "I think I know the area. You're lucky the Celts didn't catch you. They don't like outsiders in their secret places."

"Really?" Tenh-Mer gently touched a spire of one of the miniature buildings with the tip of her finger. "Well, I wasn't the only one there who wasn't one of them," she said defensively. "You won't tell Sekhmet I broke a rule, will you?"

Eros shook his head. "Not if you tell me who else you saw down there," he bargained. Gossip was fuel to many of the fires he started, and he rarely passed up a chance to collect it.

Tenh-Mer thought for a moment then gave her answer. "It was Shiva and Ceridwen," she shared. "They're such important gods they probably had permission to be there, right?"

Eros raised an eyebrow. "That depends on what they were doing there."

"Oh, I can tell you that," Tenh-Mer grinned, and Eros stooped over so that she could whisper into his ear. A smile crossed his face as he realized how valuable the information so innocently shared would be.

"Well, good for them," he said. "Now you'd better sneak back over to the stage before Sekhmet finishes her speech. I have to go see Zeus."

"Okay," Tenh-Mer said as she departed with a wave. "Thanks!"

Eros returned her wave. After one last look at Ptah's model he went directly to Zeus to share this tidbit of extremely interesting news.

━━━◦❧◦━━━

"*D*agda, ye old rogue, come out and see what I've brought." As her shout died away, Ceridwen gave the reins of the spirited horse another tug to make sure it knew she was in charge. She wished that she had a similar rope attached to Dagda, the head of the Celts. She knew he was lounging somewhere in the forest of their pantheon's district in the City, for she'd seen him swaggering off in the middle of her speech in the company of two tribal brutes rolling a barrel of whiskey. Normally, she'd leave him to his revels, but she was anxious to get rid of the gift she'd accepted from the Greek.

It was a magnificent mare, black as pitch with a fine mane that stirred in the wind like wheat before harvest. The horse was brave, too, seeming completely at home in the fae woods despite the many glowing eyes peer-

ing at it from the bushes and the strange sounds barking intermittently from the trees. Ceridwen was tempted to ride the mare, but the horse was not hers to enjoy.

"Dagda, by Cernunnos' horns, don't keep me waiting all day!"

The bushes ahead parted and two men draped in clannish colors thrashed out of the green. "Aye, woman, 'e's not deaf. Come with us," one of them slurred. The other executed a sloppy bow.

"You're drunk, Culloon," the bower said. "Pull in your tongue before the lady hexes you."

Ceridwen watched impatiently as that one straightened, brushed twigs and leaves from his attire, and adjusted his cocked cap. His motions made her question the state of her own dress. She had not expected to be delivering an animal when she donned a pretty gown designed to please the eyes of the Pantheon leaders. She hoped to inspire some of them to dream lustfully of a true female rather than a cat or a green goblin, giving her an advantage over Sekhmet and Lamasthu. After he finished setting his clothing to rights, the fussier man pulled a large branch aside and gestured for her to enter the trees. As she and the horse set off, Ceridwen took care not to snag her dress or step into anything unpleasant on the ground. A narrow but well trod path stretched out before her and she followed it as her sorry escorts tromped noisily behind.

"By the old man's staff," came the voice of the one called Culloon, "I canna say I've ever seen such fine hindquarters." Culloon fell into muffled laughter. "Eh, Donnel?"

"Shut it, ye gom," Donnel growled. Ceridwen heard the sounds of a few lackluster shoves and punches being thrown between the hooligans. She wheeled around, catching both of them in mid-swing.

"Are ye askin' to be covered in toad warts, because I'd be happy to oblige," she said. The men saw the fire in her eyes and stepped away from one another like boys confronted by their schoolmaster. "And you," she added, singling out Culloon, "had best convince me your opinion about fine form was directed toward this horse."

Culloon's jaw went slack and he tipped his head to one side, the whiskey fog impeding his sense. For his part, Donnel slowly turned and edged away from both of them. "I'll be goin' then," he said.

Culloon was saved from Ceridwen's wrath by the appearance of Dagda, who appeared, harp in hand. As the tone of the note that had transported him into their midst faded, he gruffly greeted Ceridwen. "Ah. Tis our nominee."

While his companions showed the bite of the whiskey, Dagda himself was sober as a widow. He turned a canny eye to the horse. "Speech over, is it? Or is this a talking horse?"

Dagda was big, broad-shouldered and tall. With his life-and-death bringing staff in one hand and his harp of command in the other, there was never a doubt of his dominance among the Celts. Such power allowed him to neglect the other trappings of a ruler. He was clad in no more style than his jacks, and an argument could be made that he was dressed even worse. His rough-woven tunic hung unevenly, raveling, above his dirty knees. The garment was made up of irregular, multicolored patches of wool and was cinched to his protruding belly with a wide leather belt, its many worn buckle holes attesting to the ups and downs of Dagda's weight. Ceridwen felt a brief flare of sympathy for the horse, if it was destined to carry him.

"It's said naught to me," Ceridwen said. "But ask it what you will. It's your horse."

"My horse?" Dagda asked, stepping up for a closer look at the mare. "Never seen it before. You'd best be explaining why you brought it."

Ceridwen handed Dagda the reins. "Who else could bring it? Only our people can enter here, so not anyone would be riding in on it, would 'e?"

"She's a pretty one," Dagda said with a glint in his eye. "Did you steal it? Is this a taste of the loot ye'll bring me when you're on that Council?"

"Aye," Ceridwen said sarcastically. "Those City people are all a-clamor to elect a horse thief to rule them who'll funnel their gold straight to you and the leprechauns."

Dagda laughed. "As they should be. 'twould be an improvement over what they have now. But if it's not tribute, how come we by it?" He patted the mare on the muzzle and lifted her lip for a glimpse of her teeth.

"There was a chariot race and the two drivers agreed that the loser had to give you his finest horse in memory of Cú Chulainn," Ceridwen said. "Seems neither of them ever got true satisfaction of the other. The one who lost one race would just win his wager back in the next. So they wanted the prize to go somewhere it couldn't be retrieved."

Dagda nodded his approval. "Chariot racers, eh? Was it the Egyptians or the Babylonians?"

"Must have been the Olympians, seein' as their messenger god, Hermes, delivered her," Ceridwen said.

Dagda's hand froze on the mare's bit.

"You took a horse . . . from a Greek?" Dagda muttered a curse under his breath and stepped back. "How foolish are ye? Haven't you heard the story of Troy?"

Ceridwen put her hands stubbornly on her hips. "Seriously, old man. What's going to come out of her belly? An army of pixies? If the beast was enchanted, I'd know. Just take her and count yourself lucky for it."

The mare tossed her head and pawed at the ground as if she was insulted by the slur on her character. Dagda circled her slowly, finally convincing himself that the animal was merely that, not some special construct meant to trick him. "I'll see how she runs," he conceded. "Culloon! Take charge of her."

Culloon hustled to the mare and grabbed at her bridle to lead her away. As his fingers fumbled over the brow band, they dislodged a small piece of parchment that had been tucked under it, hidden beneath the horse's forelock. The paper fluttered through the air and landed near Ceridwen's feet. She stooped to pick it up and read the writing upon it. She paled, her breath catching in her throat. The text told everything about her affair with Shiva.

"What's turned you so quare?" drunken Culloon asked, drawing Dagda's attention.

"Well? Answer." Dagda waited for less than a breath before he strode over and grabbed for the paper. Ceridwen spun away before he could seize it. Donnel casually placed himself in her way, sensing that she was about to bolt.

"It's nothing," she said desperately, even though she knew there was no way to keep the revelation on the note from Dagda now. She closed her eyes and wished she could plug her ears, but when the song of his

366

harp sounded a moment later she was forced to submit to its compulsion. Ceridwen turned and held the paper out to the lord of her realm, who plucked it from her fingers as deftly as he stroked the strings of his instrument. She felt like crying as Dagda read the message.

"So it's not the Greeks I should have been worried about," he said darkly, fixing her with a baleful eye. "If this is true, if you brought an outsider into our secret places, if you broke our first law - "

Ceridwen struggled for words to defend herself. Dagda's accusations were justified, which made them hard to refute.

"Our first law is wrong!" she blurted out. "Why shouldn't we be more open? The other realms are. It's something I could help us work toward when I'm elected."

The words hung like the hand of death between them, cold and unstoppable.

"I'll take on as if I didn't hear what you just said." Dagda crumpled the parchment in his fist. "But beyond that indulgence, I'll give you no more opportunity to undermine me. This Council nonsense ends here."

"Please, Dagda, I - "

He assaulted his harp with a forceful hand, drawing from it a dissonant chord. A veil of yellow energy enveloped Ceridwen. She struggled, pushing against the magical container that now imprisoned her like a roomy cocoon. The walls expanded like thin rubber under her palms, but she could not tear her way out. Through the golden barrier she could see Dagda and his men outside her prison.

"No, don't do this!" she pleaded, hoping one of them would listen. But Dagda struck another chord and she and her prison began to sink into the ground. "Please, Dagda, stop it!"

"Stop crying, no harm will come to ye. I'll set you free after I settle things with your blue paramour," he said. "I'll do my best to remember where I put you." Dagda stood over her magical cell, watching as it disappeared completely into the ground and her pleas could no longer be heard. He turned to his men. "Well, boys, is there whiskey left? Drink is good for forgetting women, eh?"

Culloon agreed enthusiastically. "Aye, there's still a wash in the barrel."

"Then let's to it, man," Dagda said. "Then we'll see what this horse can do." Culloon, Dagda, and the mare headed back into the wood. Donnel lingered. He stepped over to drop a copper coin to mark the spot where Ceridwen had been entombed.

"Just in case he does forget you, miss," he said.

❧⚓❧

*T*he last of the complaints and shouts died down as the Council Hall guards ushered the last group of Pantheon leaders out and shut the doors behind them. The evening's meeting had been loud and disruptive as the mass reaction to Ceridwen's withdrawal from the election sparked talk of conspiracy and injustice. Quetzalcoatl had listened carefully to the gods' heated opinions, while Zeus argued with the more emotionally stirred speakers for his own amusement. Shiva had merely sat, motionless, staring morosely at a particular spot on the wall throughout the proceedings.

"So here we are," Zeus said as servants righted several overturned tables and chairs while his personal attendant brought up a tray holding three goblets of nectar. "We're down to two candidates. And the Celts are refusing to vote at all. Certainly changes the field, eh?"

Shiva finally shook off his dour silence. "I maintain that Dagda's act is one of kidnapping and thus forbidden under the rules of election," he said. "I fully believe that Ceridwen is being held against her will."

"But not by a competing faction, Shiva." Quetzalcoatl rose from his seat and adjusted one of his bracelets thoughtfully before accepting his cup of life water. "She is Dagda's subject, and bound to whatever rules he chooses to make for his people. Her removal isn't illegal. Though clearly for you, it is inconvenient."

Zeus muffled a laugh at the way Quetzalcoatl danced around Shiva's dalliance with the goddess. He leaned over and nudged Shiva. "Cheer up, my friend. The harder they are to get, the sweeter they are to have."

Quetzalcoatl turned on his heel and looked upon Zeus and Shiva much like a stern father. "This division among the factions will only lead to increased distrust and more incidents like our last war," he lectured. "We've made a show for . . . what do you Greeks call it? Democracy? But we need to decide this election now and take the steps needed to pass our plan."

"Since when did we have a shared plan?" Zeus took a drink of nectar to steel himself. So far he'd been able to keep up the act that he'd had nothing to do with Ceridwen's fall, but Quetzalcoatl had a knack for throwing him off his guard. "What exactly do you want us to do?" he asked.

Quetzalcoatl held out his own cup and lightly gestured to it with his free hand. "Have you already forgotten our conversation about the City's nectar supply?"

"What conversation was that?" Shiva asked with a bite in his voice. "I was not party to it."

"Merely my inquiry to Zeus about current conditions within Olympia," Quetzalcoatl said. "As we all know, that flood wiped out the production site of a major supplier of nectar to the realms. Zeus, has there been any more news of Circe?"

Zeus did not enjoy the feeling of being symbolically backed into a corner and forced to confirm a weakness in his power base. He did his best to brush off the seriousness of losing Circe's factory. "There is nothing more to report. Olympia is producing no nectar at this time. Though we have an ample supply stockpiled," he muttered.

Shiva turned on Zeus. "And why wasn't this brought up at the meeting? Lack of nectar is more important than Dagda's ridiculous decrees about free association."

Zeus shrugged. "Scandals are more entertaining to expose."

"And some like exposing them," Shiva obliquely accused. "I'll track down who and how in due time."

"I'm sure Ceridwen can explain all of it," Zeus said with mock innocence. "But you might have to wait quite a while to hear from her."

Quetzalcoatl sensed that Shiva and Zeus were on the verge of a lengthy dispute. He stepped in to forestall one. "As we all agree, this nectar problem must be solved. I have discussed it at length with Lamasthu and she has promised that Babylos will step up its production. Of course, they expect to be compensated."

"With votes?" Shiva set his cup of life water aside, finding it suddenly distasteful. "I see where this is going. You want us to change our factions' minds."

"Yours will have to, Shiva, since they no longer have their candidate," Quetzalcoatl pointed out.

"But supporting Babylos? What else might they demand in return?" Shiva asked.

Quetzalcoatl was quiet for a moment as he watched the servants continue their duties, picking up litter from the floor and wiping layers of handprints from railings and door knobs. "If we are careful, and rule well," he said, "we can guide the City so that issues which Babylos hopes to exploit do not come before us for a vote, and in that way, avoid any repayment of our debt." He spread his arms open in a gesture of unity. "This means the three of us will have to work together as a unit. And that unity," he added, "must begin at once."

Shiva sighed and nodded his assent. "I will agree to this. If we allow the realms to start fighting over nectar, we will lose any shred of control the Council has. There is no option. We must have peace at any cost."

Quetzalcoatl turned to the Olympian. "Zeus?"

"Why should I concede to you?" he challenged. "I have a strong candidate. Why don't we let the election play out and see who wins?"

"We could do that. And Sekhmet might win. But why would you want to lock your realm into a partnership with Egyptos, when her defeat would allow you to look like an ally without the need to move forward as one?"

Zeus drummed his fingers on the arm of his chair, stalling. He admired Quetzalcoatl's cleverness, but hated when it turned his own plans upside down.

"Well, that would take care of an objectionable alliance." Zeus stood and stretched. "Ending it will please Hera, that's certain, and I can't say I'll miss listening to her complaints. But I'm tired of all this arm-twisting.

How many votes must we turn?"

Quetzalcoatl waved to one of his priests who had been standing silently against the wall during the discussion. He hurried forward and bowed to all three of the deities. "This scribe has a list of all the factions. Let's study it and determine the quickest path to Lamasthu's victory."

Shiva again raised his goblet to his lips. "This still feels unsavory to me," he said, after a sip. Nonetheless, he joined Zeus and Quetzalcoatl as they followed the priest to a table and stood around the parchment he laid upon it.

"There is no crime here," Quetzalcoatl insisted. "Votes will still be cast and counted."

"And what matters who wins when our block will do the ruling in the end?" Zeus rationalized. "Let's settle this quickly, Shiva, and then I'll introduce you to some nymphs who will distract you from the absent Ceridwen, eh?"

Shiva glared back at him and said nothing.

Zeus shrugged. "No? Fine. Now Quetzalcoatl, I'm not going to give you all my votes. I'd rather go to one of Chloris' flower shows than go back to the Afrik leaders and ask them to change their votes. It was too much expense and trouble getting them to agree on Sekhmet in the first place."

Quetzalcoatl and Zeus bent over the tally sheet and began to discuss the easiest factions to persuade. Shiva stood by but only gave his opinion if directly asked, and then, tersely.

"There," Zeus said after he had insisted on some changes to a new list Quetzalcoatl had worked out. "That arrangement will make the results close. We don't want Lamasthu to feel she can lord it over us after achieving an easy victory."

Quetzalcoatl nodded favorably. "You impress me, Zeus. You're showing more of a talent for political compromise than when you first joined the Council."

"Is that what it is? I thought it was self-interest," Zeus grinned.

"Same thing," Quetzalcoatl confirmed.

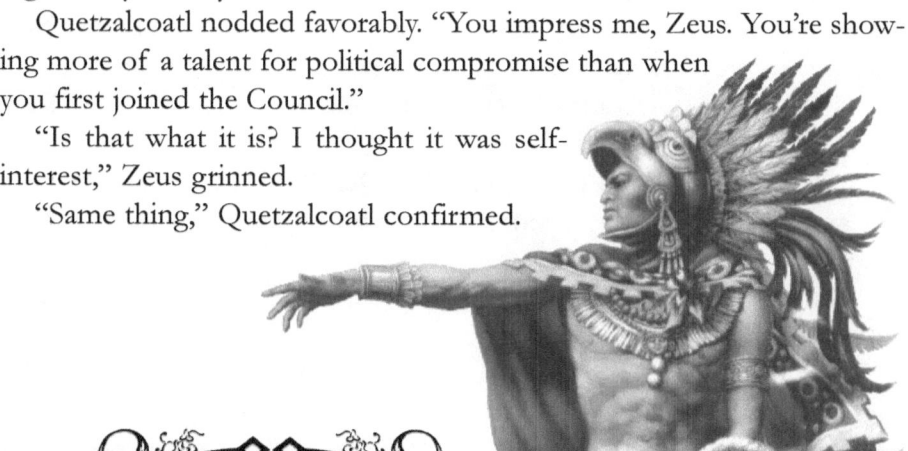

Chapter 27

A Great Deal of Trouble

azu resisted casting another glance toward the small hold of the boat. She wondered if D'Molay was still angry, if he was falling again into depression over Aavi, or if he was simply asleep. But in the end, she left her curiosity unfed. His state of mind was irrelevant to accomplishing the next step of their journey. That success or failure was entirely up to her. She knew her time had come when Quan began to fuss about the sails.

"What kind of a wind is this?" he asked. "First it blows north, then south, then north again."

Mazu could feel the result of the strange air currents as she stood and moved toward the prow of the boat. The craft would lurch forward then slide back. She had to steady herself with her staff as she took up a position near the prow and prepared to say the words that Hetepheres had revealed to her when she had met behind closed doors with the sphinx and Bast.

"Let your sails do as they wish," she told Quan. "They won't be filled by these winds. We have reached another gate. Get my barrels ready."

Quan cast a doubtful look at the rigging, but fully trusting Mazu he let go of the lines and pulled two barrels out from the pile of supplies that was lashed to the deck. Prying off their lids, he checked to make sure they were empty and free of holes or cracks. "These are fine barrels," he said.

"And if I am quick and clever enough, they again will hide me from Quetzalcoatl and his spies."

Scylla, watching from the blanket that Quan had solicitously arranged for her to relax on after suffering her last fit, spoke up for the first time since that incident.

"Why hide now? We've been traveling in the open for days," she pointed out. "And how can you fit - ?"

Mazu held up her left hand, almost as if she was testing the wind. "My enemy had no power to touch me in the realm we are leaving," she explained, looking back over her shoulder at Scylla. "But if I am seen in the one we enter, he can do as he wishes. Quan, bring the containers closer."

The servant quickly rolled the barrels so close to Mazu that they brushed against her robes. Upending them, he stood ready with one barrel lid in each hand. Scylla suppressed a giggle at his focused posture. He looked like a musician intent on clashing two cymbals together at precisely the right moment.

The boat suddenly stopped, as if it had butted against an invisible obstacle. Mazu pressed out with her extended hand. Bright white sparks danced upon her upraised fingertips. She began speaking the pass phrase. Two or three words into it, an utter silence fell upon them. Scylla could no longer hear the snap of the sails or the slosh of the water. She couldn't even hear herself breathe. She watched Mazu closely. With nothing for her ears to process, her eyes craved revelation. Mazu's lips moved as

she continued to speak the language that would allow the boat through the gate. It was a clever spell, Scylla realized, one that kept its secret words from being overheard. A large archway of white sparkling air appeared, spanning the water a short distance away. The boat was drawn toward it. She watched Quan begin to gesture frantically at Mazu to do something, but Mazu shook her head and did nothing until the boat had completely passed through the magical archway. Then, Scylla was treated to the sight of the goddess changing into a liquid version of herself which she somehow divided and poured into the two barrels.

"Oh," Scylla voiced as her question about Mazu's odd choice of a hiding place was answered. That little word seemed loud now that the silence had left them and the normal sounds of the water and wind had returned.

"I hope you were quick enough," Quan said to the barrels, securing their lids and tapping them shut. He looked toward the sky, frowning when he noticed how many clouds there were.

"Is something wrong?" Scylla asked, joining him in scrutinizing the sky. "What are you looking for?"

"Mazu's enemy is the Feathered Serpent. Clouds like those could hide him."

Scylla saw nothing unusual about the sky. She couldn't pick out a single cloud that had any recognizable shape to it, let alone one that resembled a snake or a bird. Eventually Quan also gave up his examination of the atmosphere and concentrated on piloting the boat. Watching him, she was impressed at his endurance. She felt drained; even D'Molay was probably sleeping. This man, however, seemed to have endless energy. His boasts about being blessed by Mazu had truth behind them. Scylla lay down, curling an arm under her head for a pillow.

Most of a calm hour passed as Scylla dozed lightly, aware of fragments of fleeting dreams. Sometimes she was swimming.

<hr>

*T*he message was relayed from one sky dragon to the next, all the way to Quetzalcoatl himself, who was informed as he waited for the final speeches of the two remaining candidates for Konohana's Council slot to begin. He smiled as a tiny air snake hissed word of a brief Mazu sighting on a boat emerging from one of the Lost Realm's sea gates. Quetzalcoatl motioned for his high priest, Topiltzin, to ascend the Council dais and attend him. Topiltzin athletically ran up the stairs and dropped to a bow before the Feathered Serpent. Quetzalcoatl commanded him to come closer and began whispering into the priest's ear.

Zeus, who always fell quickly into boredom while waiting for Council business to begin, took the arrival of the priest as an opportunity for conversation. "He's a quick one, but no Hermes," Zeus said, leaning over the right arm of his chair toward Quetzalcoatl. "Is he part beast to move with such speed?" Quetzalcoatl ignored his question and continued to instruct his man, which only made Zeus more determined to chat. "Well, I see now that he's a mere man. But I suppose we'll have to get used to sharing the Council Hall with monsters. What exactly is Lamasthu anyway? Did she always have claws that long? And I swear she used to have pretty legs." Zeus slouched to the other side of his chair, leaning over to tap Shiva on the shoulder. "Didn't she used to have pretty legs?"

Shiva was visibly irritated with the entire scene around him, especially

Zeus. "Ask a Babylonian, Zeus. I don't know. Quetzalcoatl," he pressed, "can we begin? Let's get this over with."

Quetzalcoatl held up a hand to forestall the start of the meeting for a moment as he finished his instructions to Topiltzin. "Have it drawn exactly as I described, and delivered immediately," Zeus heard him say. "Go!"

"Draw what? Where's he running off too?" Zeus asked suspiciously. "Do you have a surprise to spring upon us at the last minute?"

"Zeus, I can tell you in complete honesty that my priest's business has nothing to do with filling our vacancy. And Shiva is right, we should move forward on our duty."

"He's just eager to move past his scandal," Zeus laughed. "For once, it's not me in disgrace. What a novel feeling."

Shaking his head in annoyance, Quetzalcoatl rose and moved to stand next to the empty place on the dais that awaited Konohana's successor. A Council attendant saw that the ruling gods were ready to call the assembly to order and rang a bell suspended from the heights of the hall, twice.

Sekhmet's ears twitched at the sound of the sharp tones. Despite feeling like she was a piece of cheese on display for a mob of hungry rats, she was not nervous. Ptah, Horus, and Nuit had counseled her well. Her visits to the Pantheon leaders had been pleasant, and her central theme of rebuilding the City had been well received. For this last phase of the campaign, she had been thoroughly coached on what to expect, but hadn't prepared a formal speech. Who could know what the right or wrong thing to say would be? She just had to win, it was as simple as that. If Set and his faction were ever to be punished, her tail needed to be on that Council seat. Sekhmet squared her shoulders and stood a little taller at the thought of victory.

Her demeanor stood in stark contrast to that of the other candidate. Lamasthu leaned against a pillar with the fluid cling of hot wax against a candle. She looked sleepy and indolent, her tentacles curling and flexing erotically as if she was tempting the audience to join her in a sickly embrace.

In turn, Quetzalcoatl, Shiva, and Zeus nodded to the hall's chief attendant who then bellowed out, "The candidates for Council shall speak!" Sekhmet immediately strode toward Konohana's vacant chair, a bold move that was met with murmurs of approval from the audience. When she dared to wave Quetzalcoatl out of the way, Zeus slapped the arm of his chair with a hearty laugh. Quetzalcoatl managed to smile in a gentlemanly way and returned to his own place. Sekhmet looked out at the assembly and noted with satisfaction that she had caught the attention of most of the hall. She began to speak.

"Gods and Pantheon leaders. I, Sekhmet of Egyptos, stand for election to the Council. It is time for the realms to put aside their minor differences and work together to ensure that justice is done. Wars such as the recent conflict in Olympia are an unnecessary waste of life and power. Our willingness to squabble encourages villains to plot in our midst. We must be more open in our dealings with each other to prevent misunderstandings between realms. The pantheons have a duty to keep their secrets and traditions, of course, but to withhold knowledge of things that are a danger to all the realms is shortsighted and selfish."

Zeus shifted in his chair and Shiva folded his arms. Sekhmet held her breath, waiting for some verbal reaction to her words. It came as Quetzalcoatl issued a direct challenge to her speech.

"It sounds like you believe the current Council is not interested in maintaining order. You insinuate we turn a blind eye to those who work to undermine the peace. Tell us, Sekhmet, what you would have done differently during the last conflict. Perhaps you could have exercised some of this open communication you extol and warned the Council of the treasonous activities of your own son Set."

Sekhmet resisted showing her fangs. Somehow she had to appear against Set without playing into Quetzalcoatl's script that the Egyptos gods were always feuding. She decided to brush off the charge. "Had I known anything, I would have come to you. And if I am honored by appointment to this empty chair, I want the City to know that my ears and my mind will

remain open. If those in the realms truly believe we will listen, they will share their knowledge. We can solve the problems of decline in our lands and population. We can recover precious relics that have been stolen in past aggressions. We might even be able to revive our kinsmen who have faded." She took a step toward the audience, opening her arms in invitation. "Let us be true gods again, who stand undaunted by any challenge."

A hearty round of applause greeted her words. Sekhmet caught the eye of Ptah, who was watching from nearby. She wondered if he thought she had said enough to deflect Quetzalcoatl's attempt to smear her, if her choice to barely acknowledge his accusation was the right one. As the applause died down, the hall attendant called for the next candidate. Sekhmet considered not yielding her position until Lamasthu forced her to, but decided to move out of the way at once. She had plenty of time to clear the area as the Babylonian goddess seemed in no hurry to speak. Lamasthu stopped to offer respectful greetings to a number of gods in the

hall and even paused to check her appearance in the reflective surface of a polished brazier as she approached. When she finally took her place, she was silent for what seemed like a full minute.

"There. You have all had a good look at me," she began. "We Babylonians are rarely seen in these halls, so allow me to serve as an example of what gods from an ordered realm can be. My opponent, Sekhmet of Egyptos, has spoken of justice and peace. These are things that my people have always valued and continue to encourage. You do not hear of wars in Babylonia, for our vigilance prevents invasion. You do not hear of Babylonian factions fighting each other like the cats and dogs of Egyptos, for family means something to us. You do not hear rumors of ill-doings by high ranking members of our pantheon, for we guard our honor scrupulously. We are known for lending our armies to the defense of the realms. We are known for trade and commerce, providing services that all the realms desire. We are known for our code of law."

Lamasthu displayed one of her tentacles, gazing at it with a thoughtful expression. "It is obvious that I am not as beautiful or soft as my opponent. I do not have a reputation for compromise. But has it not been a relaxation of standards that has allowed so many undesired incidents to occur? The lines between right and wrong are blurring. My opponent has even been tried by the Council in the past for crimes she did not commit. I am concerned that this experience would make her reluctant to indict. Why has she not mentioned the recent great crime in Olympia, the wanton destruction by flood of the Palace of Helios? I will make it my top priority to identify, apprehend, and punish the water god responsible. Perhaps Sekhmet is simply unaware of this event. I would hope her silence on the topic isn't due to a cat's well known fear of water."

Lamasthu's joke was greeted with good-natured laughter. She dramatically bowed her head and gazed at the floor until the levity died down. When she raised her head, her eyes burned with green fire, and the crowd's smiles turned to gasps of awe.

"Elect me to this post and you will be served by a goddess who is not afraid to use her strength to right what has gone wrong. I will wade through floodwaters, rivers of blood, or clouds of fire for this City. I am not here to secure political power that my realm clearly does not need. I do not need, nor will I use, this position to even old scores with family members. I will not waste the City's time and resources on chasing dreams of the past. And now, should the Council have questions for me, I shall gladly answer them."

This time, Sekhmet did snarl. While she had been interrupted, Lamasthu had the luxury of inviting the others into the conversation. Sekhmet held her breath, hoping one of the Council members would challenge Lamasthu. Zeus leaned forward.

"Shall we test your commitment to justice, Lamasthu?" he asked. "I understand and forgive the incursion of your army into Olympia in support of Quetzalcoatl's defense of the realm. However, you control a hoard of dangerous creatures, some of whom undermined the catacombs beneath the fortress of my son, Ares. What can you do to make this right? And how can you assure our citizens that such monsters will not be set upon them?"

Zeus relaxed in his chair, confident that he had posed a difficult question. However, Lamasthu responded instantly. "I will execute all those creatures. If they are not serving the good of the City, they are serving no purpose. And should Ares have need of stonemasons to repair his building, I will supply all the skilled slaves he needs and fund the materials myself."

Her bold declaration surprised many in the Council Hall. Sekhmet heard whispers of approval, which she could not believe. Didn't they know that those monsters were Lamasthu's own children? Yet Lamasthu wanted everyone to think that she could kill them without a second thought. No mother, not even a horrible mother of horrible monsters, could truly hold this view, unless they were mad, or a liar. Sekhmet feared that Lamasthu might be both of those things.

Now everyone looked expectantly at Shiva. It was customary in these proceedings for each continuing Council Member to ask one question, and he so far had not. Shiva lifted his chin, emphasizing the blue patch that had marked his throat ever since he drank poison to save his world. "Lamasthu, if you had to choose between creation and destruction to protect our realms, which would you choose?"

Sekhmet wondered what Shiva was really asking, and she wasn't the only one. "I don't understand your question," Quetzalcoatl interrupted.

"You don't need to understand it," Shiva said mildly. "It isn't your question. Well, Lamasthu?"

Lamasthu pursed her lips in a brief pout as she thought. "I would tear down a failing building rather than build anew on a weak foundation. If we focus on destroying what is wrong in the realms, I'm sure creation will take care of itself."

Sekhmet thought Shiva, a dual lord of creation and destruction himself, seemed pleased with her answer. Zeus looked unimpressed with the word-play, while Quetzalcoatl was openly beaming at Lamasthu's crafty answer.

"Thank you, candidates," Quetzalcoatl said. "You have both acquitted yourselves well."

The hall attendant read the ceremonial instructions for voting then called for the voters to proceed to stations for casting their ballots. A large block of supporters rushed toward Lamasthu as the crowd broke up, clearly intrigued with her forceful declarations. Sekhmet felt like a lead rock had dropped into her stomach.

"Don't worry yet." Ptah appeared at her side. Sekhmet was more than grateful for his presence. "Lamasthu's throng has no voting status. They can cheer, but do little to advance her cause."

"What if I lose, Ptah?" Sekhmet said.

"Then little will change and you can live just as you did before the campaign." he comforted. "But if you win, you could change everything."

One of the Council Hall's high ranking servants approached them. "It is customary," she said in a tinny, nasal voice, "for the candidates to await the results outside. Please follow me to the sacred gardens." The woman bowed and swept her arm toward a set of arched doors, which she then started toward. As Ptah and Sekhmet followed her, Sekhmet noticed another servant attempting to herd Lamasthu's boisterous retinue in the same direction. She silently wished him luck.

They stepped outside into bright, warm sunlight. Green, flower-spotted grass stretched before them to a small, azure lake. Everything was beautiful and serene. Sekhmet looked up at Ptah. "Too bad Tenh-Mer isn't here," she said. "She'd like this."

Ptah lifted the corner of his lip to show a fang. "Look up."

Sitting upon the roofline of the Council Hall was the companion in question. Tenh-Mer waved enthusiastically to Sekhmet before flying down to meet her. The servant who had escorted them outside retreated energetically when she saw Tenh-Mer headed their way. The demoness landed solidly, her sharp, small hooves gouging the lawn.

"Sorry! I was late and they had closed the doors," she apologized. "But a nice bird-lady told me you'd come out here."

"A bird-lady?" Sekhmet asked. "Well, you can tell me about her later. Right now, I just need a moment's peace. Stay with Ptah."

"What about my peace?" Ptah grumbled. Sekhmet left him with a soft laugh and a comforting stroke of his arm.

"I'm going to look at the water," she told them. She left her friends and walked slowly down to the edge of the Lake of Remembrance.

The pool reflected Sekhmet in its still waters. She studied her face, its calm expression hiding the turmoil in her heart. In a very short time, she would know whether she had been elected. Inside the grand building next to the peaceful lake and its beautiful gardens, leaders of all the major and minor pantheons were having their culture's choice of candidate counted by a board of recorders selected from the City's peacekeeping guardians. She had seen the members of the group, but had recognized none of them. Perhaps each had been chosen for their obscurity.

Nearby, Ptah and Tenh-Mer stood in the shadow of a flowering tree. Limbs dotted with pale green leaves and purple blossoms arched above their heads. Sekhmet observed Tenh-Mer nervously picking apart a blossom as she waited, but Ptah stood with arms folded, unaffected by the election suspense. If anything, Sekhmet thought he looked a little bit bored. For a moment, she considered joining her friends, but realized it was solitude she craved. That urge worried her. If she already felt over-loaded from dealing with others, how could she stand to serve on the Council?

Tired of staring at the water, she walked down a path that led toward several commemorative monuments to treasures and heroes lost when the gods left Earth. Sekhmet paused to read the inscriptions on the gold-en plaques, but could muster no emotions beyond vague regret and appreciation. She wondered why no images had been included in the memorials. The obelisks of Egyptos were far more illustrative. Sekhmet glanced up from one of the inscriptions and noticed Lamasthu lounging on a bench. She was surrounded by priests and slaves, many of them deformed in some monstrous way. A catty thought seized Sekhmet's imagination. Perhaps those honored were, like some in Babylos, too ugly for their appearances to be immortalized. As if sensing the secret insult, Lamasthu's head swiveled and she gazed upon Sekhmet with a confident smirk upon her face. Sekhmet turned away and went back along the path the way she'd come.

She was again within sight of Ptah and Tenh-Mer. Suddenly, both of them turned and took a few steps toward something coming from the direction of the hall. Sekhmet increased her pace and soon caught up with them. "Is it over?" she asked Ptah breathlessly. He pointed to the three gods approaching them: Quetzalcoatl, Shiva and Zeus.

"I think the winner has been decided," he said. Tenh-Mer moved over to Sekhmet's side.

"Don't worry, you'll win," she said with a bright smile.

Sekhmet put a finger over Tenh-Mer's lips to silence her as the current Council members came closer. Shiva, walking in the middle, carried a folded silver and blue silk stole on a tray. Zeus walked with his hands clasped behind his back. Quetzalcoatl's hands were free, and he clapped them together as the trio stopped in front of them.

"Someone collect Lamasthu," he ordered to no one in particular. Ptah's body language made it clear that he took immediate offense at being addressed as a servant, but Tenh-Mer found nothing inappropri-ate about the request.

"I will!" she said, and hurried off, but stopped suddenly in her tracks. "Oh, wait! Where is she?"

Sekhmet pointed down the path. "Past the monuments, on a bench," she said softly.

As they waited for Tenh-Mer to return with Lamasthu, Zeus filled the tense silence with trivial conversation. Sekhmet found herself nodding distractedly as he remarked upon the unusual ceremonial dress of the Assyrians and described how a tribal representative from the Cold Realms had presented the recorders with a small, carved totem image of the candidate on whom his people had decided. Her eyes darted from one Council member's face to the next, trying to find any hint in their demeanors of how the voting had turned out. Before she could pick up a clue, Lamasthu came slinking up the path, alone.

"Is it time for me to ascend?" she inquired in a lilting, seductive voice.

"Where is Tenh-Mer?" Sekhmet asked, alarmed.

Lamasthu turned a sleepy eye upon her. "Who?"

"My winged servant," Sekhmet said harshly. "She was sent to bring you here."

Lamasthu sighed impatiently. "I saw no one. Servants can be clumsy. Perhaps yours fell in the lake and drowned."

Sekhmet moved to search for Tenh-Mer, but felt Ptah's hand land heavily on her shoulder. "I will find her," he said. He glared at Lamasthu and strode quickly down the path.

Lamasthu waved a tentacle at Ptah's back as if she was shooing a fly out a window. "Good. Now only the important people are here. What is the result?"

Quetzalcoatl and Zeus both looked to Shiva. He set the tray he carried on the ground in front of Sekhmet and Lamasthu and took up the length of cloth. As he unfolded it, he explained what would happen next.

"I will place this upon the winner as a mark of honor. Then, she will follow us into the Council Hall for the formal installation ceremony. If you have lost, you have the privilege of joining us on the dais to observe the rituals. Or, you may go about your business. On behalf of the City, we thank both of you for your efforts."

Quetzalcoatl, Zeus and Shiva all bowed to Sekhmet and Lamasthu.

Sekhmet's heart pounded as Shiva walked around behind them. She stared straight ahead at Zeus, her sponsor. When his eyes caught hers and quickly darted away, she knew she had lost. A flash of blue and silver intruded upon her peripheral vision as Shiva draped the stole over Lamasthu's shoulders. Quetzalcoatl beamed at his candidate.

"Congratulations, Lamasthu!" he said.

"It was a very close race," Zeus claimed, his fingers playing in his beard. "It could have gone either way."

"And perhaps if Ceridwen had competed," Shiva interjected, his voice sounding strained, "we would have had a different ending."

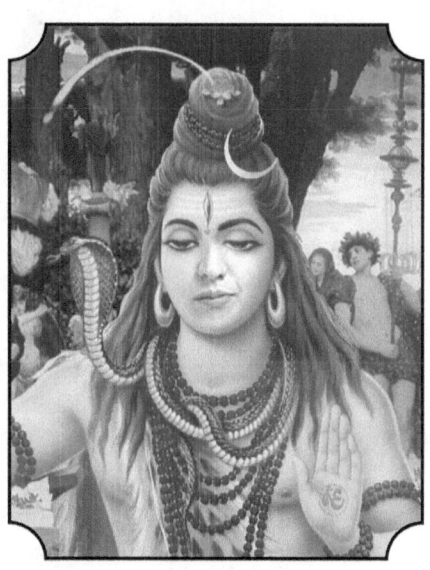

Lamasthu ran her hands down the silvery silk stole. "Ending? I prefer to think of this as a beginning." She moved away from Sekhmet, an act that emphasized she was now on a different level of power. "Shall we go in?" she asked the Council gods.

"Of course. Will you join us, Sekhmet?" Quetzalcoatl asked pleasantly.

Even though she knew refusal would imply weakness, Sekhmet could not bring herself to accept the invitation. She wished Ptah were still at her side. He would have some clever words to extricate her from the awkward scene. Instead, she kept her answer simple, and pointed.

"No. I cannot - I must search for my companion."

"Very well," Quetzalcoatl said. "Give our regards to Egyptos."

The four Council members turned away and walked toward the hall. Sekhmet stood frozen until they disappeared into a doorway. She looked down, noticing that Shiva had forgotten his tray. Anger and disappointment broke through her emotional dam and she seized the tray, throwing it violently into the gardens. Panting, she peered into the greenery with teary eyes. *Tenh-Mer, where are you?*

Finding purpose in this question, she fled down the path after Ptah.

*T*he rain had finished its work on a weakened section of limestone on the face of the neglected temple. The large chunk of stone slid free from its neighbors, sending eroded figures of cavorting naiads for a swim in the stagnant waters of Glaucus' pool. The splash of the frag-

ment's descent woke the sullen god from his slumber. His eyes lazily scanned the dirty mosaic tiles on which he lay. He saw the fallen chunk had jarred several small squares out of place. The damage didn't matter. Glaucus had long ago ceased to care about his temple. He barely cared enough to keep himself alive.

A bottom feeding fish darted past his face. Scowling, Glaucus roused and shot out of the water with a mighty flick of his fishtail. He still had great strength despite all his passive attempts to fade away. He wished that the man and goddess he had sent to bring him Circe's head would either return with it or die. Either outcome would end the magical bond that held him to his current existence. He felt paralyzed, and had begun to take pleasure in imagining clever ways to thwart the rules of Olympia and end his immortality.

Glaucus swam across his pool and lifted himself onto his decrepit throne. Staring out across the great lake, he wondering how much progress the freeman and the goddess had made in his quest. The sun was setting and the night creatures of the lake had begun their chattering. Frogs sang in chorus and night birds cooed from far above his head. The wing beats of bats were particularly loud; he tried to remember if it was the season in which they swarmed to mate. He quickly gave up the thought. The passage of time had become almost meaningless. The air above his head was again noticeably stirred by pumping wings. This time he glanced up, curious to see how many bats were circling in the broken heights of his temple. There was but one.

"Mordecai," Glaucus muttered, recognizing the creature. "I should not have thought of old quests. I should not have thought of bats. My dreams turn real and come to torment me." He watched as Mordecai flapped lower, seeking a roost strong enough to bear his weight. A column that had lost its ornamental scrollwork jutted up like a snapped off tree trunk. The creature settled down atop it as Glaucus eyed him suspiciously. "What do you want?"

"Message." Mordecai's voice creaked as if he had recently overused it. "The Feathered Serpent sent me." He reached for a leather cord looped around his neck and removed it from his body. Attached to the cord was some sort of small booklet. "This, you may like. Catch it."

Glaucus was surprised at the way Mordecai flung the item at him carelessly. He reached out, barely seizing it before it hit the water. There were several pages covered with colorfully inked designs, sewn together in a simple binding. Had the booklet been wetted, the message would have been completely lost. "What am I to do with this? Why is your god sending tokens to me?"

Mordecai adjusted his pose on the pillar as he swatted at a water fly buzzing near his face. "You're supposed to look at it," the bat said.

"Obviously," Glaucus replied sharply. Deciding Mordecai was simpleminded rather than sarcastic, he turned his attention to the message. The first page contained a detailed picture of the lake and shoreline around

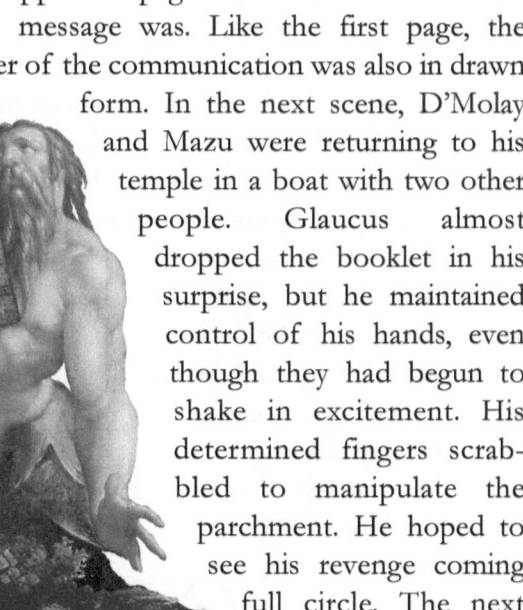

Olympia. Glaucus could even pick out the secluded cove of his temple ruin. Apparently this image had served as his address, allowing Mordecai to find him. He flipped the page over to move on to whatever this message was. Like the first page, the remainder of the communication was also in drawn form. In the next scene, D'Molay and Mazu were returning to his temple in a boat with two other people. Glaucus almost dropped the booklet in his surprise, but he maintained control of his hands, even though they had begun to shake in excitement. His determined fingers scrabbled to manipulate the parchment. He hoped to see his revenge coming full circle. The next image showed the threads of the supernatural bond that had compelled the quest breaking down. Magic, depicted by swirling curlicues of gold ink, fled toward the edges of the page. Glaucus smiled. This must mean that all would go as planned. But the picture that followed was confusing. The unknown passengers were in each others' arms, cringing away from him as the goddess challenged him and the man fled to their boat. Glaucus became disturbed by the turn of the story. Where was the head of the witch Circe that they had been bound to bring to him? Who were these other people? He glared at Mordecai, catching the creature's eye.

"Is it a good prophecy?" Mordecai asked, "or a bad one?" He idly scratched his armpit with the delicate claws of his left hand.

"This is what will happen?" Glaucus fumed. "This does not fulfill the bargain I made with them."

"The goddess cheats," Mordecai parroted. Quetzalcoatl had made him rehearse his words again and again, and the Feathered Serpent's mean priest had stabbed him with a hot stick each time he misspoke. Mordecai took great care to smoothly recite the script he had been taught. "The goddess has friends who help her break promises. They have even tricked Feathered Serpent's people."

"Mazu?" Glaucus grew a bit skeptical. Mazu was known for many things, but underhandedness was not among them. "This must be a lie. Mazu was looking for you when she took on my quest. You are just trying to get even for my telling them about you."

Mordecai shook his head insistently. "No, no. You will see the trick when it comes. And when you do, catch Mazu for Feathered Serpent. He will reward you."

Glaucus considered the bat's claim. If he was allowed to decide for himself, in his own time, he could tolerate listening to a little more of this nonsense. "What does he offer? There is nothing I want."

"He will see that what you desired to be done is truly done."

"As if you even know what that is," Glaucus said.

"Feathered Serpent knows," Mordecai shrugged. "Now I can go."

Glaucus called after the bat, but was ignored. Mordecai disappeared over the dark waters. Glaucus sighed and pitched the strange message into a dense patch of reeds that hugged the old temple stairs. Would he be betrayed again? Time, ever his enemy, would tell.

Chapter 28

The Shallows of Sadness

When Lamasthu entered the Council Hall in the company of Quetzalcoatl, Zeus and Shiva, the level of victorious cheers and disappointed howls mixed equally. The acclaim and the disdain were both music to her ears. Such strong expressions were always directed toward those who had true power; she desired no gentle support or mild rebuke. As she stepped onto the dais from which the City rulers dealt out the law, Lamasthu contemplated the retinue of attendants who had stood by her this election day. She considered which one to choose as her chief attendant in these halls. None of those sycophants were worthy. They had served their purpose during her campaign, but now they sought only to exalt themselves one over another. She resolved to look elsewhere for her attendant, to choose one who valued what she was and what she stood for more than the rewards that the City could bestow.

Her installation ceremony was conducted with pomp appropriate to the occasion. A trio of horned, winged snakes, each the size of a goat, carried her banners up to the top of the hall and draped them to hang down over her seat of authority. As traditional poems were recited and the ancient music performed, Lamasthu fell deep into thought, almost missing the cue to recite the vows required of her new office. But by the time the rituals ended she was well prepared to show everyone that her tenure on the Council would address justice. As the last note of the final trumpet flourish faded, Lamasthu stood and moved to address the crowd.

"When I asked for your votes, I promised to do my utmost to bring law and order to the realms. I marked my words, and kept in mind and heart the great offense that has been committed in the realm ruled by

Zeus." At the mention of his name, Lamasthu made a gesture of honor toward her new colleague. "My people have helped his with succor and support, but that is not enough."

"She's right!" a strained voice bellowed. Everyone turned to note Helios and his displaced courtiers in the crowd. She nodded toward the refugee-king.

"The time has come to find and punish the one who destroyed our friend's island. Helios' palace was flooded, washed away, and his own children drowned. Surely only a water deity would be capable of such an act," Lamasthu said. The crowd cheered. Quetzalcoatl had counseled her well. He had told her they would be eager for action after many seasons of a Council that did nothing but decide the occasional, non-offensive issue. She turned to the others on the dais. "All gods with control of waters must be examined. I will send the intelligent flying creatures in my realm to seek them for questioning. Will you commit your people to this cause?"

Shiva leaned forward in his chair. "Of course. But gods are gods. Most will not come willingly. What then?"

Quetzalcoatl stood, gesturing to his priest. The priest stepped forward with a glowing, golden ring.

"They shall be compelled to appear," he said, looking out over the crowd. He spotted Chaac loitering dully in the aisle and skillfully threw the ring at him. It stuck his arm and skimmed down to reform about his wrist, its color changing to bright, fiery red as it encircled him. "Chaac," he commanded. "Try to resist."

Quetzalcoatl turned to Lamasthu, nodding. She extended a tentacle toward the froggish rain god. "Come to me," she said.

Chaac hunkered down, his thick body straining to remain in its place. He grabbed the edge of a heavy marble bench as his body continued to move of its own will toward the goddess. Her tentacle waved at him again. Chaac stumbled toward the dais.

Shiva folded his arms. "I dislike such compulsion," he muttered. He observed how intently Lamasthu and Zeus watched the effect of the ring on Chaac. He began to realize just how distanced he now felt from the rest of the Council.

Chaac was soon dragged to Lamasthu's feet. The crowd applauded as Quetzalcoatl removed the ring from Chaac's wrist and thanked him for facilitating the demonstration. "Be assured, Shiva, that these rings have been enchanted for this special purpose only. All they can do is force gods with power over water to appear before us for questioning."

"So I repeat my question," Lamasthu said. "Will your flying gods join mine in this great gathering?"

Zeus nodded, studying the ring in Quetzalcoatl's hand. "Of course. And you must teach us the secret of these rings," he said. Shiva merely shrugged his agreement, still feeling resentful and out of step with the rest.

"Send your seekers to the Temple of Time," Quetzalcoatl directed, promising no revelation of the secret of the rings to Zeus. "My priests will distribute the rings to your gods."

Soon the hall was bustling with messengers being briefed on the operation. Some were sent to order flying deities to the Temple of Time while others were dispatched to request that water gods appear before the Council of their own accord. Lamasthu watched the activity unfold as a master of bees might smile down on his hive, anticipating the honey that would soon appear. She tilted her head back and looked with pride on the dark banners that hung above her. One god at time, she would bend them all to her will.

*In the heat of the afternoon, the hold of the small boat became unbearably warm, driving D'Molay to abandon its peace for fresh air. Emerging, he rested his hand on one of two barrels lashed securely to the deck, knowing that his friend Mazu had again gone into hiding. He partly felt he should apologize for his earlier anger; he more strongly wished his friends would simply believe him about what he had seen. In the end, he said nothing and moved to where Quan and Scylla sat, talking and sharing a pot of rice.

"Any for me?" he asked. Quan appeared annoyed by the interruption but gestured quickly toward a sack. D'Molay reached into it to find several more bowls. He chose one and served himself a large scoop of rice. Trying to miss the parts of his beard that were in dire need of a trim, he levered a clump to his mouth. As he swallowed, Scylla put down her unfinished meal, muttered an excuse, and moved to a blanket at the other end of the boat. Quan also started to rise.

"Sit down," D'Molay said, pinning Quan with a commanding look. "I need to talk to you about our visit to Glaucus."

Quan put down his bowl and folded his arms. "But you told me not to let her out of my sight," he protested.

"You can see her from here. And she doesn't need to hear what I have to say."

D'Molay made Quan wait while he ate most of his rice. He noticed Quan kept glancing toward Scylla. He also observed that she kept looking at

Quan. He wondered if anything had happened while he was sleeping below deck. "Did she have any more fits?" Quan shook his head in the negative. "Good. I hope they've run their course."

"Me too," Quan agreed. "She's a beautiful woman."

D'Molay had to punch Quan on the arm as his gaze lingered on Scylla. "Pay attention to me, not her. How much has Mazu told you about Glaucus and our bond to him?"

Quan rubbed his arm resentfully where D'Molay had assaulted it. "That you both would suffer unless you did what he asked. Is there more?"

"That's the heart of it. But a lot has happened since we made our deal. There's been a war, the realms have experienced all sorts of disruptions

and the usual under-handed politics go on as always. Who knows what he's thinking now? When we get to his temple, we stay in pairs. You with Scylla, I with Mazu."

"Mazu?" Quan began to shake his head in dis-agreement. "She has to stay hidden."

"Glaucus isn't going to talk to a water barrel," D'Molay said. "He'll suspect a trick if he does-n't see both Mazu and me in the flesh. We'll just have to be as secretive and as quick as we can."

Quan frowned, but found no sensible objection to voice. "I can do my part."

"Good." D'Molay stood up and looked ahead over the water. The day was pleasant, with a light breeze and a bank of thick white clouds block-ing the heat of the sun. The traffic on the great lake had increased, which meant they had traveled much closer to the City. Not far beyond their boat a half dozen others could be seen. There was a trade barge, a group of tribal canoes, and a small fishing boat. "How far are we from - "

He let his question drop as he saw several flying beings shoot out of the cloud bank. Each one made a beeline for one of the vessels. Quan scrambled up, but D'Molay put out a hand to still him.

"Don't move." Neither of them did as they watched the assorted mes-

sengers land on or near the other
ships. Soon one came near theirs.

"It's a winged man!" Quan
exclaimed. He nervously looked at
D'Molay. A slight smile had
appeared on the tracker's face.

"No, it's a god," D'Molay
contradicted.

That god was Zephyrus, the west
wind, who extended a hand to lightly grab
the tip of their boat's tallest mast. He spun
his airy form around it like a ribbon circling a may-
pole until he reached the deck. As his feet touched
the planks he solidified into the form of a dark-haired
human clad in a Greek tunic. He staggered a bit, making D'Molay wonder whether the god of the air had
no legs for the sea or if he had merely been drinking.

"Greetings! On orders from the Council, I must search this boat."
Zephyrus delivered this news with a distinct lack of serious zeal, much
like a schoolboy forced to recite a dull verse. When his eyes came to rest
on D'Molay, he brightened. "S-say! It's you! This is a surprise."

"To us as well. A search?" D'Molay moved his hand to his beard,
miming interest to disguise his alarm. Zephyrus sauntered over to the
rice pot and poked a finger into its contents.

"Of sorts. Did you hear what happened to Helios' Palace? Nasty flood.
Killed almost everyone. Made me glad I live in the heights." Zephyrus continued to pry about the boat, peeking into containers and shaking Quan's
tarps and sails. Quan started to edge toward Mazu, but D'Molay signaled
him to back off without Zephyrus noticing the silent exchange.

"I hadn't heard about that," D'Molay said. He hardly had to feign concern
as the strong god of the wind lifted and shook Mazu's barrels one by one,
listening to the liquid sloshing inside. Zephyrus sat down on one of them.

"It's the talk of the realms," Zephyrus insisted, shaking his head dis-
believingly. "Where've you been?"

The answer that jumped to his mind made D'Molay smile. "Fishing
and hunting, for the most part. What is that you're trying to catch?"

"Oh, the search, right. The Council thinks a water deity is to blame.
They've drafted a swarm of us to look for all the deities of the waterways."

"What do they expect you to do if you find one?" D'Molay asked.

Zephyrus reached into a pouch belted to his waist and pulled out a yellow crystal hoop, about the size of a bracelet. "Don't ask me how this works, but it will make them follow us back to the City. Then they'll be questioned."

D'Molay held his breath as Zephyrus twirled the ring playfully in the air with his index finger, fearing it could somehow affect Mazu. To his relief, nothing happened. "As much as we'd like a quicker ride to the City than we're getting on this boat," D'Molay said, "I'm afraid none of us are water gods."

Putting the crystal hoop away, Zephyrus then handed a green strip of gold-edged silk to D'Molay. "Attach this to your highest mast to show that I've been here. That way you won't be searched again." He stood to go. "Too bad I can't stay and have a drink with you, Tracker," he said. "I really do feel bad about all the humans that got drowned. I would love to be the one who catches this god. So I'd better keep looking!"

Zephyrus changed to his air-form in an instant and launched himself skyward. D'Molay and Quan had to grab onto masts and railings to steady themselves as the gust caused by his exit caught their sails and yanked the boat forward. They watched him until he disappeared into the clouds.

D'Molay held out the green cloth to Quan. "Get climbing." *I wonder, did Aavi somehow block the magic, or did Zephyrus not really check?*

❧⟡❧

inding the overgrown lake channel that led to Glaucus' neglected temple taxed D'Molay's memory. By the time he had misdirected the boat twice, he was as irritated by his mistakes as Quan was with his navigating. However, they did not dare allow Mazu out of hiding to help them. It would be enough of a risk to let her out when they reached the cover of the ruin. The boat nosed into another copse of tall reeds, breaking through into a small channel.

"This is it," D'Molay confirmed in relief as crumbling stone steps came into view. The place looked the same as when he and Mazu had left it. Sluggish water lapped against rocks too stubborn to wash away. Turtles sunned on cracked stones and insects bounded on their light feet across the pools. Birds squawked down at them from perches on the temple's few remaining roof beams. Their vantage point reminded D'Molay that the boat was unconcealed and easily seen from the air.

Quan tossed a rope over a leaning pillar to connect the boat with the stairway. "It looks haunted," he said. "If I were a ghost, I'd move right in."

"If only we were invisible as ghosts," D'Molay wished aloud, calculating a strategy. "The flag Zephyrus gave us should keep the Council's messengers out of our business, but if the boat is spotted by someone else, we need a cover story."

Quan put his hands on his hips and surveyed the inlet, coming to a quick conclusion. "You told that flying man we'd been fishing. This is a good spot for catching turtles. Their shells trade for a high price, you know." As if it understood his words, a turtle slid off the nearest step and disappeared into the water. D'Molay felt as if he understood the turtle's paranoia; he also felt distinctively uneasy, but hid his fears from the others.

"Help me carry Mazu inside. Then put out whatever lines will give the impression you're after turtles." D'Molay noticed Scylla watching apprehensively as he and Quan each shouldered one of the barrels. "Don't worry," he said to reassure her. "I'll send Quan right back to wait with you."

D'Molay trod carefully on the wet steps, leading Quan toward the inner chamber of the temple. The last time he had been here he was searching for Aavi. Again, he desperately wanted to see her. D'Molay frowned in frustration, feeling trapped in an everlasting cycle of discontent. Murky waters lapped at his boots as they reached a landing that stretched a short way into darkness. Beyond it was the deeper pool where Glaucus lived. D'Molay could just make out the protruding slab that served as the old god's decrepit throne.

"This is far enough," he told Quan. "Let's set Mazu free."

The men worked quickly. D'Molay pried the lid off his barrel with his knife while Quan twisted a bung out of his cask and tipped out the liquid, which ran down into Glaucus' dark pond. D'Molay pushed his barrel over, adding its waters to the mix. A moment later Mazu rose before them.

D'Molay knew immediately that Mazu had heard every word Zephyrus had said on the boat. She bore a look of poignant remorse as she stood stiffly before them. She slowly extended her right hand and coaxed the waters to form into her staff. Mazu gripped it tightly, her knuckles almost white in the darkness.

"That flood," D'Molay said quietly. "It was you?"

"Let's finish this matter," she said, turning away from D'Molay and moving on. He wondered what had really happened back in Dioscrias and worse, what would happen if Mazu was linked to it. At the moment, however, he had to suppress those worries.

"We'll take it from here. Go fish," he told Quan. He listened as the servant's footsteps receded then waded into the water. D'Molay hurried to catch up with Mazu, who stood beside the crumbling platform on which Glaucus sometimes reclined. D'Molay put a hand on her shoulder.

"Try not to think about the palace," he said. "I know what happened there had to have been an accident."

Mazu's light laugh gave D'Molay hope that she was not overwhelmed with guilt, but her next words made her position clear. "I'm disappointed in you, D'Molay. Are you going to excuse what is clearly a cruel, capricious act of a goddess just because we are friends? I'm as bad as any of the gods you've railed against all these centuries."

"That's not true," he protested. "There's a clear difference between an unforeseen complication and a willful act."

"You sound as sly as a Greek philosopher, D'Molay. But the flood that killed the innocent at the palace of Helios isn't even the worst of my crimes," Mazu continued. "And though I am not alone in doing wrong, my guilt is heavier for my knowledge of my evil."

D'Molay's brow furrowed as he tried to understand what she meant. At length, he gave up that effort and focused on the task at hand. "I don't know what to say to that, other than let's tackle one problem at a time. You can explain these crimes of yours later."

Mazu nodded, giving him a determined look. "Yes. I want to confess to everything as soon as possible. But you are right. Now, it's time to talk to Glaucus."

D'Molay called out the god's name loudly. "Come out, we've returned."

A strong wake pushed against their bodies as the god responded to the summons. Unlike Mazu's elegant emergence, that of the old fish god was raucous. D'Molay flinched as a spray of filthy, displaced water struck his face. Glaucus heaved himself onto his throne. His matted beard dripped. He pinned them with dark eyes as his tail slapped into place on the stone. D'Molay was glad Scylla was outside, spared the fearsome sight of him.

"So you're back," he said. "Good. I want to be rid of you." Glaucus noticed he had a water snake pinned beneath his hip, and eased up slightly allowing it to escape. It flailed off into the water, swimming past D'Molay unnervingly close. D'Molay forced himself to stand still as Glaucus said more. "Where is Scylla?"

"She's outside." D'Molay took care choosing his next words. "She's no longer a monster."

"You broke Circe's curse." Glaucus seemed genuinely surprised. "You did! I can feel the bond lifting."

"Yes," Mazu said, "and we have taken care to protect her on the long journey back." As she spoke, D'Molay felt a shift in the air. Somewhere in his core he felt a momentary hot twinge, a reminder of the type of fever he had suffered when he had been forced by Zeus to shirk his duty to Glaucus and track

the beast that had come with Aavi to the realms. That pain, along with a weight he hadn't even realized he was carrying, vanished. He immediately felt ten years younger and hoped that Mazu shared the same sensation of renewal. Perhaps it would improve her strange mood.

"Bring Scylla to me," Glaucus demanded eagerly. "I cannot swim past those fallen temple beams, but she can join me here in the deep channels that feed the lake."

Mazu and D'Molay exchanged a look. "Scylla has been freed from Circe's spell, but it came with a price," Mazu said. "She is a human woman now, not a water nymph."

Glaucus stared at her as if he could not comprehend the words. D'Molay tensed, fearing the god's reaction when the truth became clear. He shifted one leg back into a more stable stance and calculated how quickly he could move through the water if he had to suddenly fight or flee. Beside him, Mazu shimmered, half-liquid already, also anticipating a negative reaction. But Glaucus merely grunted and waved a hand at them.

"I was warned you would trick me," he said in a low voice. "When the bond lifted I thought the warning was wrong, but now it all comes clear. If I cannot have the pleasure of love, I will enact my plan to enjoy the satisfaction of seeing justice done."

"Mazu," D'Molay said, "we're done here. Let's go."

"No!" Glaucus roared suddenly. "You're not going anywhere!"

D'Molay blinked as a flash of gold lit up the temple. Glaucus brandished a yellow hoop like the one Zephyrus had shown him, the tool of the Council that compelled water gods to obedience. He threw it violently at Mazu and it immediately found her wrist, forcing itself past her watery fingers. Settling in place, its color changed from bright yellow to bright red. The pain caused her to drop her staff and it fell into the water. D'Molay sped to Mazu's side, drawing his knife.

"I might be able to get it off. This knife has powers." He tapped the manacle with the blade, and the bracelet glowed ever-so-slightly less red. "You see! I can - "

Scylla's scream from the boat froze D'Molay in place. Glaucus began to laugh. "It sounds like there's trouble outside. Make your choice, hero."

"Go," Mazu hissed.

D'Molay gritted his teeth and forced himself to slog away from Mazu. The dirty water sucked at his boots, slowing him. He stumbled on the wet stone as he reached the landing, clumsily dropping to one knee. Ignoring the resulting sharp pain in his kneecap, he pushed himself up and hurried on, the mocking laughter of Glaucus ringing out behind him. At the top of the exterior steps, he shouldered behind a pillar, tucking his knife away and swinging his bow into position as he took a quick peek at the boat. The reason for Scylla's scream was clear. Quan was wrapped in the constricting coils of a shining water serpent.

The snake had reflective scales which cloaked it by mirroring the world around it. At first glance, Quan seemed to be dangling magically in mid-air, but the feathery spine crest and intense blue eyes of the serpent were not reflective, allowing D'Molay to see past the rest of its camouflage. As he came   to a full realization of what he was facing, the snake   turned its head toward him. He   judged its head to be about   the size of a

horse; its lively eyes suggested there was intelligence behind its attack. D'Molay advanced. The creature slouched down toward the water, dunking Quan beneath the surface.

"Do something!" Scylla cried.

D'Molay quickly ran to the boat, calculating the best position to on deck from which to aim for the creature's head. Unexpectedly, Quan was suddenly yanked out of the water, sputtering and yelling in terror. Close enough now to board, D'Molay bounded onto the ship. This action prompted the serpent to push its prisoner back under the water. D'Molay thought he caught a glint of amusement in the thing's eyes.

Scylla was casting frantically about the deck. For lack of any better weapon, she grabbed the small pot of hot embers over which that they had cooked the rice. She was poised to fling it at the monster when D'Molay reached her side. He grabbed her shoulder and pulled her back.

"Don't attack it," he commanded. "It may kill him if we do."

Scylla wriggled out of his grip, but obeyed. As soon as she took several steps back and set down the sizzling pan, the shining water serpent again lifted its hostage into the air. Quan coughed and kicked.

"Get Mazu!" he choked.

"I can't," D'Molay called up to him. Scylla expressed disbelief.

"Why not? Where is she? What happened in there?"

D'Molay lowered his bow, keeping his eyes fixed on Quan. "Glaucus has a ring like the wind god carried. He's used to it capture Mazu. Quan!" D'Molay hoped the frantic man would listen to him. "Don't struggle! Stay calm." Quan wriggled a bit more in protest, but eventually went limp as D'Molay nodded in approval.

"What do we do? Wait until the snake gets tired of playing with him?" Scylla asked frantically.

"That's one way to look at it. But we're really waiting to see who or what comes to collect Mazu. Glaucus isn't working alone. He spoke of being warned about us. This snake was surely sent to keep us busy until his friends arrive."

Scylla exhaled in frustration. "And you haven't found out who they are? And you didn't stay to help her?"

"You were screaming," D'Molay said bluntly. "And Mazu told me to leave."

"I'm not screaming now," she countered. "Go back! Maybe she can help Quan if you free her."

D'Molay felt like a fish being played on a line, pulled first one way then another. Yet her demand made sense, as there appeared to be little he could do to the snake without risking Quan's life. He tried again to influence Scylla, speaking quietly so that Quan could not hear his words.

"If you can flee without antagonizing the serpent - "

"No. I'm not leaving him." Scylla met D'Molay's gaze firmly. He shook his head in irritation, part of him grateful that he was no longer magically bound to look out for her. D'Molay spun on his heel. Before he had taken three steps he learned who was coming for Mazu. He was not the least bit surprised.

D'Molay cursed himself for not waiting for a sunny day to make this trip as an air raft brimming with Mayan warriors descended smoothly from the cover of the clouds. Two more appeared nearby. Mazu's ruse must have failed at some point in their journey; "Quetzalcoatl has found us," he half-whispered to himself. As the flying serpents suspending the raft lowered it to a gentle landing on the lake, men released the ropes tethering them to the creatures while others grabbed long poles to propel the raft into position, blocking the channel in which their boat was tied. The reflective water snake that held Quan swam to the raft. It dropped Quan at the feet of the warrior who wore the most elaborate head dress of the group. This man gestured to several strong guards standing at his side. They grabbed Quan, tying his hands and forcing him to kneel. The shining serpent disappeared beneath the water.

D'Molay stepped up to the prow of their boat, the closest he could get to the Mayans without swimming to their raft. Any notion of fighting the dozens of warriors on the craft was ridiculous. Speech was the only weapon in his arsenal.

"Release that man," he shouted. "He is bonded to the goddess Mazu, and by the law of the City you cannot steal another's slave."

The Mayan leader smirked and turned to his men. He said several words in their language which D'Molay could not interpret. The warriors all laughed, so D'Molay concluded their leader

was mocking him.

"Where is Quetzalcoatl?" D'Molay asked. Reaching into his coat, he pulled out the Council medallion. "I carry the seal. I have the right to an audience."

The lead Mayan frowned when he saw the flying eye symbol. He called out a single word, one that sounded like it might be a name. The pack of warriors parted and a smaller man came forward to stand beside the chief. This Mayan was not dressed like the other warriors. He carried no weapon that D'Molay could see.

"Put away your token," the man said in the City's common tongue, Panthos. "Great Quetzalcoatl is in the City. Do you truly think he has time to beat the bushes for criminals himself? We are here instead, to take a water goddess to the Council to answer their questions. We have no interest in you. You and your woman can go."

"What about him?" D'Molay pointed to Quan.

The interpreter grinned, suddenly appearing more interested in the conversation. He spoke a short phrase to the leader of the warriors, who gave a short, almost disinterested response.

"It is customary to collect the key servants in a god's retinue for a Council summons, but if you would like to bargain, I will entertain an offer." The man spoke confidently. His body language indicated he was assured of his authority to negotiate.

"What's your name?" D'Molay stalled. "I like to know who I'm dealing with."

"In this tongue, my name is Smoke Monkey," he grinned. "That is what you may call me, Tracker, Freeman, Jacques D'Molay." He paused, allowing his knowledge of D'Molay's identity to sink in. "Now, what have you to offer in exchange for this slave? Cargo? Gold? Or perhaps you would like to take his place."

D'Molay thought the Mayan was aptly named. He had the craftiness of an ape and words fell from his lips with the practice of one who could blow a perfect ring of smoke from his pipe every time. It was as if Smoke Monkey already knew exactly what D'Molay would propose. D'Molay decided that the only small victory he could have in this situation was to cut short the game of words.

"Scylla, get my things from below deck." D'Molay noted with satisfaction that Smoke Monkey's face fell a bit as Scylla disappeared into the hold. When she returned with D'Molay's coat and bag, he took time to dress and equip himself properly, hoping to convey to the Mayans that he was not intimidated by his subordinate position. He cinched a small pouch tightly shut and eyed Smoke Monkey as he would a servant. "I'm ready. Release that man, collect Mazu, and let's be on our way." D'Molay stood with exaggerated arrogance, one hand on his hip.

The Mayan leader narrowed his eyes and pointed at him. He voiced a few syllables in an insulted tone, but Smoke Monkey spoke again to pacify him. The leader then grunted an order to the warrior beside him, who pulled Quan to his feet and cut the ties

around his wrists with an obsidian knife. Quan nervously inched away from the warriors to the side of the raft. One of the Mayans, egged on by his grinning mates, gave him a sudden shove. Quan toppled over and struck the water with a loud splash. A second later he was swimming frantically for the boat. Scylla rushed to help pull him aboard.

"You can't let them take Mazu!" Quan insisted, so worried about the fate of his patron that he failed to notice Scylla lightly tracing her fingers over the red marks left on his chest where the snake had seized him. D'Molay noticed Scylla blush and yank her hand away when she caught his eye.

"Let them? What miracle do you expect me to perform? All I can do is make sure they take me along. Maybe I can help her when we're back in the City and I can appeal to the Council as a whole," D'Molay said. He remembered the talk of Sekhmet's campaign to become a member of that body. If she had succeeded, perhaps he could count on her help.

"I wish I had never left the boathouse," Quan said, expressing his frustration by forcefully shaking water out of his shoes. With one shoe in each hand, he stared down forlornly at his bare feet. "What good have I been to Lady Mazu?"

Scylla, who had been watching the warriors since averting her attention from Quan, spoke softly. "D'Molay, they're coming."

They watched as the Mayans poled the raft forward until it touched both the boat and the stairs that led up to the temple. Five warriors headed up the steps. One of them carried a small, ornate box. Smoke Monkey called out to D'Molay.

"Board now. The goddess will join us in a moment."

D'Molay said farewell to Quan and Scylla. "Make sure you return this boat to the Egyptos Docks. It's only borrowed. Then make your way back to the boathouse and stay there until you hear from Mazu or me. If you don't hear from us, seek answers from Sekhmet or Bast. They might help."

Quan nodded reluctantly as D'Molay jumped down from the boat deck to the raft. He was immediately encircled by warriors who ushered him to the vehicle's center and forced him to kneel in submission. He could not see over the painted, feathered-bedecked bodies of the Mayans as Mazu was brought to the raft. He could, however, hear her voice, which was calm as she said a peculiar thing to Quan and Scylla.

"As you see, I am perfectly fine, so do not worry about me. But I would appreciate it if you both would retrieve my staff from inside the temple, and keep watch over it until I return."

Quan immediately vowed obedience to the task and Scylla expressed a heartfelt goodbye to the goddess as D'Molay wondered about Mazu's request. He had always seen her make her staff from water. It was not a normal stick that could be left behind, forgotten.

D'Molay felt the raft bob slightly as the weight of Mazu and the warriors who escorted her was added to the floating platform. A moment later she joined him in the center.

"I am sorry they've arrested you too," she said. D'Molay shrugged.

"I volunteered. They took Quan first, but not even the Mayans deserve to be stuck with him as a passenger."

Mazu smiled. "Thank you. That spares me the worry of watching out for him, and gives him the opportunity to make a new life for himself."

D'Molay was uncomfortable with the finality of Mazu's statement. "He's perfectly happy with things as they are. What incentive is there for him to change? He'll be waiting for you at the boathouse when we get out of this."

Mazu sighed. "He may have to wait a long, long time."

Four sharp tones of a flute made D'Molay flinch. Heavy wing beats of sky dragons sounded overhead as the air raft's living engines returned to duty. Warriors re-attached strong ropes to the ornate tack worn by the dragons and the craft was ready to fly again in a matter of minutes. As they ascended, bodies parted for a moment and D'Molay could see Quan and Scylla watching the raft go up into the clouds. Then the white fog of the cloud cover closed around them, snatching away their view of the world below.

"I much prefer the view from Bast's air barge," Mazu said.

"As well as the company," D'Molay agreed.

"I can't see them anymore," Scylla said. "I hope they'll be all right."

Quan lowered his upraised chin with determination. "Let's do as they said. We'll get Mazu's staff, return this boat, and get back to the City. Maybe we can help them once all that is done."

They clambered off the boat, both of them now barefoot. Stepping carefully around shards of chipped marble and stray sticks and shells, they moved together toward the entrance to the temple.

"What's it like in there?" Scylla asked.

"Wet, dark, and smelly," Quan whispered back. They reached the landing at the top of the stairs and were met with a sight that defied Quan's answer. The interior of the temple was shimmering with a silvery light. The murky waters were pristine. The columns, though still broken and jagged, were as white as they had been when they were first set into place. A platform, embellished with bright swirls of color suggesting fish and waves, dominated the chamber. Upon it reclined Glaucus. Scylla gasped and Quan froze in his tracks as the god noticed them enter and turned his dark eyes toward them.

Quan had seen a few gods in his time and a few monsters too, but none as magnificent as Glaucus. The cobalt blue of his skin, his bright copper-green wavy hair, and the brilliant gray scales of his forked tail left no doubt that he was divine. No natural thing presented colors so vibrant. Then he noticed that Mazu's staff was lying on the platform next to Glaucus. Quan's knees began to quake. The god stared placidly at them for a moment with-

out comment, as if he was watching two insects that had landed uninvited on his table. Then he cocked his head slightly to one side and extended a pointing finger.

"Woman. Attend me."

Quan reached out to Scylla as she immediately stepped forward, grabbing her tunic and stammering a warning. She twisted out of his grasp and moved toward Glaucus, compelled by his power. As each step brought her closer to the platform, Quan found a new reason to admonish himself for his inaction. What would D'Molay do? What would Mazu expect of him? Scylla now stood within five feet of the deity. Even if an answer came to him in this instant, he was too far away to act.

"I knew you once," Glaucus said to Scylla. "Do you remember me?"

Scylla dropped her head and fell to her knees. The water came up to her breasts and an unseen current caused her tunic to float up around her. "No," she answered.

Quan saw the hurt and anger flash across the god's face. Glaucus clenched his fist, and somehow Quan found the courage to take a few steps toward Scylla. But the god's fingers relaxed and his hand reached out for an odd-looking box that sat near an empty bottle on his throne.

"This will make you remember. This will restore you."

Glaucus slowly unscrewed the lid from the vessel and set it aside. He stared down into the container. "We are of the same race, Scylla. There are secret things made only for our use that have no value to the other realms. The Mayans think they bought my services cheaply in exchange for nectar and a simple herb. But they have given us a treasure. Quetzalcoatl promised me that this would give me my heart's desire - and that is you." Glaucus tucked two of his long, blue fingers into the box and extracted a golden stick. From it, pinkish tendrils curled and terminated in starbursts of white flowers. He offered it to Scylla much like a suitor would present a bouquet. Quan's stomach lurched up toward his heart, and as his insides battled, his feet used the distraction to shuffle even closer to the god and the woman.

Scylla lifted her face and held out her palm for the plant. Glaucus gently placed it in her hand. "This is the herb that restored me and reawakened my godhood. I'm sure that if you use it, your true nature will be rekindled too. Break the stem, drink the sap."

The god's talk of true natures made Quan regret his own. All his life, he had been fearful and cautious. Yet as he tried to resign himself to his character, something inside him rebelled. As Scylla snapped the herb in half, he rushed forward. He threw his arms around her and dragged her backwards. One half of the herb dropped into the water. As Glaucus raged, Quan snatched the other piece from Scylla's hand.

"This is your death!" Glaucus shouted. He threw himself from the platform and seized Quan, holding him up in his mighty arms and carrying him toward the stair landing to smash him on the stone. Scylla had been swept against the base of the platform, and the impact had brought her to her senses. She screamed out for the god to stop.

"Don't! Please! He's just a fisherman!"

Glaucus turned at her words, bemused. "I have saved many fishermen in my day. I think it's time I killed one!" He grabbed Mazu's staff and raised it to strike down Quan.

His threat gave Quan the precious seconds he needed to say the words that surged up from his soul. "I am not just a fisherman!" he yelled. "I am the favored servant of the great Lady Mazu!"

The shred of herb that was still in Quan's grip began to smoke and shrivel. A red flame burst into view as the plant was engulfed. Still holding Quan, Glaucus bellowed in pain and fell back into the water. As they both struck the pool, they fell away from one another and the burning herb dropped out of Quan's hand. Its flame remained bright, even as Glaucus weakly pushed it under the water. When it bobbed again to the surface, it started to fade and dissolve.

"How have you done this?" Glaucus moaned, dragging himself back to his platform. His hair was receding and turning a matted white. The blue of his skin was changing to a shade more like a bruise. Scales fell from his tail, floating, dead flakes in the water around him. A chunk of blood-tinged fin was caught by the current and carried toward Scylla, who recoiled and flailed through the pool until she reached Quan's side. Glaucus struggled to pull himself out of the water. He no longer sported a powerful fishtail, but the shriveled legs of an elderly man. He cried out in agony as his muscles sagged and his bones twisted. Gnarled, swollen fingers scrabbled at the stone as he coughed, struggling to breathe with dying, water-sodden lungs. Then suddenly, he fell very still, able to take a few unfettered breaths. He eyes focused and he nodded to something unseen.

"I am betrayed ... I realize now my heart's desire was to ... die," he whispered.

His head dropped and all life left him. Quan and Scylla huddled together until a low rumble began to shake the temple. Quan snatched Mazu's staff from the decayed hand of Glaucus and they ran out of the temple. The aura

of beauty was leaving the old ruin. They hurried out of the pool as it returned to a still and dirty basin. The broken columns grayed and greened to their neglected state, obelisks, then collasped, forever marking the crypt where the corpse of Glaucus lay.

Once the raft was aloft and in the cover of the high clouds, the Mayan guards settled down for the ride back to the City. They broke into small groups to talk and smoke, leaving D'Molay and Mazu with a modicum of space around their spot in the center of the raft. Other than the magical ring around Mazu's wrist, they were not bound. D'Molay grudgingly agreed that restraint seemed unnecessary. Other than leaping off the vehicle to their deaths, there was no path to freedom.

Mazu was staring silently at the red ring. "Does it cause you pain?" D'Molay asked.

"This bracelet?" Mazu lifted her arm. "It is light compared to other burdens." She turned her head to look into his eyes. D'Molay felt he was being read like an open book. "I suppose the time has come to answer the questions I've avoided until now," she continued.

The raft shook slightly as the wings of the gliding dragons carrying it struck a series of beats to keep the raft on course. D'Molay reached out to touch Mazu's shoulder for a brief moment as he lost his balance. "I could tell you were keeping secrets," he chided gently. "Why?"

"Our quest was heavy enough. But it has ended, so I cannot take advantage of that excuse any longer." Mazu pointed subtly to their human Mayan guards. "What do you know of men like these and their place in our world?"

D'Molay thought her question odd, but answered it as best he could. "Warriors? They fight. They marry, I suppose, and make more warriors." He scanned the groups of Mayans around them and his gaze settled on Smoke Monkey. "The clever ones serve as priests or scribes. But none of that is mysterious, Mazu. It's much the same for men in any realm. Even for me." D'Molay folded his arms around himself and huddled as a sudden gust of extremely cold air skimmed over the raft. Mazu did not react to the frigid wind.

"There's something else that happens to them," she went on. "Sacrifice."

D'Molay nodded. "Of course. Their realm is a bit notorious for their blood rites. But again, so are others. Mazu, what are you trying to tell me?"

"Forgive me. I am having a hard time deciding where to begin my explanation. My confession," she amended.

"Then let me help," D'Molay suggested. "Why don't you start by telling me about this flood we've been arrested for? You said it was your fault. But how?"

Mazu's spine straightened and she folded her hands in her lap. D'Molay thought the pose made her look much like a statue in a shrine. Assuming the formal position seemed to clear her thoughts.

"While I searched for you in Circe's lair, I came upon the witch. She was brewing life water, the nectar of the gods. The main ingredient in that potion comes from mortal sacrifices. It was what Aavi noticed glowing in the urns."

"Blood?" D'Molay asked. He found that odd, considering he had seen and drank life water and there was nothing bloody about it. However, he could affirm that the urns did indeed contain blood, for he himself had seen a broken one spilled of its contents.

"S-sacraficed blood...glows." Mazu struggled to speak. "I-I can say no more."

D'Molay remained silent for a moment, chewing over this information. "Is it a council bond on you?"

Mazu looked down at her hands. "Yes. Let me try to tell you about Circe. She used some dark power to process stolen spirits. T-they were broken, destroyed; their souls forever denied proper rest in their after-worlds. Ahh..." She was experiencing great pain as she tried to bypass the power of the bonding spell.

D'Molay found his jaw agape and forced his mouth shut. His mind raced as he began to put all the pieces together. "Aavi saw the urns of blood glowing. They contained...souls?" Feeling he now understood Aavi's piece in the puzzle of the urns, his thoughts turned next to Hades' Underworld. "That's why you took care to save that little girl's ghost and tried to convince the other ghosts not to go with the sibyl. You thought their souls were at risk too."

Mazu nodded and D'Molay pursued his train of thought.

"Because extracting souls from sacrificial blood isn't the only way to steal souls?"

"I don't know. But the way the sibyl was collecting ghosts seemed sus-picious to me." Mazu's fingers clenched into fists and she pounded her hands down against her thighs. "And I knowingly and willingly drank life snatched from the death of others. Even when I tried to put the vile potion aside, I was weak. I succumbed."

D'Molay remembered how she had tried to give all her nectar to Charon and how angry she was when Quan provided her with a vial in the Lost Realm. He covered one of her tense fists with his hand, comfortingly.

"You did what you had to do," D'Molay said. "It was too late to do anything for those who had been . . . used."

From the other side of the raft, a raucous chorus of laughter arose from some joke the Mayans shared. D'Molay felt like it was fate mocking his and Mazu's situation.

"What about the flood. How did that happen?"

"We battled. When Circe confirmed the truth of the nectar, I let anger overwhelm me. I pushed my powers, I called upon every drop of water I could reach to come to my aid. When I prevailed, the remorse for all the lost souls overwhelmed me and I gave no thought to putting the liquid world back to rights. The waters found their own way to the court of Helios." Mazu stared out into the dense clouds. "That will be my testimony, when the Council demands it of me."

"Exactly," he said. "It was an accident."

"No. It was neglect. Or as men characterize disaster: an act of god."

"I suppose it can be viewed from that angle. But when you reveal what you know about the sacrifices, that flood will seem less criminal, don't you think? I suspect the Council will be more interested in getting to the bottom of that."

Mazu smiled and shook her head. "You are the last person who should expect a fair hearing from our chosen kings. They surely know about all this. Their halls are filled with secrets, and they silence those who know even a hint of them, as you yourself have experienced."

The raft shuddered again and they felt it dip downward. "Don't give up hope. If Sekhmet was elected she may - "

"Sekhmet? The Egyptos cat?" So intent had they been on their conversation they had not noticed Smoke Monkey eavesdropping. "She was not chosen. The gods voted for our Feathered Serpent's friend, Lamasthu of Babylos. I hope you had no money riding on the outcome, Tracker," Smoke Monkey grinned. He adjusted his headdress and called to one of his warriors. When this Mayan stepped forward, Smoke Monkey spoke another short phrase. Then the warrior produced a rope and began to bind D'Molay's hands.

"What is this?" D'Molay grumbled. "I've given you no trouble."

"And I appreciate that. But we are almost to the City, where temptation will goad you to run. And our newest Council Member is most anxious to speak with all the water gods and their friends."

"I bet she is," D'Molay muttered, his heart in his throat. Sekhmet had lost. A dark enemy sat in her place.

"I'm sorry, D'Molay," Mazu said. "I see little on which to pin our hopes."

The air raft suddenly broke through the bottom of the cloud and bright sunlight bathed them. D'Molay looked out over the sparkling City then lifted his eyes to the blue horizon where hope lifted a pale, delicate hand in greeting.

"I know you can't see it," D'Molay smiled, "but I can." He began to pray.

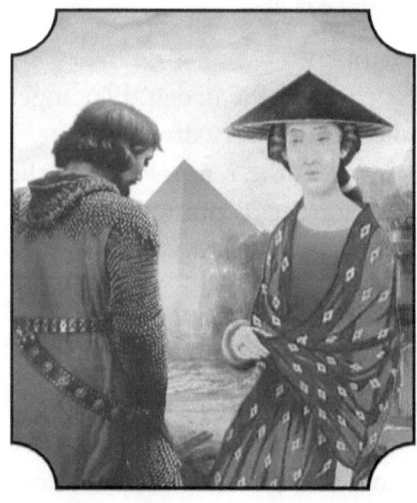

Chapter 29

Judgment Days

he gods and goddesses caught up in Lamasthu's net were brought to the center of the City. Their transport was varied and complex. Those who could take solid form arrived in carriages, astride beasts, or buoyed by flying platforms such as the Mayan air raft that carried Mazu and D'Molay. Those who could not leave their waters suffered the indignity of being displayed in large glass boxes filled with liquid set upon wheeled carts. To make things even more unpleasant, the Council had decided to let each god's innocence be decided by a single crystal guardian. The line to consult this god of truth stretched long. D'Molay noticed one deity just behind them stubbornly maintaining the form of a cloud, pelting any who came too near with stinging raindrops. Most of the gods who had been compelled by the magic rings to appear were furious, and D'Molay certainly understood their anger.

"I've always heard that the wheels of justice turn slowly," D'Molay sniped as he and Mazu stood in the barely-moving line. "Here's my proof."

Mazu untangled one of the cords of her belt, an action which brought the red band around her wrist back into view. She frowned at her bracelet. Looking up, she realized her dislike of it was a common thread shared with the other water gods and goddesses stuck in the long queue. She saw several raised fists and angrily waving hands sporting identical rings.

"Are you eager to be thrown into prison?" she asked D'Molay, turning a milder look upon her friend. "We should enjoy this beautiful day while we can. Perhaps the discerners of truth will even find someone guiltier than I before it is my turn before the crystal."

D'Molay took a deep breath, preparing to again argue Mazu's innocence in the matter of the flood, but he was suddenly overcome by weariness. His words turned to a resigned sigh. In matters like these he knew that innocence or guilt was irrelevant. What the gods in power had in mind for them had little to do with those concepts. So, D'Molay began to survey their surroundings, searching for an escape strategy. There could be an opportunity if another angry god caused some distraction. He set his frustrations aside and began to think of their situation in battlefield terms.

The field was the grand plaza before the Council Hall. In the middle of the giant Flying Eye design on the paving stones stood a single tall crystal, exactly like the ones that judged and protected the City at its gates. The enemy was the ring of City Guardians that waited by the crystal to arrest those discovered to be guilty; their generals were the four Council members that sat in stately mien overseeing the judging. As for troops to command to battle for his cause, those in line with him were either deities constrained by the rings or servants tied with more conventional bonds. D'Molay tugged at the cord that secured his wrists behind his back and tested the rope that hobbled his ankles. There was no give in either. If any fight was to come, it would have to originate from the growing crowd of spectators.

As D'Molay had this thought, he noticed three more City guardians arrive in the plaza. They briefly conferred with their comrades by the crystal before moving into the crowd. D'Molay frowned. Apparently the police force was also considering the possibility of an uprising. If something riotously convenient was going to happen, it would need to happen soon.

"You're suddenly quiet," Mazu remarked.

"I'm watching the people," he said. "If many more come, things may get unruly."

Mazu laughed. "Unruly enough to carry us off? Unruly enough to overthrow the Council? I'm pleased you've suddenly found such optimism."

"I haven't found it yet," D'Molay said. "But I'm looking."

He squinted in the bright daylight, wishing his hand was free to shield his eyes as he studied the gathering in the plaza. So far he'd spotted no familiar faces. Most of the gawkers seemed to be from the Babylos block of the City, save for several large classes of children from The Good Village that had been brought by their tutors to observe how the Council enforced the law. Several scribes from The Great Library had also come and were working their way down the line, interviewing the arrested gods for the chronicles. D'Molay suspected some of the words they had to write down were scorching their parchment. The line moved and everyone in it shuffled forward about five feet.

"Do you see your friend?" Mazu asked.

"Not at the moment," D'Molay said. "But she's not far. I feel it, Mazu."

D'Molay nodded firmly and embraced the idea that Aavi was indeed at hand. Why else would she have appeared to him as the Mayan raft reached the City? He longed to talk to her and ask why her visitations were so random. All he could do was pray that she would help him when the time was right. The line again advanced and they came close enough to the crystal judge to hear some of what was being said. Now standing before the crystal was a goddess clad in a sealskin coat with simple decorations of shells and beads. The lines of her face were deeply etched into a hard mask, though her visage was young rather than elderly. As she glared at the crystal and muttered answers to its questions, her attendant, a seal woman, ran a whalebone comb through the goddess's hair, as if comforting her during her trial. Her answers to the crystal came in a tongue D'Molay could not understand.

"Mazu, do you know that goddess?" he asked as they listened. As Mazu was about to answer, the examined goddess raised her arm high. Her red ring encircled a wrist whose hand was missing all its fingers.

"Ah, now I am sure who she is," Mazu said. "Her name is Sedna. She cares for the animals of the cold seas." D'Molay was about to ask why she had no fingers when the ring about Sedna's wrist pulsed with blue light. It began to spin rapidly around her wrist. After a few seconds of rotation it entirely disappeared. Then Sedna and her companion left the plaza, apparently cleared to leave. "I can't believe they brought someone like Sedna so far from her lands," Mazu sighed. "It's ridiculous to think she had anything to do with a flood in Olympia."

"But it's convenient to have an excuse to question all these gods, isn't it?" D'Molay took a few more steps forward as Sedna's departure allowed the line to advance. "I hope none of them have any secrets ripe for the picking."

Mazu glanced at those in line behind them then leaned in close to D'Molay's ear. "At least some of them will escape questioning when I am deemed guilty," she whispered.

"When? Is there no chance you can fool the crystal?" he asked.

"None. But I don't want to. I want the guardian to know I caused the flood, and more importantly, why."

"Of course! The secret!"

"I will tell everything I know about the nectar and the stolen souls. It's the only card I have to play against Quetzalcoatl." Mazu shifted her position so that the others in line blocked her body from the Council members' view. "I'm counting on my hunch that his purpose in convicting me

of the flood is to silence me about his quest to control Aavi during the war. I don't think he realizes that I know about the urns."

D'Molay now understood why Mazu was not very concerned about her arrest. It was the perfect opportunity to reveal the horrible crime against the mortal spirits. "What do you think the god of truth in the crystal will do when you reveal this?"

Mazu looked determined and hopeful. "The truth always comes out," she said. "And better it to come from the gods who guard it. I don't know what will happen, or how quickly, but I believe something good will result from my confession."

D'Molay's spirit began to rise to her heights, but leveled abruptly as one of Quetzalcoatl's priests jumped up from where he'd been sitting at his master's feet. He hurried along the line of gods until he reached them. Not daring to touch Mazu, he seized D'Molay instead. The man grabbed at his shoulder and pushed him out of line.

"What is this?" Mazu said. "I demand our right to proper examination by the crystal seers of truth."

"You will have that," the priest said, "but your mortal must come with me."

"Come where?" D'Molay demanded. "I've done nothing wrong."

"Did I say you had?" The priest pushed him toward the chairs where Quetzalcoatl, Lamasthu, Shiva and Zeus sat. "Walk."

D'Molay shuffled along as fast as his hampered step allowed, wondering if his summons was for good or ill. When he reached the Council's gods, the Mayan priest tried to make him kneel.

"If you force me down," D'Molay growled, "I'll have a devil of a time standing up again."

This response received a hearty laugh from Zeus. "He's right. Let him stand," Zeus said with a gracious wave of his hand.

"That seems disrespectful," Lamasthu said softly, "but if that is how things are usually done here, I will suffer it."

D'Molay tried to ignore the way her glassy eyes pinned him. He was sure she found him disgusting, but the feeling was mutual. He addressed Zeus. "May I ask what this is about?"

"It's for your own protection," Zeus said vaguely. "Quetzalcoatl, you explain it."

"Tracker D'Molay, you are under our secrecy bond. If the guardian questions you, the attempt to pull protected information from your mind could cause you great pain." Quetzalcoatl said something in his language to his priest, who began to untie D'Molay's hands and feet. "And the seer might even be strong enough to extract our secrets."

"Which is far more important to prevent than your pain," Zeus added.

Lamasthu laughed brightly. "Quite."

D'Molay rubbed his freed wrists and resisted the strong urge to look behind him to see how Mazu was faring. She may have reached the crystal. "I suppose I do know a secret or two," he said.

Shiva, who had been paying little attention to him or the others, suddenly straightened in his chair. D'Molay observed him lean forward with rapt interest just as the general murmuring noise of the crowded plaza pitched up in intensity. When a guardian bellowed a command for everyone to 'step back' he gave in to his curiosity and spun around. He was relieved to see Mazu standing peacefully in front of the crystal. But the glassy surface of the obelisk was no longer bright, no longer a focal point for supernatural discernment. It looked dark and dead, like the trunk of a tree after a forest fire.

"What has happened?" Lamasthu hissed. A different City guardian than the one yelling at the crowd ran up to the Council and bowed.

"The god of truth seems to have left the crystal chamber," he reported.

"Left?" Quetzalcoatl disputed. "I have never known the seers to abandon their duty."

"Bring the last god it examined to us," Lamasthu ordered.

A moment later Mazu joined D'Molay before the Council. "More questions?" she asked. "I can't imagine I could tell you more about the flood than I've already told your examiner."

Shiva cocked his head to one side and regarded Mazu warily. "Who are you, goddess?"

"I am Mazu. I operate a ferry on the Great Lake," she said simply.

D'Molay noticed Quetzalcoatl trying hard not to react to her sudden presence.

"Why did the god of truth abandon his post?" Shiva asked. "This intrigues me, much more than this parade of watery suspects. What did he learn from you?"

Mazu held out her arm, showing them all she still bore the red ring of restraint around her wrist. "He learned I was guilty. But when he heard how I came to be so he was reluctant to convict me."

D'Molay watched Mazu carefully. "This god of truth, he knows everything now?" he asked.

"Everything we know," Mazu smiled. "It will certainly be fun to see whom he decides to tell."

Shiva stood. "I know little of you, goddess, but your man D'Molay is under bond to keep our secrets. If he has revealed things to you, and you have in turn told others - "

"They must both be imprisoned until we get to the bottom of this." Zeus interjected. Quetzalcoatl agreed, "Yes She is dangerous, And this is too seri-ous to overlook. She may have even killed the god of the crystal, as she apparently tried to kill our friend Helios."

Lamasthu pointed a tentacle at the guardian. "Take them to separate cells. If she will not speak, we will see what we can pull out of her mortal friend instead."

"You may imprison me," Mazu said calmly. "I've enjoyed the hospitality of Quetzalcoatl's dungeons and am eager to see if your accommodations are better. But I will say nothing more."

Shiva gave Quetzalcoatl an arch look. "You have previously restrained this goddess? By what right? She is not one of yours."

"Merely some confusion that arose during the late war," Quetzalcoatl dismissed. "Perhaps I should have held her longer. By her own admission she is destructive."

"I may be guilty of destruction, but there is no confusion. Quetzalcoatl has pursued me because I discovered that he was working with Set to capture the angel and invade Ares' Fortress. He wanted to keep me from telling the Council."

"What?!" Zeus and Shiva cried out in unison.

That was all D'Molay needed to hear. He darted to the left into the thickest throng of people, with no destination in mind as he bolted.

The size of the City itself did give him some advantage. The multitudes in its streets would hamper those pursuing him. Its many neighborhoods offered ample opportunities for shelter. Still, evasion would not be easy. The compass points of flight from which he must choose included the Council building itself to the north; City guardian stations to the east and west; and the military gate to the south. He chose the eastern route. That way led to the part of the City he knew best, the quarters which were home to taverns and shops and pocketed with alleys and hidden yards.

Behind him, he heard Quetzalcoatl shout, the first of the Council to react. His cry was relayed by other voices, but D'Molay did not turn to see who or what was coming after him. He focused only on what lay ahead. As he closed on the security station, he saw only one guardian within the open, domed, gazebo-like structure. D'Molay scanned the plaza for cover in case the guard looked his way, and found it by ducking alongside a donkey cart hauling crates of leather goods bound for the shopping district. As the cart rolled along, it shielded D'Molay from the eyes of that particular City guardian, but he did not dare move at such a slow pace for very long. As soon as another thick clump of people came near, he darted into it. When a hideous stench reached his nose, D'Molay regretted his decision. After only a few strides, the putrid odor stopped him in his tracks. The miasma was so nauseating and so intense that he doubled over and began to retch. The torment was almost enough to freeze the very thoughts in his mind, but he marshaled his wits enough to realize that he had stumbled into a funeral procession.

Men with scented scarves wrapped tightly over their noses carried a platform on their shoulders. It held something rotting swathed in fine red silk. The shape under the cloth was so swollen and bloated that D'Molay was unable to determine if the corpse was human or animal. Fluids oozing from the remains soiled the crimson wrappings and dripped like slow rain from underneath the raised stretcher. In all his long years on Earth and in the realms, it was the most disgusting thing D'Molay had ever encountered; but it gave him an idea.

"There he goes!" he heard someone shout, which gave him added impetus to put his plan into action. The Halls of Healing loomed before him, and beyond that, a destination where he knew he could shake off many of his pursuers. He held his breath as he shoved mourners aside, not the least bit apologetic for the blasphemy, and raced toward the entrance to the hospital. He broke free of the funereal clump and faced an open stretch of paved street. As he raced on, breathing fresh air gratefully, a shadow darkened his path. D'Molay quickly looked up. A City guardian riding a great bird was about to thrust his staff toward him. D'Molay ducked and rolled to evade the blow - knowing even a slight hit from a guardian's staff would stop him dead. When its rider missed, the bird called out with a piercing screech and circled to give the guardian another shot at its target. D'Molay sought any kind of cover, but the nearby citizens knew better than to interfere with an apprehension. A wide, empty circle grew around him as everyone backed away.

However, there was one spectator who decided to make a difference. Whether from a sense of fairness, a dislike of authority, or merely a desire to prolong the chase for his own amusement, an Afrikan warrior tossed his large, leaf-shaped shield to D'Molay. D'Molay raised it above his body in the nick of time. The force from the hit of the guardian's staff almost knocked him over, but he kept moving, reaching the entrance to the Halls of Healing. The bird could not follow him inside and the time the rider would need to dismount would give D'Molay a slight advantage. With a feeling of relief, D'Molay ran inside the sanctuary.

Again ignoring all rudeness or offense, he barreled, shield first, through the hospital, shoving healers against the walls, throwing stands of herbs and potions out of his way, and creating general mayhem among the sick. No one tried to stop him. The indignant healers instead beset the approaching guardian, foiling his attempt to keep up with D'Molay. Healers and patients ringed around the guardian, shouting, demanding something be done about the damage the intruder was leaving in his wake.

As he rushed down a main corridor which led to an exit on the opposite side of the hospital, D'Molay dropped the shield and grabbed a roll of medicine-soaked bandages. He paused to wrap the cloth strip around his head, covering his nose and mouth lightly. The layer of protection was thin enough to breathe through but strongly protective from its soaking of herbal tinctures. He would need any safety the barrier would provide where he was headed: the contagion rooms.

416

The Hall of Healing isolated the City's victims of supernatural plagues in a separate annex. Apollo, in particular, had a bad temper and a worse habit of punishing mortals with miserable afflictions, many of which were communicable and difficult to cure. Even the compassionate act of

visiting one of Apollo's victims was often noted by the god and likewise punished, so only the most determined caregivers and loyal friends ever set foot inside the plague rooms. D'Molay burst out of the back door of the hospital confident that he could reduce the number of enemies on his tail merely by selecting the shunned building as his next refuge.

A band of Hindu fighters was rounding the exterior of the Hall of Healing and headed D'Molay's way as he set off toward the annex. The fighters shouted praise to Shiva as they sighted D'Molay and closed in, and were almost within range to strike when they realized where D'Molay was bound. Apparently Olympians weren't the only ones afraid of Apollo, for the group skidded to a halt well beyond the door to the contagion room. They reversed course, heading around the building to the back, no doubt hoping to catch D'Molay when he exited.

D'Molay shoved the heavy door to the plague house open. He would worry about the guards who would be waiting for him outside when the time came. Pushing on, he pulled aside a second barrier curtain just inside the door and stepped into a wide chamber dotted with beds and permeated with the smoke of burning herbs. After experiencing the smell of the gruesome corpse, D'Molay barely noticed the odors of the sick and the pungent scent of their cures. However, he slowed his movements and took care not to touch any of the patients. It was risk enough to be in their presence, let alone have contact with them.

Moving from bed to bed, he noticed a small corridor leading out of the ward. It contained a line of statues and shrines where those who were strong enough could pray and make offerings to regain the favor of their gods. D'Molay stalked quickly past the sculptures and altars, seeking a place to hide. A golden Buddha smiled welcomingly down at him. Taking its friendly, fat face as a sign, D'Molay squeezed behind the statue. He

417

was encouraged to find a large hollow space beneath the platform on which it sat, and hunkered down within it to wait, and think.

At least one squad of guards knew he was here, and it wouldn't take long for them to tell others. While he was safe enough inside the contagion rooms, he couldn't hide here forever. Thinking his options over, D'Molay found that his best chance was to wait several hours until nightfall. Perhaps then he could find a way up to the roof then scale down the walls in a spot where no one was watching. Satisfied he had formulated the best plan he could under the circumstances, D'Molay allowed himself to relax and recover from phase one of his escape.

At times he tensed again as footsteps paced the corridor, but always they continued past his hiding place without stopping. He had no true way of telling the time, so judging the arrival of darkness was a matter of guesswork. Eventually he relied on an increase in the smell of burning lamp oil to assure him that night had fallen on the City. D'Molay scratched the bandages that covered his nose as he ventured out again to find his way to freedom. The corridor was empty, and silent. Moving quickly by the shrines, D'Molay sought a way to the building's upper levels. He found a narrow stairway and mounted it, wincing at each loud creak the stair treads made beneath the weight of his boots. The flight deposited him, disappointingly, in yet another ward of plague patients. In the weak flames of pot lamps hanging from the ceiling, D'Molay quickly assessed their condition. All of them seemed to be deeply asleep, either drugged or near death. He counted it good fortune that none were aware enough to mistake him as a healer or a visitor, and call out to him.

At the other end of the ward, he spotted a ladder propped against the wall. Following its rungs upward with his eyes, he saw a hatch in the ceiling. It was the type of opening that often led to an attic under the roof trusses, exactly what D'Molay was looking for. He crept between the cots toward it. A dozen beds, six on his left and six on his right, had to be passed before he reached the ladder. He tried not to look at the sick as he tiptoed by, but some of them were so piteous in appearance that his eyes were perversely drawn to them. On his left, a woman was afflicted with raised channels in her skin, pale tunnels in which short, glowing worms crawled, occasionally poking their horned heads up through small holes they had chewed open. D'Molay swallowed and looked away, this time seeing a man whose arms and legs had been cursed to extend from the wrong sockets. His right leg dangled, kicking fitfully, from his left armpit. The arm that belonged there clutched fitfully at the bedclothes where a foot should be. Then he passed an extremely obese Asian man with boils on his face. He was the last he saw, for at that moment all light in the room suddenly snuffed out.

D'Molay dropped into a crouch and crawled forward toward where he remembered the ladder to be, still determined to reach the roof. He heard a loud pop and a wet, splattering sound. Loud growls and thumps confounded him and he plowed head-first into something hot, sticky and rubbery. He recoiled, fighting the grasp of unseen tentacles that grabbed hold of his arms. A torch flickered at the other end of the room, illuminating the faces of several men. From its weak light, D'Molay saw he was in the clutches of a netherbeast, one of the children of Lamasthu. It dragged him past the split-open corpse of the fat man, from which it had apparently burst, toward the men who waited at the entrance to the ward. When the beast delivered him to the humans, D'Molay recognized them as slavers and guards from Lamasthu's temple. One of them raised a club and brought it quickly down. That was the last thing D'Molay remembered before falling into darkness.

Chapter 30

The Only One

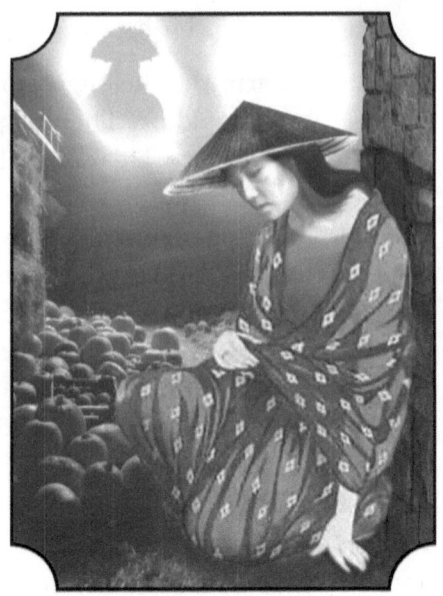

No one had come to tell Mazu what had become of D'Molay. She wasn't expecting to see her friend again. When he was pulled out of the judgment line, it seemed the Council had plans for him beyond sharing a cell with her. Mazu already missed him, yet at the same time felt free of yet another weight. He had chosen to run. His fate was in his own hands as she dealt with her own. *There is nothing I can do for him or anyone now.* She hoped that her revelation to the Council might at least start a thorough investigation into Quetzalcoatl, but she knew that it was a thin hope at best.

As the City guardians had hurried to restore order on the plaza when the crystal seer had fled, Shiva had ordered his Council guards to whisk her away to a secure place. Seeming eager to be rid of her, they had locked her in the first available room they found. She still bore the ring of restraint on her wrist, so the guards were confident that ordinary measures would be enough to prevent her escape. The place they chose was not a cell, but neither was it a comfortable accommodation. It reminded Mazu of a garden shed. The room was shallow but long, with a row of five small windows set high in one wall. Built-in shelves lifted potted plants to catch the light admitted by the windows. Beneath the windows, identical short cupboards took up the rest of the wall space. Mazu had been deposited upon a cushioned ottoman far away from the room's door. As she sat, she stared at the cupboard across from her and wondered what was inside. She leaned forward and tugged on a bronze knob on the cupboard door. The door did not yield; she noted a keyhole near its pull. The cupboard's secrets would remain hidden, in contrast to her own, which she was eager to share with everyone she could.

The door to her makeshift cell was also secured and she could hear the muted conversation of several guards outside it speaking of the near-riot taking place on the plaza. After an hour of isolation, Mazu heard the door's latch rattle as someone keyed open the lock. The door swung open and two Council guards pushed their way in, swords drawn. Mazu shook her head at them, bemused that they were ready for her to rush them in an attack. When she simply remained seated, they lowered their weapons.

"Stay where you are," one of them admonished her.

"Where would I go?" she snapped back, a bit surprised at the weary annoyance that her voice betrayed. The guards let her question stand as someone else approached. Mazu could hear the sound of a flute being played outside. As its notes faded, the sunlight cast the shadow of the figure standing just outside the open door onto the floor. The silhouette was unmistakably that of Quetzalcoatl. Mazu could count the feathers in his headdress and clearly make out the stack of bracelets and anklets that adorned his limbs. He stepped into the little room, followed by a goddess of his pantheon. Mazu wondered what part she would play in whatever interrogation or punishment was to come.

She was not acquainted with the goddess, who was beautiful, shapely, and accompanied by a green snake that was weaving itself in and out of her smooth, brown hair. Mazu pointedly ignored Quetzalcoatl in favor of studying his companion. The goddess quickly perceived Mazu's gaze and shifted her own eyes to her Mayan lord, as if she was nervous or frightened. She then clutched her right wrist with her left hand as if to keep herself from fidgeting as she stood perfectly still.

"You were a difficult catch," Quetzalcoatl said, waving the guards away. The swordsmen stepped outside, shutting the door securely behind them. "I congratulate you on evading my net for as long as you did. And your unexpected mischief at the crystal judgment - impressive! I doubt any of the gods of planning or trickery could have matched your feat. Your attempt to make me look the villain was worthy, but in the end, none will believe the word of a murderer over my word as a Council member."

Mazu rose from the ottoman and stood before him defiantly. "All I did was tell the truth."

"So? Even a murderer is capable of telling the truth."

"I didn't set out to harm the people of Helios' island," Mazu said. "I don't deny my responsibility for their deaths, but killing them was an accident. What I did was - "

"Of little consequence," Quetzalcoatl interrupted. "Mortals are easily replaced. You should be sorry for the gods you have killed, and fearful of the penalty for that crime." He took a few steps closer to her and Mazu could see a look of smug domination on his face. She felt a growing determination to wipe it off.

"What gods have I 'murdered' in your imagination, Quetzalcoatl?" she challenged. "Yes, I battled Circe, but where is any proof that she is dead?"

"Zeus believes her to be, which is proof enough for his wrath."

"When the full Council tries me," Mazu said confidently, "Shiva will find the evidence lacking. I think he already suspects the rest of you are - "

Quetzalcoatl laughed aloud. "Don't expect Shiva to save you. While he may agree that your guilt is doubtful in Circe's case, he will agree with the rest of us when it comes to Glaucus."

Mazu blinked. "Glaucus . . . Glaucus is dead?"

"Like yesterday's catch." Quetzalcoatl paused, waiting for the goddess at his side to laugh at his joke. But when his eyes pinned her, Mazu noticed she only managed a small, insincere smile. Mazu found Quetzalcoatl's accusation unbelievable.

"How could I have killed him? He was still alive when I was put on Smoke Monkey's raft." Mazu quickly reviewed the events at the old god's temple. Glaucus had trapped her with the golden ring, she had sent D'Molay away to protect Quan and Scylla, and then -

"Glaucus, please, let the past be the past," Mazu pleaded. "Scylla has been forced to change. Your anger won't undo anything."

Glaucus slapped his tail in the water and thrust a pointing finger at Mazu. "I was a fool to listen, an idiot to cooperate with you. Now I have given my trust to Quetzalcoatl. And he will keep his bargain."

Mazu's ears strained as sounds of the confrontation outside reached them. She could hear Quan screaming.

"You were not foolish to trust us," she insisted, trying to ignore what was happening to her friends. "But you will be the fool of all fools if you believe what Quetzalcoatl tells you."

"Is that so?" he questioned, pointing again. "Look. My reward comes. A reward that will give me my heart's desire."

Mazu turned to see five Mayans coming into the temple and wading down into its waters. One of them carried a decorated box. She could sense the power of something inside. As the bearer presented the gift to Glaucus, his four comrades surrounded Mazu. A wave of sadness licked at her heart. Gods were so like men at times, so easily bribed.

Mazu wondered exactly what had happened when Quan went back into the temple. What if her power had killed Glaucus and did place the blame at her feet? If Quetzalcoatl knew the details, he probably would not share them. Still, there might be some information to be gained, if she asked the right questions. "What proof do you have that I caused his death?" she demanded.

"The crystal of the head physician at the Halls of Healing detected your power signature lingering about his corpse," Quetzalcoatl said coldly. This was startling news to Mazu, but she managed to stay defiant.

"I don't know how that happened, but if that is sufficient evidence of murder then be done with me," she responded angrily. "I haven't the time to bring you and your cadre to justice. I'll let the City take care of that."

The goddess at Quetzalcoatl's side risked a subtle nod to Mazu, as if affirming her threat. This was odd, and Mazu again wondered who she was and why she was here. The goddess spoke. "If this goddess embraces her guilt, she should be offered the choices," the goddess said. The bright green snake in her hair disengaged itself and slithered to curl upon her shoulder, its keen eyes upon Mazu.

"That's correct, Ixchel," Quetzalcoatl said, revealing at last her name. "Do so."

Ixchel extended her hands, palm up, as she recited the law of the realms. "You are the condemned. You may die by battling a champion of the City's choice or you may die by giving up your life and powers to a chosen vessel."

Now Mazu understood why Quetzalcoatl's companion was here. It was customary to have the law read to the accused by one who was not involved directly in the conflict. Upon hearing the choices, Mazu scoffed at them. "You'll get no spectacle from me," she vowed, "so have whatever champion you've picked go back to his hole. And am I right to guess that you are here to steal my very life away, Quetzalcoatl?"

Mazu stared at her enemy in calm disdain. She was not afraid of ceasing to exist; the trials of recent days made that option almost a welcome one. But the thought of any remnant of herself carrying forward in the body of Quetzalcoatl turned her stomach.

"I would not be so tainted by your essence. Besides, the transfer must be to a deity of similar powers," Quetzalcoatl said mockingly.

Ixchel bowed to Mazu. "I am Ixchel, goddess of the moon, goddess of the rain. Many in our pantheon have an affinity for water, and Kukulcan honors me by offering my body as your vessel." Ixchel lifted her head, and Mazu read something eager in her eyes, as if playing her part in Mazu's execution was a personally sought prize.

"Waste no time," Quetzalcoatl said. "The City is unsettled and the Council needs to turn its attention to more important things. But I have the time to make certain that death comes to the accused. Begin, Ixchel."

"Yes, Kukulcan."

Quetzalcoatl crossed his arms and smiled menacingly, eager to see the death of an enemy.

Mazu thought of D'Molay, hoping he had used his canny skills to escape. She whispered a last blessing to Quan, willing him long life and the joys of mortal love. And when she checked her heart, she found her only regret was ever leaving Earth in the first place.

Ixchel's snake slithered down her arm and up Mazu's, wrapping almost comfortingly around it. Mazu felt the reptile's smooth warmth and took a moment to admire the bright green of its innumerable scales. Ixchel closed her eyes and seemed to brace herself.

Mazu waited expectantly, more curious than frightened about what was to come. A sharp pain rent her arm as the snake bit suddenly and viciously. The snake's green skin began to glow bluish-white with Mazu's life power. Despite her resignation to death, Mazu instinctively tried to pull her arm free of the reptile's bite. Ixchel held Mazu's arm in a desperate grip as the bright power sloughed from the snake to imbue her own skin.

Suddenly Mazu heard Ixchel's voice inside her head.

"There is no avoiding your death," Ixchel said mentally, as she took Mazu's hand. "Our thoughts can be shared during the transfer as we are both water goddesses. I must carry out your sentence. But know that I was there when you told the crystal seer the secret of the urns. I heard it all, and I will do everything I can to keep Quetzalcoatl and the others from covering up the crime against the souls. I have suspected him of misdeeds for some time."

A tear came to Mazu's eye. Could this reader of the law and enforcer of the penalty also be the ally that carries her mission forward? "I did not see you there," Mazu said, "but if you mean what you say . . ."

"I was the raincloud. I was furious that Kukulcan had me, one of the Mayan realm's most devoted deities, rounded up and put on display for his sham investigation. I was so humiliated I refused to take my normal shape."

424

Mazu smiled through her tears. "Then let us rain on his plans together, Ixchel. Seek out my allies, D'Molay, Quan, Bast." Mazu poured out her memories of those who had helped them into Ixchel's mind as her life force was siphoned away.

The transfer of energy made Ixchel strong and Mazu weak; soon there was no more struggling. Ixchel opened her eyes as she felt the other goddess give up the fight. She beheld a withered, aged woman, slumped over, taking her last breath. A single tendril of blue light skimmed down the snake's long back and disappeared into the crook of Ixchel's elbow.

Mazu's life was over. Where once a goddess lived there was now just a desiccated shell. The arm Ixchel grasped so tightly suddenly burst into a shower of powdery skin and bone, victim to her new strength. Her snake fell to the floor with the dust.

Recoiling, Ixchel scrambled away from the evidence of Mazu's fate, frantically trying to brush her hand and arm clean. The snake slithered toward her, not seeming to share her disgust with what had just happened. She gathered him up and put him back into her hair. Slowly she stood up and turned. "The sentence has been carried out, Kukulcan," she managed to say in an even voice. Ixchel waited tensely as Quetzalcoatl looked at her. She knew he was judging her new strength, testing her with his inscrutable discernment.

He smiled at her. "Well done, Ixchel. You may return to the Temple of Time and use your new powers to guide our realm. I will gather up Mazu's remains and scatter them to the four winds."

She said nothing, but bowed to him as he turned and walked off with the guards. She would do as he asked, return to the temple and wait. This would give her time to adjust to her new power and the opportunity to consult with Itzama and the others who had shared her concerns about Quetzalcoatl's rule. How much stronger would their opposition to him grow when she told them the secret of the nectar?

Ixchel walked away from the room of death and made her way out of the Council complex. On the plaza, disorder was still noticeable, with small groups of gods and mortals scuffling and shouting at the City guardians, while others ringed the blackened, abandoned crystal wondering what its state portended. Ixchel, not wanted to interact with any other being, took her raincloud form and stormed away, her own dark gloom a good match for the feeling of betrayal that was growing in the City.

"Congratulations on your High Council win, Lamasthu. A new age of greatness begins," Namtar, the hawk-like god who served Lamasthu, exclaimed. His beak turned up at the corners to form a smile. He folded his wings and bowed as she entered his office at the Slavers' Temple. "Had we known of your visit, I  would have arranged a fine gathering to celebrate your ascension."

She waved a tendril at her underling dismissively, noting a few shabby spots on his robes and reminding herself to address his unsatisfactory appearance at a more convenient time. "No, Namtar, it is time to work. I've had enough celebrations for one day. As for why I'm here, it's to tell you I put a special captive in one of the slave pens. See that he stays there until I've decided what to do with him. I also came to obtain some loyal slaves who can serve me at the Council Hall. I need a dozen guards and a new handmaid." Lamasthu strolled through Namtar's office as she spoke, her eyes seeking other areas where the feathered god might have been deficient. She noticed a basket of fruit and a memory rose in her mind. "Who was that girl that served me last time?"

"She is called Es-huh," Namtar volunteered.

"Yes, yes that one. I'll take her with me when I leave, along with the guards. Bring me some nectar and make the arrangements."

"Yes. It shall be done." He bowed again, nervously, as he backed out of his own office and closed the door.

Lamasthu walked to the balcony. Here, from the upper levels of the temple complex, she could see most of the City. She smiled, still enraptured that she was now on the Council and that real power was within her grasp. Then she heard a noise and turned, thinking Namtar had returned with some further question.

"So. Did you get everything you wanted?" The man's voice came from the other side of the room. Her eyes sought him, but it was not easy catch a glimpse of him.

Satan was handsome, but his appearance always seemed indistinct. She wouldn't be able to describe him to someone else. At times she saw him as tall, thin and blond, then she'd look at him again and he'd be stocky, and raven haired.

"I wondered when I'd see you again," she said warmly. "Yes, I have to admit, I got everything you promised. I keep expecting there to be a catch."

The man shrugged. "A catch? No, only an exchange. You signed the agreement in your own blood. It says what you owe me and what I'll give you in exchange. When you boil it all down, you simply owe me your obedience and I offer you power. It's as plain as that. You have power now . . ." He smiled expectantly.

"And you have my obedience. What is it you need done first?" Lamasthu attempted to take on a more alluring appearance as she approached. She found her benefactor fascinating, so unlike the other gods she had grown bored with over the centuries. Her features became softer and more feminine. She embraced and kissed him passionately as she ran her leg up the outside of his thigh.

He smiled and kissed her back. "Mmm, very nice. I'll keep that offer in mind, but first I want to show you something. Come with me." The handsome man took her hand. They walked out of the office and into the hallway.

"Where are we going?"

"To see that prisoner of yours." He led her down the stairs.

"The tracker? Whatever for? With the Angel gone and Mazu captured, he's of no importance now." She realized she sounded like a milkmaid in love who'd just been reminded not to forget her chores.

"You couldn't be more wrong, my dear Lamasthu," he answered as they walked through the corridors of the Slavers' Temple. In one doorway, she saw Namtar negotiating a deal but paid him no heed as he saluted her. Then they walked outside and crossed the courtyard to the slave pens. It was dark now and the first moon had just risen above the nearby buildings. A guard stood duty at the door where Lamasthu stopped. The guard bowed. "Blessings to Lamasthu, goddess of us all."

"Tell him to open it," her benefactor said, letting go of her hand.

"Open this. I would see my prisoner," she ordered, realizing that the guard seemed completely oblivious to the presence of her male companion. The guard quickly unlocked and opened the door. "Wait out here," she told the guard as she stepped through.

The door opened upon a dark narrow hallway lit by several torches. On either side were small cells with heavy iron doors. The place smelled of sweat and human waste, but neither Lamasthu nor her associate seemed to care. Lamasthu walked to the first compartment on the left. On the door was a small opening just below eye level covered by a metal plate.

Her companion whispered. "Slide it open slowly. Tell me what you see, quietly."

Intrigued, Lamasthu did as he asked and looked in. "The wretch is still there. It looks like he's praying and talking to himself," she whispered, turning to answer.

Satan casually took her hand and gave it a squeeze. "Now look again, but remain very quiet."

Lamasthu looked again. This time her eyes grew wide in shock. She gasped, but remembered his warning and managed to hold her tongue. D'Molay was still there and still talking, but now the room was bathed in a warm bright light - and right in front of him was an Angel with golden hair and large feathery wings. Glowing with a pale yellow light, the Angel floated effortlessly before D'Molay, speaking in gentle tones too quiet for Lamasthu to hear.

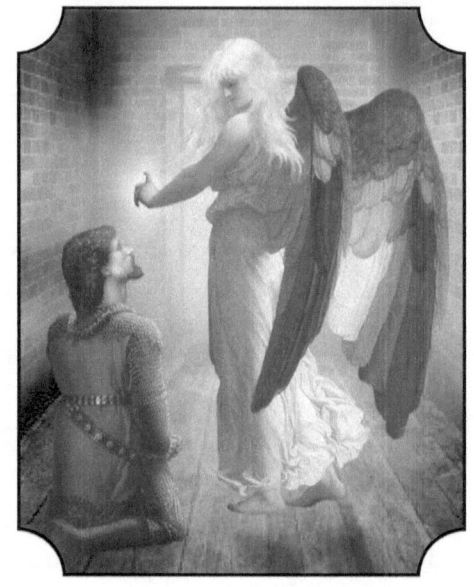

Unable to tear her eyes away from the scene, the wondrous sight disappeared when Satan took his hand from hers. The Angel vanished, leaving only D'Molay alone, praying again. Satan slid the small viewing door closed and escorted Lamasthu away from the door.

"How is that possible?" she demanded to know. "Heavenly beings are not permitted here. And why can I not see it unless you are touching me?" There was a trace of annoyance in her face as she waited for answers.

Satan held up a finger and motioned her back towards the exit. "I knew you would have questions," he said with a soft laugh. "You can see the Angel when I touch you because I have the power to see her. I doubt anyone else can, save me and your prisoner in there."

"But why is it here? I thought the Angel was destroyed at Ares' Fortress."

"I don't have all the answers. But I can tell you that your prisoner is the only Christian worshipper in the realms of the gods. I suspect that he

is some kind of conduit to Heaven, which allows her to sneak back in."
He raised an eyebrow and smiled. "Now do you see why he is still important - and dangerous?"

Lamasthu gritted her teeth. "He must be killed, immediately!"

Satan reached out, stroking her cheek as he smiled warmly. "You
need to do more than just kill him," he hinted. He began to fade until he
completely vanished, leaving Lamasthu alone in the stinking darkness.

She smiled. "With pleasure."

<hr/>

They finished the prayer together.
"...nostris; et ne nos inducas in tentationem; sed libera nos a
Malo. Amen."

"Thank you Aavi," D'Molay added.

"I only wish our prayers could unlock that cell door," Aavi said, gazing
down at D'Molay.

He smiled. "I'm just glad you're here. Waiting alone in a cell can be
maddening. I did that for seven years on Earth and it was horrible. I wonder what Lamasthu will do with me now I'm in her clutches?" D'Molay
held up his manacled hands and shook a foot secured to its twin by an
ankle chain.

Aavi frowned. "Like Set, she is a thing of evil, her intent is always
to gain at the expense of others."

"I'm not sure she has much to gain from me. What do I have that she
would want?"

"Perhaps knowledge, or simply to make sure you can't aid Mazu."

"It must be something like that," D'Molay reasoned. "Otherwise,
that thing of hers that surprised me in the contagion rooms would have
finished me then."

"Was it truly horrible?" she asked.

D'Molay laughed. "It wasn't the worst thing I saw today."

Aavi's presence turned out to be such a comfort that D'Molay found
himself somewhat unconcerned about what would happen to him next.
He was content to chat with his heavenly friend about things of little
consequence, such as taking a ride in a centaur-drawn cart or the antics
of Scylla's little monster children. Aavi listened intently to his adventures,
confessing that there were many times she wanted to appear to aid him,
but there was only so much she dared do without transgressing on the
covenant between the gods' world and her own.

After several hours of companionship they heard the latch of the door turn. Aavi started to fade away. "Don't worry. I'll be close by." Then she vanished.

The door swung open. Two Babylos guards rushed in with scimitars at the ready. "Let's go," one of them ordered. D'Molay could see there were several more outside the cell, making resistance impractical, and probably painful. In his ankle chains, he was only able to walk with small steps. Even though he cooperated, they shoved him out of the cell and he fell to the hard stone floor. Two of the guards grabbed his arms and pulled him up.

Half a dozen guards and a high priest had come to collect him. Several of the guards were no longer fully human, their arms having become tentacles and their appearance vaguely reptilian. D'Molay was placed in the middle of the group as they lined up to march out of the dark corridor.

"Where are you taking me?" he growled.

The guard hit him in the side of the head. "Shut up and walk." D'Molay did so, with a ringing pain in his ears. The moon cast long shadows of the group as they marched across the courtyard and into the main building of the Slavers' Temple.

Are they going to sell me, or transfer me to the Council? Those were the only pleasant outcomes D'Molay could imagine in this scenario. He prayed one of them would be forthcoming.

Although D'Molay had been inside the slavers' complex before, he had not been to the section to which the guards marched him. They entered a large chamber lit by torches. The stone altar at the front of the room betrayed its purpose as a temple, and standing next to it was Lamasthu, whose eyes gleamed in the darkness. Several more priests and sycophants stood by her side. Only a few mortal worshippers watched from a safe distance, their small numbers making the chamber seem empty and cavernous.

"Keep moving," the guard said, gruffly shoving D'Molay forward.

Lamasthu glared at him as he came near her. "Welcome, Christian soldier. Tonight we're holding a special service just for you."

At close quarters, D'Molay couldn't stop staring at her slimy green skin. It gave her feminine curves a strange, repulsive sheen as she moved and the torchlight illuminated the muscles underneath. She held an ornate golden dagger in her hand.

"Consider yourself privileged, for you're going to be sacrificed directly by me. I want the honor of killing you myself." She paused, giving D'Molay a moment to let her words sink in. Then, she got straight to the business at hand. "Chain him, we'll take no chances. He's slipped through our grasp one time too many - but not tonight."

The subhuman guards forced him down onto the ancient gray stone altar, which was stained with the blood of untold victims. D'Molay put up a fight, but there was little he could do in his position. He spit upon his nearest tormentor and counted that a victory.

"I know my soul will go to a better place than this," he said in defiance. "I hope the rest of the gods discover what you really are - a creature that belongs in the bottom of a privy, not on the Council!"

Lamasthu backhanded him. D'Molay's head slammed against the stone of the altar. "If they should ever judge me, you won't be here to see it."

A lustful, malicious look dominated her expression as D'Molay stared hatefully into her gleaming, yellow eyes. "As for your soul, it's not going anywhere. We gods decide where souls are needed, not you mortals. I will bathe in your blood this night, Dee-Mo-Lay, and savor the soul of the only Christian in the realms."

He turned his head away from the evil he saw in her. "One day, God will set his wrath on the sinful deities here."

Lamasthu made a dismissive noise. "We of Babylos fought the One God and his minions on Earth long ago. Now I will again do my part to keep them out of our affairs."

Two robed servants stepped forward, carrying a long red sash with cuneiforms embroidered upon it. Lamasthu held her arms out and they draped it over her shoulders. She raised the knife with both hands as she began to chant.

Ana kurnugi qaqqari,biti ellê šubat ir,
Habannat ali lu maltitka,illi duri lu manzazuka,
Dul Lamasthu, Dul Lamasthu!

431

The dread words supernaturally darkened the room as the knife she held began to glow. D'Molay pulled on his chains, trying to break free, but they were far too heavy. For just a second, he felt lighter as if he might float off the altar, but the feeling passed as Lamasthu placed one of her extra tendrilled hands forcefully upon his chest.

Alka aûšu-namir ina bab kurnugi šukun panika
sebet babu kurnugi lippetû ina panika
murui libbi ahka!

Lamasthu plunged the dagger into him. D'Molay heard himself scream as he felt the knife pierce his chest, then his heart. The pain was unbearable, endless, as a burning sensation spread from his chest. Visions of his death by flame centuries ago flashed into his mind as he felt fluid gushing up through his throat. He coughed as blood sputtered out of his mouth. The dark room got even blacker as the heat of pain became frigid and paralyzing, like the cold he'd felt in Hades. Lamasthu's glowing yellow eyes loomed over him, growing blurred and closer together, merging into one.

He was dead.

*D'*Molay lay face down on hard, rocky stone. He was cold, oppressed by a chill that was more feeling then temperature. As he opened his eyes, everything seemed misty. Darkness and blue seemed to blur together. He remembered the sacrificial altar and briefly decided he was still upon its stony plane. Then a dread familiarity struck him.

He jerked to alertness, sitting up. He saw craggy rocks and barren landscape. The sense of doom that had sparked now flared fully. He was back in Purgatory.

"Not here! No! No!" he screamed in horror. Emotions ran roughshod through him; he wanted to weep, but no tears came. He wanted to destroy himself utterly, but now no more than a spirit, he again faced the doom of wandering this hopeless realm until the judgment day. D'Molay dropped to his knees, prayed for salvation, prayed that he had done enough good deeds to earn some way to reunite with Aavi, even if he never saw the face of God.

Then behind him he heard a stifled cry and detected a faint trace of light out of the corner of his eye. Turning, he saw her near an outcropping of dark rock. Aavi was on her knees as if she too were praying. A faint golden glow emanated from her. D'Molay slowly got up and approached. As he closed in, he realized she wasn't praying, but crying, tears

streaming down her face. She seemed stunned, devastated beyond words.

"Aavi? What's the matter?" Forgetting his own sad fate, his only concern was for her.

Upon hearing D'Molay's voice, she looked up. "I failed to keep you alive and. . . I - I've discovered the horrible truth. I didn't realize it until I saw what Lamasthu was doing to you. She wasn't just trying to kill you, she was trying to consume your soul! If I hadn't interceded and taken your soul from her grasp, you would not just be dead, you would be gone, completely. Your immortal soul would have been turned into energy for Lamasthu." She stared back at him in anguish as the tears streamed down her face.

"Mazu discovered that they are stealing souls to make the nectar of the gods. That's what Circe's been doing, probably for hundreds of years. Remember the boat we traveled on with the glowing urns? The blood in those urns held the souls of people who'd been sacrificed. That's why they glowed. You were seeing the remains of their souls," D'Molay said softly.

"They've been using all that soul energy to keep their godly powers and their realms intact, long after they should have faded away. It all makes horrible, blasphemous sense now. That's why there are so many souls missing from purgatory," Aavi whispered back.

"And from the villages and farms," D'Molay added. "They need to sacrifice more and more people to keep their power and they're running out of people. My God." He gazed into Aavi's eyes and saw the pain of the entire world in them. "All those people, sacrificed to power the gods." D'Molay came forward to embrace her, holding her close for a long time as sorrow washed over them both. The gray cold of purgatory surrounded them, while one other lost spirit drifted slowly by. "But none of that matters now. I'm dead and trapped here for eternity."

They exchanged a long look and he saw her expression become intense as she furrowed her brow, her lips tightening with determination. Slowly Aavi stepped back. She looked around, as if surveying where they were. Her tears were gone and her inner strength seemed to have returned. D'Molay watched her slowly transform from a sad helpless, angel to one of immense power. It was a subtle thing; her stance, the slight stir of her hair, and the intent focus of her gaze on a distant horizon. Her wings spread open wide. The wind picked up as she began to glow brightly.

"No. This abomination cannot continue," her voice resonated. "They have broken the covenant with God. I must let the Heavenly Host know of this horrendous destruction of souls! Then, together we must find our way back to the City of the Gods."

To be concluded in book three - City of the Gods: Ambassador.

Art Credits

As tribute to the great artists of the past who created the legacy of wondrous art we are using for this series, we are attempting once again to list as many of them as we can. We hope that you have enjoyed the new way we have put this old art to use.

Note: In the listings below, the difference between 'digitally altered' and 'digital collage' is that a 'digitally altered' image is one that is very similar to the original artwork, with the addition or subtraction of some figures or objects. A 'digital collage' is an image where there are so many changes, additions or alterations as to effectively be an entirely new image.

PAGE	TITLE	ARTIST / YEAR
Cover	Among the Sierra Nevadas - digital collage	Albert Biertstadt, 1865
1	City of the Gods - digital collage	Crompton, 2012
6	D'Molay's Map of the Realms of the Gods	Crompton, 2008
7	An Arab Street - digitally altered	Frederick Goodell, c.1870
8	King Cophetua - digital collage	Edward Burne Jones, 1883
10	Assyrian Palace	Unknown, c. 1860-90
12	Digital collage	Crompton, 2013
16	Digital collage of 19th Century Painting	(Unknown) Crompton, 2012
18	Quexalcoatl (Stock image)	Unknown
20	Mayan Observatory - digitally altered	Wikipedia Commons
23	Chinese Ship 19th Century print	Unknown
27	Rime of the Ancient Mariner digitally altered	Gustave Doré, 1875
30	19th Century Engraving	Unknown, c.1850
31	Adventures of Baron Munchausen	Gustave Doré, 1865
38	18th Century Lithograph of Ares	Unknown, c.1770s
40	Dante's Inferno	Gustave Doré, 1857
41	Mazu at Helios' Palace - digital collage	Crompton, 2013
33	River Jurong, Singapore	Unknown, 1856
38	Chinese Palace	Unknown, c. 1917
39	Dover books Asian man engraving	Unknown, c. 1860
43	Emperor Honoris	John William Waterhouse, 1883
45	Engraving of boat - digitally altered	Edward William Cooke, 1828
46	Victorian Painting of Fairy - digitally altered	(Unknown) Crompton, 2012
48	Education of the Children of Clovis altered	Lawrence Alma-Tadema, 1861
49	Ulysses and the Sirens (detail) - digitally altered	John William Waterhouse, 1891
52	An Italian Man	Lord Frederic Leighton, 1864
53	The Hanging Gardens digital collage	Crompton, 2013
54	Harem Serving Girl - digitally altered	Paul Trouillebert, c. 1875
56	Set - Digital collage	Crompton, 2013
57	City Square of the Gods - digital collage	Crompton, 2013
62	Joseph Interpreting Pharaoh's dream- dig. collage	Arthur Reginald, 1893
64	Priestess	William Bouquereau, c. 1885
66	Shiva & Standing Women - digital collage	Crompton, 2013
67	A Farrier shoeing a Horse - digitally altered	Edward Robert Symthe, 1899
72	Dagr (digitally altered to be Sophia)	Peter Nicolai Arbo, 1874
75	Ruined Temple of Apollo - digital collage	Crompton, 2013
77	Digital Griffin (Stock Image)	Unknown, 2012
78	Mazu & Quan on the boat - digital collage	Crompton, 2013
81	Shepards at an ancient city gate - digitally altered	Giacomo Van Lint, 1760
83	D'Molay & Sophia in the lodge - digital collage	Crompton, 2013
85	Sierra Nevada - digital collage	Crompton/A.Biertstadt 1865
88	Adventures of Baron Munchausen - dig. altered	Gustave Doré, 1865
89	Orlando Furioso - digitally altered	Gustave Doré, 1879

More City of the Gods...

Mythic Tales: City of the Gods *(Short story collection)*

A collection of short stories centered around many of the characters from the first novel, including D'Molay, Aavi, Sekhmet, Tenh-Mer, Set, Quetzalcoatl, Bast, Circe, Sergius and other deities and citizens of the City of the Gods. With stories by M.Scott Verne, Wynn Mercere, Ken St. Andre, Randy Lindsay, Jefferson P. Swycaffer and other authors. $10.95

Pantheon #1-3 A City of the Gods Prequel

In this prequel to the City of the Gods novel, an unknown force has invaded and is destroying the realms of the gods. Drawn into the conflict, Tara, Lord Ghede, Set, Tenh-Mer & Sekhmet struggle to comprehend the sinister events foretold to cause the annihilation of men and gods alike. 32 pages B&W $3.00 each

Last Goddess #1 City of the Gods comic

The Gods left Earth long ago - or did they? At Dunwich Asylum, two evil gods secretly attempt to rebuild their powers and gain new converts on Earth. One remaining goddess of the light is reborn to try and thwart them, but is it already too late? Can this naked and confused woman rediscover her godhood and stop the coming of a reign of evil that would make Earth a living Hell? Can she adapt to the modern world after being dead for over a thousand years? Gorgeous art. Includes a missing chapter from the novel. This comic is for mature readers.. By M.Scott Verne & Wynn Mercere. 48 pages B&W $6.95

City of the Gods Map Pack

Usable with any role-playing system, the Map Pack includes: 11 x 17 full color map of the City of the Gods. 20 page booklet describing over 105 places in the city, details on the world of the Gods and 54 scenarios the GM can use to incorporate his existing game. Full color map of the realms of the Gods. 18 full color NPC cards of gods and citizens from the City. Two 32 page signed City of the Gods Comics. Plus a booklet with a chapter from the 1st CoG novel. $17.95

City of the Gods: Forgotten (Book 1)

Who is the girl who forgot? Why do the gods covet and fear her? 426 pgs $18.95

City of the Gods: Ambassador (Book 3)

Events in the City of the Gods spin out of control as word spreads about the terrible secret of the nectar. D'Molay and Aavi struggle to escape Purgatory, while a final battle for the souls of mankind begins. Is this the twilight of the gods? (This book is not yet released)

Check our website at **www.cityofthegods.com**
to order and for the latest news. Or search for us at Amazon.com

www.ingramcontent.com/pod-product-compliance
Lightning Source LLC
Chambersburg PA
CBHW020829030726
47496CB00001B/161